PI   ND

'*I'll Take New York* is like meeting up with your very best friend, **full of charm, warmth, wit and wonder, you'll never want to say goodbye.**'

Rowan Coleman

'Miranda works her magic again . . . **a sparkling, romantic, feelgood gem of a story** with massive heart.'

Julie Cohen

'Miranda Dickinson has given us yet another wonderful **warm-hearted and wise** novel with characters you can't help but fall in love with. *I'll Take New York* is **the perfect treat to snuggle up with** on a cold winter's evening.'

Ali Harris

'**Warm, feel-good and utterly enchanting,** *I'll Take New York* will magically transport you into a world you won't want to leave.'

Cally Taylor

'The characters are irresistible, the settings magical I was transported to the New York of my dreams, for the tiniest fraction of the air fare. **The perfect treat for readers who already know and love Miranda's novels – and those who have yet to discover her fantastic story-telling.**'

Kate Harrison (bestselling author of
The Secret Shopper series)

'The **perfect book to curl up with** on a cold winter's eve.'

Closer

RAISE FOR MIRANDA DICKINSON AND
I'LL TAKE NEW YORK

I'LL TAKE NEW YORK

Miranda Dickinson has always had a head full of stories. From an early age she dreamed of writing a book that would make the heady heights of Kingswinford Library. Following a Performance Art degree, she began to write in earnest when a friend gave her The World's Slowest PC. She is also a singer-songwriter. Her novels, *Fairytale of New York*, *Welcome To My World*, *It Started With A Kiss*, *When I Fall In Love* and *Take A Look At Me Now*, have all been *Sunday Times* bestselling titles. She lives in the Black Country with her husband Bob and daughter Flo.

To find out more about Miranda visit www.miranda-dickinson.com and find her on Twitter @wurdsmyth

Miranda's Novels:

Fairytale of New York
Welcome to my World
It Started With A Kiss
When I Fall In Love
Take A Look At Me Now

MIRANDA DICKINSON

I'll Take New York

AVON

AVON
A division of HarperCollins*Publishers*
77–85 Fulham Palace Road,
London W6 8JB

www.harpercollins.co.uk

A Paperback Original 2014

1

Copyright © Miranda Dickinson 2014

Miranda Dickinson asserts the moral right to
be identified as the author of this work

A catalogue record for this book is
available from the British Library

ISBN-13: 978-1-84756-234-0

Set in Sabon LT Std by Palimpsest Book Production Limited,
Falkirk, Stirlingshire

Printed and bound in Great Britain by
Clays Ltd, St Ives plc

MIX
Paper from
responsible sources
FSC™ C007454

Find out more about HarperCollins and the environment at
www.harpercollins.co.uk/green

ACKNOWLEDGEMENTS

Dear Reader

Since I wrote *Fairytale of New York*, I have harboured a secret longing to return to the City That Never Sleeps and set another story there. For the many lovely people around the world who fell in love with Kowalski's, Rosie, Ed, Marnie and Celia, I hope this book brings back happy memories and gives you new ones. If you're new to my New York stories, I hope this book steals your heart.

I am beyond blessed to be able to tell stories for a living and work with some incredible people to turn my tales into books. Massive thanks to my wonderful agent, Hannah Ferguson, for her eternal faith in me; Sammia Hamer and Katy Loftus – my editors at Avon – for their enthusiasm and hard work; and Caroline Ridding, Eli Dryden, Helen Bolton and the lovely Avon team. Huge thanks to Rhian McKay for awesome copy edits.

My heartfelt thanks go to fabulous writer friends Kim Curran, Julie Cohen, Rowan Coleman, Cally Taylor, Tamsyn Murray, Kate Harrison and A.G. Smith for their constant cheerleading and inspiration. Thanks too, as ever, to the Peppermint Massive and my brilliant friends and family for their support.

Big love and thanks to my Twitter and Facebook collaborators for their great suggestions for this book:

Cheesecake café at Grand Central suggested by Joanne Harris;

Gracie the cat named by Jill Mansell;

Snowglobe in Jake's apartment chosen by Lara Williamson;

Imelda named by Sarah Dixon;

Beads'n'Beans named by Dymphna Brennan;

Grandma Dot's book selections suggested by Julie Cohen and Rowan Coleman;

And finally, all my love to my amazing husband Bob and beautiful new daughter, Florence Wren. You are my world.

Life can bring magic where you least expect to find it. I hope this story encourages you to go looking for yours . . .

For my lovely friend Ebs.
This isn't quite the top of the Empire State,
but it'll have to do – Zupini Girls forever! xx

'New York is where you prove if what you think in theory makes sense in life.'
Miuccia Prada (1949–)

CHAPTER ONE

Stromoli's restaurant, 11th Street, Brooklyn

'Bea?'

Five more minutes . . .

'Bea, honey, why don't we just order? I don't think he's . . .'

'He's definitely not . . .'

'*Shh!* Can't you *see* she's upset?'

'What? I'm just saying . . .'

He'll be here. I know he will . . .

'I think he stood her up.'

'Could you say that any louder? Only I don't think the waiter in the restaurant across the *street* heard you . . .'

'Maybe we should wait a little longer?'

'The fact is, he hasn't just stood Bea up: he's stood us *all* up . . .'

Bea James closed her eyes and willed her gathered family members to stop voicing the thoughts in her own head. Of course, they were right. They had waited nearly two hours already and now even the laid-back waiter in Stromoli's restaurant was snatching not-so-sul.le glances at his watch.

Bea's father wasn't likely to be silenced by her mother's attempts. Even though he respectfully lowered his voice, Bea was still aware of every word. 'If we don't order soon, the kitchen will close and we'll end up at Pete's twenty-four hour diner. And you *know* what happened the last time I chanced a Reuben there . . .'

Her Uncle Gino and paternal grandfather Gramps mumbled in support.

'He said he would be here,' Bea's mother hissed back. 'He specifically asked us all to be here. We rescheduled our holiday to be here. Now why would he ask us to come if he had no intention of turning up?' She reached across the table towards Bea. 'Darling, have you checked your phone recently? Maybe he's been unavoidably delayed?'

'Or maybe he's the *schmuck* we all thought he was,' Aunt Ruby snorted. Never one to shy away from speaking her mind, Ruby had been uncharacteristically quiet this evening – until now. Bea knew this was the first comment of what would quickly become a flood.

'That's enough, Ruby! Think of poor Bea . . .'

Staring defiantly at the white linen tablecloth to avoid the concern of her family, Bea heard a chair scrape back on the other side of the table. Moments later, the vacant chair beside her – the one *he* should be sitting in right now – was occupied by the familiar hulk of her brother.

'He isn't coming, is he?' she whispered, lifting her head towards him.

Stewart's expression said it all. 'Maybe we should just

order? If Otis comes I'm sure the kitchen will accommodate him.'

'I can't believe he's done this.' Bea was close to tears. 'I've left ten messages on his mobile but he isn't responding. How dare he let me down like this?'

'Personally, I'd kick any guy to the kerb who makes me wait two hours for dinner.' Ruby's voice soared above the hum of evening diners in the neighbourhood Italian restaurant and Bea heard the stifled giggles from several of her family members. That was *it*: Otis had lost his last chance to prove himself.

'Let's order,' Bea blurted out, causing everyone to stare at her. 'Otis clearly isn't planning to join us. So please, let's just eat.'

As her family descended on the menus, much to the relief of the waiter, Bea stood. Stewart caught her arm but she smiled at him as best she could and dismissed his concern.

'I'm OK. I just need some air.'

Standing outside on the darkened sidewalk of 11th Street, Bea stared up at the heavy raindrops falling from the plastic awning across Stromoli's entrance, finally allowing her tears to fall. All she had wanted for this evening was for her boyfriend to keep his word. This had been *his* idea, not hers, and his efforts to gather her family from both sides of the Atlantic had suggested that there was an important reason why he wanted the collected James family present. He'd said he had something to say to all of them and something he wanted to ask Bea. How could it have been anything other than what everyone had suspected?

She had invested so much in this relationship, often feeling as if she were the only person in it. She had forgiven Otis when his promises fell through, plans backfired or willingness to commit waned. They'd had their problems, but then didn't every couple? She thought of the gathered members around the long table at Stromoli's, who by now were no doubt ordering everything on the menu. All of them were happily married – even Aunt Ruby, whose courageous husband Uncle Lou had signed up for just shy of forty years of wedded bliss before his heart gave up the battle last year. Sure, they argued, the women of the James family were famous for their feistiness, but history would record generations of long, successful partnerships. Bea had hoped that Otis calling everyone together this evening was a precursor to her name being added to that list. And her family had made no attempt to hide their expectation of his intentions, which – in the light of his absence – made everything a million times worse.

Grasping her mobile, Bea called Otis for the last time that night.

'Otis, this is it. I don't know what you're playing at and, to be honest, I don't care. I'm done. Don't call me again.'

Ending the call, Bea closed her eyes.

CHAPTER TWO

Departures Hall, San Francisco International Airport, California

'Are you sure you have everything?'

'I'm sure. All my worldly possessions that didn't leave for New York in the movers' van this morning are in my backpack.' Jake Steinmann forced a smile as the woman beside him dabbed her eyes with a lace handkerchief. 'Hey Pam, it's OK.'

Pam Lomas – Jake's faithful PA for the past seven years – shook her head. 'No, I'm sorry. It's *not* OK. It's not OK that your wife's given up on you like this. It's not OK that you have to abandon your whole life because of her latest whim. Can't you reconsider? You have so much in San Francisco: why leave it all now?'

Part of Jake agreed with her. It *was* unfair – but then, everything that had happened in the past month had felt that way. He shouldn't be the one to leave: as far as he had been concerned their marriage was a happy one. But realistically what choice did he have? Sure, he could stay in his adopted city and wait for Jessica to change her

5

mind. He could carry on, pretending that life was untouched by his wife's decision to leave him. But he knew, deep down, that to stay in a city in which every street, sidewalk and brick seemed imprinted with her name would be the end of him. Better to nurse a broken heart on the other side of the country.

'New York's not so bad.'

'It's the *East Coast*, Jake! Where you're just a number in a big city and nobody cares who you are unless you do something for them.'

'I was born there, remember? I may have the West Coast attitude and a better tan now but I'm a New York guy at heart.' He put his hand on Pam's shoulder as she let out a loud sob. 'Don't worry about me, OK? I'm going to be fine. My family are in the city, my friends from before I met Jess . . . I won't be alone.'

Pam gazed up at him, mascara streaking down her cheeks. 'Well, I guess I have no choice but to trust you on that. But you'd better call me, every week. I want to know everything. You promise?'

He had promised, his heart heavier than he had anticipated. Once on the JFK-bound flight, Jake closed his eyes and willed the chasm of loss to close within him. Of course, Pam was right: he wasn't the one to end his own marriage, so why should he be the one to leave?

The trouble was, Jessica didn't seem to see the injustice of the situation. Yesterday they had met for the last time, in a small neighbourhood coffee shop near her office, for Jake to hand over the keys to their Russian Hill house. He had hoped the finality of the act might coax a little understanding from her, might somehow break through the steel-strong walls she had erected around her heart. But even as they made polite small talk about Jake's plans for his New York relocation, it was clear all Jessica cared about was getting on with her life. *Her life* – which consisted of nothing changing other than her gaining more closet space in her bedroom and considering the possibility that she might let out the spare room to help pay the bills. Her comfortable job in interior design, the expensive social life she pursued, her Cabriolet and her weekend yacht would all remain. 'It's easier this way,' she had said, as if she were discussing a subject she cared nothing about.

Easier for you, Jess. Not for me . . .

He hated the lightness of her attitude, the way she smiled after every flippant comment, regardless of the pain each one inflicted. He should be glad she wanted to leave him. He should be celebrating . . .

And yet, even as he had watched her stride away along Mission Street and out of his life forever, his heart still ached for her. He told himself this was inevitable: after all, only six weeks beforehand he'd thought he had the happiest marriage in the world. *I'm still in shock*, he decided. *It hasn't sunk in yet . . .*

But now, as the lights of San Francisco Bay fell away from view through the aircraft windows, it suddenly felt very real. He was leaving the life he had so carefully built over seven years behind him, with no guarantee he could successfully rebuild it on the other side of America.

I won't be alone, he had assured Pam as they stood by the departure gate. But now, twenty thousand feet and rising above the Californian coast, Jake Steinmann felt more alone than he ever had before.

CHAPTER THREE

Hudson River Books, 8th Avenue, Brooklyn

Bea looked up at the oversized clock above the counter. Five more minutes and then she was leaving.

She had known it was Otis calling last night even before the answer machine clicked into action, but she had no intention of picking up. His voice sounded pathetic and insincere as it entered her apartment where she was hiding after the debacle at Stromoli's:

'*Bea – it's me. I am so sorry. Give me a chance to explain, please? I know I screwed up. You have every right to walk away. But don't do it until I've had a chance to explain. Give me an hour tomorrow and I'll make it up to you, I swear. I can come to the bookstore. We'll talk. And you'll see why I couldn't be there tonight. I'll call your family and explain, too. I feel awful, Bea, you have to believe me . . . Hell, please pick up the phone? I know you're there . . .*'

Changed into her faded PJs and huddled up in her favourite chair – the dress she'd expected to be proposed to in screwed into a ball beside her bed – Bea had stared at the answer machine. 'Go away,' she told the grey box with its blinking red light.

'*Just meet with me tomorrow? I won't stop calling until you say yes . . .*'

'Leave me alone!'

'*I'm not kidding, Bea. If I have to sit outside your apartment night and day I'll do it . . .*'

Tired and bruised from the mortifying family dinner, Bea couldn't bear the thought of Otis turning up in the early hours. As sleep was unlikely anyway, contending with a belligerent boyfriend would definitely ensure she was good for nothing in the morning. Admitting defeat with grudging disappointment, she had answered the phone.

'Fine. I'll meet with you tomorrow afternoon.'

'Bea – it's so good to hear your voice . . .'

Oh no, Otis, your wounded puppy routine won't work this time . . . 'I'll be leaving at five p.m. Be there before then or we have no deal.'

She should have said no last night. But Bea wanted answers – and she wanted to see his face when she challenged him. Now, facing another Otis Greene no-show, she knew it: she had clearly been wrong to trust him. He had let her down. *Again*.

'Maybe you should wait a few more minutes?'

Bea turned to her business partner and best friend. His eyes were earnest behind the wide-rimmed hipster glasses he wore. '*Maybe* he should have been here twenty minutes ago. I've waited long enough, I think.'

Russ wrinkled his nose. 'Ten more minutes.'

'Five.'

'OK, five. But he'll be here, Bea. I know he will. Just *be* patient, *Bea* . . .' He sniggered at his own joke, his laughter fading when he saw Bea's expression. 'Sorry.'

After three years of running a business together, you would think that Russ O'Docherty would have grown tired of his 'be-slash-Bea' jokes. But unfortunately her business partner (and unofficial partner-in-crime since she'd arrived in New York to study at Columbia University) was writing comedy scripts and performing stand-up in his spare time, with Bea (and her increasingly complicated life) a seemingly constant inspiration for his material.

Bea took a deep breath, the comforting scent of paper, print ink and furniture polish filling her lungs. For her it was the most delicious smell in the world: the tantalising aroma of a bookshop. For as long as she could remember, Bea had dreamed of one day owning her own bookstore. She had loved books all her life. *Real* books, not electronic ones. Books you could carry in your bag and read on the subway. Books you could pretend to read in neighbourhood coffee shops while people-watching. Books you could snuggle up with and lose yourself in. Books you could fill your apartment with – packed onto shelves, propping up tables and piled up reassuringly by the side of your bed. If she left home without a book, Bea felt naked, bereft. But then, working in a bookshop meant there were always new friends to make and take home.

Friends who never let her down. Friends she could trust.

Her heart contracted again and she wished hard that she didn't care whether Otis turned up or not. But she loved him: she had loved him for five years and even though she was angrier with him today than she had ever been before, she knew the moment he swept into the bookstore his handsome face would tempt her to forgive him. *Again.* He knew how to get under her skin and it was this ability alone that had saved their relationship many times before. Bea couldn't deny their chemistry – and when he arrived today she would have to fight hard to resist it again. If he ever turned up, that was.

'I just – I'm sick of this, Russ.'

Russ slung his arm around her shoulder. 'I know. What you need is a distraction from staring at that clock. I've been thinking about maybe introducing a coffee corner by the window – what d'ya think? I mean, what could be a better combination, hmm? Books and coffee: like mac and cheese, Cagney and Lacey, New York and angst. Come on, admit it, that made you smile . . .'

Bea shook her head. Russ knew her better than anyone and even his lame jokes had the power to break through her dark mood. 'I like the idea. If you think we can afford it?'

'I've looked over the accounts and I think it's possible, yes.'

Hudson River Books had been a dream Bea had shared with Russ from their earliest conversations at university. It became their favourite daydream in long English Lit classes, discussions about what it would look like and debates over which authors they would stock going on late into the night; continuing in study periods and lunch breaks spread out on the lawns surrounding the campus buildings. Much of what customers saw today in the little redbrick shop on 8th Avenue had been planned years before on diner napkins, on the back of lecture notes and in countless notebooks covered in their dreams over the years. Russ often said he thought the atmosphere that many of their customers remarked upon was because it had been their passion during the early years of their friendship.

Bea felt her heart sinking as she consulted the clock again. Despite her anger, she had so wanted Otis to come through this time. Just once, to stay true to his word. For *her*. Accepting the inevitable, she picked up her bag and coat. 'That's long enough. I'll see you later, OK?'

Russ dropped the stack of new books he was cataloguing and hurried around the maple wood counter to block her escape. 'Wait. Just a few more minutes? I know there's a good reason Otis is late.'

'I can think of a great reason: he isn't coming.'

'Bea . . .'

Irritated, she held up her hand to silence him. 'Stop defending him! All Otis ever does is make big promises he can't deliver. He's let me down too many times and I've had enough.'

'Enough of what?' A rush of street noise hurried into the bookstore as Otis Greene strolled in. He checked his watch. 'OK, so I'm a little late.'

'*Twenty-five minutes* late,' Bea returned, fully intending to push past the tall, elegantly dressed man and leave.

'Bea, let me explain. You wouldn't believe the trouble I had getting here. Roads are jammed, buses can't get through. Finally I caught a cab but it got stuck so I had to run the remaining five blocks to get here.'

For someone who had endured such a troublesome journey, Otis didn't seem very concerned – or out of breath. Russ smiled a little too enthusiastically between Bea and Otis, rubbing his hands together. 'Good, good. So, I'll get coffee and you two can – *talk*.' Still grinning, he hurried out of the bookstore, flicking the OPEN sign to CLOSED on his way out.

'Otis, I—'

'You're beautiful, Bea. Come here . . .'

He moved towards her but Bea shrank back. Otis' smile was all the evidence she needed to approach the conversation with caution. She didn't trust him – not like she used to, at any rate – and was determined not to let him win this time. Even if her heart was tugging at the sight of him in his smart business suit, dark eyes brooding as they held hers . . .

Stop it, Bea James! He has a lot *of explaining to do.*

'Baby . . .'

'Cut the crap, Otis. Where were you last night?'

'I had to view a new artist's collection. The gallery wants to take him on before the Manhattan dealers try to steal him. This guy's the real deal: I couldn't lose him.' He reached out to touch her arm, but she avoided his hand. She was angry and he needed to know it.

'And you couldn't have called me?'

'I was in the middle of negotiations. I – uh – lost track of the time . . .'

'Do you know how long my family waited at the restaurant to meet you? *Two hours.* I'd worked so hard to get them all there after what happened last time. Mum and Dad had even rearranged their holiday to come –

their dream American holiday they've been planning for years. They don't get the chance to visit me in the US very often but they came because you asked them. Do you have any idea how mortified I was when you didn't show up?'

Something Otis deemed to be remorse flickered momentarily across his face. 'Bea, I'm trying to apologise here.'

'Well, try harder. I don't believe you, Otis! You said you were serious this time. You *promised* you would be there.'

'I know I did and I'm sorry. I *said* I'm sorry, Bea. I'm sorry I missed last night and I'm sorry I was late today. But I'm here now: what more do I have to do?'

A lot more, Otis, Bea thought, *a whole lot more . . .*

CHAPTER FOUR

Jake's apartment, 826B Jefferson Street, Williamsburg

Dear Mr Steinmann,

My client, Mrs Jessica Steinmann, wishes me to inform you of her decision to file for divorce, on the grounds of irreconcilable differences. I require a response from you or your counsel within 28 days' receipt of this letter. Provided you have no objection to this action being progressed, please sign the enclosed agreement in order for divorce settlement proceedings to begin . . .

Irreconcilable differences.

In other words, his wanting to remain married to the woman he loved versus her desire to be rid of him as soon as possible. *Provided you have no objection* – or, to put it more precisely – *regardless of your objections.*

Jake had half-expected Jessica to see her lawyer within a month of his relocation to New York, but a day after? Even for his headstrong ex, that was fast. He wondered if she had met someone else already, the thought twisting his stomach before he quickly dismissed it. Whether she had or not, there was no point in torturing himself. The lawyer's letter was enough to hurt him.

He groaned and threw the brown envelope across the polished cherry wood floor of his new apartment. Divorce papers were the last thing he needed today.

His phone buzzed and, turning away from the offending envelope, he walked to the window as he answered the call.

'Jake Steinmann . . .'

A familiar voice yelled back. '*Jake-a-a-a-yyy!* How's it hanging, dude?'

He rubbed his eyes and looked out at the dreary March day. Williamsburg might be an up-and-coming neighbour-hood, but today it appeared more down-and-out. 'Hey, bro.'

'You sound like death,' his brother observed.

'And you *still* haven't learned tact, Edward. Tell Rosie she has more work to do on you.'

Ed's chuckle made Jake smile, despite his mood. But then his big brother had always possessed an annoying ability to do that. 'Rosie loves me for who I am. That's why she's planning to keep me around for a while.'

'Good for her. How *are* the wedding plans?' The mention of the 'w' word in the light of today's unwelcome mail made Jake wince as he said it.

'Fancy a beer?'

'*That* good, huh?'

Ed lowered his voice. 'I'm going out of my *mind* here, J-Man. I'm not kidding: if Dad tries to force any more random relatives onto our list, I won't be responsible for my actions. Did you even know we had a Great Aunt Eunice?'

'No, I didn't. Are you sure Dad isn't smuggling in his crazy golfing buddies under assumed names?'

'It's possible. That man will be the death of me.'

Jake smiled at his brother's frustration. 'Hey, look at it this way – at least Dad's getting into the spirit of the Steinmann–Duncan nuptials. It wasn't so long ago he was convinced you were gay . . .'

Ed's groan was identical to Jake's earlier utterance. There was one thing to be said for the Steinmann brothers of New York: they knew how to groan. But then groaning was a Steinmann clan survival tool – and with a family like theirs, every verbal protest was precious.

Jake knew what his brother had suffered from their father's ignorance. Ed's decision to shun the Steinmann family tradition of psychiatry in order to train as a florist hadn't been well received by their father. In fact, it was true to say that had Ed Steinmann announced he was growing his hair, becoming a Liberal and moving to a hippy commune in Goa his father would have taken the news better. For years Joe Steinmann had mocked his middle son's chosen profession, in public and in private: at the annual Steinmann Christmas gathering, at birthdays and anniversaries, graduations and summer holidays in the family's lake house in upstate New York. No matter how many women Ed dated (and there were *many*), no matter how successful his career, all Joe Steinmann saw was his middle son defying his true calling. Never mind that the prospect of Ed Steinmann as a psychiatrist, counselling the great and good of New York, had a high probability of ending in abject disaster. Never mind that Ed's idea of compassion was a night of beers and a good baseball game. For years, Joe could only see the betrayal he perceived in Ed's actions and not the man his son was becoming.

Rosie Duncan had changed all that. Even though Jake had long before moved his practice to San Francisco to be with Jessica, he had seen the change in his brother beginning when Ed had confided that his feelings for 'a specific someone' had started to grow. Of course, Jake had known immediately who it was: on his trips back to New York, the way Ed's face lit up whenever he mentioned Rosie's name had given more away than he'd intended. Working together in the Upper West Side florists' store Rosie had inherited from an old Polish man (who by all accounts was legendary), every story Ed relayed to his brother seemed to include the confident English woman.

The details of how they'd finally got together were sketchy in Jake's mind as he considered it now – although this was probably due to the empty, Jessica-shaped ache that currently robbed his head of pretty much everything else. However it had happened, Jake knew that he had never seen Ed so at peace, so completely in love and so permanently happy before. In turn, Rosie had charmed Joe from their first meeting and it was almost as if through her eyes he was able to see his middle son for the first time. Jake respected Rosie for that almost as much as he did for the change she had wrought in his brother. He had a lot to thank his soon-to-be sister-in-law for.

'Threaten to set your fiancée on Dad,' Jake suggested. 'If anyone can rein him in, it's Rosie.'

'Ha. I'll mention it to her, maybe. But I'm serious about that drink, Jakey. I haven't seen you since you came back and I miss my little bro. Besides, I need to get out of Kowalski's for a while. What with the wedding plans and Marnie's swollen ankles this place is threatening to become Oestrogen Central. *Ow!*'

'What happened?'

'Rosie hit me . . . What? I'm on the *phone*, baby . . . Really? J-Man, my beautiful wife-to-be wants to speak to you . . . Passing her across now . . .'

'Hi Jake.' The soothing tone of Rosie's English accent seemed to reach down the phone line to hug him and instantly Jake began to relax. 'Welcome home.'

'Hey, sis-in-law-to-be. Just how crazy is my brother making you?'

Rosie's groan was a good one: she would fit right in to the Steinmann family. 'Between you and me, on a scale of one to ten he's almost reached eleven. *Please* take him out for a bit? I need to try to smooth things over with your dad and Ed isn't helping.'

'Well, all right. But only because it's you.'

'Thank you, you're a star! Listen, how are you? How's the new home?'

'Still new. And quiet. And the removal guys seem to have mislaid my coffee machine somewhere between San Fran and here.'

'Hang in there, you'll find it.' There was a definite pause. 'Have you heard any more from Jess?'

Jake stiffened his spine against the sinking feeling his

19

almost-ex-wife's name caused nowadays. 'I heard from her today, actually. That is, I heard from her lawyer.'

'Oh Jake, no! I'm so sorry. I know it's clichéd but if you need to talk '

He laughed. 'I'm good. I think maybe me taking Ed out of your hair for a couple hours might be good for both of us.'

'You're right, it would. But please call me if I can help at all.'

'Thanks, Rosie. I'll remember that. Put him back on, OK?'

There was a muffled remark as the phone was passed back to his brother and Jake could picture Ed and Rosie giggling together, surrounded by flowers in their Upper West Side neighbourhood florist store.

'I think I should be worried about the outrageous way my fiancée flirts with you,' Ed said. 'What? It's *blatant*, Rosie Duncan!' Jake could hear the amusement in Rosie's voice as she made a comment in the background, then Ed laughed. 'She just said if you'd been free when she was single she might have picked a different Steinmann. Cute. So are we going out to play, bro?'

Jake cast a glance around the bleakness of his new apartment: at the depressing cardboard boxes waiting to be unpacked and the bland décor he hadn't chosen. It didn't feel like home at all and right now he didn't think it ever would. He needed to be out of here, before the too-quiet rooms and endless self-analysis in his mind sent him crazy. 'Yes, we are.'

CHAPTER FIVE

Hudson River Books, 8th Avenue, Brooklyn

'Babe, all I want is to make it up to you.'

They had been battling for almost an hour and Bea could feel her resolve beginning to wane. Through it all Otis had stared directly at her in that startling, confident way of his – a weapon that was devastatingly disarming when used to its full effect. He had reached for her hand and managed to hold it for a few seconds before her anger resurged and she pulled it away. Now he was sitting a small distance from her, wearing an expression that begged her to move closer. She rubbed her eyes and wished she had been able to make it out of the door before he had arrived.

'I'm just so tired of fighting,' she said, her thoughts becoming words before she could stop them.

'And so am I. We've been here before, Bea, and we've always made it back.'

'Maybe this time is different.'

Why was her love life so complicated? Why, when

everyone around her seemed capable of finding halfway decent partners, did she struggle? Bea didn't consider herself a demanding girlfriend; neither did she experience problems meeting men. But somewhere between the initial spark and the middle of a relationship the problems began – growing and tangling and balling up until she found herself with an unsatisfactory, untrustworthy partner in a situation more akin to a battle of wills than a productive partnership.

'I don't see why. Sure, I screwed up: I admit it! But we can move on from this, Bea. I want to make amends.'

'Amends? How, exactly? Are you going to go and personally apologise to every member of my family who waited for you in the restaurant last night?'

He couldn't hide his wince from her. 'If necessary.'

'My parents set off on their trip this morning. You might catch them somewhere in upstate New York if you're quick.'

'Baby . . .' He ran a frustrated hand through his dark hair and gave her his best 'pleading puppy' look. Ordinarily, this would have worked, Bea relenting at the sight of his contrition.

Not today, Otis, she told herself sternly. *Today I need answers for everything.*

'And my brother was baying for your blood. Which, considering Stewart is officially the most laid-back person in the city, was no mean feat.'

Her older brother Stewart – who had never been particularly fond of Bea's boyfriend – reckoned his sister was attracted to the wrong kind of men. This, of course, was easy for him to surmise, especially given how loved-up he was with his older partner, Celia. Since the pair of them had met at the *New York Times* where he was a staff writer, writing as Stewart Mitchell (their mother's maiden name) and Celia was a star columnist, they had been virtually inseparable, settling into the easy rhythm of a deeply contented pairing in which they still remained. Just like every other couple in the James family.

Staring at her grovelling partner, Bea felt a well of unease rising within her. She loved him, but how much did he really feel for her? He'd said it himself: they had been here many times before. Surely after five years something should have changed? She *wanted* him to step up, to make good all of his overblown promises that never managed to come to fruition. Was she kidding herself that it was possible? The more she looked at Otis Greene, the louder the white noise in her head grew.

This is ridiculous. It's never going to change. I deserve more than this.

Otis edged closer, his earnest dark eyes searching her face for an invitation. 'Baby . . . What can I do to make this good with us?'

She was tired. Too tired to ride the merry-go-round any more. 'I don't know. I think I need some time to think.'

'So take some time. Call me when you want to continue this discussion.' It was defensive but Bea suspected Otis was relieved to be excused from any further apologising he might have been called upon to do tonight.

'No, that's not what I meant.'

'Then *what*, Bea? What are you saying?'

What am I saying? Bea considered this, her heart thumping. She didn't want to be in this argument again. Ever. Slowly, it began to dawn on her.

'I'm saying . . .' she began, picking her words as if tiptoeing across a minefield '. . . I think we're done. We keep returning to the same problems and I – I just can't go over it any more. I need to be *me* again, Otis. Not some paranoid half of a relationship that isn't going anywhere. I think this is it for us. I'm sorry.'

Otis blinked. This wasn't how it worked: he made apologetic noises; Bea gave in; serenity was restored. Bea's response seemed to throw a spanner in the works. Dropping his gaze, he stepped back. 'If that's what you want.'

Surprised by the strength of her own conviction, Bea stood tall. 'It is.'

The silence in the bookshop was louder than the angry lines of traffic on 8th Avenue outside. Bea retreated behind the counter. Otis stared up at the high ceiling as if expecting to find answers to this new situation written there. Outside, the heavy raindrops battered against the bookstore windows and the world beyond them.

'Then I should go?' It was more of a question than a statement of intent.

'We both should.'

Otis began to reply but the crash of the bookstore door snatched his attention. Dripping wet, Russ O'Docherty clutched a fast disintegrating cardboard cup-holder as he struggled to close the door without losing three teetering coffee cups in the process.

'Sorry I took so long. It's like Armageddon out there . . .' He stopped when he saw their expressions. 'Oh boy, are you guys not done?'

'Actually, I was just leaving,' Otis replied, the lightness of his tone knocking the wind from Bea's stomach. He helped himself to a coffee cup and turned back to Bea. 'Call me when you're ready. Remember I love you.'

Russ watched his friend leave and held out his hands in surprise. 'What happened?'

Bea slumped in the grandfather armchair beside the counter. 'I think we broke up.'

Shocked, Russ hurried over and hovered hesitantly by her side. 'Really? Only he said, "I love you." Usually guys don't choose that line when they're breaking up with someone.'

'I think I might have broken up with him.' Tears welled in Bea's eyes as the frustration of the past week overwhelmed her. 'The thing is, I don't think I can do this again, Russ. I'm the laughing stock of my family: the only James to fail at relationships. And I really don't want this to be all I end up thinking about.' She looked up at her friend, who took the hint and knelt by her, taking her hand. 'My business is doing great, the rest of my life is pretty good. I don't want to be the kind of woman who is ruled by her love life, you know?'

'You're not,' Russ assured her.

'I feel like I am.'

'Yeah, well, you're not and that's all there is to it. I've watched you work so hard to make this place a success, and I know how many people love you, Bea. Most of New York would kill for that kind of résumé. And I don't think you're a failure. So here's one person who isn't laughing at you.'

Bea shook her head, a small smile breaking free. 'Thanks.'

'Otis made a mistake. A big one, I'll admit. But deep

25

down he does love you: I'm sure of it. I think maybe you should focus on what makes you happy for a while. Maybe when you do that, you'll be ready to try again.'

Russ' unquestioning loyalty to his friend would have been touching in any other setting, but today it wasn't helpful. Irritated, Bea stood and moved away.

'What if I don't want to try again? Hmm?'

'I'm just saying you *might* . . .'

'What is it with you and Otis?' Bea demanded, knowing this wouldn't help the situation but compelled to challenge her best friend's stance. 'Why must you always defend him?'

Russ rose to his feet and faced her. 'He's my friend, Bea. Of course I'll defend him. But it shouldn't make a difference whatever I say. You have to decide if you want to be with Otis or not.'

'Can't you see what he's done to me? Don't you think he was wrong?'

'Of course I do . . .'

'Then *why* not support me? Does our friendship mean so little to you?'

'This isn't about us, Bea, so don't make out like I don't support you.' Russ sighed and took off his black-rimmed glasses to wipe the rain-splattered lenses on the bottom of his vintage rock T-shirt. 'I've supported you for as long as we've known each other. You know I have. Sure, I think Otis was out of line when he let you down in front of your family. And yes, I agree, this isn't the first time you've been disappointed. I told him he's a Class A jerk for not putting you first, actually – not that you'll believe me. I warned him he'd lose you if he didn't

26

straighten up his act. But above that, I can't do a thing to change who he is or any of the decisions he makes.'

Bea stared at him, hating Russ for his logical view of life. It had always been his secret weapon. The worst of it was, it made sense. He wasn't to blame for Otis' bad decisions and he was perfectly entitled to be friends with whomever he wanted.

'It would just be nice to have you on my side,' she replied, her voice small and vulnerable as she spoke.

'I don't take sides, Bea. But I'm not a heartless individual either. You know I care about you and I want you to be happy. Heaven knows you deserve it. Take some time out. Figure out what it is you want and whether Otis can provide it or not. In the meantime, I'm your friend and I'm here for you. OK?'

'OK.'

'Good.' He popped his glasses back on. 'And the rain must've made me psychic because I bought you a peppermint mocha.' He held out a cup, a wry smile returning. 'Did I make the right choice?'

There was no point arguing any more. And the coffee smelled good. Still convinced she and Otis were over, Bea nodded at Russ. 'You did good.'

CHAPTER SIX

Kowalski's, corner of West 68th and Columbus, Upper West Side

The small silver bell chimed out over his head as Jake walked into his soon-to-be sister-in-law's florist shop in the pleasantly chic neighbourhood in the Upper West Side. A rush of floral fragrance assaulted his senses from the rainbow-hued display in galvanised steel buckets. Jake loved it here – and completely understood why his brother had chosen to give his skills to the neighbourhood florists' instead of the high-tech, faceless floral boutiques in New York City. There was a peace about the little store that few other shops in Manhattan had, a sense of timelessness that made even the busiest customer linger.

A pretty, heavily pregnant young woman with shocking pink streaks in her hair screamed from behind the counter and hurried towards him.

'Jake! Oh, it's *so* good to see you, honey!' Hugging him with her large belly was a challenge but she made an enthusiastic attempt at it.

28

He laughed, despite being almost knocked off his feet by Rosie's kooky assistant. 'Great to see you, Marnie. And look at you! How long till D-Day?'

She pulled a face. 'Six weeks. I'm kinda hoping it'll be earlier but my obstetrician told me it might be a week over.' She rubbed her back. 'I feel like I'm carrying a moose, not a couple of babies. I blame Zac's quarterback genes. But anyway, how are you?'

Jake ignored the sinking feeling when he saw Marnie's smile morph into concern. It was barely a month since his separation from Jessica had become public knowledge and already he dreaded receiving the identical expression from everyone he met. He knew their concern was well meant, but it still made him wince. It was as if somehow the fact his wife had chosen to live her life without him was cause for the whole world to pity him, as if he was less of a man.

'I'm good,' he replied, his voice already bearing the singsong notes of someone who really, *really* didn't want to discuss it any more. 'I'm here to rescue your boss from the whining Steinmann charm of my brother.'

Marnie grinned. 'Good call. Any longer and there might not have been a wedding at all.' Throwing her head back, she yelled, '*Ed! Jake's here!*'

'Thank goodness for that!' a familiar voice replied and moments later the welcome smile of Rosie Duncan lit up the store as she walked in from the workroom. With her dark eyes, dark brown hair and pale English rose complexion, Rosie was striking to look at, even though her demeanour revealed how little she realised it.

'Hey sis-in-law-to-be,' Jake grinned, dispensing with

29

the tradition of respectable cheek kisses and scooping her into a huge embrace instead. 'Boy, am I glad to see you.'

'Tough day?' she asked, the smile not leaving her face, for which Jake was unspeakably grateful.

'As much as ever,' he replied, happy that, with Rosie at least, this was sufficient to draw a line under the subject.

'And now it's going to get tougher having to spend time with the love of my life,' she laughed. 'Are you sure you can handle my fiancé?'

'Leave him with me. There's nothing Ed can throw at me I haven't seen before. I used to be his wing-man back in his dating days – and believe me, once you've pulled your brother from a New York bar brawl pretty much anything else is mundane.'

'You are a godsend, Jake Steinmann,' Rosie laughed, squeezing his hand. 'He's been driving us *insane* all day.'

'I thought I knew how grouchy he could be after all these years working with him, but he's reached new depths of pessimism,' Marnie agreed.

'Sounds like my brother. Is he ready?'

'As I'll ever be,' Ed replied, striding into the store and planting a kiss on Rosie's head. 'Thanks so much for the glowing summation of my current state of mind there, girls.'

'We're only saying what we see,' Rosie smiled up at him – and Jake felt his heart tug as he saw the way she looked at his brother. Had Jessica ever looked at him that way? He thought she had, yet the pain of recent events clouded his memories. But Ed deserved to be happy, he reminded himself. One happy Steinmann had to be a good thing for the world . . .

'Hmm. Well, I'll let you off this time, Ms Duncan.'

'Excellent. You do that. And don't depress your brother.' She jabbed a finger into Ed's chest, before turning to Jake. 'If he gets too much, just shove him in a cab and send him back, OK?'

Jake chuckled. 'Deal.'

The bar Ed had chosen was one Jake vaguely remembered visiting before – probably to watch a baseball game with his brother before Jessica had swept into his life and taken him to the other side of America. It felt odd to be thinking of things he had done pre-Jess, especially as all of his recent thoughts had been consumed with memories of their marriage. But it was a positive change, he decided. And something positive in his life was way overdue.

They settled at a booth and ordered beer. Even though it was early, Jake was glad of the cold buzz the bottle gave him. A little bit reckless, drinking in the daytime, he reasoned. Jessica would *not* have been impressed . . .

'You literally saved my life,' Ed grinned, clinking the neck of his beer bottle with Jake's. 'I feel bad leaving Rosie in charge of wrangling wedding guests but, trust me, she's a better man than me for the job.'

'You're lucky, you know,' Jake replied, taking another swig of beer. 'Rosie's a wonderful woman.'

'She is.' Ed seemed to glow in the darkened bar booth. 'I have to pinch myself every day. I *know* how lucky I am.'

'I'm happy for you. And, hey, I'm sorry I wasn't in

town for your engagement party, man. There seems to have been a lot happening in New York that I missed.'

Ed frowned. 'What engagement party?'

'Yours and Rosie's?' Jake stared at his brother. 'Don't tell me you guys didn't have an engagement party?'

'No, we didn't. We got engaged and then had a string of big wedding orders at Kowalski's so we – didn't get round to it.'

Jake couldn't believe what he was hearing. Surely the momentous event of Rosie and Ed agreeing to marry each other should be marked? He thought back to the lavish engagement party he and Jessica had enjoyed in an exclusive New York club – so expensive that it rivalled the wedding for extravagance. Back then it seemed the most natural thing to do. The expense was an expression of the enormous impact Jessica's acceptance of his proposal had on his life; to spend any less wouldn't have done their engagement justice.

'And Rosie was OK with that?'

Ed shrugged. 'It was her idea.'

'I find that hard to believe.'

'Then you clearly don't know my fiancée very well. Rosie's practical. She didn't want the hassle of organising a party when we were flat out at Kowalski's.'

Jessica would never have stood for that. From the earliest days of their relationship Jake had learned that everything his partner did was designed to be seen by others. One hundred and fifty guests to the exclusive engagement party; two hundred guests to their wedding at her parents' house overlooking beautiful Half Moon Bay; and no expense spared at either. Both events had been reported in the society pages, the beautiful people of New York and California gathered in black tie and ball gowns for the eager lenses of the national press. Of course Rosie was different, but Jake still felt a pang of sadness that she had been denied the opportunity to celebrate her engagement.

'I have an idea,' he said, even as it was still forming in his mind.

'Oh?'

'Let me throw you guys a party. Consider it my belated engagement gift.'

'I couldn't ask you to do that, man.'

The more he considered it, the more Jake believed his idea to be a great one. 'I'm serious, Ed. Let me do this for you. You and Rosie have been rocks for me lately. I just want to repay your kindness. What do you say?'

Surprised, Ed hugged his brother. 'Yes, then. Thanks, bro.'

Jake smiled as they pulled apart. It was a brilliant idea: allowing him to express his deep gratitude for the support he'd received from Rosie and Ed while also giving him something completely non-Jessica-related to focus on. Besides, it had been a while since he had felt like celebrating. This could be just what the doctor ordered.

You're a genius, Jake Steinmann, he congratulated himself. *This party is the start of something new . . .*

CHAPTER SEVEN

Celia and Stewart's apartment, 91st Street Upper West Side

Bea stepped out of the yellow cab and gazed up at the bay windows of the traditional New York brownstone building. She loved this street and had taken every opportunity to visit since her brother Stewart had moved in here with his girlfriend Celia. The leafy boughs of London Plane trees rustled in the light breeze above her head and gave the street an air of serenity and calm, despite the constant buzz of Manhattan traffic at the end of the block. It seemed a world away from Brooklyn and the perfect place for Bea after the events of the day. Right now, she needed familiarity and comfort – and her brother was the one who could provide it.

'Bea! Come on up,' Stewart's voice crackled through the door intercom and Bea headed inside the elegant brownstone. He was waiting for her as she reached his floor, leaning casually against the doorframe of his apartment. 'Coffee's on and I have muffins from M&H Bakers.'

'Sounds wonderful,' Bea smiled, taking off her coat and walking inside. The apartment was light and airy, bearing more evidence of her brother's taste since he and Celia had recently redecorated. In addition to the floor-to-ceiling bookcases that separated the living room from the dining area, a collection of Stewart's beloved gadgets, games consoles and gym equipment had been assigned a place near the hallway that led to the bedrooms. True to form, his things were arranged haphazardly, more than a little at odds with the ordered regularity of Celia's belongings. But, much like their unconventional relationship, it worked perfectly.

Bea and Stewart settled on chairs by the table in the large bay window and Bea helped herself to a triple chocolate muffin, the scent of freshly brewed coffee making her mouth water.

'Have you eaten lately?' Stewart asked, inadvertently sounding like their mother.

'Not much,' Bea replied through mouthfuls of chocolate sponge. Perhaps it was being so far away from Brooklyn – and Otis – but her recently absent appetite had made a sudden return. She laughed when she saw her brother's amusement. 'It must be the magic of M&H.'

'Now, *that* I can't argue with. Seriously, Bea, how are you doing? You left so quickly after the meal the other night.'

Bea felt her heart sink. 'Well, I didn't want to hang around. Not with Aunt Ruby's loud damnations ringing in my ears. Public humiliation isn't something you want to prolong.'

'You weren't humiliated, sis. Your boyfriend on the other hand . . .'

'He's not my boyfriend.' Bea's sudden admission made her appetite evaporate once more. 'Not any more.'

Stewart took a few moments to process this. 'Really? Are you sure?'

'Yes.'

'Only you've said this before and . . .'

'It's definite this time. I'm done with Otis and his broken promises. I just can't do it any more.' She shook her head. 'Russ thinks I'm being hasty, of course. He's convinced we're destined for each other. But he should try dating Otis. I'm tired of the stupid roundabout of my love life, Stew. I've decided to get off it for good.'

'Wow.'

'I know.'

Stewart refilled their coffee mugs. 'So what's the plan now?'

'Focus on the things in my life that work. Russ is talking about putting a coffee bar into the bookshop and I have lots of ideas for promotions and evening events. Also, I'm thinking of looking for a bigger apartment.'

'Moving uptown at last, eh?'

Bea laughed. 'No fear. It's Brooklyn all the way, baby! I like where I live. I'd just like somewhere with a bit more room.'

'It all sounds good. But you haven't answered my question, Bea: how are you really?'

Bea thought back to the night of the doomed family meal – the uniform disappointment of her gathered family members, the sympathy in their expressions that she really didn't need to see, and the crushing realisation that, once again, Otis had let her down. How was she meant to be after an experience like that?

'It was mortifying,' she confessed, staring into the dark depths of her coffee. 'A whole history of happy-ever-afters around the table and I couldn't even get my boyfriend to keep a promise he'd made to all of them. It made me feel like a failure, through no fault of my own. And more than anything else, it made me realise that I'm the exception in the James family: I'm destined not to find a decent relationship.'

'Bea . . .'

'I mean it, Stew. Let's face it, by the law of averages it had to happen to someone eventually. It would be impossible to have so many generations of childhood sweetheart success stories without one blip. That's just what I am. A blip.'

Her brother's laugh was gentle but still stung. 'You're being melodramatic. This is *one relationship*, Bea. There's no unwritten rule that every member of the James family has to find true love at their first attempt. If that were true, I'd have been sunk years ago. The point is we all get there in the end. Otis isn't The One: that doesn't mean there isn't someone out there who might be.'

Bea wanted to believe him, but she couldn't see anything beyond the possibility of years of disappointment stretching into the future. Frankly, there were other things she would rather expend her energies on. Things that had at least a hope of success attached to them.

'I don't know if I can be bothered to look for them any more.'

Stewart took his sister's hand across the table. 'Then stop looking for now. You need to be good to yourself, sis. I hate seeing you down.'

'Am I missing something good?' The door to the apartment slammed and Bea looked up to see the flamboyant figure of her brother's partner approaching.

'Hi Celia,' she smiled, standing to receive a hug.

'Honey, how *are* you? I was so worried after that *awful* dinner.' She placed her hand on Bea's forehead as if expecting to find a raging temperature. 'Are you well?'

'She's fine,' Stewart laughed, rising to fetch another mug from the kitchen. 'Put my sister down before you strangle her.'

Celia pulled up a chair and sat beside Bea. 'The man is an *oaf*, Bea darling! He's not worthy of you. I hope you tore a strip off him when he finally showed his face.'

'I did more than that,' Bea replied, secretly touched by Celia's overblown concern. 'I told him we were over.'

Celia's eyebrows shot heavenwards. 'Oh? Well, I'm proud of you, honey! Men like that have to learn that women aren't doormats to be abandoned at a moment's notice.'

'Can you abandon a doormat?' Stewart grinned at Bea, but Celia wasn't listening. For a full five minutes she launched a scathing attack on Otis Greene's lack of manhood, complete rudeness and inability to be the man Bea needed him to be.

'You're better off without him. Why waste your life on a loser?'

Why indeed, Bea smiled to herself. 'Enough about that, anyway. How's everything with your book?'

Celia heaved a dramatic sigh as Stewart kissed the top of her head, placing a fresh mug of coffee in her hands. 'Exhausting. But I think we're almost there. My publisher insists on making last-minute changes to my manuscript that make no grammatical sense whatsoever – I swear they think I don't know how to write. I'm only a senior *New York Times* columnist for heaven's sake. What the hell do I know?'

'When do you publish?'

'In a month. Of course, I'll be glad when it's out on the shelves, but I'm not convinced I'd do it again. Still, if it worked for Nora Ephron, I have to hope it'll work for me.'

Bea decided to ask the question she had been mulling over for a few weeks. If Celia agreed, it would be the first major event Hudson River Books had ever held – and could be the start of a whole new chapter in the bookshop's success. If not, it was back to the drawing board.

'I've been thinking – and please feel free to say no – but how would you like to hold the launch of your book at my bookstore? We'd love to have you and I could arrange everything.'

Celia exchanged glances with Stewart and beamed brightly at Bea. 'Now that is just *perfect*! I was only saying to your brother last night I thought your place would be ideal. Of course! Pencil it in!'

Bea felt as if the sun had just broken free on a very dark day. 'That's wonderful! Why don't you come down to the bookstore soon and we'll go through everything you'd like?'

Celia offered a perfectly manicured hand and Bea shook it. 'You just got yourself a deal, lady!'

As Celia and Stewart began to talk about their respective days at work, Bea gazed out of the bay window to the street below. This was the positive sign she had been longing for – and she was determined to make it a success.

CHAPTER EIGHT

Private loft apartment,
Upper West Side

The loft apartment looked like a movie set. As the owner gave Jake a tour, he couldn't help but be impressed by the space. Architect-designed and full of light, the apartment smelled of money – every detail an indicator of taste and expense. Frosted glass met industrial slate and polished cherry wood floors. Generous couches in neutral tones were arranged around exposed brick walls. Glass and brushed steel staircases rose from either end of the room to a mezzanine above, with bedrooms situated off it. Two-storey glass windows provided the most amazing view of the Upper West Side – at night the lights of the city would meet the stars and guests could wander out onto the slate balcony to admire the view. It was perfect.

'And you don't mind if we clear some furniture for the party?' he asked.

Eric Reynolds, the owner of the gorgeous living space and an old friend from Jake's Yale days, nodded. 'No problem. We do it often, actually. My practice holds all its business functions here so we've become old hands at furniture removal.' He slapped a friendly hand on Jake's back. 'You know, it's good to see you, man. I thought we'd lost you to the West Coast forever.'

Jake laughed, but his heart was heavy. 'Me? Never! Always an East Coast fella.'

'Good. We should do a weekend at the Hampton house some time. Laura would love to see you.'

'How is the family?'

Eric chuckled. 'Growing. Suddenly I'm the father of three teenagers and I have no idea how it happened. The boys are good, though, even if they have relegated me to "old man" status in backyard basketball matches. And Laura hasn't changed in twenty years. So, what do you reckon?'

Jake looked up at the light flooding in from the glass roof of the apartment. 'It's perfect. Ed and Rosie will love it. And I hope you and Laura can join us?'

'Unfortunately, we're out of town that Friday. But we'll expect you all at the house soon, OK?'

In a coffee shop around the corner from the apartment, Jake pulled out his Moleskine notebook and ticked 'VENUE' off his to-do list. Remembering that Eric Reynolds had an apartment he let out for events had been a masterstroke this morning and a large part of Jake's planning conundrum solved. Now what remained was a bar, waiting staff and a caterer, perhaps a DJ, maybe some mood lighting. Jake looked at his list and congratulated himself. This party planning was easier than he'd imagined.

He sipped his flat white and glanced around the coffee

shop interior. A long line stretched along the counter towards the door but the speed of service meant that even those at the back of the queue weren't visibly rattled by having to wait. That said, compared with San Franciscan coffee shop customers, this queue would appear uptight. Jake shuddered as a familiar thud of reality echoed through him. *Everything* had seemed easier on the West Coast – the sunshine and laid-back atmosphere permeating every aspect of life. Except for his marriage, which should have been the easiest thing of all. Why did Jessica leave him? What happened to change how she felt about him?

Jake groaned. Speculation was pointless. Jess had her reasons – whatever they were – and he was powerless to change her mind. He could go over and over the situation until the end of time and never find the answers. Jessica simply didn't want to be his wife any longer. The unsigned divorce papers in his still-unpacked apartment were irrefutable evidence of that.

He turned his attention back to the neatly written to-do list. *This* was what he should focus on, something removed from his marriage situation.

Make this a success, he wrote in bold, confident letters, *and the rest will follow*.

Alongside the list of engagement party tasks, Jake had written an extensive list that would take even longer to complete. When he moved from San Francisco he had left more than his marital home behind. Along with his friends and lifestyle he had also left his business – a thriving psychotherapy practice that he had built from scratch.

Even now, he regretted having to leave his hard work on the other side of the US. Still, at least the money from its sale would go a long way to seeing him established in New York. And, as Ed had joked, there were fewer places in the world more in need of mass therapy than Manhattan.

'It'll be a goldmine,' he'd assured Jake. 'They'll be lining up outside to dump their neuroses on you.'

Jake hoped Ed was right. Certainly their father and eldest brother Daniel had profited handsomely from dealing with the minds of the Big Apple, so there was no reason to suppose he wouldn't do the same.

If only it were that easy. Finding the right premises was a challenge. Too close to the centre of New York and he could be lost in the city blur; too far away and he would just be lost. He needed to be where people needed him and were willing to pay for his services, so affluent areas were preferable. But affluent areas spelled expensive rents and to place his fledgling business in the wrong area would prove costly indeed.

Deep down, Jake hated that money was always the bottom line. When he graduated from medical school he had entertained lofty aspirations to treat everyone, regardless of income. And, for a couple of years, he had worked in volunteer practices, offering psychological assistance to the police and community outreaches in addition to his junior partner position at a local psycho-therapy unit. He had almost burned himself out in the process, but had felt a deep sense of pride to be doing the right thing.

Then, he met Jessica. And everything changed. Her father was a powerful businessman in the city and only too happy to send wealthy colleagues Jake's way. With the profits from his new clientele, Jake was soon able to set up his own practice, moving wholesale to San Francisco a year later when Jessica was offered a position at a West Coast interior design agency. Since then, Jake's business had focused solely on private clients – and he had become comfortable with the safety and security it afforded him.

Maybe he had become *too* comfortable with everything. Maybe that was why Jessica left . . .

He shook the thought away. He hadn't changed: she had. He needed to focus on rebuilding his business. Premises and good staff, definitely a great PA, maybe a practice partner in time – all of these things he had control over and could ensure he made a success of.

He spent the afternoon calling recruiters and realtors, his list getting longer as appointments to view premises and meet potential staff built up. Back in his apartment and pleased with a productive day's work, Jake closed his notebook and stretched his aching arms above his head as the light began to fade over the Williamsburg skyline. He poured a glass of bourbon and relaxed back in his favourite leather chair – one of the few pieces of furniture he had brought from his previous home. The apartment grew dark as streetlights flared into life, casting an eerie orange glow around the bare walls. A single shaft of white light from a neighbouring building's security lamp illuminated the table by the window – and the dreaded brown envelope confirming the end of his marriage. Taking a long sip of bourbon, Jake let pain wash over him as he closed his eyes.

CHAPTER NINE

Hudson River Books,
8th Avenue, Brooklyn

'Celia Reighton is a *legend*!' Russ stroked the journalist's latest column in the *New York Times*, which was spread across the counter in Hudson River Books.

The column was a wry take on the Mayor of New York's recent speech at a fundraiser in which he mistakenly referred to Donald Trump as 'Sir Donald'. A furore had broken out, Manhattan's journalists having a field day at his expense while political opponents claimed this as evidence of the Mayor's unsuitability for the job. Celia, in her inimitable fashion, was musing on the Mayor's secret plan to 'Olde-Englandise' New York:

One has to wonder what's next? Will suits of armour be seen on Wall Street? Will corsets be compulsory at New York Fashion Week? Before we know it, our esteemed Mayor will have the whole of Manhattan as a giant, Disney-esque theme pub. My advice? Be sure

to sign up for those jousting lessons now, before the
rush begins . . .

'I think I actually love her,' Russ laughed.

'Well, hands off. My brother's already claimed her.'

'Shame.' Russ studied Bea. 'You look better today.'

'Thanks. I feel better.'

'Did you and Otis talk?'

Bea ignored her irritation. '*No*. We have nothing else to talk about. I've been thinking: Celia's book launch could be the first of many evening events Hudson River Books could host. I thought we could collaborate with the Comedy Cavern and do an open-mic style event nearer the summer, if you're up for it?'

'Well look at you, Ms Businesswoman of the Year! It's all good, Bea.'

'Thank you.' Pleased with herself, Bea looked around the bookstore. It was coming together at last.

'When is Ms Reighton arriving to look around?'

'About ten. But Stewart said to expect her any time between now and two p.m.' Bea smiled. 'Time-keeping isn't her forte, apparently.'

Russ looked hurriedly around the shop. 'Heck, I need to tidy this place for when she arrives. We can't have a *New York Times* star columnist seeing the bookstore like this.'

'Like what? It looks great.'

Russ stared at Bea. 'So *you* say. But we're talking New York *royalty* here. I'm not settling for anything less than perfect.'

Bea giggled as her friend set about cleaning the already clean shop. She was used to Russ panicking but today he was doing it at an entirely new level. Bea understood his nerves: she too was a little daunted by the task. It was a coup to host Celia's event, but, knowing her reputation and respect within the literary community of the city, the prospect of famous authors, socialites and powerful journalists eating canapés and drinking wine at Hudson River Books was slightly terrifying. She was excited though: if the bookstore could pull this off, anything was possible.

As predicted, Celia breezed into Hudson River Books just after one o'clock, by which time Russ was more tightly wound up than a spring. Not wanting to risk her colleague exploding in Celia's presence, Bea despatched him to the local coffee shop to fetch drinks. At least this way she could guarantee ten Russ-free minutes to talk about the important things with Celia.

'I *love* this place!' Celia said, walking around the bookstore and inspecting the bare-brick walls, comfortable leather chairs and informally arranged bookshelves. 'It's so inviting, so warm and welcoming. Every bookstore should be like this.'

Bea had overheard similar conversations between customers over the last couple of years but it was wonderful to hear it said directly to her. It was what she and Russ had worked so hard for: to create a store that people wanted to linger in. Cosy beanbags, cushions and chairs were arranged throughout for customers to sit and enjoy their books; special genre-themed zones changed regularly so there was always something new to discover; quotes from Books of the Month were chalked up on thought-bubble-shaped blackboards around the store; and they had even devised a 'Take A Chance on Me' book service, where a pile of titles wrapped in brown paper with labels hinting at the stories within invited readers to discover an author they might not have read before.

As Celia continued to enthuse about the fixtures, fittings and ambience of the bookstore, Bea beamed with pride. She remembered making her Grandma Dot laugh when, as a little girl, she had earnestly asked if the local bookshop in her home town might let her live there if she asked nicely enough. She had even devised a back-up plan if the bookshop declined her idea: the local library's children's section had very comfortable patchwork beanbags that could easily make a bed. As long as books surrounded Bea all the time, she wasn't fussy about where she lived. Now she was living out her childhood ambition – almost. Hudson River Books was definitely the kind of book-filled space that she would happily spend every hour of her life in.

Aware of the brief amount of time she had before her colleague's return, Bea sat on the large black leather sofa in the corner that would soon house Russ' coffee bar and invited Celia to join her.

'I've been thinking about the book launch,' she said, pulling out her notebook and scanning the list of suggestions with the shaking tip of her pen. 'I'd love it if you would do a reading for us. I thought, with your permission, we could reproduce some quotes from your book and hang them around the walls. We have some bespoke frames that we use for seasonal promotions and Russ is a graphic design whizz.'

'I like it. Go on.'

Encouraged, Bea shared more items from her list. The French bistro opposite the bookstore had agreed to serve mini versions of its popular dishes as canapés and provide as much wine as the guests could drink, while the small stationery store further down 8th Avenue had offered to hand-print invitations for the event and supply matching goody bags for all attending.

Celia listened to Bea, nodding enthusiastically. 'You've really thought about this, haven't you? I must say, I'm impressed. Stewart told me how much this event means to you. Talking of which, how are you? Has that awful man tried to contact you?'

Slightly taken aback at the speed with which Celia had changed the subject, Bea took a few moments to reply. 'I – um – I'm fine and no, thankfully, Otis hasn't been in touch. But then I did tell him we were over, so it's little wonder he's left me alone.'

Celia folded her hands in her lap and fixed Bea with a look that made her a little nervous. 'You know what you need? A night out. Great company, good wine – get away from all thoughts of relationships and enjoy yourself.'

Bea had to admit that sounded good. Lately all she had done was dodge thoughts about Otis and her failed love life. 'I'd like that.'

Celia's smile illuminated the store. 'Excellent! My good friend is having a party in the Upper West Side, Friday night. It'll be full of interesting people and I hear the private venue is to *die* for. Say you'll come.'

Bea laughed at the unexpected invitation. What else would she be doing on a Friday night, anyway? 'OK. I'd love to.'

That evening, Bea sat alone in her cosy apartment in the Boerum Hill neighbourhood of Brooklyn. To the casual observer, the only differences between her business and her home were a few more chairs, a kitchen sink and a bedroom; the rest of the space being devoted to books. Russ jokingly referred to Bea's apartment as a 'flat-share' arrangement: 'It's nice of the books to let you stay. Do they charge you reasonable rent?'

Bea smiled now as she sipped a large mug of hot chocolate and ran her fingers along the spines of her books. Since ending her relationship with Otis she found she was enjoying being alone. The days following the awful family dinner had given her time to reflect on her recent life and what she had seen hadn't been pretty. She realised she had become so focused on tackling potential problems Otis could cause that she had been neglecting her own life. She had been a fire-fighter rather than the trailblazer she wanted to be. That was going to change.

Bea couldn't remember the last time she had been able to think only of herself. Between her final year of university and the start of this week she had lurched from one doomed relationship to another, with barely time to catch her breath in between. On one hand it proved she was a woman in demand – as Stewart had often said – but the problem was the *kind* of men lining up to date her.

She caught sight of her reflection in the vintage mirror she had bought last year at the Brooklyn Flea market.

Well, no more, she told herself. *From now on, it's all about me.*

She meant it, too. Why should her life revolve around relationships? Who wrote that rule, anyway? More than anything, Bea wanted to be known for who *she* was, what *she* could achieve. Placing the responsibility for her happiness on someone else was only going to lead to more heartache. Her family might have the monopoly on successful relationships, but she didn't have to join them. It was her time to be whoever she wanted to be. And right now, she wanted to be happy being herself.

Her reflection started back, singularly unconvinced. Otis Greene still had a heavy hold on her heart. She let out a sigh. Clearly this was going to take some getting used to.

The shrill ring of her 1950s red Bakelite phone made her turn from the mirror.

'Hi, Bea James?'

'Sweetheart! It's Mum. Can you hear me?'

'Loud and clear.' Bea smiled and all of a sudden wished her parents hadn't set off on their long-planned trans-American adventure the day after the family meal. 'How are you both?'

'Your dad is driving a forty-two foot Winnebago, so he's like a kid, as you can imagine. And I'm a happy navigator with my lovely new maps. More to the point, how are you?'

'I'm good.' She hesitated, wondering how much to tell her mother, before reasoning that Stewart would most likely fill her in on all the details even if she didn't. Better to bite the bullet. 'Single, again. But it's the right thing.'

'Good.' Her mum's reply didn't miss a beat. 'I'm sorry we had to leave so quickly, darling. Thing is, your father has a list as long as your arm that he wants us to get through before we fly home.'

'It's fine; I know you've been dreaming about this trip for years. Where are you now?'

'Philadelphia. Next is Boston and New England. I suspect he has the historical tour worked out for every place we visit, but that's what I get for marrying a history lecturer. Are you sure everything is OK?'

'Yes, I'm sure.'

'Because if not I can tell your dad to turn the Winnebago around right now.'

Bea could hear a muffled retort from her father and missed him incredibly. 'You're not getting out of Dad's magical history tour that easily.'

'Rats. Oh well, you can't blame a girl for trying. I'll check in next week, though. That's if your dad hasn't bored me off the face of the planet.'

'She loves it, Bea-Bea! Love you!' Bea's dad called out.

'Love to you both. Tell Dad to drive safely and let you have a day off for shopping in Boston.'

'I will. That's why I love you! Bye, Bea!'

When the call ended, Bea looked around her book-strewn apartment, which suddenly seemed too quiet. *I'm fine*, she told herself. *Absolutely fine.*

CHAPTER TEN

Chez Henri, Upper West Side

'Smoked salmon with wilted spinach and cumin,' the waiter announced, placing a small tasting plate of beautifully constructed canapés in front of Jake. 'We also have gazpacho and lime shots and bourbon-marinated beef with wasabi glaze.'

Jake stared at the table covered in white plates with sumptuous edible art and sighed contentedly. Party planning definitely had its perks, not least in Manhattan, and he congratulated himself on the fortunate position he found himself in. He could quite happily do this every day for the rest of his life.

'It looks wonderful,' he smiled, noting the pride of the chef standing beside the table. 'All of it.'

'Please,' the chef invited, keen to see his potential customer sample the dishes laid before him.

Every tiny mouthful was an explosion of flavour, layer upon layer of taste experiences that delighted the palate and seemed designed to excite every one of Jake's senses.

Eric had been right about this place. Chez Henri's food could rival the best in the world and was definitely the hot ticket in New York. No wonder the chef was rumoured to be on his way to achieving a Michelin star for his creations.

Feeling a little uncomfortable with the scrutiny of the chef and attendant waiting staff, Jake turned to Henri DuChamp. 'Why don't you join me and talk me though your dishes?'

The waiter and three waitresses exchanged looks of surprise, but Chef Henri's expression didn't flicker. With a gesture of his hand the waiting staff retreated to the kitchen and he sat down.

'Merci, Monsieur.'

'Call me Jake, Henri, please.'

Henri laughed. 'Thank you, Jake. This is unusual, but I must confess I prefer it.'

'You don't get to do this often?'

The chef shook his head. 'Most people like to be waited on.'

'Ah,' Jake smiled. 'Well, I am *not* one of those people. The thing is, I'm organising an engagement party for my brother and his fiancée. They're very special to me and I want the event to be relaxed, happy and characterised by awesome food.'

'Then in my opinion, these dishes here would be the best for the occasion,' Henri replied, pulling plates from the far side of the table. 'We will begin here and you tell me what you like. Together, we will create the perfect menu.'

'Sounds good, Henri.'

The chef beamed and then, checking that none of his staff were listening, he leaned closer to Jake. 'But you know what would make the tasting even better?'

Jake expected Henri to recommend a fine wine, expensive champagne or rich cognac. 'What?'

Henri chuckled. 'An ice-cold *beer*.'

'A beer? Henri, I like your thinking.'

'And that, Jake, is why we are going to become firm friends . . .'

'Bro, this is too much.' Ed shook his head as he read the list of dishes Jake had selected for the engagement party. 'Rosie and I would've been happy with a bar somewhere . . .'

'I know you would. But if it had been left to you guys to plan this party it wouldn't have happened. Which is why you asked me. And which, Eduardo, is *why* you're having what I decide you're having.'

Ed whistled and leaned against the florist store counter. 'Rosie will flip out when she sees this. I haven't been able to take her to dinner for months; it's like you're bringing all the food we've missed to one party.'

'But you think she'll like it?'

'Like it? She's likely to forget she's engaged to me and marry you instead.' He put the menu on the counter and shook Jake's hand with the handshake they had devised as teenagers: hands clasped low, switching to holding thumbs, finished with a fist-bump. 'Thanks, man.'

'Hey, my pleasure. Now all I need from you is a list of all the people you forgot in the initial guest list.'

Ed's sheepish expression confirmed how well his

brother knew him. 'There were a couple I missed off . . .'

'What's this?' Ed and Rosie's multi-hued assistant picked up the list, her other hand protectively resting on her considerable baby bump.

'It's the menu for the engagement party on Friday, Marnie,' Ed said.

'Goat's cheese? Brie? I can't eat this, Ed!'

Ed stared at her. 'Who says you're invited?'

Marnie stuck out her chin. 'Rosie did. And Jake. And *you* for that matter.'

'When?'

'Yesterday.'

'Ah.'

'Exactly. I can't believe you wouldn't consider the needs of your very important pregnant friend.'

Ed groaned. Jake jumped in to save his brother from the terrifying fury of Marnie Andersson's pregnant indignation. 'But we did, Marnie.' He took the paper gently from her clenched fist and drew her attention to an extra set of dishes printed on the reverse. '*These* are specially designed with the specific needs of your pregnancy diet in mind. No unripened soft cheese, no egg yolk, no rare meat or fish, no alcohol.'

Marnie squeaked and hugged Jake as best she could around her belly. 'You're a darling! If I wasn't with Zac . . .'

'And almost eight months pregnant,' Ed pointed out.

'That wouldn't matter.' She shrugged off the suggestion. 'He looks like Henry Cavill, only with blue eyes. The twins would love him.' Happy, she waddled away to greet a customer who had just arrived.

Jake felt his cheeks burning. 'Wow.'

'She's an original,' Ed agreed. 'And, thankfully for you, *very* in love with Zac, otherwise known as the Fit Guy.'

'Can you tell I'm relieved?' Jake's heart was thudding nevertheless. Despite the growing acceptance of his new single status, he wasn't quite ready to be propositioned by a heavily pregnant woman. He grinned at his brother, who handed him a mug of smoky coffee from Kowalski's ancient-looking coffee machine. 'Hasn't Rosie retired that thing yet?'

Ed feigned offence. 'Shh! That's a very valuable member of our staff you're abusing. Trashing Old F would be sacrilege. Besides, as long as he makes great coffee, who are we to judge how he looks?'

'I hear you.' He tasted the coffee and was again surprised by how excellent a brew could come from such a dubious coffee maker. 'OK, what?'

Ed was looking at him intently and the instant sinking sensation Jake experienced could only herald one thing: he was about to receive a 'concerned older brother chat'. He had learned it from their father – a past master at the serious Steinmann conversation switch – although Ed would vehemently deny it if Jake ever pointed this out to him.

'Have you dealt with – *it* – yet?'

Jake folded his arms. 'It?'

'Come on, man, you know what I mean. The letter. From Jessica's lawyer. That, I'm guessing from your expression, is still in the envelope it arrived in?'

Jake wished his brother didn't know him quite as well as he did. Of course he hadn't replied to the letter. He'd told himself he was too busy and had made sure the engagement party preparations demanded as much of his time as possible. Between that and his to-do list for establishing his new Manhattan practice, what time was there left to deal with lawyers who only wanted to fleece him anyway?

'I'll deal with it.'

'Yeah, sure. When do you reckon that'll be, hmm? Five years? Twenty? You need closure on this. As soon as you can.'

Irritation rising, Jake prepared to face him down. 'Easy for you to say. Before you met Rosie you never had a relationship last long enough for lawyers to notice. Apart from the ones you were bedding, that is.'

'Ouch. You cut me deep, bro.'

Ed was mocking him, but Jake didn't care. He was so sick of the entire world feeling entitled to tell him how to live his life: Jessica and her lawyer, Jake's father, Ed, his own lawyer Chuck – even the lady who sold him coffee at his new neighbourhood coffee place had somehow learned that he was going through a divorce. What right did any of them have to advise him, however well meaning they were? 'Of course I'll answer the damn letter.'

Ed held up his hands. 'Hey, it's your call. Just don't leave it too long.'

In the cab heading back to Williamsburg, Jake was still fuming. He knew Ed was right, but the truth of it was that he didn't want to start the process that would inevitably lead to the end of his marriage. Jessica might have made herself undeniably clear when she walked out on him, but while they were still legally bound to one another there remained the possibility that – just maybe – there was a chance they might be reconciled. Jake hated the stubborn hope within him and wished that he didn't still yearn for Jess to reconsider her decision. But, he reasoned, you didn't spend almost ten years of your life loving someone only to let go of them so easily, did you?

He stared out at the grey Manhattan afternoon; the vivid yellow of New York cabs on either side of him appearing like splashes of sunlight against the leaden palette of the passing city. *I'll sign the papers soon*, he decided. *But I'm not ready yet.*

CHAPTER ELEVEN

Hudson River Books, 8th Avenue, Brooklyn

If it was possible to have a coronary induced by new culinary machinery then Russ O'Docherty was going to need a paramedic. Bea watched her colleague unwinding bubble-wrap from the bookstore's new espresso machine with the kind of breathless reverence normally reserved for priceless works of art, expensive gifts and beautiful women.

'She . . . is . . . *stunning* . . .'

'How do you know it's female?'

'Are you kidding me? Look at her curves, the shine on her chrome, the delicate curve of her milk arm . . .'

Bea shuddered. 'That's just creepy now. It's a *machine*, Russ, not Marilyn Monroe.'

Russ clicked his fingers and stared at Bea as though she had just shared the meaning of life with him. 'That's perfect! We'll call her Marilyn.'

'We will?'

'Sure! Men will want to worship at her feet, women

will want to hang out with her and bask in her beauty.'

'O-K . . . Well, when you're done worshipping her, perhaps you can help me clear the corner where her shrine will be? The carpenter will be here in an hour.'

Reluctantly, Russ left the gleaming object of his affections to begin packing boxes of books as Bea dismantled a shelving unit that was making way for the new coffee bar. He shook his head as they worked, casting wry glances at Bea. And, while it pained her to admit it, Bea loved him for it. This was the way things had always been between them since the day they first met in a mutual friend's dorm at Columbia. They had gone under the auspices of studying for a group project, but somebody had found a bottle of vodka and the gathering had quickly descended into hook-ups and hilarity. Attempting to avoid the advances of a particularly persistent English Lit major, Bea had headed for Russ, who looked like the only other person in the room who was as uncomfortable as she felt. Acting quickly upon seeing her predicament, Russ pulled her to him for a hugely theatrical stage kiss, sending her disappointed would-be suitor sulking away. When Bea recovered from the shock of his sudden embrace they struck up a conversation, and Bea discovered a kindred spirit with a wicked sense of humour whom she quickly felt an affinity with.

They had once tried to recreate the fake kiss for real, not long after their graduation when, both despondent after recent break-ups, they ended up drowning their sorrows in beer and cheap takeaway pizza at Bea's apartment. It was a spontaneous moment that very nearly progressed further than either of them was prepared for, but before clothes were removed, Russ had pulled away. Bea had understood completely – the sudden awkwardness of their kiss sobering her – and they had never spoken of it since. Russ relied on Bea to be his closest friend and Bea felt the same. Their relationship represented the nearest thing to a successful partnership that either of them had experienced and therefore was not something they were willing to risk.

'Look at this,' Bea said, keen to take her mind off the sudden recollection of their historic drunken clinch. She held up a slightly faded hardback, its cover protected with the kind of plastic sleeve usually seen in libraries.

Her colleague's expression instantly softened. 'Oh, hello old friend! I didn't realise Sid was still with us.'

Bea gave the cover an affectionate pat. 'I think HRB would collapse if Sid ever left.'

Motorcycling For Life by Sid 'Wolfman' Wolkevic was the very first book Bea had unpacked as she and Russ had prepared to open their store, just over three years ago. At the time it had been the cause of their first argument in Hudson River Books, as neither of them would admit to ordering the book from the distributor. Since then, the book had periodically appeared on different shelves around the bookstore and, consequently, had become something of a phenomenon.

'We should put him somewhere prominent,' Russ suggested. 'Or make him a one-off sale item. See if we can re-home him at last.'

Bea stared at her friend. 'Or maybe we could just hide him on a new shelf and see if he finds his way to another one?'

'You don't want to let Sid leave, do you?' Russ grinned, knowing he was right.

Bea hugged the book. There was no use denying the fact. 'He's like one of the family now. I'm not sure how I'd feel if someone tried to buy him.'

'So take him home.'

'But he lives here.' Bea knew she was being sentimental, but *Motorcycling for Life* had become as much a part of the fixtures of Hudson River Books as the exposed brick walls, worn American oak floorboards or brushed steel lamps that hung from the high ceiling. Knowing that there was one book in their stock that never changed was oddly comforting, as if demonstrating to Bea that the hope and ambition with which she and Russ had founded the bookstore was unchanged too.

'It's one of the countless things I love about you,' Russ replied. 'Fine, you find Sid a new hiding place and I won't look. That way his legacy will be preserved.'

'Thank you.' She checked her watch. 'How do you feel about us closing a little early this evening? Once the carpenter has built the bar the bookstore will probably be full of sawdust anyway.'

Russ put the pile of books he was sorting into a box and folded his arms. 'Did you hear that?'

'Hear what?'

'I swear the tectonic plates beneath us shifted.'

'Come on, it's not that unusual for us to close early.'

'Hello? This is so unusual the Discovery Channel is commissioning a show on it. May I ask why?'

Bea groaned. 'Celia and Stewart have invited me to a party this evening, that's all. Is that a problem?'

Russ shook his head, but was still looking at her as if she had just grown another nose. 'No problem at all. I have a gig later anyway. I could use the time to work on my material. I was *kinda* hoping you'd come. You've been to every other one. You're my one-woman receptive crowd, after all.'

Bea instantly felt like the worst friend in the world. Since Russ had embarked on his part-time onslaught on the local comedy club circuit, he had encountered more than one hostile crowd and, even though Bea was pretty sure she could recite his entire routine in her sleep, she had made a point of going to his stand-up gigs as often as she could. 'I'm sorry, Russ, I didn't know. Celia suggested it a few days ago and I think going somewhere different might be good for me.'

'Go. It'll do you good. Just – just don't go looking for someone to replace Otis yet, OK?'

Bea couldn't believe what Russ had said. Had he listened to nothing during their many conversations about her new single status that week? Did he honestly think she would dash into another relationship when the dust was still clearing after the collapse of her last?

'I am going to get out of my apartment and try to live a little,' she stated, aware of the defensiveness in her reply. 'I have no intention of replacing anyone.'

'Hell, Bea . . .'

Realising his mistake, Russ moved towards her but Bea, rattled by his obvious loyalty to Otis and inference that she couldn't function without a boyfriend, turned and headed towards the back stairs which led to the office above the bookstore. She thought he might follow her but was relieved to see him return to the half-packed boxes as she left the shop floor.

She was still annoyed three hours later as she stood in her bedroom deciding what to wear for the party. Russ had apologised in all but words when she had finally rejoined him in the store, but it irked her that he could know her so well yet understand this aspect of her life so little. She held up a black skater dress with a red patent belt. Otis had never really liked it; although the few times she'd worn the dress her other friends had complimented her on it. That was enough of a reason to choose it, she decided. Stuff Otis. Tonight was about her embarking on the next phase of her life – where relationships didn't cloud the issue and she could be true to herself. It would be good to be selfish for a change. Finding a pair of red patent heels, she nodded at her reflection in the bedroom mirror.

Tonight is all about Bea James, she told herself. *Get ready for me, New York!*

CHAPTER TWELVE

Private loft apartment, Upper West Side

They were *all* couples.

Why hadn't he noticed this when he was sending out the eighty invitations for the party? Jake mentally kicked himself for being so naïve. *Of course* they would all be couples! People their age generally were. He and Jessica had fitted the demographic until recently and all their friends in San Francisco were either remarrying, having kids or just loved-up.

As Chez Henri's polished waiting staff buzzed about the beautiful loft apartment, Jake watched each new couple arrive. The elegant champagne flutes they were furnished with at the door seemed to underline their quiet satisfaction with their situation in life. And each one reminded Jake that he could no longer be counted among their ranks.

He shook his irritation away. It would be *fine*. He was the party organiser and, as such, could legitimately busy himself with anything that looked like it could be part of his job. The evening would pass quickly, he could give Rosie and Ed the celebration they both deserved and everyone would be happy. He remembered countless conversations with his clients over the years about facing their fears head-on: *The longer you hide from what you fear, the more seemingly insurmountable it becomes . . . When you put yourself in challenging situations, you find you have what you need to cope within you . . .* He knew he was doing the right thing by being here. Jess was gone and he shouldn't give up his life simply because she wasn't a part of it any more.

A polite burst of applause drew his attention back to the apartment's entrance lobby and Jake smiled as Rosie and Ed entered. He was struck by the way his brother looked at Rosie, a regard magnified by the company around them. Jake momentarily forgot his own battles, filled with deep love for the beautiful couple walking towards him.

'This is amazing, Jake.' Rosie kissed his cheek and Jake drew her into a hug. 'It's so lovely of you to do this for us.'

'It's my pleasure. And you look incredible, Ms Duncan.' Jake was struck by how a simple red silk strapless dress was transformed on his soon-to-be sister-in-law, the vivid material contrasting with Rosie's pale English rose skin, dark wavy hair and deep chocolate eyes. She was radiant. No wonder Ed looked like the kid that got all the candy from Santa Claus.

Rosie giggled and gave a little twirl. 'I'm glad you approve.'

'Hey, I'm pretty impressive too,' Ed said, running a

hand down his pale blue shirt. 'Rosie says it brings out the colour of my eyes, you know.'

Jake laughed. 'You look great, bro. Now, make yourselves at home, eat, drink and be happily engaged. If you want to make a speech I'd suggest waiting till nine when most people have arrived.'

He watched the happy couple wander away and smiled to himself as they received the warm congratulations of their friends. Many people in the room tonight knew what both Ed and Rosie had travelled through in their lives before they found each other. Consequently, the atmosphere in the party was one of genuine support and celebration.

There are worse places I could be tonight, Jake thought. Watching two of his most favourite people in the world being loved by so many guests was far from a chore.

He accepted a champagne flute from a passing waiter and enjoyed the chilled bubbles as they slipped down his throat.

'Jake.'

He turned to see Chef Henri standing beside him. 'Hey, Henri. Everything looks good.'

Henri didn't smile. 'We're one member of waiting staff short,' he apologised, his annoyance plain to see. 'It is late notice but, apparently, unavoidable. Of course we will rectify this in your bill . . .'

Jake clapped a hand on the chef's shoulder. 'I'm not worried. We have a beautiful event, your food is the best in the city and everyone here is smiling. If there's a rush for the bar, I can pitch in.'

'I can't ask that of you . . .'

'Sure you can. Call it a crazy demand from your client.'

The chef wasn't convinced. 'I am sure it won't come to that. But thank you for your understanding.'

Jake chuckled to himself as he walked through the small clusters of guests. The prospect of working the bar at least gave him a legitimate job to do if the large number of couples became too much for him.

'Jacob Steinmann!' A deep voice boomed across the room, closely followed by a balding, rotund man in his early fifties. 'Do you ever age?'

Jake shook hands with his former practice partner. 'On the inside I'm one hundred and forty. How are you, Bob?'

Bob Dillinger laughed. 'Good, good. What's this I hear about you setting up a rival business in Manhattan?'

'All true. I'm going to steal every one of your clients. Except I don't play golf as well as you do, so I fear my world domination attempt is doomed to failure.'

'You really should learn now you're back in the land of the living,' Bob said. 'Got premises yet?'

Jake shook his head. 'I'm seeing a couple of places on Monday morning.'

'Take my advice: choose your location with care. The city's a different animal since we worked together. You know if you need referrals you can count on me, I hope?'

'That means a lot, Bob. How's business for you?'

Bob's chocolate brown eyes twinkled. 'The financial crisis has been kind. Some people need reassurance; some just need a badge for their hang-ups. People have exchanged their job titles for professional psychosis lately.

I swear thirty-five percent of my clients need recognition instead of therapy. Which means rich pickings for us guys as long as you don't mind needy rich people.'

Jake hated to admit it, but he'd witnessed the same thing in his West Coast clients. Therapy was the new cosmetic surgery: cheaper than a facelift and easier to brag about at parties. 'We do what we can.'

'That we do, Jake. And hey, I'm truly sorry to hear about you and Jessica. So unexpected. Barbara and I were shocked when we heard.'

And there it is. Jake felt the thud of disappointment as his old foe reared its head once more. 'It's been tough. But we'll get through it. I'm looking to the future and so is she.' *Please let that be enough*, he added silently, knowing full well it wouldn't be.

'Still, being single in Manhattan is no easy run. I mean, look around you. Can you see anyone else single in this room?'

Every defence in Jake rose like sheets of steel. 'I hear Chef Henri's on the lookout for Wife Number Three.'

'Bad news for you, then.' Bob slapped his hand a little too enthusiastically on Jake's back. 'Don't sweat it, man. You'll bounce back. In the meantime, if you need setting up on any dates Barbara can put you in touch with lots of lovely ladies from her club. Just say the word and she'll play Cupid.'

'I'll bear it in mind.'

'Good, good. Ah, I'm being summoned. You take care, Jake.'

Jake maintained his smile until Bob had disappeared into the crowd, letting out a sigh and downing the rest

of his champagne in a single gulp, then reaching for a
fresh glass when a waitress passed by. It was going to
be a *long* night . . .

CHAPTER THIRTEEN

Private loft apartment, Upper West Side

As soon as Bea entered the expensive loft apartment, her heart sank.

Couples. As far as the eye could see.

In the middle of the room, a tall, good-looking man with an endearing mess of dark hair and vivid blue eyes was tapping a fork against his champagne glass to summon the guests' attention. Bea took a glass from the smiling waiter and huddled between her brother and Celia as the room fell silent.

'Hey, everyone. Now you know I'm not one for long speeches so this will be short and sweet. But I just wanted to thank you all for coming this evening and, especially, to my bro over there for arranging this whole event.'

The guests clapped and over their heads Bea saw a hand rise in acknowledgement.

'But the main reason we're here – as you all know – is a long overdue celebration of the best day of my life so far.' He turned to a beautiful dark-haired woman in a stunning red dress beside him. 'Rosie, when you agreed to marry me I couldn't believe my luck.'

A chorus of 'ahh's came from the guests, closely followed by spontaneous laughter.

The man raised an eyebrow. 'Wow, you guys are more pathetic than I am.'

'Get on with it!' someone yelled.

'OK, OK. I'm going to be serious for precisely one minute and then we can all enjoy the night.' He smiled at his fiancée and a reverent silence claimed the room as every guest witnessed exactly how he felt about her. 'Rosie Duncan, I love you. And I can't wait to make you Mrs Steinmann this Christmas. You are all I want in life and to know I'm yours is better than breathing.' He reddened and laughed at his own words. 'And so, before I embarrass myself and everyone else beyond rescue, I'll just say please raise your glasses to wish us the best.'

'To Rosie and Ed!' the crowd replied as one, crystal champagne flutes lifting around the room.

Bea's skin felt damp and cold as sickening reality hit. *This isn't just a regular party. It's an* engagemen*t party*. How had Celia failed to mention this small detail? And how did she think going to an engagement party in a room full of couples she didn't know would help Bea forget everything that happened with Otis?

Looking into her glass she realised she had already emptied it. Right now, getting drunk seemed like the perfect option . . .

'See? I told you that you'd love these people!' Celia said, swapping Bea's empty glass for a fresh one without question.

'It's an *engagement* party,' Bea hissed back.

'Of course it is, honey. Rosie is one of my dearest friends and she and Ed are just *such* an adorable couple, don't you think?'

'They seem very happy . . . But that's the point, Celia: they're a couple. Just like everyone else in the room?'

Celia waved her hand. 'Nonsense. Several of these gorgeous waiters must be single. Look at them, Bea! I'd say your luck's in this evening . . .'

Bea resisted the urge to scream. Celia had a heart of gold but she could make the Dalai Lama lose his cool. 'I didn't come to find a man,' she said carefully. 'I came to get away from Brooklyn for a few hours.'

'Well, in that case, the couples shouldn't bother you at all, honey! Drink champagne, eat some of this fabulous food and relax. You'll thank me for bringing you here, I promise.'

As Celia wafted away in a cloud of Chanel No. 5, Bea looked around the party. The full-length windows at the opposite end of the apartment gave a wonderful view of the Upper West Side, the lights from surrounding buildings a stunning mosaic set against a blue-black cloudless New York sky. She moved towards it, the beauty of her adopted city stealing her attention. Whatever else happened in her life, New York was the constant. The city could change and forge a blazing path of progress, but the vibrant heart of the Big Apple beat as surely as it ever had. It was the city that had called to Bea many years before as she dreamed of it in her family home in Shropshire, and being part of New York had been the reason for all of her decisions since the age of seventeen.

It had painted an East Coast note in her accent, bled into her emotions and laid claim to her heart.

I was wrong about the party, Bea said to herself, *I do have a friend here.* She smiled at the breathtaking nightscape. *Hi, NYC. I'm so glad to see you . . .*

'It's beautiful, isn't it?'

Bea looked across at the blond-haired guest beside her. She guessed he was in his thirties, although in this part of New York it was impossible to tell. He might just have a very good surgeon . . .

'Stunning. Must be fabulous to live somewhere like this.'

He smiled, revealing a perfect set of brilliantly white teeth. 'It is. Forgive me, I haven't introduced myself.' He held his left hand out, the light from the halogen spots above them glinting across the wide gold band on his third finger. 'Wes Avery.'

'Bea James.'

'Pleasure to meet you, Bea. So how do you know the happy couple?'

Given that this was a private engagement party for a couple Bea didn't even know, she had been dreading this question. 'They're good friends of my brother's partner, Celia.'

'Celia Reighton? Wow, I didn't realise I was in the company of a Reighton clanswoman.' Seeing Bea's confusion, he laughed. 'I know her well. So *you're* Stewart's single sister, huh?'

Great. 'I suppose I must be.'

'I've been hearing about you from Celia. Seems she's keen to get you hooked up.'

That figured. Bea kept her smile steady while secretly planning how she would exact her revenge on Stewart's partner. 'I see. Well, I'm in no hurry to . . .'

Wes' hand appeared at the small of her back, the sudden – and uninvited – contact causing Bea to quickly step away. 'Hey, don't sweat it. Being single is an advantage. Just because people arrived here in couples, doesn't mean they all want to *leave* in one.' His thousand-kilowatt smile fixed squarely on her. 'Listen, I have a *great* loft a few blocks from here. If you ever want a personal, private view of the Upper West Side, call me.' He thrust a business card into her hand and sauntered away.

Stunned, Bea stared at it. Had a married man just propositioned her? This evening was getting better and better . . .

'Sis, you've got to try the sashimi,' Stewart said, stopping when he saw Bea's horror. 'What? You don't like raw seafood?'

'I do . . . I just . . .' She swallowed as the full impact hit her. 'A married guy just gave me his card.'

Stewart pulled a face. 'Eeww. I hope you sent him packing?'

'Of course I did.'

'Good. I'm afraid Celia is playing Millionaire Matchmaker for you. I've told her to stop, but you know what she's like once she gets an idea in her head.'

Bea raised her eyes to the apartment's high ceiling. 'Fantastic. So not only am I fair game for adulterous Lotharios but I'm now your girlfriend's pathetic pet project. I think I might just go, Stew. I don't know anyone here and it should be a celebration for Celia's friends.'

'You've been here less than an hour. And whether you like it or not, this is what being single in Manhattan is like. Better to get used to it and learn to enjoy yourself, I reckon. Stay. Try the sashimi. It'll change your life.'

'Maybe later.'

Her brother shot her a look. 'OK. But if I come back in half an hour and you're still moping here I'm going to force-feed you gourmet food.'

'Fine.'

Forget sashimi, Bea thought. *What I need is a drink . . .*

CHAPTER FOURTEEN

Private loft apartment,
Upper West Side

'*So* sorry to hear about Jess, man. I thought you two were made for life . . .'

Jake could feel the edges of his smile fraying and longed to change the subject. But this had become the sole topic of conversation with everyone he had talked to during the last hour. It was, of course, an unavoidable hazard; most of Ed's friends had known Jake since childhood and therefore were fully appraised of every aspect of his life. And those who didn't know every available detail were only too happy to be shocked by it tonight. Everywhere he walked in the elegant apartment, he could feel the pitying eyes of almost a hundred guests following him. How had this outcome not occurred to him when he was drawing up the guest list for this evening?

'Shame you didn't invite more single women,' a well-meaning friend observed. 'Even the waiting staff are all guys.'

Jake shrugged. 'My bad. Anyway, I'm not looking.'

His friend's blonde companion tittered. 'This is *Manhattan*, Jake. *Everybody* is looking.'

'Especially the ones who shouldn't be,' another friend quipped, his remark allowing the group now gathered around Jake to laugh and not feel so awkward about the situation.

Jake wished for light relief to rescue him in the same way, but none appeared. 'They're welcome to the search. I'm not in the game.'

The blonde's nipped-and-tucked features fell as far as they could. 'Don't ever say that,' she breathed. 'You shouldn't deny yourself, Jake! You're still young and . . . *virile* . . .' Her ill-disguised survey of *just* how young and virile Jake was left him reeling and he mumbled something unintelligible to make his escape.

This place is nuts! How had his good intentions towards Ed brought him into the minefield he now found himself in? He looked up to the apartment's mezzanine where his brother and Rosie were looking happy and relaxed, sharing conversation with friends. At least they were enjoying tonight. This was *their* night, Jake reminded himself, not his. It would have to be his mantra for the rest of the party. That, and bourbon . . .

He remembered a client he had worked with back in his Russian Hill practice in San Francisco, who went to every social occasion convinced the rest of the guests knew his deepest, most secret thoughts.

'They watch me, Dr Steinmann. They say pleasant things, but I can feel them scrutinising me. Like a *bug*.'

'Why do you think they would want to do that, Ray?'

'Are you kidding me? Do you *know* what I'm capable of thinking? They know it all, Doc. I can't hide.'

Jake had spent months assuring Ray that small talk was a way to pass the time and socialise without asking too much of either party; that everyone had their own set of hang-ups and insecurities to deal with; and that it was impossible to see anyone's innermost thoughts, however obvious they may seem to be. But even on their last session before Jake packed up his San Franciscan life, Jake hadn't been entirely assured that Ray had accepted it.

Now, surrounded by familiar faces that *did* know Jake's business and were making valiant attempts to guess his innermost thoughts, he felt a new affinity with his former client's predicament.

'Jake . . .' Chef Henri was wringing his hands beside him. 'I am so sorry, but . . .'

'The bar?'

'There is a considerable queue. Do you mind?'

Heart lifting, Jake could have kissed the apologetic chef but resisted, settling instead for slapping him amiably on the back. 'I'm there.'

Swinging his jacket over one arm, he rolled up his shirt sleeves and strode through the guests towards the bar, which had been set up beneath the mezzanine, next to a floor-to-ceiling window looking out towards the beautiful night-time cityscape. Seeing the buildings and lights of the Upper West Side comforted Jake: while he'd loved his adopted city of San Francisco, he had always carried a secret longing for New York. His father's favourite saying was true: Steinmanns were born with Big-Apple-shaped hearts.

'Hey, New York,' he smiled, pausing for a moment to take in the view. 'Looking good.' Taking a deep breath for the first time that evening, he turned towards the bar and jumped into the fray.

'Scotch straight up, no ice.'

'Manhattan – one olive.'

'Red wine for me and a white for the lady . . .'

It had been years since Jake last worked a bar, but he quickly found his rhythm. It was good to find he hadn't lost the skills he'd acquired during his last year at Yale and the distraction it gave him was priceless. Finally, he could lose himself in an activity that required no deeper thought than which bottle and glass to select. Maybe this was the ideal career for him, he mused as he worked. Psychiatry was far too introspective for his current state of mind . . .

The next hour flew by, Jake relishing the almost constant stream of thirsty guests vying for his attention. But as ten o'clock neared, the queue dwindled until the bar was almost empty. He helped himself to a long drink of cola, realising how thirsty his efforts had made him, and once again his eyes strayed from the bar to the night view from the huge window. There was much to do to re-establish his life in the city, but Jake knew he could make it a success here. This was his home: always had been. And that counted for a lot. Frank Sinatra had it pegged: if he could make it in the city that never sleeps, he could pretty much make it anywhere. He had spent too long feeling as if he was skulking back home, defeated. This had to stop – and tonight was as good a time as any.

'White wine, please.'

Turning back to the bar, Jake smiled at the pretty redhead with eyes the colour of the winter sea. 'Sure. Any preference?'

She stared at him, a weariness that didn't seem to belong to her claiming her expression. 'Large glass?'

He suppressed the urge to laugh. 'I'm sorry, I meant French? Australian?'

'Alcoholic.' She dropped her gaze to the empty glass on the bar. 'Please.'

Intrigued, Jake pulled a fresh glass from the box behind the makeshift bar and gave it a quick polish with a tea towel. 'Tough night?'

'You could say so.'

'Ah. I see.' He poured wine almost to the brim. 'That enough?'

She raised her gaze, the smallest trace of a smile appearing. 'Perfect.'

'Enjoy.'

The woman gave a quick glance over her shoulder. 'Actually, mind if I hang out here for a while?' Her accent was difficult to place: the characteristic New York inflection was there, but something else lay beneath it. Boston, maybe? No. Washington?

'Be my guest.'

Smiling her thanks, she pulled up a stool and sat down, hunched over her drink like the old men at Harry's sports bar where Jake and Ed had wasted so many of their Saturday afternoons before Jake met Jessica. Was she hiding from someone? An overbearing partner, maybe? That didn't seem likely. She didn't look like the kind of woman to be subservient to anybody . . . Maybe her guy was of the too-intense ilk, smothering her with his affection?

Realising what he was doing, Jake pulled his thoughts to a halt. He knew nothing about this woman, but her muted demeanour told him she didn't need the psycho-analysis of a total stranger tonight.

'How's the wine? Doing its job?'

'Seems to be.'

'Good.'

Did she even want to talk? Jake hesitated to ask another question – but to his surprise, the woman stared directly at him.

'Everyone here is in a couple. I mean, everyone. Nobody told me. If they'd told me I wouldn't be here.'

'It's not surprising, considering the occasion.'

The woman shook her head. 'Of course. But the thing is, I didn't know what the occasion was. I thought it was just a party. My brother's partner omitted the key point of who the party was for.' She let out a long sigh. 'And now I feel like an idiot for not asking. I just thought it was a normal, Friday night party in the Upper West Side. How was I to know it was going to be the Couple Centre of the universe?'

English! That was the clipped note in her voice! Jake congratulated himself for identifying it. 'If it helps, I didn't figure on there being so many couples here, either.'

'Well, there you are! I should be happy you're in the same boat but I actually feel sorry for us both. What kind of world do we live in where everything is so domi-nated by relationships? Does this city only function in

84

multiples of two? I don't think so.' She downed half her glass and coughed a little. 'I'm sorry. I'm just *done* with it all.'

'Done with this city?'

Her frown softened. 'Oh no – never with this city. It's the only thing you can rely on. I mean I'm done with the whole couple thing. You think it's what you want, and you spend all your time pursuing it – but for what? To be disappointed, let down and ultimately dumped upon. I can't believe it's taken me so long to see it, but this week I've realised something: I don't need the hassle any more.'

Jake stared at her, suddenly wondering if Paranoid Ray was actually right. This woman – who knew nothing about him – was repeating almost word for word the thoughts that had been running through his head all evening. Without waiting for an invitation, he grabbed the wine bottle and refilled her glass.

'I'm Jake,' he said. 'And I know exactly what you mean . . .'

CHAPTER FIFTEEN

Private loft apartment, Upper West Side

Bea couldn't believe it. Was there really someone else in New York who thought relationships were a waste of time? She could feel the edges of her consciousness beginning to blur and resolved to drink slower. The barman's confession intrigued her and she wanted to know more. There was honesty in his startling blue eyes that seemed to draw her in . . .

'I'm Bea. Thanks for the wine.'

'You're welcome.'

They looked at each other for a while, the sounds of the party around them filling the air. For the first time that evening, Bea felt understood by someone else. Russ had done his best to sympathise with her, but beneath his kind words and pep talks lay the unmistakable desire to see her reunited with Otis. Celia and Stewart had listened, but they couldn't mask their ultimate aim to see her as happily coupled-up as they were. Even her mum, speaking soothing words from the bumpy freeway as her dad drove their rented Winnebago across the United States, clearly thought her daughter just needed time before she found the man of her dreams. When it came down to it, nobody had tried to see it from Bea's point of view. Until now . . .

Sure, he was a random barman in a party neither of them wanted to be at, but at least one person in the whole of New York City understood. And right now, that seemed to Bea like the most precious discovery.

'So – how do you know?' Bea asked, before she could think better of it, quickly adding, 'If you don't mind me asking?' when she saw the slight droop of his shoulders.

'About relationships? Because I received divorce papers this week.'

Instantly, Bea felt awful. Choosing to walk away from a relationship was one thing; having the decision made for you was something else. 'Gosh – I'm so sorry. I shouldn't have asked . . .'

'No, you should. It's OK. Pretty much everyone else here knows already, so there's no reason why you should escape the bulletin.'

'That's awful.' Bea wished the floor would open and swallow her up. Her one interesting acquaintance in the room was now smiling so sadly at her that she felt like she'd just kicked a puppy.

'Yours isn't divorce, then?' The joke was clearly intended to make her feel better and Bea appreciated it.

'We didn't make it as far as marriage,' she smiled, finding the act of sharing such personal information with a relative stranger surprisingly liberating. 'And I called it in the end.'

'How long?'

'Five years.'

Jake shook his head. 'That's tough. My marriage was seven, with three years before.'

'Wow.'

'I know.'

'I probably should be sitting at home tonight, wishing for him back. But actually, I don't want him back. Not like we were. It's taken me standing in a room full of couples I don't know and toasting a happy couple I don't know either to discover that. The more I think about it, the more I think relationships and me are incompatible.' She checked that Jake was still smiling at her. He was. At least that was something. 'It might sound strange, but the thought of not being in a relationship isn't scary to me any more. I have so much in my life that's already working: why focus on an aspect that just makes me unhappy?'

'I hear you. I'm sick of trying to explain that to people. Truth is, I don't think I want another relationship.'

'Me either!'

'I mean, when the one you think was The One turns out not to be, what hope is there, huh?'

He had a nice laugh, Bea thought. Maybe it was the wine, but the more she talked to the barman, the happier she felt. 'I am so glad I met you tonight, Jake. I was beginning to think I was losing my mind.'

'When, instead, we are probably the only two sane individuals in the room tonight.'

'In the Upper West Side!'

'In the whole of New York!'

Bea's heart was racing. 'People are so dead set on finding someone else to share their lives with. But they forget there are so many things you can do when you're single that you can't do when you're in a relationship. Like assuming the sole use of the remote control.'

Jake chuckled. 'Amen, sister. Or heading out for dinner on a whim without having to check schedules . . .'

'Going to the cinema by yourself and eating all the popcorn – I love that.'

'Or reading the Sunday paper all day without interruption.'

'Only going shopping when you feel like it – and never having to feel guilty about dragging someone else along.'

'Long baths on a weeknight listening to Lou Reed . . .'

'Watching five episodes of a box-set in one go . . .'

'Setting out from your apartment on a Saturday morning and wandering wherever you want to.'

'I love that! I haven't done that for years.'

'Me either. Know what, Bea?'

'What?'

'We should start again.'

Bea smiled, despite the blush she knew was now spreading across her cheeks. 'We should.'

'Because we live in the best city on earth,' Jake said. 'Why wouldn't we want to explore it?'

'Exactly. I love this city.' Bea turned to the stunning night view from the tall window. 'Look at that: isn't it the most amazing view?'

'It is. There's a big city out there, just waiting for us.'

'And we've wasted too much time being trapped by someone else already.'

Jake nodded, an unmistakable fondness in his expression. Bea recognised it instantly because it was how she felt. 'Gotta love this city.'

'Absolutely.' Her earlier consternation forgotten, Bea looked back at her surprise ally. 'I'm really glad I met you this evening.'

'Me too. It's refreshing to find someone else who understands where I'm coming from.'

Jake offered the bottle to Bea, but she declined, enjoying the conversation far too much to be distracted by any more alcohol.

Snapping his fingers, Jake grinned at her. 'Hey, you and I should make a pact.'

'What kind of pact?'

An impish twinkle danced in his eyes. 'That we will never get involved with anyone, ever again.'

A few days ago, this suggestion would have horrified Bea. But after all she had experienced tonight – and the enjoyable conversation she was having with the barman – Bea was keen to agree. 'Absolutely. I'm done with relationships.'

'OK, here it is: we solemnly swear that no matter what, we will avoid relationships. That we are through trying to find true love. From now on, it's about us, celebrating the parts of our lives that work and not obsessing over those that don't. We will be successful, happy, self-fulfilled individuals, who don't place responsibility on anyone else for our happiness. Nobody writes the book of our lives but us.'

Bea loved that idea. So often in her life she had felt at the mercy of unseen scriptwriters who blindly dictated the ebb and flow of her happiness. The only author of Bea James' life story should be herself. 'That's brilliant.'

'Then are you willing to agree to The Pact?'

She grinned at the audacity of it. 'Yes, I am.'

He held out his little finger. 'Then we must solemnly seal it. With a pinky shake.'

'A what?'

He couldn't hide his amusement. 'Trust me. This is the only way.'

Giggling, Bea locked her little finger with his. 'I hereby agree to The Pact.'

'No more relationships for Jake and Bea.'

'No more relationships for us.'

It was a beautiful moment: an unexpected gift of understanding between two people who barely knew each other. It felt deeper than the light-hearted banter of strangers and significant in a way that surprised them both. It was the end of a struggle and the beginning of a new chapter in their lives. And, with her finger locked with Jake's, Bea suddenly didn't feel alone any more . . .

Much later that evening, watching the lights of the city passing by the taxi window, Bea was lost in her thoughts. Celia and Stewart had waved her off, reasoning that her quietness was due to fatigue and maybe a little too much wine. Bea barely said two words as the cab pulled away, waving absent-mindedly as she tried to work out how she was feeling.

She *should* have felt elated by the twist the evening's events had taken. She *should* have felt justified in her new decision to live life for herself. But beneath the glow of an evening unexpectedly well spent, a gaping hollowness refused to be filled by any of the above. Why did she feel like she'd missed something?

Should she have asked for his number? It would have been nice to have a friend in New York who didn't have an ulterior motive for pairing her up with someone.

But then, Bea told herself, maybe Jake was being polite. He was serving at the bar at a private party, for goodness' sake; it was his job to entertain the guests. She didn't doubt that he had enjoyed talking to her, but what if that came from a longing to make his work shift pass more quickly? It was entirely possible. And why did it matter, anyway?

Of course it doesn't matter, she told herself. It was a bad night made better by a barman with a crazy pact. One of Manhattan's unexpected surprises. And it was over now.

CHAPTER SIXTEEN

Vacant office suite, McKevitt Buildings, Broadway

'I'm sure you'll agree, it's a great property,' the real estate agent nodded encouragingly at Jake. 'Competitive rates, excellent square-footage, close proximity to the better business areas of the city and the scope for a wide catchment area for your practice.'

'Great . . .' Jake replied, but he wasn't really listening. He was still smiling from the conversation he'd enjoyed last night. This pact idea had legs: and finding the right premises for his business was the perfect place to start.

'But please, don't take my word for it,' the over-eager agent rushed, 'let me show you around and I assure you the property will speak for itself.'

Jake followed the agent around the empty office space, barely noticing the freshly painted walls and brand new carpet at his feet. It was light and airy, in the right location and with more than enough scope for his practice to expand in time – but he had made all of these observations within minutes of arriving and now his brain could focus on other things. As the agent eulogised the benefits of the building, Jake's thoughts returned again to last night.

Why didn't I ask for her number?

He had seen her wave goodbye as a man he presumed was her brother hurried her out of the apartment, so at least he knew she hadn't fled the moment she'd had the chance. But in the cold light of day, was her participation in their conversation little more than classic British politeness? She was alone at the party and so was he: she was also a little worse for wear from champagne and wine and he had drunk more bourbon than he'd intended. Was it simply a case of shared experience to get through an otherwise excruciatingly embarrassing event?

'Dr Steinmann?'

Jake stared dumbly at the real estate agent. 'What?'

'I said, staff. Will you be having any?'

'Yes. I'll start recruiting as soon as I secure premises.' The thought of finding an assistant even half as competent as the wonderful Pam Lomas he had left back in San Francisco filled Jake with dread. Pam had done everything for him bar actually counselling his clients. She knew what he would ask for almost before he thought to ask for it, ran the office like a well-oiled, military machine and was the kind of person you would happily entrust your life to in an emergency. There was nothing about his practice that Pam didn't know. Would he ever find someone with her level of loyalty and commitment in a city where trading up to a better job was a constant goal?

'Then you can do no better than choose McKevitt

Buildings as your practice base,' the agent beamed, proud of his closing argument.

Jake stared at the agent's self-satisfied smile and wondered if he would ever feel as much pleasure in his New York practice as the weasel-like little man clearly did in his profession. 'OK. Thank you, Mr . . . ?'

'Howell-Brown,' the agent reminded him, thrusting another business card into his hand. 'Eugene Howell-Brown. I'm sorry. Did I forget to mention it?' The question was loaded with accusation and Jake momentarily regretted forgetting the agent's name so easily.

He did his best to return to the matter at hand; thinking about last night coupled with his hangover wasn't helping him this morning. 'Forgive me; it's been a busy morning. I like the office, so I'll take it.'

Eugene Howell-Brown forgot his passive-aggressive consternation and instantly sprang into action. 'Wonderful! You will not regret this decision, Dr Steinmann. Now all I need from you are a couple of signatures and I'll arrange for you to have the keys . . .'

Out on the too-bright sidewalk outside, Jake paused to take a breath. He needed to focus, to work his way through the list of tasks he had assigned himself today. There were recruiters to meet, office furniture and décor to choose and a million and one other jobs to attend to. But right now, they could wait. Before any of it could happen, Jake needed coffee.

In the sanctuary of a warmly lit coffee house nearby, he ordered an enormous black coffee. As he found a table hidden from the hubbub of other customers, his phone rang.

'You haven't called me. And you said you would.'

Jake smiled as the soothing voice of his former PA warmed his ear. 'What can I tell you, Pam? I'm a disgrace.'

'I was worried about you. You knew I would be. So? How's life in the City That Sneers At You?'

'And New York sends its love right back at you.'

'Be serious.'

'It's good. A little weird to be back, but I haven't been ridden out of town yet.' Jake took a long sip of coffee and closed his eyes. 'Actually, I just signed the lease on a new office building.'

'Where?'

'Just off Broadway. Near the Lincoln Center. It's a good space: I think you'd approve.'

Pam's snort made Jake grin. It was no secret what she thought of the East Coast in general and Manhattan specifically. In her college days she had interned at a law firm in New York for two months while staying with her aunt and the experience had apparently traumatised her for life. She had often said that the only native New Yorker she had ever liked was Jake. Coming from a woman as set in her opinions as Pam, this was the ultimate compliment.

Jake decided to move to safer territory. 'How's the new job? Is your new employer as devastatingly handsome as I am?'

Now it was Pam's turn to laugh. 'He's tidier. And pays me more. But no, he isn't a patch on you. You're very hard to replace, Dr Steinmann.'

'Oh, if only that were true.' He didn't mean to say it out loud; but of all the people who could have heard it, Pam understood more than most.

'Tell me she hasn't—'

'Afraid so. I've had the papers for a week.'

'And you're going to sign them?'

'I don't know. I haven't signed them yet. I will, I guess, just not yet.'

'That woman doesn't deserve you,' Pam retorted. 'I'm sorry, Jake, but you don't pay my salary any more so I can say it. You're better off without her. Sign the papers and get on with your life.'

Her forthrightness took Jake aback – in all the time they had worked together Pam had been very guarded in her comments on his private life, even though he often guessed what her opinions were. 'You think?'

'I do. In fact, I think it's the only way. You talk to your clients about closure all the time: I've heard you. You can't make her change her mind. But you *can* change your response to it.'

Jake laughed despite the sinking feeling Pam's words caused. 'Pam Lomas, are you psychoanalysing me?'

'Maybe I am, Doctor. Maybe you need to hear it. Look, I can't tell you what to do. I just care about you and I know you're not happy. Ultimately it's up to you how you move on. But you *need* to move on . . .'

When the call ended, Jake stared into the dark depths of his filter coffee. He hadn't expected to hear it from his former employee, but Pam was right: he needed to take control of the situation. If only he'd reached this conclusion last night, when the possibility to take a new step had presented itself . . .

CHAPTER SEVENTEEN

Beads & Beans craft and coffee store, Brooklyn

'So, let me get this straight: you spent all night talking to a cute guy and you *didn't* ask for his number?'

The look on Imelda Coulson's face said it all. Bea groaned as her friend observed her from the top step of a rickety stepladder, a cluster of knitted clouds in her hand.

'Of course I didn't,' Bea replied. 'And I never said he was cute! It was just nice to meet somebody who understood my point of view.'

Imelda snorted and began to hang the clouds from small hooks in the ceiling. 'A point of view that you're hiding behind.'

'I'm not hiding . . .'

'Yes, you are. Admit it, honey: if Otis hadn't stood you up that night you'd still be with him and you'd still be a firm believer in relationships.'

The mention of Otis made Bea wince. She might have succeeded in telling everyone else she didn't miss him but she had a long way to go to convince herself. She didn't *want* to feel this way. She wanted to feel as happy being single as she had spent many hours telling Russ, her parents and Imelda she was. But she had invested five years of her life in building something with Otis. It was unrealistic to think she could walk away from that unscathed.

'That's immaterial. Otis *did* stand me up and it was the last straw. He isn't going to change and I'm not prepared to put my life on hold waiting for a miracle.'

'But you're still in love with him?' Imelda pulled no punches and Bea was winded by the direct question.

'Maybe I am. Or maybe it's been slipping away from me for months, only I wasn't prepared to notice.' She sighed and moved to the side as Imelda descended the steps. 'There's no point trying to work that one out. I just want to focus on me for a change. Is that so wrong?'

Imelda's expression softened and she put her hand on Bea's shoulder. 'Of course it's not wrong. I just want you to be happy.'

'So do I. That's why I want to find out how to do that by myself.'

'O-K . . .' Imelda shrugged, about as satisfied with Bea's answer as Bea was. 'How's Russ been?'

That was a good question. Russ had veered between insisting that all Bea needed was time to forgive his best friend and standing staunchly alongside her in her decision. At least he seemed to have finally got the message that Bea didn't want to talk about it now, after a week of berating her at every opportunity. Bea was relieved to feel the pressure lessen: what she wanted now was to focus on the bookstore.

'I think he knows not to push me on it.'

Imelda smiled as she sorted through a basket of knitted meteorological symbols for her window display. 'The guy cares about you. In his own klutzy way. And I think he's a little embarrassed about his friend. After all, if it wasn't for Russ, you and Otis would never have met.'

A brief memory of the party where Russ had introduced Bea to his 'legitimate single friend who most definitely isn't gay' flashed across Bea's mind and she felt her stomach twist in response. Otis Greene had caught her attention immediately, with his velvet-smooth olive skin, dark eyes that seemed to call her closer and toned body visible beneath the contours of his well-cut shirt and jeans. When he smiled, it was as if a pause button had been pressed on the rest of the scene in the bar: suddenly it was just him and her, smiles spreading as their eyes drank in the sight of one another. Bea had fallen hard and fast for the handsome art dealer – a fact she could trace back to that first meeting – and that initial surge of emotion had carried her through years of not-so-perfect times.

She didn't want to still love Otis. She wanted to push him and everything in her life connected to him into the Hudson River and walk away, never looking back. But Bea knew her own heart. That was why striking out on her own was so important.

'I understand why Russ tried to get us back together. I do. He's stuck between Otis and me and I don't suppose it's ever been a particularly comfortable position.'

'Shame you didn't ask for the barman's number, then,'

Imelda winked, twirling a large knitted raindrop around her forefinger as she ascended the stepladder again. 'Could have solved a *lot* of problems . . .'

'It doesn't matter anyway: we made a pact.'

'Who did?'

'Me and the barman. We're swearing off relationships for good.'

Imelda groaned. '*Bea* . . .'

'No, it made me feel better, Immi. I've wasted too much of my life chasing something that hasn't happened. My life is worth more than that. It was good to find someone else in this city who sees it like I do.'

'Trust you to find a cute guy who *doesn't* want to date you,' Imelda laughed. 'Hey, I'm not making fun of you. If it makes you happy, go for it.'

'I think it will make me happy.'

'Good, then. Now, do you have time for coffee before Russ sends out a search party?'

Russ had practically bundled Bea out of the bookstore that morning, seeing how distracted she was by the events of the night before.

'You're no use this morning. Go for a walk or something.'

Bea had instinctively headed for Beads & Beans, the quirky craft and coffee shop owned by the third Musketeer to her and Russ. Imelda Coulson had been Bea's firm friend for almost five years and was as unconventional as her business suggested.

Imelda's store was a riot of colour, filled with every craft item imaginable. Rainbow skeins of embroidery silks and wool were packed next to roll after roll of beautiful ribbons and trims. Almost an entire wall was filled with tiny wooden drawers containing buttons, charms, quill papers, sequins and fastenings, each drawer front bearing a hand-painted sign. Next to the haberdashery supplies were thick bolts of brightly patterned fabrics – shimmering satins, cool cottons and thick, luxurious velvets. In the centre, tables and chairs were set out, each one painted in a different pastel shade and customers congregated here, indulging in crafts while enjoying coffee and cakes on hand-painted crockery.

Bea loved it here: the strong sense of creativity and fun mirrored the boundless positivity of the store's proprietor. It was impossible not to smile when you were surrounded by so much colour and possibility. She had first met Imelda at a mutual friend's Christmas party and they quickly struck up a friendship, Bea drawn to Imelda's fiercely optimistic stance on everything. They had talked about owning their own businesses one day and Bea never doubted that Imelda would succeed in her ambition. Then, around the time Russ and Bea were looking for properties to set up their bookstore, Imelda's wish had unexpectedly come to pass.

Suddenly made redundant from her job at a Wall Street bank, she had seen it as a sign to move her life forward and had opened the business she had long dreamed of, uniting her two loves of great coffee and crafts. Only in Brooklyn could this unlikely pairing have worked. Surrounded by unusual, artisanal shops and kitsch cafés, it was a perfect fit. Imelda hosted children's parties at weekends and various groups of craft enthusiasts and local people interested in learning new skills during the week. Everybody else came in for coffee and the unique experience of sitting in a place alive with activity and fun.

'So how long were you and the barman talking for?'

Bea shrugged. 'An hour, maybe? I wasn't exactly watching the time.'

Imelda peered over the rim of her oversized coffee cup. 'Unusual to have a conversation that lasts a whole hour which doesn't mean anything, don't you think? Especially if you're *still* thinking about it this morning. Just what did you talk about?'

Bea couldn't hide her smile at the memory. 'Everything and nothing. How much we loved New York, how embarrassing it was to be single at an engagement party filled with happy couples and . . .' She trailed off as the pinky shake pact came to mind.

'And what?'

'And then he suggested The Pact. And it was the most perfect idea I'd heard in ages. So I agreed.'

Imelda's expression didn't flicker, leaving Bea in no doubt of her opinion. 'So now you need to hope that your pact-buddy will be tending the bar at the next party you go to.'

Bea had to admit that it would be good to talk to the barman again. Their conversation about the benefits of singledom had been a lot of fun. 'As if *that's* likely to happen. Apart from in your head.'

Imelda grinned. 'Hey, my head is a nice place to be, believe me. I'm just saying, honey, it's possible that last night was an opportunity you were meant to take. And in my experience, if life wants you to take a certain road, you'll end up coming back to it time and time again. My great-aunt Lavinia always says life is like the baggage carousel at the airport: if you don't collect your case first time around it will keep passing you until you do.'

Bea wasn't sure if Jake could be compared with a suitcase – or if Imelda's batty great-aunt's philosophy carried any grain of truth – but it made her smile nevertheless.

'Excuse me, do you have air-drying clay?' A customer peered over the counter.

'We do,' Imelda replied, casting a wink in Bea's direction as she headed into the store to find it.

On her own again, Bea considered what her friend had suggested. Meeting Jake had been a fluke.

Hadn't it?

The thought was still playing on her mind that evening when Bea finally arrived home from the bookstore. Feeling better after talking with Imelda, she had returned to Hudson River Books and thrown herself into work, much to Russ' relief.

It was almost seven p.m. when she turned her key in the front door of her apartment, swinging the paper bag of Chinese food onto the breakfast bar before taking off her coat. The thought of what had happened last night and the possibility that it might be the start of a new chapter of her life intrigued her. Not that she thought for a minute that Jake had anything to do with her future. But the very fact that she had met somebody engaging and different when only days before she had been at her lowest ebb was enough to give her hope. Relationships might be a thing of the past for her, but at least New York had proved it still had the ability to surprise her. Perhaps if the luggage carousel of life was turning in her favour, a new friend might be on the way . . .

CHAPTER EIGHTEEN

Jake's new office, McKevitt Buildings, Broadway

Jake studied the long list of possible PA candidates in his notebook, acutely aware of how long this day was going to be. In the week following Rosie and Ed's engagement party he had been making a determined effort to focus on practical matters, with an impressive rate of success. All around him, plastic-wrapped office furniture, still-boxed computers and a rather impressive counselling couch were testament to his recent activities. He had already confirmed details of the final design with his interior decorator and the team of painters would begin work in two days, leaving him this window of time to recruit new staff for the practice.

But there was where the problem lay: the search for a suitable replacement for Pam was proving tricky. The recruitment consultant Jake had contracted from a prestigious Manhattan personnel agency had assured him that all the shortlisted candidates were amply qualified. According to the CVs laid out on his new desk, the excellent SAT scores, Ivy League degrees and proven aptitude for clinical administration promised great things. But so far this morning, Jake had been faced with a seemingly never-ending stream of humourless, ambitious airheads bearing no resemblance to the ideal-on-paper candidates whatsoever.

'My inspiration is Kim Kardashian,' one candidate had earnestly informed him, 'because of her *business acumen*.' She had emphasised the words as if to add gravitas to her argument. Jake, his smile as steady as he could keep it, had nodded knowingly as he carefully drew a definite line through her name.

Another woman had blatantly misread the job description before applying for the post and was most surprised to learn that a psychiatrist did a vastly different job to a *psychic*. Yet another laughed when Jake asked whether she enjoyed the challenge of office administration, answering: 'Are you nuts? It's like dying slowly on your feet. I just need a job until my agent finds me the right movie . . .'

How was it possible for so many supposedly well-educated young women to be so devoid of personality, common sense or intellect? Jake strongly suspected the recruiter's mention that the prospective client was a newly single young doctor with expensive Manhattan offices might have had more to do with the interviewees' enthusiasm to apply for the job than their natural aptitude.

'Why do you want to work at this practice?' he asked the latest candidate, a softly spoken twenty-something who had listed Friedrich Nietzsche as one of her major life influences on her résumé but, when pressed, couldn't recall any of his theories.

'I think working for you could meet my career aspira-tions.'

'Which are . . . ?'

'To progress my career in an interesting and challenging environment.'

Jake suppressed a sigh. 'Listen, Madison, forget the accepted interview responses and just talk to me. I want to know about you as a person: what interests do you have? What beliefs do you live by? What makes Madison Montgomery who she is?'

Madison blinked. 'Working here?'

Switching into analyst mode, Jake leaned towards her and softened his voice. 'Apart from that. I'm curious as to why you applied for this position. What excites you about working in a psychiatry practice? Do you have an interest in the field? I notice in your résumé that you mention several philosophers as key influences on your life '

Madison was having a hard time disguising the growing panic in her eyes. After a few excruciatingly long moments of silence, she sighed. 'I just need a job, OK? I can organise an office and your diary. I can field calls, prioritise tasks and act as a point of first contact between you and your patients – sorry, *clients*. But beyond that, I don't care whether you are a doctor of psychiatry or a CEO of a Dow Jones listed company.'

And there it is, Jake congratulated himself for seeing this coming the moment Madison entered the room. 'Great. Thank you for your honesty. I'll be in touch.' He watched her leave the room without so much as a parting thank you and sank back into his brand new office chair.

Maybe the recruiter he had chosen was wrong for the task. He knew there were bright, intelligent candidates in New York. So how come none of them wanted to work for him?

The list of names was nearing the halfway mark now. That was something. He checked his watch and stood, wandering over to the window overlooking Broadway where a flurry of yellow cabs was backed up in early afternoon traffic. The Lincoln Center was draped in huge banners advertising the New York Ballet's upcoming season. A lone dancer appeared to be jumping across the grey concrete expanse of the building and the undulating ripples in the banner's length gave the impression that she was flying. It was an intensely positive image that Jake instantly liked, as if the dancer represented the creative, driven spirit of the city thriving in its hard landscape. He smiled. There was a good reason he had chosen to return to New York. It would be tough, but he was tough. Growing up here had woven stubborn drive into his DNA and that counted for a lot. It would get him through his divorce; spur him on to find success in his new practice; and then, who knew?

Three hours later, any vestige of enthusiasm Jake had for appointing a new PA had evaporated like the steam rising from Broadway drains in the early evening air. *Nothing* – not even someone he could train to love the job. He'd had three offers of telephone numbers, a crash course in how *not* to write a résumé and several hours' experience of identical stock answers, but nobody had even come close. In frustration he had dismissed the final eight candidates, who vacated the premises with little more than resigned disinterest. Were his standards too high? He half-wondered if the problems stemmed from a subconscious need to sabotage his new business before it had begun. Without a decent PA, how could he hope to offer the level of service his San Franciscan clients had enjoyed? Tired and irritated, he dismissed the thought. If he was going to end the day without his first employee it wasn't for lack of trying.

This was getting him nowhere. He decided he would call it a day and go and find somewhere to eat, his empty stomach not helping his mood at all today. He screwed up the unsuccessful candidate list, tossed it in the wire waste paper basket and prepared to leave.

'Am I late?'

Jake turned to see a smartly dressed black woman standing in the doorway. She made direct eye contact with him as she waited for his reply. *That* was a first today . . .

'Uh – no . . . Please come in.'

'The agency gave me the wrong address,' she stated, offering her hand. 'Desiree Jackson.'

'I'm Jake Steinmann. Dr Jake Steinmann.'

'Good to meet you. *Finally*. I swear the personnel agency is staffed by high school kids.' She pulled a chair from the line that Jake had set around the wall of the reception area and settled opposite Jake, who sat quickly in the leather chair behind the desk. 'I doubt very much you have my résumé, if their sense of direction indicates anything.' She opened a leather document case and handed him a couple of neatly stapled pages. 'Here.'

Jake accepted it, his mind whirring. She had *taken a chair* from the line. Without waiting to be asked to sit It was a small detail, but it showed initiative. And, having been denied anything to be impressed by all day, Jake was taken aback by this. He skimmed over the details on her résumé, but there was something about the confident woman's attitude that made him like her immensely from the outset.

'You'll see from my employment history that I had a break of two years to raise my son,' Desiree continued. 'During that time I raised him alone, working nights preparing accounts and paperwork for friends. For the last year I have worked at a law firm on the Lower East Side.'

'And your reason for leaving?' Jake asked, trying to regain the initiative in this conversation.

Desiree nodded at her résumé. 'It's all there. They're downsizing. Which, translated, means they're letting me go.'

'Oh. I'm sorry to hear that.'

'Don't be. I walked out and I won't be looking back.'

I really like you, Jake thought, his spirits beginning to lift. 'I see. What attracted you to this position?' *Please don't say 'because it's a job'* . . .

'The mind is fascinating. What makes people act the way they do; why they make the choices they make. I know a little about psychology. Mostly serial killers.' She smiled when she saw Jake's surprise. 'I like real-life police cases. My kid thinks I'm crazy. But I want to know what turns a regular person into a killer.'

Jake coughed to disguise his laugh. 'Well, I have to tell

you we do very little work with psychopaths here. Most of my clients will be dealing with wrong attitudes and learned behaviours, perhaps stemming from trauma in early childhood. The FBI rarely asks for my assistance.'

Desiree shrugged. 'It's all from the same place, isn't it? The mind.'

If you don't want this job I will beg *you to take it . . .*

'I guess it is. Did the agency brief you on the required duties of the job?'

'They mentioned you were a young, single doctor,' she answered, grinning at Jake's groan. 'Beyond that, I kinda figured out what you'd need.'

Jake could believe that. Desiree Jackson was a breath of fresh air, her chutzpah and no-nonsense attitude exactly what Jake was looking for. It was as if Pam had sent her especially for this new role and Jake would be crazy if he didn't appoint her immediately.

'Then I only have one more question: when can you start?'

Desiree smiled broadly. 'Right now, if you want.'

CHAPTER NINETEEN

Hudson River Books, 8th Avenue, Brooklyn

The day of Celia's book launch arrived, sending Bea and Russ into a frenzy of activity. While Bea had laid much of the groundwork for the evening already, there was a list of things yet to be sorted that had grown rather than shrunk all week. Finally, with less than an hour until the event, Bea emerged from her makeshift dressing room in the bookstore office, smoothing down the skirt of her new aubergine velvet dress.

'Will I do?' she asked Russ.

Russ did a Muppet-style double take and dropped the pile of books he was carrying. 'Wow.'

Suddenly self-conscious, Bea put her hand to her hair where a vintage slide was uncomfortably placed. 'Stop it.'

Russ chuckled as he bent down to collect the books. 'You look good. Stop worrying.'

'I'm not worrying, I just wanted look the part.'

'Well, you do.'

113

'Are you getting changed?'

Russ looked down at his faded red and white striped T-shirt, skinny jeans and red Converse trainers. 'I am changed.'

'Russ!' Frustration rising, Bea glared at him. 'This is one of the most important events we've ever hosted. We *need* to make a good impression . . .'

Knowing argument was futile, Russ dropped the pile of books on the counter and headed towards the office. 'OK, I get it! If you can't handle my über-cool look, I'll change it. But it's your issue, remember, not mine.'

Bea ignored his parting shot and set about arranging Celia's books on the table she had decorated for the book signing. She and Russ had been dancing on the edge of an argument all day, neither one finding the pressure particularly easy to handle. At times like these, they both knew it was best to discount anything the other said and certainly never take any of it to heart. From final exams at Columbia University to establishing Hudson River Books, this approach had paid dividends over the years. Today was no different, Bea reminded herself, tempted as she was to hit back at her best friend.

When Russ re-emerged he was dressed in dark jeans, a pressed midnight blue shirt with a thin red tie and the polished black shoes he only wore for first dates, family events and meetings with the bank manager. 'Enough, Ms Fashion Cop?'

'Better.' Bea looked at the clock above the counter. 'What time did Celia say she was coming?'

'Don't ask me,' Russ retorted, closer to a fight than Bea had realised. 'I thought *you* were the darling of Ms

114

Reighton. She barely said three words to me when we were planning this.'

'She was just focused. She gets like that.'

'You'd know.'

Bea shrugged off her irritation and headed to the new coffee station, which had been draped in gorgeous silver lamé fabric from Imelda's shop. Trays of wine glasses were already laid out across it, borrowed from Stromoli's that afternoon. The caterer would be arriving soon and Bea wanted to ensure there was adequate room for the trays of New-York-inspired canapés next to the wine. Forty minutes passed in a blur of checklists and last-minute finishing touches. Except for a few anxious moments when one of the caterers realised he'd only brought half of the party food and had to dash back to his unit to pick up the remainder, Bea and Russ remained impressively calm and in control.

'Darling, this is *just perfect*!' Celia gushed, when she eventually swept into Hudson River Books like the Queen of Sheba. 'I *love* it. Everything.' She put her hand on Bea's shoulder. 'I knew you would be good, but this is wonderful!'

A little stunned by the glowing endorsement of her event organisational abilities, Bea managed to smile in return, but when she tried to reply Celia was already off on a mini-tour of the bookshop. Russ followed in her wake, trying to point out everything he and Bea had arranged for the evening before Celia saw them.

Bea laughed and turned her attention to the growing numbers of guests who were arriving. Some she recognised from their author photographs, others from the staff photos of the *New York Times*. A few she had seen at the engagement party – which, inevitably, made her think of Jake. She wondered which event he might be working at this evening. Would he be having an identical conversation with another single guest somewhere in the city? Remembering their pact, she enjoyed the memory before carefully packing it away behind the box of responsibilities for this evening. After all the time and hard work she and Russ had invested in making Celia's book launch a success, she owed it to both of them to give the event her full attention.

The new coffee bar looked fantastic. Imelda had surpassed herself with sourcing great fabric and Russ had worked late last night hand-painting a sign to officially name their latest venture:

R'n'B's JOE STOP

It had amused Bea no end when she'd seen it, not least because Russ had kept the name a secret until he unveiled the sign. She loved him for many things, but his creativity remained what she most admired. Back at university, they had volunteered together for the drama society and ended up making props and decorating sets for the lavish productions laid on three times a year. As their ambition was always far grander than the available budget, their ingenuity at making plausible objects out of items they could beg or borrow for free had come to the fore. Many a time they had taken part in semi-illicit dumpster raids behind the university kitchens and offices to find discarded cardboard, plastic bottles and other rubbish to transform into expensive-looking props. Bea became chief finder, while Russ used his creative spark to see the potential in whatever his best friend could pilfer from the trash.

Thankfully, her days of jumping into skips and wheelie bins were long behind her, but Bea and Russ' flair for creativity now characterised their business. The quotes and quips on the hand-drawn blackboard signs around the bookshop walls changed weekly, sometimes bestowing great wisdom from famous authors, other times denoting temporary special-interest areas in the store. The recent Zombie Corner, for example, had been a great success with the large contingent of students and artists in the area, although the sight of fifteen black-clad readers with zombie-style white contact lenses had given her nightmares for a week. Today, the former Undead reading zone had been replaced by the 'Upper West Side Words' corner, filled with books from the literary community of the area, championed so strongly by Celia.

'Bea, honey, I'd like you to meet a very good friend of mine.'

Bea instantly recognised the smiling lady standing next to Celia and Stewart as one half of the happy couple from the engagement party. 'Oh, hi.' She thought for a moment, then added, 'I'm sorry I didn't get to speak to you at your party, but congratulations on your engagement.'

Rosie Duncan smiled. 'No problem. Thanks for coming.'

'So – welcome to my bookstore.'

'This is your place? It's lovely.'

'I own it with Russ.' She scanned the crowd of guests and spotted him standing proudly behind the new coffee bar. 'He's serving coffee over there.'

Rosie nodded politely. 'Books and coffee – *great* combination.'

'As is *flowers* and coffee,' Celia interrupted, giving Rosie an unnecessary push towards Bea in her excitement to contribute. 'Rosie owns Kowalski's florists', in the Upper West Side. You remember that stunning floral display I had for my birthday? Rosie *made* that.'

Rosie waved away the compliment. 'If it was up to Celia everybody in New York would be forced to buy their flowers at Kowalski's. She's very kind.'

'I am,' Celia grinned. 'Now I have to *circulate*. So, *talk*, both of you.' And with that she was gone, leaving a fragrant rush of Chanel No. 5 in her wake.

'There goes the One Woman Whirlwind of the Upper West Side,' Rosie chuckled. 'But then, being Stewart's sister, I bet you get to see that phenomenon all the time.'

A waiter stopped between them with a tray of mini Reuben sandwiches and Bea and Rosie both took one.

'I do,' Bea smiled. 'She took some getting used to when I first met her.'

'I've known her for years and I'm still getting used to it! So, whereabouts in England are you from?'

'Northbridge, in Shropshire.' It was nice to talk to a fellow English person after her many years in New York. 'How about you?'

'A little village called Stone Yardley, in the Black Country. Not sure if you've heard of it?'

Genuinely surprised, Bea nodded. 'I have, as a matter

of fact. My Grandma Dot has friends in the Stone Yardley WI. She's a bit of a daredevil, despite being in her early nineties.'

Now it was Rosie's turn to be taken aback. 'They *all* are, aren't they? My mum told me they went on a coasteering break in the south of France last month: a group of pensioners dressed in wetsuits jumping off cliffs into the sea – for fun! I laughed for a week when I heard that . . .'

Bea found herself liking Rosie intensely. At the engagement party she had been too caught up in her own self-consciousness to see what a confident, funny woman the florist was; now, as they chatted about their English roots, she was surprised to find how much they had in common. While she didn't want to presume anything, Bea felt that Rosie could become a good friend. She'd had the same instinct when she first met Russ and Imelda. Grandma Dot called it 'The Common Spark'.

'People are like flint,' she once told Bea, long before New York called her away from England, 'and they walk around in life meeting other pieces of flint. Every now and again they find one they can create a spark with: the angles are just right and everything aligns. Then everything else is easy.'

Grandma Dot had a certain way with words that Bea hadn't witnessed in anyone else, but each of her slightly left-field analogies contained wisdom beyond their strangeness. She missed her very much and often thought of her grandmother still working in the second-hand bookshop she owned in Ironbridge, just across the street from the actual iron bridge itself, the iconic symbol of the Industrial Revolution. Despite being in her nineties and employing both a shop manager and staff, Bea's grandmother refused to take it easy at home, preferring to oversee the day-to-day running of the bookshop. Dot had problems with her hip and, consequently, couldn't travel as easily as Bea's other English family members. Because of this Bea felt the distance between them more acutely than she did with her parents.

'You know, it's been so lovely to talk to you,' Rosie said, mirroring Bea's thoughts. 'And not just because we're both Brits. If you ever fancy popping to Kowalski's for a coffee and chinwag, you'd be very welcome. We have great coffee.'

Meeting Rosie and hearing her talk so animatedly about her business, Bea was keen to see the famous florist shop. 'I'd love that.'

Rosie grinned. 'Fantastic! Here's my card – just give me a call when you want to visit.'

The sound of a glass clinking in the middle of the store drew Bea's attention to Russ, who was standing on a chair.

'Ladies and gentlemen, on behalf of Hudson River Books I would like to welcome you to this special event. Tonight we honour one of New York's finest: a writer whose view of the city has entertained and informed us for many years. We celebrate the launch of her very first collection of columns, a book that already has "bestseller" written all over it. And, by the way she's glaring at me, I can tell I've said enough . . .'

Laughter bounced around the guests and Russ beamed, the performer in him lapping it up.

'So, I give you . . . Ms Celia Reighton!'

Warm applause filled the bookstore and Russ stepped aside to let Celia take the floor. She refused his offer of the chair to stand on and instead raised her glass.

'I think I'm tall enough without that, thank you. Friends, it means the world that you're here tonight. This book has been a long time coming – or a myth in the making, if you listen to my editor . . .' A short, wiry-looking woman nearby laughed in agreement. 'But miracles do happen, as Elspeth discovered when I finally delivered my manuscript.'

'It was worth waiting for,' Elspeth replied, eliciting a benevolent smile from Celia.

'See? That's why we make a crack publishing team! I have many, many people to thank for the contents of this book – most of whom will never know what they inspired or recognise themselves from my descriptions – but that's what makes New York its fabulous, cantankerous self. In particular I want to recognise the great input I've received from the unique wit of our city's cab drivers.'

Celia's guests laughed again, knowing only too well the caustic observations of yellow cab drivers she frequently referred to in her column.

'Most of all, I have you all to thank. My closest and dearest friends are in this room: both those I've known forever and those I've just met. I appreciate your support and I hope you will all think of this poor, starving writer and part with your greenbacks to make sure I can feed Stewart for the next few months . . .'

Celia's signing table became the focus of the guests

for the next hour, keeping Russ and Bea busy with replenishing boxes of her new book, *My NY*, as they rapidly emptied.

'This is going to blow our monthly sales record,' Russ beamed at Bea as she passed him another box of books. 'I'm glad we ordered so many!'

Bea had to agree, amused by the way Russ had conveniently forgotten his heated argument earlier with her about the number of books she was ordering in. It didn't matter now: this evening was a resounding success, proving to all present that Hudson River Books could hold its own with important literary events. That in turn could open up all kinds of possibilities. And Bea was determined to take advantage of every one . . .

It was almost one o'clock in the morning when Bea arrived back at her apartment, exhausted but very happy. The evening had been a resounding success, sealed with Celia's delightedly tipsy approval and an end-of-night hug from Russ, signalling that all was well between them again. As they cleared the party debris long after the last guest had left, Russ had put down the rubbish bag he was carrying and approached her.

'Hey, I was a jerk earlier. Forgive me?'

'There's nothing to forgive. We were both stressed – it's what we do.'

Russ gave a wry smile. 'It is. But I was still a jerk. And you were right: about the number of books, about what I was wearing, all of it.' He held out his arms. 'Hug it out?'

Bea grinned at the memory as she changed out of her evening dress and kicked off her high heels to sink her feet into the welcome comfort of her slippers. Russ might be the worst person to try to win an argument with, but he would always eventually admit if he was wrong. That was part of what made them such a good team: they were as evenly matched in disputes as they were in collaboration. Most people didn't understand this: Imelda was convinced one day they would find a subject on which neither was willing to back down and that would be the end of their friendship. Even Otis – firm friends with Russ for nearly ten years – had been flummoxed by their relationship.

'How can you fight like that and not hate each other?' he would ask Bea whenever she arrived at his apartment glowering after the latest run-in with her best friend.

Bea had tried to explain many times that she and Russ would always veer from felicity to irritation and back, but Otis couldn't see what she could in their unorthodox friendship. The point was, Russ had been her closest ally through the highs and lows of the last fifteen years of her life; and that counted for a great deal.

Still buzzing with adrenaline from Celia's book launch, Bea settled down in front of late night television with a snack and a huge mug of hot chocolate. She picked up her laptop from the coffee table and absent-mindedly flicked through her unopened emails. Nestled between offers from clothing companies and notifications of the latest book reviews from national newspapers was a message that made her heart flip.

From: Dot.James@severnsidebookemporium.co.uk
To: Bea.James@hudsonriverbooks.com
Subject: Every little thing

Hello darling Bea,

Of course I heard about your awful ordeal (your mum filled me in) and I had to check how my favourite granddaughter is doing.

First of all, let me say that I am disappointed beyond words in that young man. I hope you have sent him running with a flea in his ear. You deserve more, sweetheart, but then I think you've probably come to that conclusion already. We are, after all, cut from the same cloth, you and I.

So, how is life in that big city? I know it's where your heart belongs but I must confess that at times like this it feels far too far away for comfort. I remember our many talks about matters of the heart in my bookshop during your teenage years and I wish it could be as simple now for me to be of help to you. Back then, we would hide in the old leather armchairs I inherited from Great-Gramps and raid my secret sweetie tin, which went a long way to solving whatever dilemma we were discussing, as I recall. How I wish we could do that now!

Your mother has promised to help me put that Skype thing on my computer when she and your father get back from their holiday adventure, so at least I will be able to see you. Whoever thought we would be able to talk through computer screens to one another! I'll feel like I am in *Star Trek*, I'm sure of it.

For now, tell me your news. How are you feeling? What are your thoughts about Otis and your future? Send me a message as soon as you can, if for no other reason than to appease your fretting grandmother.

Fondest love, my darling,

Grandma Dot xx

Bea was struck with a deep longing to see Grandma Dot again. It had been far too long since they had both been on the same side of the world and she missed her grandmother's unconventional take on life. Most of her school days had been characterised by the conversations they had shared in Great-Gramps' armchairs, munching Love Hearts and Refresher Bars in secret. Her mum would have been shocked to see how much sugar her mother and daughter consumed during Bea's visits to the Severnside Book Emporium.

The truth was, right now Bea needed Grandma Dot's wisdom. With Celia's book launch done – and her main distraction removed – Bea's thoughts returned to the conversation she'd had at Rosie's engagement party. Imelda's insistence that Bea should have procured the barman's number hadn't helped to remove the memory of Jake and the pact they'd made; neither had the growing realisation that very few people understood her reasons for staying single from now on. During the short amount of time she had talked with Jake, she had enjoyed the experience of being understood.

It shouldn't have mattered – it was a small thing after all – but Bea wondered if she had maybe missed an opportunity. That was enough to create an itch in her brain and she knew if she didn't do something about it soon, it could become far bigger than it should be.

There was only one thing for it . . .

From: Bea.James@hudsonriverbooks.com
To: Dot.James@severnsidebookemporium.co.uk
Subject: Re: Every little thing

Hi Grandma Dot,

It was so lovely to hear from you! How are you? Any news on the dreaded hip operation? I hope they get it sorted for you soon.

I'm fine, honestly. The family meal was the last in a very long line of straws for Otis and me. And, actually, I feel better knowing that a line has finally been drawn underneath that season of my life. It's freed me to focus on the bookshop and on the areas of my life that I know I can make a success. I'm very content and the rest of my life is going well.

Except for just one thing. And this is where I need your advice because it's just possible that you are the only person who will understand it.

Recently, I met somebody. I think he had the potential to be a good friend. We talked about loving New York and how embarrassing it was to be the only two single people at an engagement party (yes, that's another one for the Life Experiences file!). I liked his sense of humour and he seemed to be amused by mine, too. I can't remember when I last felt so understood by someone. And yet, I actually know nothing about him, other than he is going through a divorce and despairs of relationships as much as I do. It's silly, but I wish I knew more.

The problem is, I didn't ask if he would like to talk again some time. He didn't ask me, either, so quite why I feel it's a missed opportunity confuses me. It could just be part of the fallout from the end of my relationship with Otis, of course. But I feel like I need to make friends with people who know me right now, not who I was with Otis. What do you think? Have I completely lost the plot? I would love to know what you think. I promise I will have copious amounts of sweets handy when I read your reply, so it will almost be as good as our chats in Great-Gramps' armchairs . . .

Miss you lots,

Bea xxx

She pressed send and leaned back against the sofa cushions.

How do I get myself in these situations?

The question bounced hollowly around her head and didn't find an answer. Tired and frustrated with herself, Bea put her laptop back on the coffee table, knocking off something which fluttered to the floor. She bent down to pick it up, reading the inscription on the elegant business card:

ROSIE DUNCAN – Proprietor
Kowalski's Florist
~ Where beautiful things happen ~
Corner of West 68th & Columbus, Upper
West Side, New York

Bea turned the card over and over in her fingers, her mind returning to the conversation she'd had with Rosie that evening. If it was a new friend she needed, Rosie would be a strong contender. They had a lot in common and it would be good to talk to a fellow Brit in New York.

'Pop in anytime you fancy a chat,' Rosie had offered. 'We have great coffee . . .'

Bea smiled as she made her decision.

She was going to Kowalski's.

CHAPTER TWENTY

Jake's practice, McKevitt Buildings, Broadway

Desiree Jackson was a one-woman wonder. In the short time since Jake hired her, she had already revolutionised the way he ran his business. And that was some feat, considering that his business wasn't even operational yet. Even though Desiree had no experience of managing a psychiatry practice, she had taken to the task like an incredibly forthright duck to water. Her instincts were spot-on and there was very little advice or guidance Jake could offer to better her service.

She wasn't just good at her job; she was *scarily* good at it.

As she whizzed around the reception area, Jake retreated to the safety of his office to call Pam.

'How's the new girl?' Pam asked.

'She's not a girl. She's a *woman*. And she terrifies me,' Jake whispered, keeping one eye on the door in case Desiree came in.

'Ah, you got a *good* one.' Pam's amusement made

Jake feel even more useless. 'Let me guess: you're hiding out in your office right now so you don't get under her feet.'

Man, you're good, Jake smiled. 'Maybe.'

'I'll take that as an affirmative. You did the same on my first day at your practice, remember?'

Oh no, I really am that predictable, aren't I? Jake was aware of his blush even though Pam couldn't see it. 'I'd forgotten,' he lied, laughing at his own failings.

'It's a natural reaction. Now, quit hiding and go act like the employer.'

'I'm not sure how to.'

Pam laughed. 'You'll figure it out. Go!'

Jake ended the call, stared at the office door and prepared to walk out. He had just taken hold of the handle when it jerked downwards, pushing him back as the door flew open.

Desiree shrieked and clamped a hand to her heart. 'Are you *trying* to give me a heart attack?'

'I'm sorry, I was just . . .'

She rested against Jake's desk, breathing heavily. 'It's OK. I didn't see you. I'm looking for the new patient files. I believe they arrived yesterday?'

'Sure, I put them under the reception desk this morning.'

'Oh.' She stared at him. 'Well, I didn't know.'

'I didn't get a chance to tell you. But they're there, I assure you.' He took a breath and remembered Pam's advice. 'Why don't you sit down?'

Desiree frowned. 'What did I do?'

'You haven't done anything – apart from be too adept

130

at your job already. Please – you haven't had a break since you arrived today.'

Still suspicious, Desiree sat on the new consulting couch, her long painted nails digging into the edges of the cushion as if tethering her in the wake of an oncoming storm. 'So, I'm sitting.'

'Good.' Jake tried to think of what to say that might make him sound suitably in charge, but quickly gave up. 'I just wanted to thank you. You've been incredible since you arrived and I appreciate everything you're doing.'

Desiree observed him carefully. 'But . . . ?'

'No buts. You're great.'

'So, why the chat?'

'Uh – to thank you?' This wasn't how Jake had intended the conversation to go.

'Oh.'

'O-K, then. So . . .'

'Can I say something?'

'Sure, go ahead.'

His PA's expression softened a little. 'You have a lot on your mind, don't you?'

'Do I?' Jake was suddenly on edge. Where was this heading? 'I guess in my line of work that's an occupational hazard.'

'That's not what I mean. You've been preoccupied for a while. I've seen it: you do and say the right things, but your head's somewhere else.'

'I'm setting up my practice, Desiree, there's a lot to think of.'

'It's more than that. Forgive me; I just have a sense

for these things. Can I ask, are you thinking about your divorce?'

The question hit Jake like a freight train. 'I – um . . .'

'It's OK if you are. I mean, it's huge. You're dealing with a *death*, after all. Death of dreams; death of a relationship. Difference is that when someone we love dies they usually don't hire a lawyer to take half your house.'

It sounded like something he would say to his clients, but Desiree's forthrightness hit closer to home than Jake was comfortable with. His feelings for Jessica were too raw to be picked over so keenly, especially by his employee. Stuffing his feelings behind his smile, he rebuffed her assertion. 'I appreciate what you're saying, but I'm fine. If my head's been somewhere else it's not because I'm missing my ex, OK?'

'OK, whatever you say, boss.' She stood up. 'Am I good to go now?'

'Sure.' Feeling like his mother had just reprimanded him, Jake motioned for her to leave.

Desiree paused in the doorway, and turned back. 'Why don't you take a break, huh? I think you're ready for one and I've got everything covered here.'

'I can't just leave you to do all the work,' he protested, but Desiree was having none of it.

'Then go buy lunch for us. I have a lot to do and, frankly, you're getting in the way.'

Jake conceded defeat. Desiree had the spirit of Pam all right: eminently capable, bossy and, frustratingly, always right. Besides, it would be good to get out of the office for a while to escape the never-ending list of things to do and the muddle of emotions waiting in the wings.

Yellow cabs buzzed in and out of the lanes on Broadway like an army of irascible bees when Jake emerged onto the sidewalk. Horns blared and the rumble of Manhattan seemed to come from somewhere deep beneath his feet, reverberating up through the streets and buildings and up towards the sky. The busyness of the city had always calmed Jake before he moved to the other side of America: now, it was a characteristic he was acutely aware of. Some aspects of New York life he had been able to settle back into like the old leather sofa at his brother's workplace, but some were taking time to reacclimatise to. It was natural to experience this, Jake reminded himself. After all, it had taken a good twelve months for him to get used to the laid-back nature of the West Coast. He had walked around San Francisco feeling like an uptight alien, frustrated by the unending positivity and relaxed nature of everyone around him. But pretty soon he had begun to make friends there and learned that West Coast residents worked and played as hard as their East Coast compatriots, only in their own way. After all, with the ocean on your doorstep, no day was too much to bear. Meetings took place on yachts or in summer houses on the Pacific coast; business deals were signed over great seafood overlooking the Bay; you could even meet your stock trader on the golf course with blue waves crashing on the nearby cliffs. New York by comparison was one great conurbation of stress.

And yet, Jake adored New York. Its ornery cantankerousness made it fun to love – like a tiny niece or nephew that disliked being hugged. You loved it and you embraced it, even though it seemed to hate your regard.

He crossed Broadway and wandered down one of the side streets, the smell of roasted meat drawing him away from the city artery. Passing several delis and restaurants, he was drawn to an A-board on the street decorated with front covers of classic books.

Spend your lunch break with the greats! – the sign invited him. Jake smiled. Back in San Francisco one of his favourite Sunday morning activities was wandering down to the quirky second-hand bookstore a block from his home. They served great coffee and encouraged their customers to browse the shelves while they enjoyed their morning caffeine hit. He missed the thoughtless ease of it and was keen to see if the bookshops in Manhattan were as wonderful as he remembered.

His eyes took a few moments to grow accustomed to the dim lights inside, but soon he saw wooden shelves filled with books and smelled the familiar scent of dust and printers' ink. Instantly, he felt at home. He moved further into the shop and saw that a large table had been set up in the middle of the bookcases, where several workers from the nearby offices were huddled over piles of books as they ate their lunch. Maybe he would join them from now on, he mused. It could be the beginning of a whole new tradition in his workday. He liked that. Possibility was definitely what he should be thinking about. He had given far too much headspace to everything he had lost.

He picked up a faded paperback copy of Ernest Hemingway's *To Have and Have Not* and was flicking through it when something caught his eye. At the back of the shop a woman was unpacking a box of books, her shoulder-length auburn hair catching the light from the halogen spots above the counter. Jake froze.

It couldn't be . . . could it?

Had Bea mentioned she worked in a bookstore? He tried to remember, but the details were sketchy in his mind. Then the realist in him kicked into action. What were the chances that the woman he had met once before in another neighbourhood would be working one street away from his workplace? It was a classic case of transference: he was projecting an imagined scenario onto a real-life situation.

But then, what if it actually *was* her?

Unlike everyone else at the party, Bea hadn't flinched when he'd mentioned Jessica; she hadn't judged him, merely shared her own bad experience and her determination to move on. Jake wanted to move on, too. If this was where she worked he could have an ally right across the street from his new practice. It would be good to know he had a friend on hand to cheer him onwards.

Grasping the book, Jake made his way towards the counter. A man stepped from the other side of the bookcases, blocking his way. In the limited space between the shelves, Jake was forced to perform an awkward do-si-do dance with him to allow both of them to travel in their intended directions. Unexpected obstacle overcome, he took the final few steps . . .

And then, she turned.

'Hi. Can I help you?'

It's not her. Everything within Jake sank as the woman-who-wasn't-Bea smiled. Embarrassed, annoyed at himself for believing in an impossible situation, and with no other option but to buy the book he held, Jake managed a weak smile in return.

'Just this, please.'

'Sure.' She picked up the book. '*Great* book. My favourite of his, I think.' She pulled a brown paper bag from underneath the counter and put the book inside. Handing it back to Jake, she said, 'Did you find everything you were looking for today?'

Mortification growing, Jake nodded and handed over a ten-dollar note, grasping the bag and heading out of the bookstore before the woman could give him his change.

Outside, he let out a groan, raising his eyes to the Manhattan sky.

What's wrong with me?

He had to put thoughts like this out of his mind and focus on what was important. Even Desiree, who had known him for exactly one week, had noticed his distractedness. If he was ever going to have a professional relationship with his new PA, he had to get himself back in the game.

Remembering the errand he was meant to be running, Jake walked back towards Broadway, stepping into a small deli to order sandwiches and coffee. As he waited in line with the disgruntled conversations of waiting customers mingling with the hiss of the espresso machine, he tried to gain a rational hold on his wayward thoughts. The only way to get past this mind block was to confront it. Bea had come to the party with her brother, that much he remembered. As he didn't remember seeing a Bea on the guest list when he was sending invitations, she had to be a 'plus-one' of one of the invited guests. And, as Rosie and Ed had prepared the invitation list, they *had* to know which one of their male guests might have invited his sister to the party.

The queue ahead of him was moving slowly, so he took the opportunity to make a call.

'Jake-e-e-y! How ya doin'?'

'I'm good, bro. Listen, I need to pick your brains on something. You free for a drink after work?'

Ed's chuckle made Jake smile. 'Always for you. Harry's at six?'

'It's a date.'

Ending the call, Jake knew the die had been cast. One way or another, he would have an answer this evening . . .

Harry's Bar was quiet when Jake entered later that day. The after-work crowd had left and it was too early for the evening drinkers who usually filled the place. With no sign of Ed, Jake took a seat by the bar and ordered a bourbon and water. All afternoon he had debated whether this was the right course of action to take. Would Ed laugh at him? Could it open a Pandora's box he wasn't ready to deal with? On the other hand, if it settled the matter once and for all, surely it was worth it?

A sharp slap on his back heralded his brother's arrival and Ed swung onto the bar stool next to him.

'I'll have a beer, thanks,' he told the barman, 'and – *wow* – whatever my bro's having.'

'Same again,' Jake confirmed, sliding his glass forward.

'The hard stuff already? Man, your day must've been

137

worse than mine.' Ed's smile softened his concern. 'Is the bourbon anti-Jess medication?'

'No. Nothing like that.'

'So – the papers?'

'I haven't signed them yet. But I will.'

'OK. So what gives?'

Jake could feel the rich spirit warming his stomach, wondering too late whether he should have eaten before he started drinking bourbon. 'I have a problem I need help with.'

'Hey, shouldn't I be saying that to you, Dr Steinmann?'

'You'd think. This is a subject I believe you are better qualified to answer, Eddie.'

Ed swigged his beer and grinned. 'Ah. So it's a *dating* question.'

Jake resisted the urge to cringe. He might have been thinking of Bea for the last couple of weeks but it wasn't anything more than curiosity. It was certainly *not* a dating opportunity. 'No. At least, not in the way you mean.'

'You're not making this easy. You wanted to talk to me, remember?'

'You're right: I did.'

'So – *talk*.'

'At the engagement party, I met someone . . . OK, now you can stop with that face immediately. We talked and, I dunno, I thought we made a connection. As *potential friends*, Edward. I'm done with relationships. The thing is, I don't know who she was.'

'Did she mention her name?'

'Bea. She said her name was Bea.'

Ed frowned. 'I don't recognise it. But then I'm bad with names, you know that.'

'Sure.'

'Any more information?'

Jake sighed, already feeling this conversation was doomed to failure. 'Not much. She had red hair, sea green eyes, loved New York – which I liked, obviously. She was originally from the UK. Oh, and she said she worked in a bookstore, only I can't tell if she actually said that or if my mind added it. She wasn't on the guest list, but she said her brother had invited her.'

'OK. So we need to figure out who brought their English sister . . .' Ed thought for a moment. 'No one comes to mind, but don't panic. Rosie knows more of the people we invited than I do. Do you mind if I ask her?'

'Not at all.'

'Leave it with me.' Ed smiled at his brother. 'I gotta tell ya, bro, I'm proud of you.'

'For what?'

'For getting back out there so soon after Jess. You don't need to sit waiting for her to hurt you any more. It's good to get back in the game.'

Jake finished his drink and refused the barman's offer of another. 'I don't want to find this woman for a date. I just think we could be friends. And it would be good to meet new people who only know me right now – no Jess, no life in NY before her.' He meant every word: the thought of being able to start a friendship with a clean sheet was very appealing. It would grant him much needed respite from the heartache of his impending divorce. He deserved that. 'My life has changed, and I'm changing with it. I just think if I'm going to figure out who Jake Steinmann is now, it would be good to talk with somebody who can say what they see. Know what I mean?'

'Kinda. But I'm curious: why are you not considering dating her? She sounds like a beautiful woman, who was obviously interested in you. Seems to me like a heck of an opportunity to pass up, Jake.'

Jake thought back to the party and the pact he had made with Bea. 'She doesn't want a relationship,' he said.

'What? How do you know?'

'I know because that's what we spoke about: how much we hate relationships. She'd just come out of a long relationship and she said she was done with them.'

Ed dropped his head into his hands. 'Oh *man* . . .'

'I agreed with her. Jess has ripped my world apart – and for what? So she can have her own way and discard me in the process. I don't want to go through something like that again.'

'Bro, it was her *choice*. You couldn't change that if you tried . . .'

'I know that. Point is, I thought my relationship was strong, that I was successful as a husband. Turns out I was wrong. Sure, it was her decision, but if I couldn't see it coming – and I honestly *never* saw it coming – then what's to say I wouldn't get it wrong again?'

The barman brought Ed another bottle of beer, which he started drinking. 'I think you're missing the point here. A divorce isn't a reason to give up entirely. It's just one closed door. How do you know this woman couldn't be the love of your life, huh? Exactly. You *don't* know.'

Jake began to think he might be losing the advantage. Changing tack, he appealed to his brother's better nature. 'Thing is, I liked talking to her. She made me laugh, bro, and you know how long it's been since anybody did that.'

'Hey, if that's what you want then I'm happy to help. Besides, it will be good to think of something other than *wedding* preparations . . .' Ed pulled a face. 'I swear, Rosie's a saint for dealing with the crazy people we seem to have invited to our wedding. They're driving me insane. It's gotten so bad that she's banned me from talking to them when they call.'

'Thanks. I appreciate it.'

'I know you do. Leave it with me and I promise Rosie and I will figure out who this woman is.'

Arriving back at his Williamsburg apartment, Jake felt calmer than he had since the party. Of course, Rosie and Ed might draw a blank; but at least wheels were in motion. Walking from the kitchen with a large glass of water, Jake's gaze fell on the brown envelope on his dining table. It had been a constant reminder of everything he had lost and suddenly he wanted it out of his sight. Grabbing a pen, he sat at the table, pulled out the legal papers and signed them. From now on, his life was about moving forward, not looking back. This was a necessary part of the journey, which needed to be dealt with. Whatever happened next in his life, the experience of the last few weeks had taught him that he needed to live for *now*, not in perpetual limbo anticipating what might never be.

'There, Jess,' he said to the divorce papers. 'That's what you wanted. Now let me get on with my life.'

His pulse was racing as he replaced the document in its envelope and sealed it. He would send it first thing tomorrow morning. Feeling a little shaky from his brave act – and the inevitable tearing it caused in his heart – he picked up his glass, switched off the light and made his way to bed.

CHAPTER TWENTY-ONE

Hudson River Books, 8th Avenue, Brooklyn

From: Dot.James@severnsidebookemporium.co.uk
To: Bea.James@hudsonriverbooks.com
Subject: RE: RE: Every little thing

My darling girl,
   What a conundrum!
   This young man sounds as if he made
quite an impression upon you. But I quite
understand your reticence about inviting
anyone else into your life so soon after
Otis.
   On the other hand, I think your need to
be seen for who you are on your own is a
good one and should be heeded. Friends
are like books: you can never have too
many. We meet people throughout our lives
that resonate with different aspects of who
we are. Breaking away from a relationship is

a tough thing but will bring out new things in you that new people can share. Maybe the young man at the party has unlocked that need in you to spread your social circle. It could well be that he was just meant to be there, on that night, to make you realise you were changing. You have to decide if you just need new friends or if he *is* the new friend you want in your life.

Whatever you decide to do, I know you'll follow your heart. You always have, my love, and I consider it one of your best features. Don't let your recent disappointment deter you from pursuing new friendships. The man you met at the party may well be the key to your next great life adventure. I think you need a friend who appreciates who you are with no prior knowledge of your life. In my experience, life tends to send us new acquaintances to show us who we are becoming. It might be the handsome barman, it might not. The most important thing is that you find what makes you happy and pursue it with all your heart.

Keep me in the loop, darling. I'm crossing everything crossable for you.

Fondest love,

Grandma Dot xx

'Would you mind if I take this afternoon off?' Bea asked Russ next day. Since her decision late last night – and the email she had received from her grandmother this morning – Bea had firmly decided on visiting Rosie. If she needed new friends, Rosie seemed the obvious – and safer – choice.

'*This* afternoon?' Russ asked, aghast.

'Yes. You weren't planning on taking it off, were you?'

'No.'

'So is it all right if I do?'

Russ handed Bea a large paper cup of coffee from the bookstore's new espresso machine. 'Are we talking the *whole* afternoon?'

Bea couldn't decipher his mood: was he complaining or simply surprised at her sudden request? 'Yes, all afternoon. Is there a problem?'

'*Yes*, there's a problem,' Russ retorted. 'The problem is that you never take time off. Not unless you're sick – and even then I've had to send you home when you've insisted on working.'

Bea was on edge enough this morning without having to endure her friend's sarcasm. 'Russ. Do you mind, or not?'

'Of course I don't. I'm just shocked you asked. Is everything OK?'

Bea sipped her coffee. 'Everything's fine. But I'm tired after Celia's event and I thought I should take it easy today.'

'Good call. You deserve it.'

'Thank you.'

'You're welcome. Just promise me that you'll have fun

whatever you do. Knowing you a day off mightn't happen again for another five years . . .'

All morning, Bea kept herself busy with stock ordering, invoice filing and countless other mundane tasks that would distract her from her plan. What would she say to Rosie? 'Shall we be friends?' sounded so needy . . . If she thought about it too much, she knew she would back out at the last minute. But Grandma Dot was right: she had to follow her heart.

At midday, Bea found Rosie's card and called Kowalski's. A young woman answered and passed the call over to Rosie when Bea asked to speak to her.

'Hello, Rosie Duncan speaking.'

'Hi Rosie, it's Bea James. From Hudson River Books? We met last night.'

'Oh, hello! Nice to hear from you.'

'I was wondering if your offer of coffee and a chinwag was still open?' *Please say yes*, she silently willed.

'Today? That would be wonderful! What time shall we expect you?'

Bea looked at her watch, not wanting to sound too eager. 'I could perhaps get to you for about one-ish?'

'Brilliant. See you soon.'

With everything in place, there was only one thing left to do. Collecting her bag from the bookstore office and saying goodbye to Russ, Bea stepped out onto 8th Avenue and hailed a cab.

'Where to, lady?' asked the driver.

'Upper West Side, corner of West 68th Street and Columbus Avenue, please.'

Settling into the back seat, Bea watched Brooklyn pass

by and Manhattan loom ahead. It was exciting to imagine what Rosie's store might look like and she felt deliciously naughty to be heading there on a weekday when she should be at work.

'This is it: corner West 68th and Columbus,' the cab driver announced. 'My mother uses this florist.'

'I'm visiting the owner, actually.'

'Rosie? You'll love her. My ma loves her so much she sends her Christmas cards.'

Bea paid the driver and stared up at the frontage of the Upper West Side flower shop. Like everything in this neighbourhood, the shop had a bespoke awning over its entrance and a beautifully chalked A-board on the wide sidewalk, bearing the message:

WELCOME TO KOWALSKI'S

In front of the shop, buckets of arranged bouquets provided a riot of colour against the greyness of the building and Bea could see a rainbow of blooms through the window. It looked chic but inviting, not like some of the florists' shops in the city, which usually had 'boutique' in their title. Kowalski's was the kind of florist you weren't afraid to enter.

A little silver bell rang out as she entered and Bea looked up to see it swinging above the doorway. The shop was busy, with three customers at the counter and another couple browsing the bank of flowers in galvanised steel buckets. From behind the counter, Bea saw Rosie wave and beckon her over.

'Hi Bea! Let me serve these customers and I'll be right

with you. Take a seat by the window and make yourself comfortable.'

Bea sat on a battered, brown leather sofa placed in the large window overlooking Columbus Avenue and took off her coat. She was a little apprehensive but made a concerted effort to relax. The comfort of the sofa and the incredible aroma of flowers and greenery, together with the smell of freshly brewed coffee helped to calm Bea's nerves. An odd metallic clunking sound came from behind the counter, like a robot falling slowly down a metal staircase, but neither Rosie nor the very pregnant woman with blue-black hair next to her seemed to notice.

While she waited, Bea watched Rosie serving her customers. She appeared to know and be on first-name terms with everyone, asking about their kids, their grand-kids, their new job, or their latest holiday. The whole shop felt like a community hub, where customers were family, and Rosie made every conversation personal to each one. This was definitely Rosie's store: from the little Bea had learned about her since the party and their chat at Celia's book launch, she could see her positivity and sunny nature in every aspect of Kowalski's.

It reminded Bea of her own store and she instantly felt affinity with Rosie. From Hudson River Books' inception, both Bea and Russ had been adamant that their bookstore would be inclusive, welcoming to all and, most importantly, a place people would always want to return to. Being an independent business, they'd had to work hard to offer the kind of service large chains and online retailers couldn't, especially as it was impossible to compete on price alone. Luckily for them, 8th Avenue was part of a neighbourhood where local people loved the difference of independents; where creativity was a selling point rather than an expensive distraction from discounts. Brooklyn residents liked to feel businesses were designed for them and were willing to be more adventurous than their Manhattan counterparts. Consequently, the whole area had recently seen an explosion of new, diverse businesses, which sat alongside long-established, family-run shops and restaurants, faithfully frequented by generations of Brooklyn customers. It was tough to succeed there and many new ventures failed, but if the neighbourhood took you to their hearts you thrived.

The last of the customers left with their purchases and Rosie headed over to Bea, handing her a steaming mug.

'Present from Old F,' she said, laughing when she saw Bea's confusion. 'Sorry. Our resident coffee machine. You might have heard him working a few minutes ago.'

'Oh, *that's* what it was,' Bea smiled, accepting it. 'I thought something was dying.'

'That's what a lot of my customers say. Until they've tried his coffee.'

'It is good.'

'Thank you. Anyway, it's good to see you. So, what do you think of Kowalski's?'

Bea looked around again. 'I love it. It's beautiful. And your customers certainly seem to love it, too.'

'Yes, we're really lucky on that score. The previous owner made an impact on many people's lives and started something in this neighbourhood that they have wanted to see continue. Ed and I both feel the responsibility of that and we've worked hard to maintain it.'

'It certainly seems to be working,' Bea replied, seeing the way her compliment made Rosie beam with pride.

'I love your store, too, by the way,' Rosie replied. 'Celia had been raving about the bookstore for weeks and I was excited to see it. You and Russ have created a really unique place. He's a nice bloke, by the way. You two seem very comfortable together.' Her eyes widened in shock as she realised what she'd said. 'Oh, I'm sorry! That was very presumptuous of me.'

Bea laughed. 'It's OK, you're not the first person to think we're a couple. We're just business partners and really good friends.'

'I'm sorry. That's how Ed and I started out, that's all. I keep forgetting we're the only ones daft enough to turn a working friendship into a relationship. But your closeness shows in your business – I think that was what I was trying to say.'

'Thank you. We're just starting out in many ways, but I'm proud that we seem to have become a favourite for local people. If we can establish something they want to return to again and again, I think we'll be there for the long haul.'

'That's a great thing to aim for,' Rosie smiled. 'But I'm guessing you didn't visit today to swap business tips.'

Bea could feel the redhead blush creeping up the back of her neck. How desperate was she going to appear if she told Rosie the real reason for being there? Conjuring up Grandma Dot's words in her mind for courage, she took a deep breath. 'I'm trying to make new friends in the city. The thing is, I've just left a long-term relationship and I feel like I'm changing as a person, but the

150

friends I have – and they're great friends, honestly – don't seem to see the changes in me. It's made me think that I need to widen my social circle; meet people who will see me for who I am now, not who I have been before.' Embarrassed by her own words, she laughed. 'And that sounds *totally* needy. I'm sorry.'

Rosie surveyed her, amused. 'It's not needy at all. I'd say it's very sensible. When I first arrived in New York I didn't really know anyone, except Celia, and even then it was the most tenuous of acquaintances. All my friends I made here only knew me from that moment and it was refreshing to be able to be myself without people knowing everything about my life.'

Bea felt a rush of gratitude. 'That's what I think I'm looking for. Maybe it's a British thing: we don't like putting ourselves out there.'

'Oh, I understand that completely. But once you're in New York you meet people who don't mind asking to be your friend. In many ways it can be easier to make friends here than in England for that reason. Although you do get some nutters marching up to you sometimes.'

'Like me,' Bea smiled.

'Don't be daft,' Rosie laughed. 'Listen, you're welcome here any time. And if you fancy hanging out some time, that would be lovely. Nice to be able to chat about British stuff without someone assuming you live in a castle or know the Queen.'

'Do you get that too?'

'Oh, all the time! That or, "You're from England? My cousin is from Scotland, do you know her?" I know we're meant to be a small island, but not that small!'

'When I first met Russ, he was convinced I was distantly related to the Royal Family. I think he thought everyone in the UK was.'

'That's sweet. So how do you find running a business with your friend?'

'It's great, most of the time. Sometimes we clash but I think that always happens when you've known someone for a long time. He doesn't understand why I broke up with my boyfriend, unfortunately: they've been friends for a while.'

Rosie grimaced. 'That must be awkward.'

'It is, a little. But I know I made the right decision and I have to stick to it. That's why I'm giving up on relationships.'

'Really?'

Bea nodded. 'It's something someone at your engagement party suggested, actually.'

Bea could tell that this intrigued her new friend. 'Oh? Who was that?'

'The barman.'

Rosie laughed. 'Things *have* to be bad if you're taking advice from a barman.'

Considering how it would sound to Bea if the roles were reversed, she had to agree. 'I know. But your barman was . . . different. Apparently he was going through a divorce and felt exactly the same. We had a great conversation about it and then he suggested we make a pact to swear off relationships. So, we did.'

'Wow. I had no idea we had such a philosopher in our midst! But you aren't serious about this pact, are you? It seems a little *drastic*.'

'Actually, I am. I wish I'd been able to talk to the barman for longer, to be honest. It was good to meet someone in the same boat as I am.'

'Maybe you should have asked for his number.' Rosie winked at Bea as she took her empty coffee cup. 'The bloke sounds like a true original. More coffee?'

'Love one, thanks.' Bea watched Rosie walk behind the counter. It was good to be able to chat with someone new, but why had she ended up talking about Jake? It was only natural, she decided; meeting him had created a desire to include new people in her life, which was the main reason she'd come to Kowalski's today.

This is all part of becoming the person I want to be, she told herself. *New life, new outlook, new acquaintances . . . Who knows where this will take me?*

CHAPTER TWENTY-TWO

Jake's practice, McKevitt Buildings, Broadway

'Provided you're satisfied with our practice protocol, I see no reason why we can't shake on it now,' Jake smiled at the psychiatrist sitting opposite him, mentally crossing another item off his to-do list. It had been a good morning, with progress made on several fronts, but this was by far his greatest achievement. Even Desiree had to be proud of this one . . .

Dr Tom Stephens grinned a wide, white smile and reached across Jake's desk to shake his hand. 'I'm looking forward to working with you, Jake. I'm excited about where you want to take this practice.'

'Great. Listen, talk with Desiree and she will arrange everything you need for your office. It's going to be good sharing the business with you. I have to say, you come highly recommended by my former practice partner.'

Tom laughed as he stood. 'Bob Dillinger is a kind man. Especially as I regularly win our golf tournaments. He speaks highly of you, but I'm sure you know that.'

He shook hands again with Jake. 'I'll arrange to move in during the next week or so. You won't regret this, Jake.'

There were many things Jake might live to regret, but he was certain that appointing Tom Stephens as his junior partner was not one of them. As soon as he began to plan his new practice in New York, Jake had decided he wanted another professional to share the workload. Dr Stephens came with an impressive client list and several specialist qualifications, all of which would help to boost the practice and widen the scope of services they could offer to the people of New York. It was a financial gamble, but Jake had learned from experience that the right mix of personnel in a psychiatry practice could reap big rewards. Might as well start as he meant to go on . . .

The intercom on his desk telephone buzzed. 'Hey Desiree.'

'I have your brother on Line One,' his PA informed him.

'Thanks. Put him through, would you?' Jake waited for the click as the call was transferred. 'Eduardo! To what do I owe this honour?'

'I've got news, Jakey-boy. Are you ready?' He inserted a dramatic pause for effect. 'We found her.'

Stunned, Jake sunk back into his chair. 'Do you mean . . . ?'

'Rosie figured it out.'

'And?'

'Her name is Bea James. She's the sister of Rosie's friend Celia's partner, Stewart. They brought her to the party. And she doesn't just work in a bookstore, she *owns* one.'

'Where?'

Ed laughed. 'I knew you'd love me.'

'I do. Where can I find her?'

'Her bookstore is Hudson River Books, on 8th Avenue in Brooklyn. So go get her, bro!'

'I'm not going to "get her". I'm going to see if she'd like to chat some more.'

Ed groaned. 'Whatever. Just go.'

Jake didn't need to think about his next move. Leaving the office in Desiree's very capable hands, he hailed a cab on Broadway and headed towards Brooklyn . . .

Rain had started falling when the cab turned onto 8th Avenue, coming to a halt outside a small bookstore. Jake had somehow expected it to be bigger, but as he ducked out of the cab onto the sidewalk he felt a surge of anticipation power through him.

It seemed surreal after weeks of thinking about the woman from the party that she could have, in hindsight, been so easy to track down. He looked up at the wide window filled with a display of 'Early Summer Reads', each book accompanied by a handwritten endorsement of its virtues. It made him smile and he remembered how good it had felt to talk about his divorce with Bea. If he could count on a friend to understand and help him move on with his life it could make all the difference. Ed and Rosie might think this was about him dating again, but they were wrong: right now, Jake needed a like-minded friend.

The rain was soaking into the collar of his jacket, thin trails of icy water sneaking inside and running down his spine. He had no idea what he was going to say to her, but he had come this far. Taking all of his courage, he pushed the door open.

Soft jazz music was playing as Jake walked into Hudson River Books, and instantly the smell of fresh coffee met him like an old friend. He was amused by how much the bookstore reminded him of Rosie and Ed's florists', even though the stock differed greatly. Perhaps it was the exposed brick walls, or the cheerful, handwritten chalkboard signs. Or the sense of welcome the entire shop seemed to emit.

He moved further inside, noticing the customers engrossed in their latest book purchases around the store, and the kids' book corner, where a young mother was settled on a huge, acid yellow and lime green beanbag seat with her small daughter, reading a Shirley Hughes' *Alfie* book. The store that had appeared small and restrictive from the street actually stretched back much further than Jake expected, allowing for reading areas to be dotted between the shelves. Every aspect of the bookstore had been designed to entice customers to linger, to take their time choosing the word-worlds they wished to enter and then indulge themselves using the shop as a sanctuary. Jake had been impressed by the second-hand bookstore near his office, but Hudson River Books was a world away from it.

A tall man Jake guessed to be in his early thirties was serving behind an industrial-looking steel and wood sales counter halfway down the bookstore and, with no sign of anyone else, Jake approached him.

'Hey. Can I help?'

Jake instantly felt foolish for even being there, let alone for the enquiry he was about to make. The man behind the counter was wearing an Andy Kaufman T-shirt beneath a slim-fitting pinstriped jacket and peered at him through dark-rimmed glasses. Here in this part of Brooklyn he looked completely at home, while Jake, in his work suit and tie, felt like a fish out of water. This wasn't helping the situation, he told himself. He needed to ask for Bea, talk to her and leave.

'I hope so. I'm looking for Bea James?'

The quirkily dressed man observed him carefully. 'Can I ask what for?'

He probably thinks I'm a salesman in this suit, Jake grumbled silently, wishing again that he'd had the good sense to change before he dashed over to Brooklyn. Williamsburg wasn't far away, for crying out loud: *why* hadn't he thought to make a detour to his new apartment?

'I met her a couple of weeks ago at an event and I finally got round to saying hello.'

'I see.' The way the man looked Jake up and down, he felt like he was under suspicion for an as yet unidentified crime.

The silence was excruciating. Jake pressed on, hoping politeness would win him favour. 'I'm Jake – Jake Steinmann.' He extended a handshake and, after a brief hesitation, it was accepted.

'Russ O'Docherty. I own this place with Bea.'

'Good to meet you. Great store you have here.'

The most fleeting of smiles passed across Russ' face. 'Thank you. We've worked hard to make it a success.'

'I can tell.' He was making conciliatory small talk now, but at least it was better than the silent scrutiny of Bea's business partner. 'Your customers seem to like it.'

'They do. We're very popular in the neighbourhood.'

'Great.' Non-contentious subjects thus exhausted, Jake nervously glanced at his watch. 'So – can I talk to Bea, please?'

'No can do, I'm afraid.'

What is your problem? 'Pardon me? Why not?'

'She has the afternoon off.' Jake could swear he saw a glint of triumph in his opponent's eyes. 'But if you care to leave a message . . . ?'

Battling the crush of disappointment bearing down on him, Jake grasped the lifeline. 'Yes. Thanks, I'll give you my card.' He fumbled in his suit jacket pocket for a business card and hastily scribbled a note on the back of it. Handing it to Russ, he thanked him – although he wasn't entirely sure what for – and walked quickly out of the bookstore.

Not wanting to return home just yet, he ducked into a coffee store a few doors down the street. He needed to process what had just happened; make sense of it all.

As he sat with his cinnamon latte, the full weight of what he had just done descended upon him. It had made so much sense when he received Ed's phone call – that irritatingly optimistic streak in his nature convincing him that it was the only course of action to choose. Now he felt like a jerk for leaving a lame message on a business card for a woman he didn't know ever wanted to see him again. What would she think when she saw it? *If* she saw it: the disdain of her business partner

159

didn't fill Jake with hope that Russ would be inclined to pass it on.

He stared out at the unfamiliar street in a neighbourhood he had never previously visited, wearing a suit that made him stand out like a polar bear in the desert – and wished he had never come. Jessica would pity him. He pitied himself. Why was what she thought of him still important?

Perhaps the stress of an impending divorce battle had skewed his judgement. He was obviously searching for something and had projected that onto Bea, as if she were the antidote to the emptiness inside him. She wasn't; that much had been proved this afternoon. He had to get a hold of himself and focus on making it through the final stages of his separation from Jessica, for his own sake and for that of his clients, who would be walking through his office doors soon. How could he hope to counsel anyone when his own life was a mess?

It had been a painful experience, but necessary. He needed to forget this episode of his new life in New York, move on and get a grip. As he finished his coffee he allowed himself a final wistful thought of what might have happened if he had met Bea today. Then, banishing it to the furthest reaches of his mind, he began the slow walk home.

CHAPTER TWENTY-THREE

Bea's apartment, Boerum Hill, Brooklyn

Bea was still smiling when she arrived home later that afternoon. Her time away from the bookstore had been the tonic she needed, not least because of the fun afternoon she had spent at Kowalski's with Rosie. They had chatted like lifelong friends and she couldn't help but feel better for the experience. Surrounded by the beautiful colour and aroma of flowers, she had felt at peace; and the surprise of finding a new friend in a street in New York she had never visited before made her smile. It had been a wonderful day.

It was good to feel positive again. Since she had broken up with Otis, Bea had realised how down she had been. It stretched back months, not days; a slow-growing fatalism caused by letdown after letdown. At the time, she believed she was happy, but if she was honest with herself she knew she had been surviving, not thriving. The engagement party conversation had shown her that; so had meeting

Rosie today. Bea liked the positive version of herself and was determined to pursue it.

She was about to head into her kitchen to make a pot of tea when a faint mewing sound from the living room window caught her attention.

'Not again,' she muttered as she drew up the sash to reveal a shivering ball of smoke-grey fluff clinging to the wrought iron fire escape outside. 'Now what are you doing out here, hmm? You know you're scared of heights.' With practised flair she clambered out of the window onto the metal platform, not minding the four-storey drop to the street below between the open grid-work. She had made this trip many times before, each one connected to the terrified cat she now scooped into her arms. 'You never learn, do you?'

The cat shivered against her, burying its head in the crook of her arm as she climbed back into her apartment and shut the window. 'Right, Gracie, let's get you home.'

Bea picked up her keys and put them in her jacket pocket as she closed the door to her apartment and headed across the hall to 12B. Unlike all the other doors in the apartment building, 12B's bore a jaunty name plaque:

AVONLEA
Welcome One & All

Gracie the cat was still clinging to Bea as she knocked the fox-shaped doorknocker.

'One minute . . .' a singsong voice called from inside the apartment.

Bea grinned and waited. After the sound of several bolts being slid back and a chain unfastening, the door opened and a short, rotund lady with a mass of white curls beamed up at her.

'Beatrix! What a lovely surprise!'

'Hi Giesla. I have someone I believe belongs to you.'

Giesla tutted and held her hands open to receive her cat. 'Were you up to your old tricks again, Gracie? We spoke about this. You shouldn't go out the window. You hate it.'

Apparently recovered from her ordeal, Gracie began to purr, gazing lovingly up at her owner.

'She won't learn, of course. Gudrun and I keep hoping the experience will deter her.'

'Maybe you two should think about not leaving the window open?' Bea suggested, as gently as she could. 'Then Gracie wouldn't be tempted to venture out onto the fire escape.'

'Who's at the door?' a gravel-edged voice demanded from inside the apartment.

'It's Bea from 12C,' Giesla called back. 'She brought Gracie home.'

'Invite her in!' the voice called. 'Don't leave her on the doorstep.'

Giesla blushed. 'I am *so rude*! Won't you come in, Bea dear?'

'Of course. But I can't stay long, I'm afraid,' Bea replied quickly. She had learned from bitter experience that it was best to state a time frame before stepping across the threshold of 12B.

Giesla and Gudrun Niequist were sisters, both in their

seventies, who had lived in the same apartment for forty years. They had been the first neighbours to knock on Bea's door when she moved into the apartment block on St Marks Place, in the Boerum Hill neighbourhood, and had remained her closest allies. She had seen a lot more of them this year, mostly due to their rescue cat Gracie's sudden desire to explore the fire escape that snaked down one side of the apartment building. Bea had been called upon to rescue Gracie when the cat had first ventured onto the metal platform just beyond the kitchen window in the sisters' apartment. Neither lady had been able (or willing) to go out onto the fire escape to rescue the hapless moggie, so Giesla had knocked on Bea's door in a panic, believing Bea to be young and fearless enough not to be fazed by a trip out of the window. Thankfully for Bea, heights had never bothered her; both she and Stewart had been keen rock climbers in their teens, making their mother squirm when their father took them climbing on family holidays, laughing at her panic as they dangled from ropes on cliffs, mountainsides and climbing walls.

Since then, Gracie had become more adventurous: walking around the side of the apartment building only to realise where she was and panic outside Bea's window. Were it not for the shaky state of the cat whenever she was rescued, Bea could swear the cat did it on purpose. Recently, as spring had become early summer and the metal platform began to attract heat, Gracie had marooned herself more frequently, and Bea was growing tired of being the apartment's unofficial pet rescuer.

Giesla and Gudrun's apartment had last been decorated

in 1968 and, though a little faded, it still evoked the spirit of the groovy Sixties. Walking into the apartment was like travelling back in time, the only link to the twenty-first century being the new packaging of old favourites such as Oreos and Twinkies in their kitchen cupboards. It was fascinating: from the psychedelic orange and pink lava lamps on either side of the large fireplace in the living room, to the bright Biba print curtains shielding the long, thin windows.

Bea loved it here, even though she always ran the gauntlet of being unwittingly detained by her neighbours, who liked to keep her talking for as long as possible. She strongly suspected the reason for this was to break the monotony of each other's company they had endured for years. While it was obvious that they loved each other, their constant bickering revealed the stresses of living with a sibling. She and Stewart had attempted to share an apartment for a year after Bea graduated and had come perilously close to disowning one another as a result.

'I made apple cake,' Gudrun said – although with the gruffness of her delivery it sounded like a complaint rather than a pleasant offer. Nevertheless, the news made Bea happy. Gudrun Niequist's Swedish apple cake, made from a recipe handed down from their grandmother in Uppsala, Sweden, was legendary in the apartment block. Giesla and Gudrun made it their business to know everyone's birthdays in the building and so, as regular as clockwork, a cake tin would arrive at your front door on your special day. Their gift was always apple cake and it was always delicious.

'Sit, sit!' Giesla urged Bea, her cheeks flushing red. She reminded Bea of the Fairy Godmother in Disney's *Cinderella*, all soft curves and curly, pure-white hair. By contrast, her sister was what Grandma Dot would call 'a streak of tap water': tall, thin and angular, the only resemblance to her sister being her ice blue eyes and snow-white curls. 'How is life with you?'

Bea, sitting in a G Plan chair, accepted a slice of cake from Gudrun and smiled at the sisters. 'Good, actually.'

'And your young man?' Giesla instantly ducked as Gudrun shot her a stern look.

'We broke up,' Bea replied, adding quickly, 'but it's a good thing.'

'So, you are single and sensible, like we are,' Gudrun nodded wisely, still not smiling.

'That's right. And I think it suits me.'

'It is by far the best way. Giesla and I have never needed a man to enjoy our lives. Isn't that so?'

Her sister's head drooped. 'Yes.'

'And your bookstore?'

'Doing well, thank you. We held an important book launch last week and it was a sell-out event. Russ and I have put in a coffee bar as well – you two should come over and try it.'

Giesla brightened. 'Oh, I'd love that. We should do that, Guddi.'

'Maybe we will.'

Gracie – now transformed from the shivering fluff ball Bea had rescued into a contented cat with a purr like a pneumatic drill, jumped up onto Giesla's lap and instantly went to sleep.

'Gracie seems to have recovered, anyway,' Bea said.

Giesla stroked the sleeping cat. 'She's happy to be home. And we have you to thank for that.'

'We need to put that cat on a leash,' Gudrun hissed.

'She's still learning, Guddi.' Giesla leaned towards Bea. 'The rescue shelter said she'd had trauma in her last home. When they first had her, she hid in her cage for a month. I think it's good she feels adventurous.'

Her sister sucked her teeth disapprovingly and stood up. 'I will fetch the coffee.'

Giesla waited until Gudrun had gone, then reached over and clasped Bea's hand. 'What my sister said – about being happy single: don't listen to her.'

Bea stared at her neighbour, surprised by the change in her demeanour.

'I mean it, dear. Being single *sucks* . . .'

To hear this word coming from a sweet old lady was hilarious, but Bea hid her smile. 'Does it?'

'Trust me. I know.' She raised her head a little, listening for her sister's returning footsteps on the wooden floor, then returned to Bea. 'I had a man. Once. I loved him.'

'Oh Giesla, I didn't know that.'

'I've never told anybody. His name was Enrique. He worked the bar in our father's restaurant, back in Duluth. My dad loved him – like a son – but he would never have agreed to us marrying because Rique was Puerto Rican. Back in those days, that mattered to some people. It didn't matter to me: I was sixteen and thought he was the most beautiful man I had ever seen. We shared one night . . .' She blushed and her gaze dropped to the sleeping cat on her lap. '. . . Nobody knew. I met him after my dad had gone to bed. It was – *magical* . . . Rique wanted me to run away with him, but I was a good girl. He left the next day and gave me an address to find him when I was ready. Of course, I never found the nerve . . .'

Bea was taken aback by the old lady's confession. 'I'm sorry to hear that.'

'It is the single biggest regret of my life,' Giesla said, her eyes glistening in the glow from the mantelpiece lava lamps. 'I should have followed my heart, but I didn't. I put my sister and my family above my happiness.' Her grip on Bea's hand tightened. '*Promise me*, Bea dear, that you'll never stop believing in love? Because without it,' she indicated her time-frozen apartment as if it were an omen, 'what do we really have?'

An hour later, Bea arrived back home, grateful of the chance to be alone. Giesla's words had unsettled her, although she couldn't pinpoint exactly why. She hadn't given up on the possibility of love, just the search for it right now. The decision she had made at the party was the right one. *I'm not like Giesla Niequist*, she told herself. She felt for her neighbour, of course, but it was a completely different situation.

Next day, Bea found Russ had already opened the bookstore when she arrived for work.

'Enjoy your leisure time?' he enquired, a sly grin spreading across his face.

'I did, as a matter of fact. I went to the Upper West Side to meet a friend.'

Russ grimaced. 'And they let you in? I thought you needed a visa to enter that neighbourhood.'

Bea ignored his prejudice. It was a well-known fact

that once upon a time Russ had harboured dreams of living there, only to find the price of apartment rents prohibitive. From then on, he had condemned the entire area of New York as money-obsessed and snobbish. 'They must have liked me, then, because I was *invited* in.'

'Get you, Ms Fancypants.'

'How was everything here when I left, anyway?'

A strange flicker passed across her best friend's expression. 'Funny you should ask. I had a visit from a very interesting stranger.'

'Oh?'

Russ folded his arms. 'Looking for *you*.'

Everything seemed to freeze around Bea as she stared at him. 'Did they say why?'

Russ couldn't have looked any more accusatory if he was wearing a barrister's wig and gown. '*He* said he met you a while ago and promised to look you up again.'

Bea felt giddy. 'I see.'

'He left a note.' Russ held up a business card, but as Bea reached for it he pulled it back, evading her grasp. 'So when were you planning on telling me about him, hmm?'

Bea was mystified. 'I don't know what you mean.'

'Obviously you met the guy and told him where to find you, which in my book constitutes a desire on your part to see him again.'

Embarrassed and feeling vulnerable, Bea glared at him. 'First of all, I haven't told anyone "where to find me". I've met a lot of interesting people lately; it could be any one of them. What's with your attitude, anyway?'

'I just thought you and Otis were working things out,

that's all. Seems a little sudden to be finding a replacement, don't you think?'

'We *broke up*, Russ! We're not working anything out. I told him I didn't want a relationship with him and I meant it. I don't want a relationship with *anybody*, not that it's any of your business.'

'He's my friend, Bea. If you're playing him, I owe it to him to say so.'

This was the final straw. 'And what about what you owe to *me*? I've been your friend for years: does that count for nothing? Otis and I are *over*. And whether you agree with me or not, that's the way it is. Now hand over the card, please.'

Russ was clearly rattled by Bea's outburst, but gave the card to her. 'For the record, I'd just like you to know that I'm not your personal answering service, OK? And if you intend on telling any other strange men where you work, I'd appreciate a heads-up. So I can arrange to be *out* when they arrive.' He picked up a stack of books and stomped away from the counter.

Trembling with anger, Bea stared at the card.

Dr Jake Steinmann MD, PhD, EdD, APA
Suite 7, McKevitt Buildings, Broadway, NY

The name screamed out at her, knocking the wind from her stomach.

Jake – was here in my store? How was that even possible? But Dr *Jake?* Bea stared at the list of qualifications after the name. Jake wasn't a doctor, he was a barman – wasn't he? She tried to remember if he had either confirmed this as his profession or hinted that serving drinks wasn't his career at all during the party. But he hadn't said anything: of that she was certain.

Confused, she turned the card over and her heart jumped as she saw Jake's message:

Hi Bea,

Remember The Pact? From the party? We shook on it but I didn't get to say goodbye. I'm sorry. I'd like to discuss our list of Pact benefits further, if you'd like to? My number's on this card, if you do.

Jake

It was definitely him. Bea's heart thudded loudly in her ears as she reread the message. She couldn't work out how Jake had found her – or quite comprehend that, at the same time she had been telling Rosie about him, he had been standing here, asking about her. Maybe Grandma Dot was right: maybe they were destined to be friends . . .

'Are you calling him?' Russ asked, arriving back.

Her defences rising immediately, Bea snatched the card from his view. 'I don't know what you mean.'

'He wants to discuss your "Pact", whatever that is. Yes, I read the message. What, you think I wouldn't?'

'Leave it, Russ.'

'Just what did you agree with this guy you'd only just met? Does Otis know about it? No, I didn't think so. Think about what you're doing, Bea! You're doing exactly what you've always done: go rushing out after the end of one relationship straight into another. And who will pick up the pieces when it all goes wrong? Me.'

Bea couldn't believe what she was hearing. 'Well *thanks* for the vote of confidence.'

'I know you, Bea! This is what you *do . . .*'

'You know *nothing*!' Bea countered. 'I haven't gone looking for another relationship because I don't want another relationship.'

'The guy didn't get your memo,' Russ returned, stabbing his finger towards the card in Bea's hand. 'He seemed very interested in you.'

'As. A. Friend!'

'So you say. Are you going to call him?'

Bea was filled with an intense desire to be rid of this conversation, hurt by her friend's accusations and confused about Jake's sudden initiative in trying to find her. Not wanting to prolong the argument, she opened a drawer in the counter and flung the card inside, slamming it shut. 'No, I'm not. Satisfied?'

'But he came looking for you. What if he returns?'

'Then I'll deal with it.'

'Bea . . .'

'I have work to do.' Without giving Russ a second look, she hurried to the office and kicked the door shut.

This is all too much, too soon, she decided. *I don't need the hassle: not from Russ and certainly not from Jake.*

CHAPTER TWENTY-FOUR

Jake's apartment, 826B Jefferson Street, Williamsburg

Dear Dr Steinmann,

Thank you for returning the documents pertaining to your divorce from my client, Mrs Jessica Steinmann. I am writing to inform you of the next steps of the process.

At my client's request I am writing to ask you to provide, through your legal counsel, full financial information regarding the joint assets accrued during the time of your marriage. This is in order to begin negotiations regarding the acceptable split of assets. My client is keen to expedite this as soon as possible. I am sure you will understand her desire to complete proceedings without delay.

I look forward to hearing from your legal counsel.

Yours sincerely,
Don Sheehan

Jake had put off opening the latest letter from Jessica's lawyer for days, but decided to bite the bullet on Sunday morning when he returned from buying coffee and bagels for breakfast. Even as he stood in line at the small neighbourhood coffee shop beneath his apartment building, Jake had been dreading what he might find in the innocuous brown envelope waiting for him at home. His worst fears were justified when he read it: Jess wanted to settle the divorce as soon as possible.

He didn't care about the material things. She could have the house and the Jeep they had bought together for weekends at Half Moon Bay. All the possessions he cared about he'd packed into the removal truck before leaving for New York. He had his Bob Dylan albums, medical books and prize comic book collection; beyond that he didn't much care for anything else. The other stuff was too bound up with memories of Jess: he couldn't hope to move on if he were surrounded by pieces of their shattered life together.

But the clipped practicality of the lawyer's letter made the divorce into little more than a necessary procedure – as mundane and meaningless as a tooth filling or a wart removal. No emotion, no acknowledgement of years and dreams invested in a marriage Jake thought would last forever: just a dismissive nod to nearly ten years of his life invested in an ultimately doomed venture of the heart.

What made it worse – much as he hated to admit it – was that he'd had no word from Bea. It had been a few days since he left the message he now couldn't bear to think of on his business card. Had her achingly cool colleague not passed it on? Or had Bea taken one look at it and thrown it in the trash?

She wasn't the answer to his future happiness: of that much he was already certain. But he had hoped that it might be an interesting, positive aspect of his new life in New York, that maybe a new friendship, on his own terms, might offer an escape from the Damoclean sword his divorce felt like over him. Of course, it was unrealistic to expect a woman he'd only ever had one conversation with to firstly remember who the hell he was and, secondly, be keen to become a friend.

He knew he was feeling sorry for himself: had he been hearing the thoughts in his head coming from a client he would have advised them to deal with their emotions and move on. It was a classic case of 'physician, heal thyself', but he was tired of trying to rationalise his feelings. So he allowed himself to wallow. With nobody to witness it or try to remedy the situation, this was something he could indulge in for a while.

His appetite had been quashed by the contents of the letter, so the bag of still warm bagels lay untouched on the kitchen counter. Retreating to the comfort of his old leather armchair he had bought at the Brooklyn Flea market years before Jess arrived in his life, he nursed his extra-large coffee and stared out at the Williamsburg rooftops beyond the window.

When the door intercom buzzed, Jake jumped awake. Checking his watch as he stood up, he realised he had been asleep for almost an hour.

'Hello?'

'Jake-e-ey! Let me in, will ya?'

Rubbing sleep from his eyes, Jake pressed the door entry button, trying to ignore the dragging nausea in his stomach. He was happy to see Ed, but his rude awakening coupled with the dark cloud over him today made him dread the prospect of a brotherly chat. He unlatched the door and slowly walked back to his chair, downing the last of his stone-cold coffee to try to wake himself up.

Moments later, Ed bounded into the apartment, as effortlessly messy as always – the 'just-got-out-of-bed' look suited him where on others it would look untidy.

'Hangover?' he grinned, when he saw Jake's face.

'I wish.'

'Good job I brought coffee, then. And bagels – oh.' Seeing the unopened bag on the kitchen counter, Ed shrugged and added the brown paper bag in his hands to the collection. 'Ah well. Great minds, bro.'

Despite consuming enough coffee this morning to wake the dead, Jake gratefully accepted the new cup from Ed, enjoying the scent and the heat of it in his hands. 'Thanks, man.'

'You look like hell.'

'Once again, thanks.'

Ed's eyes fell on the lawyer's letter, which had dropped to the floor at Jake's feet. 'Ah, I see the Devil's been in touch.'

'Part of the necessary process, apparently. Go ahead – read it. It's so damned impersonal it could refer to anything.'

Ed scooped up the letter and scanned its contents. 'Whoa. They don't pull any punches, do they?'

Jake rested back in his chair. 'Lawyers never do. Hers

is the worst kind, too. He represented her last year when one of her former employees accused her of unfair dismissal. Don Sheehan *annihilated* the guy. He's a professional piranha and he won't stop until he wins.' He glared at his coffee cup, picturing the sickly, insincere smile of his wife's attorney. 'In that respect he and Jess are well suited.'

Ed pulled up a chair from the dining table and faced Jake. 'Perhaps she just wants it all done quickly to let you move on,' he suggested. 'I can't believe Jess means any of this personally.'

The sentiment was intended well but lit the blue touchpaper of Jake's anger. 'Oh, sure. I guess when she decided to quit our marriage she was only thinking of my wellbeing.'

'Dude, that's not what I meant . . .'

'And, hey – maybe she decided she wants pretty much everything we have in order to make my life simpler, huh?'

Ed held his hands in surrender. 'OK, OK, forget I said anything.'

Jake relented. This wasn't his brother's problem and he had no right to make it so. 'I'm sorry. I'm just so over this whole thing.'

'Understandably. But –' Ed's grin returned as he produced a small white card from the pocket of his brown leather jacket '– *this* might help.'

'What is it?'

'A business card.'

Jake rolled his eyes heavenwards. 'I can see that. Whose card is it?'

Ed wiggled the card just out of Jake's reach. 'A certain redheaded beauty you might remember from a party you tended the bar at.'

Had it not been for Jake's current state of mind, he would have jumped from his chair and snatched it right away. But as it was, his confusion caused by this sudden turn of events kept him seated. How had Ed managed to get Bea's business card? And if she was so keen to see him again, why hadn't she called? 'Where did you get it?' he asked, carefully.

'*She* brought it to *us*,' Ed exclaimed, almost bouncing off his seat with excitement. 'Well, to Rosie, to be exact. They met at Celia's book launch and seem to have bonded as ex-pat Brits.' He shook his head. 'Trust Rosie to find the only other Brit at the party. Apparently, Bea mentioned you. She thought you were a barman, by the way.'

Jake's head reverberated with all the information forced upon it today. First, Bea hadn't called, then Jessica's sleazy lawyer had shouted his demands, and now Ed had Bea's business card. What did it all mean and, more than that, what was he supposed to do about any of it?

'Wait a minute: when did she bring it to you?'

'On Thursday afternoon. Rosie invited her to come visit us; the next day, Rosie got a call from Bea and she came over. And mentioned *you*.'

Jake stared at Ed, the pieces of the past few days clicking into place. 'Thursday afternoon? But that's when—'

'When I called you and you high-tailed it across the city to find her,' Ed confirmed. 'How "kismet" is that?'

'So –' the information was slowly filtering through Jake's neural pathways '– when the guy at the bookstore said she had the afternoon off, she was at your store?'

'Mm-hmm. I'm telling you, Jakey, the women in New York City can smell a newly single guy from miles away. You think being separated is a burden; trust me, bro, to single women in this city it's like nectar.'

'What are you talking about?'

'Think of it this way: you had a woman you never met before going to great lengths to get in contact with you, after only one drunken conversation. Most guys would commit a felony to get that kind of reaction! I see this as the start of your rebirth, man; the reincarnation of Jacob Steinmann!'

'For the last time, I don't want another relationship! It's – *interesting* – that's all.' Jake took the card from his brother and stared at it. 'All the same, I wonder why didn't she call me?'

Ed shrugged. 'Woman's prerogative?'

Jake shook his head. 'I'm not ready for this.'

'Ready for what? For starting to live your life again?'

'No, *this* – the uncertainty, the second-guessing. That wasn't why I wanted to see her again.'

Ed raised an eyebrow. 'It wasn't?'

'No. I just liked talking with her. She doesn't want a relationship any more than I do, and that was – *refreshing*. I thought if I met her again I could put her out of my mind. Maybe she thought the same about me. Which is why she hasn't called.'

'Shouldn't *you* call *her*?'

'No.'

179

'Why not?'

Jake stared at Ed. 'Because it has to be her decision. I don't want to force my friendship on anybody.'

Ed groaned. 'You're impossible. And wrong. But it's your life.'

'It is.' Ed's tone irritated Jake, much like everything else had done today. Not wanting to fight with his brother, he firmly changed the subject. 'Do you feel like finding lunch somewhere? I want to get out of here for a couple of hours.'

Ed's relief was palpable, never being a great fan of confrontation himself. 'That's the best idea you've had today. And I'll quit bugging you about the girl, OK?'

Jake smiled at his brother. 'Now, that's the best idea *you've* had.'

CHAPTER TWENTY-FIVE

Hudson River Books, 8th Avenue, Brooklyn

'Bea. You have a parcel.' Russ appeared from the bookstore office waving a small package wrapped in brown paper.

Chalking up a blackboard for the children's section with details of a storyteller's visit, Bea didn't turn to see what it was. 'We get parcels every day. It's probably a sample book from a publisher. Just leave it on the desk and I'll deal with it later.'

'Well, I *would*, but somehow I don't think this is a promotional package. It has *cartoon mice* all over it.'

Bea's heart did a flip and she put the blackboard down immediately, brushing chalk dust from her hands as she hurried over to Russ. 'I'll take that, thanks.' Seeing her business partner's expression she grinned. 'As you were.'

Denied the details he was craving, Russ glared at her. 'This is from that guy, isn't it? The one with the personal message business cards and bad suit.'

'No, actually. It's from someone you don't know.'

Determined to leave Russ hanging, Bea hurried into the bookstore office and closed the door. The jaunty little mice, drawn in black ink with tiny pink dots in their ears and the tips of their noses came straight from her childhood memories. They were looking up to, parachuting beside, and hanging off, a hand-drawn label on which Bea's name and the bookstore's address had been written in a beautifully ornate hand. Instinctively, Bea raised the package to her nose and inhaled deeply. There it was: the faintest scent of violets . . .

From as far back she could remember, Bea had received surprise parcels from her grandparents. Grandpa George would choose a gift – always a book – and Grandma Dot would wrap it, decorating the brown paper packaging with tiny drawings of mice. The parcels would arrive at odd times during the year, without warning. Sometimes the books would come from the places around the UK where they holidayed, such as the small bookshop in St Ives, a place much beloved by her grandparents. Or sometimes, Grandma Dot would find books in her own shop to send. Both Stewart and Bea received the parcels, but for Bea they helped to fuel her ambition of one day running a bookshop like her grandparents did.

Grandpa George had died ten years ago and, as the parcels had been his idea in the beginning and something he had always done with his wife, Grandma Dot hadn't sent one since. Until now.

Bea held the parcel as if it were made of solid gold, suddenly overcome with the heartfelt sentiment from her grandma. She almost didn't want to open it, but curiosity got the better of her. Carefully, she peeled back the sticky tape and unwrapped it. Inside was a small blue leather hardback book, wrapped in a handwritten letter and tied with a white satin ribbon. When she took the ribbon away, she could see that the book was an edition of poems by John Keats. A bright yellow bookmark from the Severnside Book Emporium – Grandma Dot's bookshop – marked a place near the centre of the book's pages; and when Bea opened the book she found Keats' poem 'To Hope'. Her grandmother had underlined two lines of the poem in soft grey pencil, with one of her signature mice pointing to the excerpt with a quill pen:

> Sweet Hope, ethereal balm upon me shed,
> And wave thy silver pinions o'er my head!

Bea remembered Grandpa George reading poetry by Keats, Byron, Shakespeare and Rossetti on Christmas Eve when she and Stewart were children. Her parents would light a fire and turn off the television so that Grandpa could treat everyone to his recital. Bea could almost smell the satsumas she and her brother munched on as the strange James family tradition played out, not really understanding the words then but loving the togetherness of the event. Grandma Dot had always professed herself to be an admirer of novels over poems, but her husband was a firm fan of poetry, so the festive reading was something she supported.

Unfolding the letter that had been wrapped around the book, Bea blinked back tears as she read her grandmother's message:

Dearest Bea,

I know it has been some time since the Book Mice visited you, but I felt this occasion was apt for them to make a comeback.

I thought a great deal about our email conversation last week, especially regarding your conundrum with the young man you wanted to find again. I decided that I couldn't really reply with any great gravitas using email. So I have devised another method . . .

I am going to send you letters on the subject because, forgive an old woman her foibles, but I firmly believe matters of the heart - be they platonic or not - should never be discussed using email. Love, in all its forms, is timeless: therefore old-fashioned post is the only way.

And so, my plan begins.

For my first letter, I have enlisted the help of one of Grandpa George's 'chums'. Do you remember he used to refer to famous poets like that? He considered them his friends, 'as all writers of words that touch our hearts should be considered'. I often wonder now if he is passing his eternal days in the company of Lord Byron, Betjeman, Owen, et al. I like to think he might be.

I chose this poem because it seemed appropriate. When there is so much to doubt in this world, hope can be our saving grace. I certainly believe it is yours, Bea. Whatever you have decided to do regarding this young man, I know your aptitude for hope will strengthen your resolve and guide you onwards.

You have had your heart broken badly. You need time, space and care to recover from the experience. But this shouldn't deter you from finding new friends and believing in great things to come in your future. I am not just referring to relationships, but to life in general.

I won't go into detail yet, with this being my first letter, but there is a very important reason why I know you mustn't ever let go of hope. It has been a secret in my life for as long as you have known me, but I sense a great parallel between our lives now. I will reveal it to you in my letters.

Until the Book Mice bring your next delivery, keep hope as an 'ethereal balm' upon you and let me know how you are getting on.

Fondest love,
Grandma Dot xx

At that moment, Bea loved her grandmother more than she had ever done before. It didn't all make sense, but the intention was such a lovely one that she was determined to take it as it was meant.

Hearing the whirr of the espresso machine in the store, Bea quickly gathered up the book, letter and ribbon and put them safely in her bag. She would consider Grandma Dot's advice later: for now Hudson River Books required her undivided attention.

'Good parcel?' Russ asked, handing an enormous cappuccino to their first customer of the day.

Bea smiled, her heart light and happy. 'The *best*.'

At the end of the day, Russ turned the OPEN sign around to the CLOSED side and stretched his arms over his head.

'Just how long was today?' he yawned, stretching his arms above his head. 'It's always worse when we're quiet in the afternoon.'

Usually, Bea would have agreed. The day had indeed dragged, but the arrival of Grandma Dot's package had given her such a boost that she'd barely noticed it. Russ, on the other hand, had been only too aware, taking every opportunity to moan about how quiet the store had become.

'At least it's over now,' she replied.

'What was in that package?' Russ asked. 'Whatever it was I could use some of it. You've been like a spring lamb all day.'

'It was a surprise. From my grandma. She used to send us letters wrapped around books when we were kids, always with her cute little mice drawings on them. She calls them her Book Mice. I haven't had one for years but she decided to revive the tradition.'

'That's cool. The only thing my grandma ever sent me

186

were gift tokens for JC Penney,' Russ grinned. 'I used to trade them with Mom for cash.'

'Trust you to do that.'

'What can I say? There wasn't much the teenage me wanted from a department store where my mother bought our underwear. You want a coffee before we leave?'

Bea shook her head. 'No thanks. It's still a nice day outside: I think I'll go for a walk before I head home.'

It was only a short walk from the bookstore to Bea's apartment, but today she turned in the opposite direction and walked a few blocks down until she reached Prospect Park. Birds were singing as she walked away from the traffic and past the 3rd Street Playground, where parents watched their children playing in the still, warm May sunshine. Bea had always loved it here, the park reminding her of the Coronation Gardens in her home town of Northbridge. She loved watching people from all walks of life coming together in one of Brooklyn's green spaces, to run, to walk, to sit on benches and read. On Sunday mornings a Tai Chi class performed their graceful routines metres away from the frantic cries of an extreme fitness boot camp. On fine weekends, art students from the local night school would meet for a communal picnic to paint, and every day without fail, regardless of the weather, the faithful, neighbourhood dog-walking community would pound the pavements and green spaces with their excitable canine companions. It was a magnet for everyone in this area, from those fortunate (and affluent) enough to live overlooking it, to those who enjoyed a break from their everyday city lives in its leafy surroundings.

Bea found an empty bench and sat; content to watch the world and their dogs pass by. Knowing that Grandma Dot was thinking of her gave her a surprising strength. Even thousands of miles away, the bond between Bea and her grandmother was as sure as it ever had been and the reappearance of the Book Mice parcels would only make it stronger. She thought about everything that had happened since the night Otis had stood her entire family up: the protracted end of their relationship, the party, Jake and the new friend she had found in Rosie as a result. In its own way, each one was important for her to have experienced.

That was what Bea loved about living here: that even the worst experience could be turned into a positive. It was something about New York she had learned as soon as she arrived. You could knock a New Yorker down, but they always came back stronger. It was true of 9/11, when the very resolve of the city had been tested to breaking point. As a student in the city, Bea witnessed first-hand the defiant resilience of its people; and in the years following she saw New York pick itself up and run again. If the city she loved could do it, so could she.

A buzzing from her handbag broke Bea's train of thought. Reaching in, she retrieved her mobile phone and answered the call.

'Hello?'

'Hi Bea, it's Rosie. How are you?'

'I'm good, thanks. How are the wedding plans?'

Rosie groaned. 'A lot more complicated than they have any right to be. I'm desperately in need of a night off.

Which is why I'm calling, actually. What would you say to joining Ed and I for dinner this Friday?'

The invitation was a surprise, but Bea didn't hesitate to accept. The prospect of a night out with her new friends was just what she needed. 'I'd love that.'

'Excellent! Come to the store about seven thirty and we'll go from there.'

As Bea walked back to Boerum Hill, she smiled to herself. Maybe Grandma Dot was onto something with her belief in hope. Rosie and Ed were proof that unexpectedly good things could come from bad experiences and, if more positives like this were in her future, Bea was ready to move towards them.

CHAPTER TWENTY-SIX

Hudson River Books, 8th Avenue, Brooklyn

On Thursday evening, after what felt like the longest day at the bookstore, Bea turned to Russ as he collected his coat from the office.

'Got anything planned for tonight?' she asked him.

'Other than trying not to stress out about the new stand-up routine I'm meant to be writing, no. Why?'

Bea had been thinking about it all day: part of her new single life should include hanging out with her best friend more often. The process of getting over Otis had made her wary of spending time with Russ, fretful that he would bring up her former flame whenever they spent any time together. It was time to lay that particular ghost to rest. Her friendship with Russ meant more than that. Added to this, she wanted to tell him about the dinner invitation for tomorrow night with Rosie and Ed. If her life was changing, she wanted Russ to witness it.

'I think we both deserve a treat. So I'm calling it: Mister Wong's!'

Chinese food from Mister Wong's – the tiny front-room-sized takeaway kiosk below Russ' apartment – had long been a tradition for Bea and Russ. It was the best for miles, cheap and plentiful. And even if Bea had to endure Russ' 'if Mister Wong's is wrong, I don't want to be right' quip every time they visited, it was worth it for the fantastic collection of dishes in white takeout boxes Russ spread out across the coffee table in his apartment.

'Egg rolls *to die for* . . .' Bea grinned as she piled her bowl high with spicy, fragrant goodies. 'I think he gave us extra again.'

'He likes it when I bring you,' Russ replied, holding up a box. 'We have double duck chow mein again *and* a whole portion of pineapple fritters we didn't order. I call it the Bea James Effect.'

Bea giggled. 'Maybe that's my problem: all this time I've been searching for Mr Right when I should have just dated Mister Wong.'

'No way! Trust me, Bea, the key to our bountiful Chinese feast is his *unrequited* love for you. If you ever got together with him it could seriously hamper that. I'm not having him take out his relationship frustrations on our food order.'

'Not to mention the small detail that Mister Wong is at least seventy years old.'

'Well, yes. And *that*.'

They munched their Thursday evening meal in amiable silence, the soft sounds of jazz floating from the small stereo on the breakfast bar. After the busy week at the bookstore, hanging out with Russ was the perfect tonic. The 'Mister Wong's Night' rule was that no business talk was allowed to pass across Chinese food: a very early caveat put in place to protect areas of their friendship when they first went into business together. It was important to both Bea and Russ that they never lost sight of their friendship. At times, this proved difficult, but both were committed to protecting their relationship outside of Hudson River Books.

One thing was certain, Bea thought as she reached for her third egg roll: she and Russ were finding it increasingly easier to be friends outside of work with Otis not around. He had always been the elephant in the room whenever Bea had the opportunity to spend time alone with Russ and would also frequently arrange something at the last minute to scupper her plans, especially on nights when she'd agreed to hang out with her best friend. Russ had never openly resented this when it happened, but now Otis was no longer between them, Bea could tell he had relaxed.

'This is nice,' she smiled. 'I've missed this.'

His eyes were very still in the darkened apartment. 'Me too. I'm sorry for pushing the Otis thing, Bea. You have every right to live however you want. Honestly, I'm glad to have you to myself at last.' As if sensing a change in the air between them, he quickly added, 'You know, for the extra service from Mister Wong's and all.'

It was a ham-fisted attempt at a compliment, but Bea appreciated the gesture.

'Love you, too,' she grinned.

Russ turned his attention to his plate of food to shield his embarrassment. 'So, got any plans for tomorrow night? I have a terrible stand-up script you could browse if you wanted.'

'Ooh, tempting, but no thanks. Actually, I've been invited to dinner.'

Russ took off his glasses and wiped them on the hem of his T-shirt. 'Oh?'

'With Rosie Duncan – you met her at Celia's book launch.'

'I did?' The penny dropped and Russ pushed his glasses back onto the bridge of his nose. 'Oh, I *did*! So you're playing gooseberry to the loved-up couple from the engagement party, huh? What a night *that's* going to be . . .'

Bea helped herself to a sticky pineapple fritter. 'Actually, it's going to be lovely. I like Rosie and we have a lot in common.'

'Ah, the Brit thing.'

'Yes, the Brit thing – and also we see the world in a similar fashion. Rosie's made her mark in this city, has a fantastic business and is blissfully happy with Ed. I like that she's accomplished so much and loves the city like I do. So, I'm looking forward to seeing her and getting to know Ed better, too.'

Russ raised his chopsticks. 'You go, girl. It's good to see you getting out and meeting people.' He pulled a face. 'Man, it's finally happened: I've turned into my mother. But you know what I mean.'

Bea did: and as they laid waste to the feast from Mister Wong's, her anticipation began to build for tomorrow night's dinner.

Friday at the bookstore passed in a blur and soon Bea was back at her apartment, dressing for her dinner date with Rosie and Ed. She felt content and happy, the warm evening mirroring her sunny mood as she dressed in a dark blue sleeveless dress and matching flats, teaming it with a short-sleeved pale blue cardigan. Grandma Dot's letter and book lay on her coffee table and she smiled at it as she collected her bag to leave her apartment. She would write back tonight when she returned, she decided. It had been years since she had last handwritten a letter, but if it was good enough for her grandmother, it was good enough for her. Besides, there was a definite romanticism to the exchange of real letters and Bea loved the idea of communicating with her grandma this way.

The window was open in the back of the yellow cab as it passed across the Brooklyn Bridge and Bea took a deep breath as the familiar skyscrapers of New York rose above her. She loved New York at all times of the year, but in summer the city seemed to come alive. The streets and parks were filled with people during the day, markets appeared at weekends and tables from bars and restaurants spilled customers out onto the streets in the evenings. Driving up through the city, Bea could see people beginning their Friday evenings out and felt happy to be joining them.

Tonight was going to be a fun, relaxed time with people who expected nothing more from her than the pleasure of her company, which was such a pleasant change for Bea. When she had been with Otis there had always been another, unspoken agenda playing out; with Russ the conversation invariably returned to his life, his hang-ups and his semi-successful relationships; Imelda was good company providing her on-off boyfriend Janek wasn't on the scene; and even with Stewart and Celia, Bea often felt like an invited audience to the two-person performance of their life.

West 68th Street was quieter than the last time she had visited, but Kowalski's looked as inviting as before. Bea was surprised at how familiar the florist shop was, even though she had only visited once. She knocked on the door, smiling when Ed unlocked it and invited her inside.

'Hey, you must be Bea. I've heard a lot about you.'

'All good, I hope?' Bea asked as Ed kissed her cheek.

'Naturally. Come in, Rosie's looking forward to seeing you.'

Bea followed Ed inside, the beautiful scent of fresh flowers assaulting her as she entered the store. Even without customers and with most of the lights extinguished, Kowalski's felt like a special place.

'She's in the back,' Ed grinned. 'Take a seat and I'll go fetch her.'

Bea settled on the leather sofa and waited. The sound of traffic outside was muffled and late evening sunlight streamed into the shop, illuminating the lines of galvanised steel buckets against the opposite wall. The exposed brickwork glowed red, contrasting with the dark green foliage in a steel trough on the floor. Everything about Kowalski's exuded peace this evening and Bea felt happy and calm. It was going to be a great night . . .

A knock at the front door caught Bea's attention and she leaned forward to see if Rosie and Ed had heard it.

'Um, Rosie? Ed? There's someone at the door,' she called out, but there was no answer. The knock came again. Bea stared at the door, wondering what to do. She could just ignore it: after all, this wasn't her store and opening hours were over. But the person on the other side seemed very intent to come in. She stood and wandered over to the workroom entrance but, finding the door shut, didn't want to venture further inside.

The knocking intensified and, not wanting to ignore it, Bea decided to answer the door. If it was somebody wanting flowers she could advise them that the shop was closed; if it was someone else she would figure out what to do. Having run her own business for three years she was well versed in dealing with bolshie members of the public. She hurried across to the door, turned the lock, opened it – and lost her breath.

'Oh.'

Jake Steinmann stared back at her from the street. 'You!'

'What are you doing—?'

'What are *you*—?'

Bea's mouth was completely dry and she knew she was staring at him. But the shock of seeing him again, coupled with the fact that she was standing in the doorway of a shop she didn't own, stole her ability to rationally respond.

Jake appeared to rally before Bea did. 'I'm here to see Ed and Rosie.'

'Right. Me too.' Bea didn't move.

'Ah.' Jake shuffled awkwardly. 'So, can I – come in?'

Mortified, Bea backed into the shop as Jake followed her. They stood facing each other in the middle of Kowalski's, neither knowing what to say. Bea could hear her heart crashing inside her chest and the swift flow of her breathing as she struggled to find words. She was completely unprepared to deal with this and felt ambushed by its sudden occurrence.

'They're in the back,' she managed, hoping that Jake would venture where she hadn't and leave her for long enough to be able to gather herself together. But Jake didn't seem to take the hint. Instead, he remained where he was, leaving Bea feeling like she had nowhere to hide.

'I visited your store,' he said. 'I left you my card . . .'

'I know. Um, thanks.' This was more excruciating than pulling teeth without anaesthetic.

Jake ran a hand through his hair and looked over Bea's shoulder towards the closed workroom door. 'Are you sure they're still in there?'

'I don't know. Where else would they be?' Bea watched as Jake marched behind the counter and flung the workroom door open.

'*There* you are. I think you need to come out here.'

Bea heard Rosie giggle and she and Ed emerged like naughty children, sporting identical grins.

'Would I be correct to assume this –' Jake pointed to Bea, then back to himself '– isn't a coincidence?'

'You two *know* each other?' Ed asked, aghast – his purported innocence not fooling anyone in Kowalski's.

Jake glared at him. 'Bro—'

'We set you up,' Rosie relented. 'But let's face it: you both wanted to see each other again. Jake, you asked Ed about Bea; and Bea, you mentioned how much you'd enjoyed speaking to Jake at the party. Except, as you might have guessed, Jake is Ed's brother and not a barman. I just didn't see why it should then be so difficult for the two of you to meet again.'

197

Bea should have felt touched by Rosie's initiative – it was well meant after all. But instead, she felt cheated. This evening was supposed to be about a no-pressure, relaxed time out with new friends. Instead, it had become an embarrassing set-up with a guy who obviously didn't want to be there any more than she did. And now she was trapped. She could make her excuses and leave, but where would that leave her fledgling friendship with Rosie? Alternatively, she could stay, but what could be worse than being forced to socialise with someone who didn't want to be there, either? This evening had changed from a great Friday night out into the worst way to kill time: a blind date neither she nor Jake wanted to be on . . .

'I can't believe you did this without consulting us,' Jake said, his blue eyes sparking with barely controlled anger. 'It's embarrassing. You've put both of us in an impossible situation.'

Bea felt awful. 'I should probably go,' she stated, clutching her bag like a shield.

Ed moved towards her. 'Please don't. My brother is an idiot. Believe me, he wanted to see you again.'

She could feel a lump building in her throat and had no intention of crying in front of people she barely knew. This evening had been a disaster already before it had even begun: now all she wanted to do was get away as soon as she could. 'I'm sorry, I—'

'Stay *exactly* where you are!' Rosie's command was so sharp that everyone turned to look at her. 'All I am offering is the opportunity for the two of you to talk. I've booked a table at Monty's a few blocks from here. Ed and I have made other plans. Now, I'm sorry if you both feel ambushed, but it's obvious you enjoyed each other's company at the party. It isn't a date; it's an opportunity. So take it, for heaven's sake. What do either of you have to lose?'

Silence fell in Kowalski's, the last of the evening sun fading as the streetlights outside glowed into life. Jake turned to Bea and shrugged, the smallest beginnings of a smile appearing. Still reeling from Rosie's revelation, Bea managed to smile back.

'Would you like to have dinner with me?' Jake asked.

Bea almost refused, but Jake's softened tone and earnest gaze changed her mind. 'That would be lovely, thanks.'

Rosie squeaked and clapped her hands, while Ed looked like he needed a lie-down. 'Fantastic! I'll call you a cab.'

'I don't mind walking,' Jake suggested.

'Me either,' Bea replied, glad of the opportunity to get some fresh air. At least if she was walking she could concentrate on that, rather than having to be cooped up in uncomfortable silence with Jake in the back of a cab. They walked quickly down Columbus Avenue, neither one making more than occasional small talk. When they reached Monty's, Jake looked as relieved to have arrived as Bea felt.

The Italian restaurant was small and intimately lit, each table covered in a red check tablecloth and hidden from view of other diners with dark wood dividers. Bea's heart sank as she and Jake were led to their table, which could have come straight out of a romantic movie scene. All that was missing was an engagement ring and enthusiastic violinist . . .

'This is awkward,' Jake said, peering at Bea over the top of the burgundy leather menu handed to him by the waiter. 'And also proves that my brother has *dreadful* taste in restaurants.'

'Perhaps he and Rosie love this place,' Bea began, the ridiculousness of the situation causing her to burst out laughing.

Surprised, Jake followed suit. 'I'm sorry,' he said, 'for all of this.'

'Why? It wasn't your fault.'

'I got Ed involved by saying how much I'd enjoyed talking to you at the engagement party. I didn't know he was going to play matchmaker with Rosie, mind you.'

'Well, I told Rosie about you, so I suppose I'm as much to blame.' She smiled at Jake, the unease of the past thirty minutes finally beginning to wane. 'I had fun that night. And I wanted to see you again to thank you for making the evening a great one when it could have been the worst night of my life. I was a little surprised to find you were a doctor, though – I thought you were a barman.'

Jake laughed again. 'I understand why you would have thought that. I was serving drinks behind the bar, after all. I thought you worked in a bookshop, not owned one.'

'I own it with my friend, Russ. You met him when you visited my store.'

'Ah. No wonder he wasn't impressed with me. He's obviously protective.'

'Yes. Something like that . . .' Bea was amused by Jake's opinion of her best friend. Russ liked to think he knew everything about Bea's life – a fact only magnified during the time she and Otis were together. Well, it served him right for assuming she couldn't keep secrets from him. Maybe the experience would prove to Russ that she was far from predictable . . .

The waiter returned to take their order, his too-white smile and bushy moustache straight out of a Disney film.

'Sir, are you and your beautiful *laydee* ready to order?'

'I think so,' Jake replied, amused. 'Ladies first.'

'I'll have the Fusilli Milanese, please,' Bea said.

'An *excellent* choice for a lovely *laydee*,' the grinning waiter exclaimed. 'And you, sir?'

'Sounds good to me. I'll have the same.'

'*Bella*. You would like wine, too?'

Jake selected an Australian Cabernet Shiraz from the wine list and Bea could see him struggling not to laugh.

'*Excellent*. I will leave you two alone now.' With a parting wink at Bea, the waiter disappeared.

'Interesting fella. I wonder which part of Italy he comes from,' Jake chuckled. 'My guess is somewhere north of Queens.'

Bea giggled, the sparks of her previous meeting with Jake reappearing. After an unpromising start, the evening was turning out surprisingly well.

Food and wine arrived and both of them began to relax in each other's company. Bea noticed Jake's habit of making intense eye contact when he was speaking, his doctor's training evident in the way he studied her responses. He listened intently, too, leaning slightly forward to emphasise how carefully he was taking in what Bea said. Unlike their first meeting, they exchanged more personal details of their lives as they spoke, Bea feeling confident to do this, having shared humiliation with him at the hands of their well-meaning friends. As they spoke, her original hope that she and Jake could be firm friends returned. She liked Jake's view on life in general; his sense of humour was never far away from anything he said. It was refreshing to hear someone else's point of view, especially when her own group of friends had remained the same for years. Jake wasn't predictable, yet so much of what he said resonated with Bea's own worldview.

When dessert arrived, Jake pushed his plate across for Bea to taste as naturally as if they had been friends for years. Bea did this with Russ – largely because neither of them could make a decision when they went out for cheesecake, waffles or ice cream – but when she first met him it had taken months until he'd willingly offered to share his food.

'So, be honest: did you freak out when you received my card?' Jake asked. 'It's OK if you did.'

'A little, maybe. I was more taken aback than anything else. It also didn't help that Russ is my ex's biggest fan, so he wasn't happy I was keeping secrets from him. Not that I was, obviously. He just thinks I tell him everything, when sometimes I don't.'

'He cares about you. That's a good thing, isn't it?'

Bea folded her napkin and laid it on the table. 'Most of the time. Occasionally it can become a bit claustrophobic. He wasn't happy when I broke up with Otis – my ex. But then *he* didn't have to go out with the bloke.'

Jake sniggered, then apologised. 'I'm sorry. "Bloke" is such an English word.'

'Since we're being honest, how did you know where to find me?' Bea asked. She had been mulling over the question since Jake's card had arrived at the bookstore.

'I asked Ed if he could figure out who you were. All I could remember was your red hair, that you'd been invited to the party with your brother and something about you working in a bookstore. Rosie worked it out in the end because she'd met you at Celia Reighton's event. She asked Celia, who told her where I could find you.' He gave a wry smile and looked down at his empty dessert plate. 'I must confess, I regretted leaving that message.'

'Why?' Bea studied his expression carefully. Was this where Jake admitted he'd thought better of contacting her? Had Rosie and Ed forced his hand this evening?

'Because it was a lame thing to do. And because I haven't done anything like that for – *years*.' He raised his eyes to hers, that searching intensity there again. 'I thought you'd think me a jerk.'

'I didn't. I was surprised, but it was a pleasant surprise.' Bea liked Jake's vulnerability, which seemed so at odds with the confident persona he projected.

He smiled. 'I'm glad.'

Bea wanted to ask so many things; to find out when Jake had last done something so spontaneous; to discover why his marriage had ended; to know his thoughts on the future. She wanted to continue their exchange of reasons not to date again – that having been the thing she'd enjoyed most about the first time they spoke. Their conversation tonight was more personal than it had been then, but it was still the polite, non-threatening past-timing of new acquaintances. So why did Bea feel as if she had known Jake for years? And why did she want more?

This is good, she reminded herself. *It's more than I could have hoped for.* She smiled as she remembered Russ' favourite motto he had practically chanted like a mantra during the two years they planned the bookstore, before it even came into being, when Bea wanted so much to get started and launch into their new business: *Baby steps, Bea. Baby steps . . .*

She was enjoying this evening: her wish to see Jake again had been granted and her hopes about the possibilities for their future friendship had been confirmed. From the little he'd said about his ex-wife and divorce, she could understand his need to establish The Pact – and knowing that he had sworn off relationships made her feel safe. Tonight was a *great* night, she told herself. Beyond that, who knew?

CHAPTER TWENTY-SEVEN

Monty's Italian restaurant, Columbus Avenue, Upper West Side

Jake had not been prepared to meet Bea again today, but the evening was turning out surprisingly well. She was as funny, good-natured and sweet as he had remembered, and seemed happy to share more personal details of her life with him. Seeing Bea in a different environment to the engagement party gave him a fresh perspective on her character – and he liked what he found.

He had so nearly walked out of Kowalski's this evening. Angry with his brother and Rosie for blatantly setting him up, he was ready to leave. But Bea's crestfallen expression and the realisation that she was as surprised and embarrassed as he, made him relent. Jake could be accused of many things, but being unkind wasn't one of them.

For the first part of their meal, he had been asking himself the same question: had he agreed to it out of genuine interest for him or concern for her? Only a few days ago he had been so adamant with himself that he was putting Bea out of his mind; yet here he was, now, enjoying a meal with her. What was that all about?

He imagined counselling himself in his new consulting room: one Jake Steinmann lying on the leather couch, while another sat in the high-backed chair nearby, taking notes as he asked questions.

Why do you think you have a connection with this woman? Is she a diversion to stop you thinking about your wife? What is the real reason for being here this evening?

Bea was telling him about how she and snotty Russ had conceived the plan to run a bookstore when they were fellow students, laughing at their early ambitions for the place, which included a live music venue, licensed bar and vintage record store crammed in between the bookshelves. He liked Bea's laugh. It bubbled up from a place deep within her, gurgling out like a fountain, and was impossible not to join in with, even if you didn't get the joke. He couldn't remember the last time he had heard Jessica laugh. Hers had invariably been at someone else's expense and the stories she told highlighted the failings of others rather than the follies of her own life. Bea, by contrast, possessed that uniquely British self-deprecating humour which took delight in the absurdities of life. It was never cruel or biting, but rather an all-inclusive wit that caused a smile rather than affront. Jake was fascinated by it, having never had the opportunity to experience such humour at close quarters before.

Scrap that: he was fascinated by *Bea*, period. Being able to enjoy dinner with a beautiful woman completely unhindered by the usual date pressures of expectation and silent agenda was a brand new experience for Jake and he felt comfortable in Bea's company. Swearing off relationships with her at the party might just have been the best decision he had made this year.

As dinner ended and they finished their coffee, Jake wondered if he should ask the question that had been burning a hole in his head all evening. Would she agree? Was this a one-off or a precursor to more? She might refuse, of course: she was a sweet person who wouldn't want to hurt his feelings but not want any more contact than they had already shared. He had to be prepared for that. After all, when he'd first seen Bea at Kowalski's, he had been seconds away from declining dinner with her. There was only one way he would find out for certain: and with the minutes to their parting ticking away, he knew he was running out of time.

After much insistence when the bill arrived, they split the amount and walked out of the restaurant sharing jokes about the comedy Italian waiter who was still grinning at them like a Pearl-Drops-sponsored Lothario as they left. Out on Columbus Avenue a natural lull appeared in their conversation – and Jake seized his chance.

'How about doing this again some time?' He cringed as shock painted Bea's face. 'I'm not hitting on you,' he added, dismayed at the awfulness of his chosen words. 'I had fun tonight and I think you did, too?'

Bea nodded, an unmistakable pink flush appearing on her pale cheeks. 'Definitely.'

'Besides, we've talked for a whole evening without continuing our list of non-relationship benefits. I think it's something we should continue, for the good of mankind.'

Bea raised her eyebrows. 'For the good of mankind? Wow. That's some responsibility.'

'It is. We owe it to the poor, unfortunate single souls of New York to carry on the good work we have begun, don't you think?'

She laughed. 'I think maybe we should. I believe you have my number.'

'And you have mine.' It was Jake's turn to blush.

'Good. *So . . .*' She looked up the street, the red lights of cabs illuminating her hair like a crimson halo. 'I should probably get a taxi home.'

'Where are you headed? We could share one?' The question was out of Jake's mouth before he could stop it. Now she really *might* think he was hitting on her . . .

'Boerum Hill, Brooklyn. You?'

'I'm in Williamsburg.'

'Oh.'

For a moment, neither of them spoke. Jake kicked himself for even suggesting a shared cab ride home. What was next: *come up for coffee*?

'I'm sorry. I—' he began, but to his surprise, Bea nodded.

'Sounds like a plan. I didn't realise you lived so close to me . . .' Blushing again, she stared at her feet. 'Now that sounded like I was hitting on you.'

Seeing Bea as vulnerable as he felt, Jake relaxed. 'We made a pact, remember? Nobody's hitting on anyone when it comes to us.'

As they sat together in the back of the yellow cab, Jake couldn't hide his smile. Bea hadn't run a mile, hadn't refused his admittedly *very* forward offer of a joint ride home and hadn't even batted an eyelid when she learned Jake lived only a short distance away from her. That *had* to be a good sign, right?

She was watching the lights of the city pass by, shadows between them passing across the contours of her face as she gazed out of the window. Jake realised he was staring and made himself look away.

'It's been a great night,' he said. 'I'm glad we met again.'

Bea turned to smile at him. 'Me too. So, what do you fancy doing next time?'

Wow. He hadn't expected that question to come from her, especially as he had been working up the courage to ask it himself since they had got into the cab. The lights of Times Square loomed into view and he saw Bea's wistful expression. Seeing how much she loved the city gave him an idea.

'We should *do* this city. And I mean, really do it. Tourist things, our own personal things; heck, buy a guidebook even.'

Bea's reaction was as bright as the lights passing by the cab windows. 'Oh, I *love* that idea! I could show you my favourite places in New York and you could do the same. I mean, you were born here: there must be places you know about that I've never seen; and you might be interested in my British viewpoint on New York's delights.'

Jake could feel adrenaline pumping through his body as the idea grew in brilliance between them. 'Awesome. Let's do it. How about we begin on Sunday with one of yours?'

Bea considered this, delight claiming her expression. 'Great idea. I'll think of something between now and then. This is going to be so much fun!'

The cab reached Jake's apartment block and he took Bea's hand. 'This is my stop. Where shall I meet you?'

'How about I catch a cab and meet you here, about eleven a.m.?' she asked. 'That is, if you don't mind?'

'Sounds perfect. I'll be waiting on the street.' He looked into her eyes and for a moment wondered if he should kiss her cheek. Thinking better of it, he gently squeezed her hand. 'Thanks for a wonderful evening. I'll see you Sunday at eleven.'

She squeezed his hand back and let go. 'See you then – *friend*.'

Jake laughed as he opened the cab door. 'OK then, *friend*.'

Watching the cab pull away, Jake waved and stared after it until the lights disappeared into the next street. Something important had happened tonight: he could feel it. Uncertainty remained, but the bright sparks of possibility blazed within him. Sunday couldn't come soon enough . . .

CHAPTER TWENTY-EIGHT

Beads & Beans craft and coffee store, Brooklyn

'It *has* to involve food,' Imelda grinned, tossing a bundle of red and white ribbons to Bea for her to sort and wind around wooden bobbins for the new window display.

'Why?'

Imelda cast her a pitying look. 'This is *New York*, Bea. Everything good in this city revolves around food. Think about where your favourite places to eat are. It's as good as any a place to start.'

She had a point: and Bea was fast running out of ideas for where to take Jake for their first New York trip tomorrow. At a loss for what to do, she had come to Imelda's craft store during her lunch break. Imelda was always a great sounding board for ideas and would be bound to think of something Bea hadn't considered yet.

'I love the Reubens at Katz's Diner,' she said, 'or the dogs at Gray's Papaya. But are those too obvious?'

Her friend shrugged. 'You said interesting places in the city; you didn't mention they had to be original.' She frowned. 'OK. There's something else going on here, am I right?'

Embarrassed by her own train of thought, Bea averted her gaze. 'No.'

'*Bull*. Don't ever try lying for a living, Bea, you'd starve in a day.'

'I'm not lying,' Bea began, but she could tell Imelda had got the measure of her. 'I don't know. It just feels important to choose somewhere – *right*.'

'Right for what? You aren't proposing to him, honey. You're just showing him what you love about New York. And, as I recall, there's a lot you love about this city. Perhaps it would be easier to begin with what you don't love, seeing as those aspects are significantly smaller?'

Bea had to laugh. Imelda had accused her of wearing rose-tinted Manhattan spectacles on frequent occasions before, but Bea genuinely hated very little about New York life. It came from years of longing to see the Big Apple, from her earliest memories in England and her fascination with everything American when she first arrived as a starry-eyed teen fifteen years ago. Of course the rents were astronomical and the traffic awful; the weather could be prohibitively harsh in the winter and equally as unforgiving in the height of summer; New York people had precious little patience at the best of times and were never happier than when they were bemoaning the downsides of living in one of the world's most famous cities. But for Bea, most things still had their peculiar charms, even on frustrating days. She had only to remind herself that she had achieved her dream of making the city her own and had established her own business within it to appreciate how lucky she was to be here.

'I'll think of something,' she said, handing the completed bobbins to Imelda who was balancing in the small window setting up a summer picnic display.

'Thanks. Grab that knitted sun, would you? Oh and could you attach some invisible thread so I can hang it, please?'

Bea searched through the white wicker basket Imelda had given her and pulled out a large, golden yellow knitted sun with a smiley face embroidered in black wool. 'Did you make this?'

'I was up until three this morning finishing it,' Imelda grimaced. 'The things I do for my business.'

'This is *genius*,' Bea giggled and turned the sun over in her hands. Today, she felt an affinity with the grinning celestial body. The events of yesterday had been glowing brightly in her mind and she couldn't help but smile when she thought of Jake. She was looking forward to seeing him tomorrow and desperately wanted to pick somewhere great for their first shared New York experience. Her mind was still a blank, but she was determined to think of somewhere she wanted to show him.

'You can have him when this display's over,' her friend offered. 'Maybe put him up in your kids' section.'

'I'd love that, thanks.'

Imelda gave her an evil grin. 'You could call him *Jake*.'

'Immi . . .'

'Give me a break, Bea! You've met up with the cute barman-who-is-not-a-barman again – who was all you talked about last time we met – and now you don't want to give me details?'

Knotting the thread above the knitted sun, Bea handed it to Imelda. 'Fine, what do you want to know?'

Imelda's face lit up. '*Everything*. Let me hang Jake up in the window and we'll chat over camomile tea.'

In reality, there wasn't much to tell, other than they had been set up, eaten dinner in the cheesiest Italian restaurant on the Eastern seaboard and had decided to see each other again, strictly as friends. It had been a quietly successful evening with a pleasant outcome and the promise of more to come. Yet for Bea, it felt significant: as if this was, as Grandma Dot had intimated in her letter, the key to an important new stage in Bea's life. She was excited about spending time exploring the city she adored with someone who felt the same way.

'Just how serious is he about this pact of yours?' Imelda asked, cutting to the heart of the situation as she had a habit of doing.

'Very serious. It was what got us talking in the first place and he mentioned it again last night.'

'I see. And how serious are *you* about it?'

Bea frowned. 'I'm serious, too.' She could see Imelda was far from convinced. 'I mean it, Immi. It was so good to be able to share an evening out with an interesting, engaging man with no expectation that either of us wanted anything more than friendship. I haven't experienced that before, not even with Russ. There's always been a bank of questions waiting behind every conversation, even if neither of us care to go there now.'

'And it doesn't help even a little bit that Jake is drop-dead gorgeous?'

Bea had to smile. 'He *might* be pleasant to look at . . .'

'Aha!'

'But so is New York,' Bea added, thwarting her friend's triumph. 'And I don't want to date New York.'

'Forgive me if I don't believe you.' Imelda handed Bea a mug of fragrant tea. 'You just keep telling yourself you only want Jake as a friend. Time will tell if you're kidding yourself or not.'

Imelda's words stuck in Bea's mind as she returned to Hudson River Books. Maybe Jake was gorgeous – actually, there was no maybe about it – but the bottom line was this: Jake liked her as a friend and wanted to spend time with her. And Bea needed a friend so much more than another complicated matter of the heart. As far as she could see, this was the perfect arrangement.

Sunday morning was a little overcast, with the promise of sun later that day. Bea was pleased at least that rain hadn't been forecast, due to the open-air nature of her chosen destination. She still wasn't entirely sure of her choice as the yellow taxi headed into Williamsburg, but it was too late to change her mind now.

Jake was waiting on the sidewalk outside his apartment building as he'd promised and looked comfortably casual in jeans, white T-shirt and grey flannel jacket. Bea was pleased she had also opted for jeans this morning, reflecting the relaxed nature of what she hoped would be a fun day out.

'Morning,' Jake smiled as he climbed into the cab. 'Long time no see.'

Bea giggled. 'That's the kind of joke my dad loves.'

'Ouch.'

'It's a compliment. Sort of.'

Jake nodded. 'I'll take your word for it. So, Tour Guide Bea, where are we headed?'

'Before I tell you, let me say that I thought it was best to begin with obvious places first. It's somewhere I went to the very first week I arrived in New York and it was my childhood dream to see it.'

'Empire State?'

'Good guess. But no.'

'Statue of Liberty? I should probably tell you now that I'm not the biggest fan of the Staten Island Ferry. Or boats of any type, to be frank. They challenge my "in-control Doctor of Psychology" persona.'

'Ah. Good job I steered clear of boats, then.'

Jake grinned. 'That's a relief.' He looked out of the cab window. 'Well, I'm guessing as we've come over the Hudson River that our destination is not a Brooklyn landmark. Would I be correct in assuming it's in Manhattan?'

'You would. It's really obvious – I hope you aren't disappointed.'

Jake touched her arm. 'Hey, Bea, relax. Wherever we're going I'm experiencing it from your perspective: no matter how many times I may have visited before, I won't ever have seen it through your eyes. That's the point of this exercise: for me anyway.'

It was a good answer. Feeling happy, Bea smiled back at Jake. 'OK, then.'

'But you're not going to tell me where we're going?'

'Nope. It's a surprise.'

Jake looked towards the cab driver, whose grin could be clearly seen in the rear view mirror. 'And I guess you won't enlighten me either?'

The driver gave a Manhattan shrug. 'I'm sorry. You heard the lady.'

Sunday traffic through central Manhattan was heavier than Bea had anticipated and by the time the cab pulled up on the corner of 5th Avenue and 59th Street, she was buzzing with excitement.

'Here we are, people,' the driver announced.

Bea handed him the fare plus a generous tip. 'Thanks for not telling.'

'Hey, my pleasure. You kids have fun, now.'

'Are you taking me to the zoo?' Jake asked as they stood on the sidewalk beside the entrance to Central Park. Horse-drawn carriages queued alongside them, jostling for position with tourist coaches and New York City buses and the corner was alive with bustling crowds. The sun had begun to break through the clouds and a light summer breeze had sprung up. Bea was pleased with her choice: she couldn't have ordered a better day to bring Jake here.

'No – unless you want to go there?'

Jake's laugh was full and hearty. 'I haven't been to the zoo since my seventh birthday. I ate too many doughnuts and threw up by the ape enclosure. Not my finest hour. But hey, maybe I'll take you there to reminisce.'

Bea pulled a face. 'I'll look forward to that, then.' She nodded in the direction of the park entrance, where a group of portly tourists in ill-advised outfits of pressed shorts and tucked-in polo shirts were gathered around a tourist map. 'Shall we go in?'

'Lead the way, Ms James.'

They passed the group – who were now arguing about whether or not to buy hotdogs from a nearby stand before they attempted to enter – and strolled into the park, the dappled sunlight through the trees passing over their heads. It was beautiful and at last Bea relaxed about bringing Jake here: yes, it was an obvious choice to come to Central Park, but when she'd arrived in New York City it had been the very first place she had visited on her first weekend. She had never lost the sense of wonder at finally standing in the place she had dreamed of so many times before.

'So, why Central Park?' Jake asked, casting a glance at Bea as they walked along winding paths, flanked by iconic black cast iron lampposts.

'Why not?'

'Good point. But you've brought me here because it's one of your favourite places, so why does it mean so much to you?'

They rounded a corner in the path and the trees opened up to reveal a large expanse of water surrounded by lush greenery, framed by famous buildings beyond the trees.

A huge grin broke out across Jake's face. 'Ah, OK. I get it. The Pond, right?'

Bea's heart skipped as it always did when this view appeared before her. 'The Pond. I know it's a tourist cliché, but it means a lot to me. It's beautiful and I feel like it's been a part of my life for as long as I can remember.'

Bea loved this part of Central Park at any time of the

year but today, with china blue sky overhead and bright summer sunshine, it looked especially beautiful. The Pond – more of an ornamental lake rather than the small patch of water its name suggested – was surrounded by green lawns where New York citizens and tourists alike were sitting enjoying the sunshine. Jake and Bea walked through a gorgeous palette of greens, from the weeping willow trees and artfully arching tree boughs to the sunny grass spaces and deep green reeds surrounding the expanse of water. Even though it was busy today with a steady stream of city dwellers taking a break from the bustle of their New York day, this part of Central Park still exuded a relaxing serenity.

Bea stopped by the water's edge, gazing across the Pond to the iconic, ivy-covered bridge at the other end. This scene was as familiar to her as the photographs from her childhood, showing summer picnics on the banks of the River Severn with Stewart, Grandma Dot and Grandpa George, because it was the subject of a large poster Bea had in her bedroom from the age of ten. In her version the Pond was a black and white winter landscape, the lit lamps around its paths illuminating the bridge in the shadow of the Plaza Hotel. She had gazed upon it every night before she slept; and as soon as she had known she was coming to New York to study at Columbia University, the thing she had been most excited about was standing in the spot where the photograph had been taken. On her first Saturday in New York, seventeen-year-old Bea James had stood exactly where she was with Jake now, and had sobbed unashamedly as her long-held dream came true.

The memory of that moment made her blink back a rogue tear and she became aware that Jake was watching her.

'I'm sorry.'

'What for?' He looked closer. 'This place means a lot to you, huh?'

Bea sniffed. 'It does. It was the first image of New York I ever saw when I was little and I still have to pinch myself that I can see it for real now, any time I like.'

She wondered if her new companion would be amused by her sudden sentimentality, but Jake's smile was warm and comforting. 'It must feel wonderful to know you have achieved your dream.'

'It does. But then I'm proud of everything I've achieved in New York.'

'And rightly so.'

They found a bench beside one of the famous lamp-posts where the path curved slightly, and sat watching the ever-moving crowds passing over the grey stone bridge. Behind it, New York's famous buildings framed the skyline: giant sunbathing monoliths of stone and glass perfecting the scene.

'I always think the bridge looks as if it's floating above the water in the summer when the bushes and trees at each end are in full leaf,' Bea said, not minding whether Jake was amused by her observation or not. 'It looks like a green-mottled rainbow arcing between two green clouds.'

'You know, I never noticed that before. But I kinda see what you mean,' Jake grinned.

'Have you come here a lot in the past?' Bea asked,

keen to know which parts of the city they both had an affinity with.

'Actually, no. I grew up in the Upper East Side and we rarely visited as kids – apart from my fateful visit to the zoo, that is. I spent time in the park later on, especially when I was working at my first practice, but it was nearer the Lake and it was only ever to go for lunchtime runs or to grab a half-hour lunch break.'

'How about at Christmas? Surely you must've come ice-skating?' Bea couldn't imagine anyone lucky enough to be born in Manhattan not heading straight to the Wollman Rink as soon as the first flurry of snow fell. It was the ultimate New York winter scene, even though she herself had never ventured out on the ice there. Instead, she and Russ would watch other people's dodgy ice moves on the Rockefeller Center Rink each year when they did their Christmas shopping together.

Jake seemed to flinch as he stared across the Pond. 'Oh you know, sometimes. Usually when I was trying to impress a girl.'

'Did it ever work?' Bea meant the question as a joke, but when she saw that Jake didn't smile, she quickly changed the subject. Maybe this was a little too personal a question to be asking so early on in their friendship . . . 'I've actually never skated on the Wollman Rink.'

Jake's blue eyes were still as they looked at her. 'No?'

'I've never found anyone to go with. Russ likes the Rockefeller Rink at Christmas and my ex didn't skate. I blame too many hours spent watching *Serendipity* for making me love the idea.'

'Think that'll happen?' Jake asked. 'Now you've sworn off relationships?'

Bea hadn't considered this. 'Oh. Well, perhaps I should add that to the list of things I'll do by myself now I'm not looking for anybody else to share the experience with.'

'Good idea.'

'You can join me, if you like.'

Jake stared at her. 'Eh?'

Replaying the question in her mind and realising, with horror, how much like a chat-up line it sounded, Bea quickly qualified it. 'I mean, as an avowedly single person in the city you could exercise your right to skate in Central Park at Christmas without the need for anyone else. We could add it to The Pact.'

'A Pact addendum?' Jake appeared to be considering this. 'I like it. We should make a list on our travels. That is, if you'd like to do this again?'

It was the easiest question Bea had ever answered. 'I'd love to.'

CHAPTER TWENTY-NINE

Jake's practice, McKevitt Buildings, Broadway

'I'm telling ya, Doc, it's like I see that woman and my brain vacates the building.'

The middle-aged man on Jake's couch gave a dramatic sigh.

'And why do you think that is, Tony?' Jake pencilled a note on his pad.

'I have no idea.'

'OK. How long has this . . . situation . . . been happening?'

'I first saw her when I changed my local deli. I'd been going to Joshua's on East 65th, but there was a disagreement over my bill. Stupid checkout guy said I owed him fifty bucks, but I checked my purchases and I know I had the right money. So I said to myself, "Tony," I said, "you ain't gotta give that place your custom no more." So I switched delis to Harvey's on East 59th. And *that's* when I saw her.'

Jake resisted the urge to smile. But then, he had been

fighting smiles all day. For a Monday morning with a full list of brand new clients, this was as close to a New York miracle as it was possible to be. Tony De Vitis, a high-flying owner of a real estate agency, was the third client of the day, and it appeared had a severe case of unrequited love for a checkout girl in the neighbourhood deli where he now shopped. Jake listened and made notes as Tony described the object of his affections and his frustration at not being able to tell her how he felt, but his own thoughts were far away from his client notes.

Spending Sunday in Bea's company had been a revelation. He was astonished at how much they had in common, and how candid she had been with him about her reasons for loving Central Park. He felt as if he had been given a guided tour of her innermost thoughts; and while all they had done was wander through the sunlit park, pausing at a hotdog stand to grab lunch and, later, a Belgian 'Dinges' waffle from a bright yellow food truck, the time they spent together carried a significance beyond the sum of its parts. Bea was great company, her sunny personality and sense of humour made her a joy to be with. For a precious few hours, Jake had forgotten his recent troubles – the divorce process that Jessica's lawyer was no doubt gleefully entering into and his own struggle to feel at home in a new apartment in its unfamiliar neighbourhood – and just been in the moment. It was a long-forgotten freedom that he had surrendered in the name of love and responsibility. But to have it back, even for a brief time, was more of a gift than his new friend could ever realise.

'I'm afraid that's the end of today's session,' he told

Tony, checking the time on the wall clock over his consulting couch. 'Same time next week?'

Tony rolled to his feet. 'Sure. Thanks, Doc. It helps to talk to somebody who listens.'

Jake stood and shook Tony's hand. 'That's my job. Take care.'

Desiree was making light work of a mound of papers on her desk when Jake emerged from the consulting room.

'Good session, Doctor?' she asked.

Jake helped himself to a fresh mug of coffee from the percolator on permanent duty in reception. 'Very productive. Book him in at the same time for the next four weeks, would you?'

'No problem.' Desiree made the booking on her computer, holding out her mug to Jake as she typed. 'Black coffee straight up.'

Jake grinned and poured coffee into it. 'Yes, Ma'am. How are the files looking?'

'OK, I think. I've filed them a little differently to the old system, just so you have the most recent to hand first. It'll make finding them easier. And I've added a greater search function to the database. That way you can identify the regular clients and those who need a little encouragement to come back. I propose we initiate a practice newsletter, keeping your clients in the loop, so we can monitor responses.'

'Desiree, you're a machine.'

His PA seemed pleased with the comparison. 'Why thank you, Dr Steinmann.' She took a sip of coffee. 'And you make great coffee.'

It was a strange choice of compliment, but Jake was quickly learning that any positive comment from Desiree was worth a hundred from anybody else. 'Thank you.'

Desiree leaned back in her chair, nursing her coffee mug. 'So, who's the lady?'

'Excuse me?'

'I mean, I'm *assuming* it's a lady.'

'I don't follow . . .'

'The *smile*, Jake! You've been smiling since you got here. When you left on Friday you had the world on your shoulders. So, what changed over the weekend?'

Her perceptiveness took Jake by surprise and he knew he'd been busted. Keen not to reveal too much to his PA, he shrugged. 'I had a good weekend, that's all.'

Desiree's chocolate brown eyes narrowed. 'That's *all*? You sure about that?'

'Yes, *Dr Jackson*, I'm sure. I met up with friends Friday night and yesterday I went to Central Park.'

'Central Park makes you *this* happy? You should buy a condo there.'

Jake laughed. 'Who are you, my mother? It's a good thing if I'm happy, isn't it? Far better than the alternative.'

'For sure. It's just that this is the most content I've seen you. I wanted you to know that.'

'I appreciate it. Thanks.'

Walking back to his office, Jake thought about Desiree's observation. Was it *that* obvious? More worryingly, just how withdrawn had he been for the last month? Of course he couldn't help the anxiety and injustice he'd felt about having to start again in New York while Jess happily filed for divorce. But he hadn't realised quite how evident it was to other people: and especially not to someone he hadn't known for very long.

But the fact that Desiree had not only noted but also commented on the change in his mood was significant to Jake. Was it possible that one weekend could make such a difference? It had been so refreshing to spend time with Bea, their ongoing list of reasons to avoid relationships growing as they walked around Central Park. For a few hours, thoughts of Jess had disappeared and Jake had been able to be himself. This new friendship with Bea was *definitely* good for him . . .

Now the challenge for Jake was to find a suitable location for their next venture into the Big Apple. He had laughed when Bea confessed the heart-searching she had gone through when planning yesterday's day out, but now he was experiencing exactly the same dilemma. He almost asked Desiree for her ideas, but quickly thought better of it. The less she knew about his new friend, the better.

Instead, he called the only other person who would understand.

'I don't get why it's such a big deal for you,' Ed said, stealing the basketball from his brother's hands and looping it up and over into the basket in the yard at the back of Kowalski's. 'You snooze you lose, bro! What's that – sixteen–ten?'

Jake pulled a face, wishing he had brushed up on his backyard basketball skills when he had an actual backyard in San Francisco. Ed was pummelling him into the ground and even the distraction of where to take Bea next couldn't be wholly blamed for his lack of skill today. 'You're too kind: it's sixteen–nine.'

'So pick up your game!'

Ed tossed the ball to Jake, who squared up to challenge him for the basket.

'It's important because Bea really thought about where we could go on Sunday.' He bounced the basketball towards the basket affixed to the rear wall of Kowalski's, managing to weave past Ed to score. 'Mojo's coming back!'

'You wish,' Ed laughed, flinging his arms out in an attempt to steal the ball. 'She took you to Central Park, dude. That's hardly a groundbreaking choice. Every tour bus in Manhattan heads to Central Park.'

'It was important to her. That's why she chose it.' Jake groaned as Ed whipped the ball from his hands, slam-dunking it for his seventeenth point. 'Anyway, that's the whole point of this. We share our favourite places: there's no rule says they have to be *original*.'

'All the same, yours should be,' Ed returned, laughing as his brother tried several moves to steal the ball. 'Denied again – oh, and again!' This time Ed's shot was misjudged, bouncing off the wall to the right of the hoop.

'As are you,' Jake laughed, grabbing the ball while Ed protested. 'I want it to be good, you know? It should mean something to me like the Pond in Central Park does to her.'

Ed rolled his eyes. 'The only memorable thing that happened to me at the Pond is when a date dumped me because I made a joke about the ducks looking like they needed orange sauce.' He shrugged. 'Back when I was in denial about Rosie and dating half of Manhattan, obviously.'

'I heard. Even in San Francisco you were a legend.'

'The Pond. *Man*. There must be something about Steinmanns in denial at that place.' He winked at Jake, stealing the ball once more and scoring his eighteenth basket.

'How am I in denial?'

'Oh, I think you know.'

Jake glared at his brother, who was at that moment performing a victory lap of Kowalski's backyard. 'If this is about Bea . . .'

'Who else?'

'She doesn't want a relationship. And neither do I. We made a *pact*.'

'Pact *schmact*. If that woman turned around tomorrow and offered herself on a plate to you, I swear you'd discard that pact of yours quicker than Dad discards acquaintances at his golf club. And you *know* how fast that is.'

Jake dodged his brother to snatch the basketball back and fling it into the basket. 'Not as fast as I was just then.'

'You're hardly beating me, bro. And don't change the subject, Dr Steinmann. You know I'm right.'

Out of breath, Jake bent over to rest his hands on his knees. 'I just want a friend. And I think Bea and I could have fun *as friends*. Is that so hard to believe?'

Studying his brother's expression, Ed slapped his hand on Jake's back. 'No. Not at all. You've been through hell with the Jess thing and I think it's time you had some fun. You deserve it, bro. You know I just want to see you happy.'

'I am happy. Happier than I've felt for months.'

Anything else Ed might have wanted to say was shelved as he smiled at Jake. 'Then that's all that matters.'

CHAPTER THIRTY

Corner of 42nd Street and Park Avenue

Bea stepped out of the taxi and felt her heart skip a beat. 'Really? This is where you want us to visit?' She had been anticipating this day for a week, wondering which part of New York he would take her to. But she hadn't guessed it might be *here*.

Jake seemed to be studying her reaction far more carefully than he had before. 'This is it. Do you mind?'

For a moment Bea thought her heart was going to burst right out of her chest. 'Are you kidding? I *love* this place!'

Relief spread across Jake's face. 'Great! I thought you might think otherwise.'

'It's impossible not to love it.' Bea gazed up at the beautiful carved stone exterior of Grand Central Station, which seemed to glow from within against the leaden grey sky. Until she had moved to New York, she'd only known about the famous interior of New York's major train terminus from guide books and friends' photographs: when she'd visited for the first time she had been blown away by the classically ornate exterior of the station, looming proudly above the corner of 42nd Street and Park Avenue. It was grand in every sense of the word.

Nevertheless, Bea wondered why Jake had chosen this place for their second New York adventure. He had hinted in the cab driving up from south of the Hudson River that their destination was one for which he had great affection, but refused to be drawn any further. She guessed she was about to discover more inside.

They walked into the crowded concourse with its starry-night-sky ceiling and long windows made so famous by an old photograph – since proved to be a fake – showing huge streams of sunlight flooding into the station's interior. Like so many parts of New York, Bea and Jake's first instinct was to look up. And they were amply rewarded when they did.

'It's gorgeous,' Bea breathed, suddenly very aware of how close Jake was standing to her.

'It is.'

'So, why bring us here?'

Jake spread his hands. 'Why not? I mean, *look* at it. You've seen it in movies and photographs, but until you stand in the concourse at Grand Central Station you can never truly appreciate what a wonderful building it is.'

Bea cast a sideways glance at Jake. 'That's very profound.'

'It is. But that's because I didn't say it.' Seeing Bea's confusion, he smiled. 'That was what my grandfather said to me when we came here. I was five, I think, Ed was seven and our eldest brother Dan was eleven. Grandpa brought us here one Saturday as a treat. He loved trains and told us with great affection about the steam locomotives that used to run in and out of Grand Central. Turned out he met Grandma here, in the Thirties, when both of them were teenagers. She lived in upstate New York and had arrived on a day trip with her sister. Grandpa was at the station to meet a friend – who, incidentally, never showed up – and he chased a thief who stole Grandma's handbag as she stepped off her train. It caused quite a commotion by all accounts: but by the time Grandpa and several cops apprehended the culprit, Grandma had already decided that Grandpa was the man she would marry. They began courting soon after and were married a year later.'

Bea adored the story and could imagine Jake's grandfather in his trilby and greatcoat chasing the thief through the crowded concourse. It was like a scene from a classic film, with Grand Central the evocative backdrop. 'That's such a lovely story.'

Jake laughed. 'It *was*, the first time we heard it. Trouble was, Grandpa never could remember telling us the story and so, every Thanksgiving and every Christmas Day, when the Steinmanns were gathered around the dining table, Grandpa would drag out the old story. Thing is, none of us had the heart to correct him. So we just learned to "ooh" and "aah" in the right places. It became an important feature of our family get-togethers.'

'And that's why we're here?'

'Partly. But also because of the awesome cheesecake at Junior's.' His smile had all the cheekiness of a little boy and Bea couldn't help but smile back.

'They have a Junior's in Brooklyn, you know,' she said.

233

'Sure they do. But nothing beats sitting in Grand Central Station eating unbelievably good cheesecake.' He offered his arm to her, making Bea think of Fred Astaire in *Easter Parade*. 'Shall we?'

'Why, thank you, sir.' It was a delightfully old-fashioned gesture and Bea accepted without hesitation.

The cheesecake restaurant was busy when they arrived, filled with travellers and tourists. Jake and Bea chatted while they waited for a seat and Bea was surprised by how at home in Jake's company she now felt. Sharing one of her favourite places with him a week ago seemed to have moved their friendship to a deeper level; one that Bea wasn't used to experiencing so early on in her acquaintance with someone. Jake opened up about his childhood memories, growing up in New York, his love for his grandparents and the tempestuous relationship with his own father.

'Don't get me wrong: Dad's a great guy. But he's ambitious – always has been – and that ambition was magnified onto us kids. The Steinmann boys weren't allowed to get Bs and Cs in their school papers; it was straight As or serious trouble. Of course it meant we all excelled at our studies, but the cost was that school and high school weren't fun. That's where Grandpa came in: he was the bringer of fun in our lives, even though he was more qualified and, arguably, more successful than Dad ever was in his profession. When we had days out with Gramps, he would make sure we had as much fun as possible. It was our secret from Dad – although I think Mom always knew what we got up to. The best way we learned to deal with Dad's burning ambitions for us all was to live hard and play harder.'

'Was that difficult for you, living up to your father's expectations?'

Jake smiled. 'Now you sound like you're doing my job.'

Instantly, Bea stared down at her cherry cheesecake. 'Sorry.'

'That was a compliment. It was never a problem for me, largely because I decided early on that I wanted to follow Dad's profession. My brother Daniel had already begun his studies and it looked like fun. I think my decision saved me, in Dad's eyes anyway. Ed, on the other hand, was constantly at odds with our father. Still is, in many ways. I think that's why Dad's struggling a little with Ed and Rosie's wedding plans. Dad's being his usual "immovable object" self and Ed sees red every time. Even though my brother is older than me, I always felt protective of him. He excelled in art and design, practical subjects that let him use his hands and express his creativity. He wasn't interested in science or psychology. Dad just couldn't see that: I think he figured if he pushed Ed harder, he'd eventually relent. Of course, Dad didn't realise Ed was every bit as stubborn as he was. And so, the war always raged.'

'I can imagine it must have been hard for Ed to refuse the family profession. My brother and I didn't have that to contend with, thank goodness. I always wanted to run a bookshop because my Grandma Dot has always been a bookseller. Stewart was always the one with an eye for a story when he was at primary school, so he'd pretty much decided that was what he wanted to do when he grew up.'

'I'm glad I knew early,' Jake admitted. 'Seeing what Ed went through with Dad galvanised that. So, I know you have one brother. Any more James family siblings?'

Bea giggled at Jake's unconscious suggestion that she might have more family members hidden away. 'Nope, just the two of us. And you have two brothers?'

'Yes. Daniel's six years older than me and there are two years between me and Ed. Dan lives in Michigan now, so I don't see him so much, apart from Thanksgiving and Christmas.' He smiled at her. 'Well, look at us exchanging family stats. Where should we go next? Family pets? Academic prowess?'

'I don't know I should share such personal information with you yet. My pets are *precious* to me. Or they would be, if I had any.'

Jake smiled. 'I hear you. We should start small and work our way up. Do you think you're ready to share another slice of cheesecake with me? That chocolate fudge nut is calling my name from the cabinet there.'

Arriving home in the early evening, Bea realised that she had been smiling all day. Jake had been charming, funny and great company. She liked that at no point had she wondered what he was thinking of her, or worried about what the future held for them. She was able to simply enjoy his company. This was far better than the dating carousel she had always clambered back onto when relationships ended. The Pact was what made it all work: being friends with Jake was a million miles away from wading through new dates with anybody else.

She flopped onto her sofa and kicked off her shoes. *I like the new Bea James*, she thought. *I'm content, I've found a great new friend and I'm having the best time. What more could I want?*

The apartment was silent, save for the distant rumble of traffic and the slow ticking of her kitchen clock. And somewhere way in the back of Bea's mind, a tiny note of discord began to chime.

'I'm perfectly content,' Bea said out loud, as if even her own home didn't quite believe her. 'This is a perfect arrangement.'

The apartment said nothing.

CHAPTER THIRTY-ONE

Kowalski's, corner of West 68th and Columbus, Upper West Side

Jake listened to the huge argument in full flow around him but it was as if he were floating in a bubble above it all.

'What do you want me to say, Rosie? I *tried* to get Dad on side and so did you. If he's playing hardball it's nobody's problem but his.'

'I know that, but he's holding up every arrangement we've made so far. I *need* this to be sorted, Ed,' Rosie countered. 'I'm so far behind with everything. And then there's this place: we're both rushed off our feet since Marnie had the twins; we're under-staffed and I can't find temporary cover because there aren't enough hours in the day to hold interviews. Something needs to budge, and soon.' She gave a brief smile to the startled lady buying a bunch of multi-coloured gerberas as she handed over her change. 'Thank you, Laura. I'm sorry about this.'

'Hey, don't apologise, Rosie. When I was planning my

wedding I almost killed my fiancé. No, I'm serious. I had a frozen leg of lamb in my hand and I almost swung for him.'

Ed momentarily forgot his fury, staring at the primly dressed middle-aged customer. 'Wow, Laura.'

Laura shrugged. 'It happens. I thought better of it, we married and next February we celebrate twenty-five years together. You will get through it, believe me. Just make sure you take care of each other, OK?'

Ed watched her leave and turned to Rosie. 'I'm sorry. I love you, Rosie. Promise me you'll never bludgeon me with frozen meat?'

Rosie laughed. 'You're forgiven and I love you too. And I promise I'll clear the freezer of possible weapons next time Jake takes you to the bar.'

Hearing his name, Jake drifted out of his thought bubble and rejoined them. 'Does that mean I need to take him out again?'

Ed shot a comedy scowl at his brother. 'Don't do it on my account.'

'Aw, man. You know I love hanging with you.'

'Hmm. Besides, I hear you might be too busy to come out with your big bro now a certain *friend* is commanding your time.'

Rosie grinned conspiratorially and snuggled up to her fiancé. 'This sounds much more interesting than our wedding venue problems. What's happening, Jake?'

Jake blamed his current state of mind for walking him right into this ambush before he could realise what Rosie and Ed were doing. 'Nothing's happening. Bea and I are just enjoying hanging out.'

'*Frequently*,' Ed added. 'How many dates have you been on now, hmm?'

'They're not dates,' Jake returned, annoyed that Ed couldn't see their friendly meetings for what they were. 'We're just exploring New York together. As friends.'

'Sure you are. So how many *friendly explorations* have you been on, exactly?'

'To date, four. She's taken me to Central Park and a quirky stationery store she loves on the Lower East Side. I've taken her to Grand Central and last Saturday we went to the old baseball ground where you, Dan and me played as kids. See? We're just sharing places we love in the city. No big deal.'

Ed and Rosie looked at each other, amused.

'It sounds lovely,' Rosie said, beaming. 'And you seem to be enjoying yourself.'

'I am. Thank you.'

'So what's next on the Friendship Tour?' Ed asked. 'Empire State? Ellis Island?'

Jake didn't like the mockery in his brother's tone of voice. 'Maybe. Who knows? It's her turn to nominate, so I won't know till I get there.'

'And you'll get there on . . . ?'

'Sunday.'

'Ah.'

Jake groaned the Steinmann Family Groan, much to Rosie and Ed's amusement. 'Please stop bugging me. I like spending time with Bea. It's good to have a new friend who doesn't know my entire history. And it takes my mind away from – well, you know.'

Rosie's smile vanished. 'Oh no. Have you heard more from that awful solicitor?'

'Not yet. But it can't be long before he gets in touch again. Knowing what a hurry my wife is in to be shot of me.' He saw their reaction and wished he hadn't been quite so frank. 'Hey, it's not a problem. Just a necessary part of the process. It'll do us all good to be done with it as soon as possible. So, what's the issue with Dad?'

Ed's expression darkened. 'He's being deliberately obstructive. We were all systems go for having the wedding at their house – at his suggestion I might add – and then I dared to suggest that, as we were paying for everything else, we should have final say over the guest list.'

Rosie squeezed Ed's arm. 'He did it nicely, believe it or not. But it hurt Joe's pride I think and he's now said unless he has complete control of the wedding, we can't use the Steinmann house at all. It's hopeless, Jake! I even went out there on my own last week to try to reason with him. But you know your father: when he's decided something he's an immovable force.'

Jake could see that neither Rosie nor Ed were likely to find a resolution to the problem with Dr Steinmann Sr. Perhaps it was time to send in a psychological professional. 'Why don't you let me have a word with him?'

Rosie and Ed blinked at him, his offer sinking in.

'You'd do that?' Rosie asked.

'Sure, if it means you guys are able to enjoy planning your wedding again,' Jake replied. 'I haven't seen Dad for a couple of weeks, so I'm due a visit. I'll use the opportunity to put your case forward.'

Rosie looked close to tears as she threw her arms around Jake. 'It would mean so much! Thank you!'

'Take your invisible lightsaber,' Ed joked without smiling. 'Once you two get locked in a battle of the brains I can see it becoming a duel worthy of Darth Vader and Obi-Wan.'

The leaves were beginning to transform into their autumn colour when Jake drove out to Long Island the next day. Hiring a car, he headed out to his parents' home, enjoying the freedom of the open road once the city was behind him.

When his mother and father first bought the house in Hampton Bays, their sons had put it down to a whim and predicted they would be back in the city within a year. But much to everyone's surprise, Martha and Joe Steinmann took to Long Island life like well-heeled ducks to water. Joe's health had been tested by a heart scare four months before they bought the coastal property and while his personal dietician and trainer had brought him back to a healthier lifestyle, Joe had developed a passion for beach walks. Martha was involved in the local community society and their lives became dominated by charity functions, bake sales and weekend regattas. Jake liked the change in his parents, while Ed and Dan took great delight in mocking their new life choices.

He turned onto the coast road overlooking the Atlantic Ocean and drove past pricey bay properties until he reached a tree-lined driveway leading up to a large house. The tall cedar trees framing the property made the white-painted wood frontage glow, even on an overcast day like today. It was an impressive property in every sense, from the row of hand-blown glass lanterns on either side of the drive to the enormous swimming pool on the right-hand side and the long, whitewashed jetty leading from the boathouse on the left out into the sea. In this respect, it was every inch Dr Joe Steinmann: everything on show, demanding your attention.

Martha Steinmann flung open the door before Jake reached the front steps. 'Jacob, darling! How was the drive down?'

Jake hugged his mother, inhaling the familiar scent of cinnamon and violets on her clothes. 'Good, Mom. Where is the Dragon Master?'

Martha's smile revealed more than she realised. 'In the Ocean Room. I hope you can knock sense into him, Jake. I've given up.'

'Leave him to me.'

His mother kissed his cheek. 'You're an angel. Now I'm meeting the girls in town for some much needed coffee. Will you stay for dinner?'

'Sure. Say hi to the ladies for me.'

'I will. Try not to murder your father.'

Jake strolled through the wide marble lobby with its two-storey-high ceiling into a large, open-plan living room with wrap-around windows looking out to sea. His father was seated on one of the many white damask sofas in the centre of the room and took off his reading glasses as he stood to greet Jake.

'Son, this is an unexpected pleasure. I could hardly believe it when your mother said you were visiting us again. That's twice in a fortnight, after years of seeing you only on holidays.'

They shared a brief, backslapping hug and sat down together.

'Your mom made us coffee,' Joe Steinmann said, folding his newspaper and indicating a cafetiere and plate of homemade cake on the large oak coffee table. 'She's gotten into baking again after all these years. Help yourself.'

'I'll do that.' Jake filled two bone china mugs and passed one to Joe, taking a large slice of cake and sitting beside his father. 'This is good cake.'

'You know your mom: never does anything half-heartedly. I swear she'll be supplying half the coffee shops on Long Island before long.' Joe laughed loudly at his own joke. 'She's meeting the Hampton Bays Centenary Sisters this morning, would you believe? I have no idea what they do, either. Are you staying for dinner?'

'If you'll have me.'

This pleased his father no end. 'Excellent! I have some new yacht brochures to show you. Thinking of testing out the old sea legs again. What do you think?'

'I think if it makes you happy, you should do it.'

'And *that's* why you're my favourite son!'

'This is good coffee, Dad,' Jake said, glad of the smoky caffeine hit this morning.

'New blend from the coffee merchants I found in Garden City. It's Peruvian-Guatemalan. I bought out their supply when your mother and I visited last weekend. I think I'm their best customer.' He revelled in the taste of his coffee, then put his cup and saucer down on his knee and looked at Jake. 'But you didn't come here to consult on coffee blends and yacht brochures, did you?'

The veteran psychiatrist had kicked into action and Jake prepared for another mind-battle. 'You're right, I didn't. I came to see you and Mom.'

'But more than that: what's on your mind, son? The divorce must be taking its toll.'

'I guess so, although I haven't heard back from Jess' lawyer yet.'

'Don't let her walk all over you, Jake. I know you want the affair signed off as soon as you can, but defend your share. You invested far too much in that marriage to hand it all over to Jessica. She might think she can win, but you must stand your ground for what's rightfully yours.'

Jake didn't want to have this conversation, but it afforded him useful thinking space to work out how to tackle the main subject he had come to discuss. 'I'll try to.'

'Who's representing you?'

'Chuck Willets.'

'Ah! Good choice. That man saved my practice when Dean Graham tried to sue. What does he suggest?'

'That I wait and see what Jessica's lawyer lays down first. I'm happy to follow his lead.'

Joe nodded thoughtfully, stirring another lump of sugar crystals into his coffee. 'Don't tell your mom,' he said quickly when he saw Jake's disapproval. 'She's got me up to my eyes in tofu. Sugar in my coffee is the one treat I have left.'

'You should think of your heart, Dad. You know what Dr Keller said.'

'Dr Keller is a mean old man,' Joe returned. 'And what he doesn't know he can't steal from me.'

Jake laughed. 'Your secret's safe with me.'

'Thanks, son.'

Seizing the moment, Jake turned on the offensive. '*Although*, if you don't back down on Ed's wedding arrangements, I may be forced to say something.'

Joe Steinmann stared at his youngest son. 'Blackmail, Jake? I didn't give you my years of psychological knowledge to let you resort to cheap tricks like that.'

'Oh, and your insistence on taking over the wedding isn't a cheap trick?'

'Certainly not!'

Jake leaned a little closer to his father. 'Well, it looks that way from here. What's the real problem, Dad? You surely can't disapprove of Ed's choice of bride?'

'Of course not. I love Rosie like a daughter already.'

'Then why the *High Noon* standoff? You really upset her when she spoke to you last.'

'She may be perfect for Edward, but she was asking too much.'

Jake put his coffee cup down on the table. 'Rosie was asking to be able to have a say in her own wedding. Is that unreasonable? You *know* what planning this wedding means to her and how imperative it is that their big day is as happy and trouble-free as possible.'

Joe dismissed this. 'I know, of course I know. I've heard the story a thousand times. Their day will be happy. They just need to appreciate that this is my house and my rules apply here.'

'Dad. Be reasonable, huh? They're not asking for

money or crazy wedding arrangements. They're not going after an embarrassing theme or inviting scandal into your home. All Ed wants is to marry the love of his life in your beautiful house, surrounded by the people that mean the most to him. Sure, it's two days before Christmas, but all the family members they want to invite will be staying here for Christmas anyway. You don't have to do a thing . . .'

'And *that's* the problem!' Joe exclaimed suddenly. 'All of this will be going on around me and what am I expected to do? Nothing! I will not be in charge of my own house! And it isn't just the closeness to Christmas: the planners will be here for days before; they will move *my* furniture and rearrange *my* home and I will be expected to exist in the middle of their chaos. What makes you think I'll be comfortable with that?'

Jake could hear his father's reasons but sensed that none of them pointed to the underlying problem. 'All of what you've said is valid and understandable. But all of it would be easy for you to overlook if you were happy with the wedding taking place here. There's something you're not telling me.'

His father appeared momentarily stunned by Jake's suggestion. Then, slapping his hands on his knees, he stood and marched to the window overlooking the sweeping lawn strewn with autumn leaves and blue-grey Atlantic beyond. 'I don't have to take this from you, Jacob. I didn't take it from Edward or Rosie. It's unfair to suggest I'm attention-seeking.'

Aha! Jake congratulated himself on making his father

admit the real reason for his behaviour. 'Is that what you want here, Dad? Attention?'

Joe pulled a face. 'I never said it was.'

'I think you'll find you just did. Do you feel Ed and Rosie are freezing you out of their wedding plans?'

'No.' His answer was quiet and the telling question mark his voice added revealed how close to the bone Jake's assertion was.

'Dad, come on. You're talking to a psychiatrist.'

Joe harrumphed, his breath clouding the windowpane in front of him. 'That suggests that I'm no better than a child.'

'Does it? Is that how you feel about your reaction to the wedding plans?'

'Cut the crap, Jacob! I know how this works: I've been asking the questions for long enough. Yes, OK? I can't rationalise it and on paper it looks like a bid for attention, but I feel like a visitor in my own home. Your mom spends all her time going over details with Rosie; Edward has organised marquees and catering and music; even you organised their engagement party. What's my job in all this? Where do I get my chance to contribute? Handing over my home is not the level of participation I expected in this wedding. I suggested they hold it here because I wanted to be part of the day. But every idea I've had has been shot down in flames or laughed out of the room. Like I'm nothing more than a caretaker handing over the keys.' He shook his head. 'And listening to myself I hear a spoiled brat throwing his toys out of the buggy because he isn't the centre of attention at somebody else's birthday party.'

Jake walked over to his father and laid his arm gently around the older man's shoulders. 'And that reminds you of how you had no say in Ed's career choice, doesn't it? Don't give me that look, Dad: I know where this is coming from. You felt you should have contributed more to his professional career, and you're still smarting that he didn't follow you into psychiatry. Aren't you?'

Joe Steinmann's expression was defiant but his eyes had reddened. 'It all happened such a long time ago . . .'

'Doesn't make it any less painful.'

'No. I guess not.'

Jake sighed. This was very tricky ground for him to cover: the feud between Ed and his father had become ingrained in Steinmann family behaviour. Addressing it would take more time than a day on Long Island could offer.

'But if you think Ed has rejected your role as his father, you're wrong. Ed adores you: he always has. If he didn't care so much for what you thought of him, do you think he'd have stuck around for as long as he has? He's been willing to attend every family occasion for twenty years, even though he knew that every time the subject of his chosen career would rear its ugly head. He has endured countless jibes about his sexuality because he chose to work with flowers; and, sure, he may have fought back, but he has never, ever deserted the family because of it. Plenty of others would. And now he wants to share the happiest day of his life with you – in *your* house. Do you think he would have even considered that if he didn't want you to be there?'

Joe said nothing, the clouds of his breath coming quickly against the window glass.

Sensing his words had hit home, Jake took a step back. 'I'll go make us more coffee, shall I?'

Joe nodded, swallowing hard as his youngest son turned away.

Rosie's face was a picture when Jake visited her and Ed's apartment to share the good news.

'I don't know how you did that, but thank you! I was beginning to think we'd have to postpone the wedding.' She hugged Jake tightly. 'You're fab! I'm so happy you're going to be my brother-in-law!'

'The feeling's mutual,' Jake smiled, kissing the top of Rosie's head as she hugged him. 'What matters now is that you two get back to having fun planning your wedding . . .' He broke off as a vivid memory of he and Jessica kissing on the floor of his apartment surrounded by lists and seating plans returned. Their perfect wedding at her parent's house overlooking the beach at Half Moon Bay was made all the more fun by how happy everyone had been, encouraged by all the personal touches he and Jess had built into the ceremony: tiny candle lanterns strung through the tall maple trees that surrounded the garden; a 'wish-tree' where guests could hang their blessings on the new marriage; Tom & Jerry cartoons playing all evening in one of the four sitting rooms; boxes of blankets around the garden for the evening festivities; and hot chocolate with marshmallows served at midnight. Every aspect had been planned to elicit the biggest smiles. Consequently, the wedding day was a truly happy, laughter-filled, intimate event still talked about years later by those lucky enough to be there.

The memory of it was a stark reminder of how much he still loved her – in spite of everything.

Jake flinched as a shard of pain jabbed his heart. Had their wedding day been *too* perfect, he wondered? One thing was certain: he wouldn't be making that mistake again.

Rosie broke the hug and grinned up at him. 'Listen, Ed and I talked about this and we would really love to invite Bea to our wedding . . .' Before Jake could protest, she continued. 'And I know it's early days for you two – *as friends*, obviously – but you've done so much for us and I wouldn't want you to feel alone on our wedding day.'

'Rosie, I—'

'Hear me out, OK? Bea's a sweetheart. You get on with her so well and it's clear from your mood lately that her friendship is something you're really enjoying. All I'm suggesting is that the two of you might enjoy the wedding more if you can have a kindred spirit there. Promise me you'll consider it?'

Damn Rosie Duncan! It was impossible for Jake to deny her anything when she looked up at him with her big, brown, British eyes. She knew it, too, a smile already playing on her lips as she waited for his answer.

'I'll think about it.'

'Excellent. I'll leave you to mention it to her. If it feels wrong or the moment doesn't arise, don't ask her. But if it *does* . . .'

'Sure. I get the idea.'

He hated his soon-to-be sister-in-law for knowing him so well. Even as he feigned practised disinterest in Rosie's idea, his heart was inexplicably light.

Maybe I will ask her to the wedding. It could be fun . . .

CHAPTER THIRTY-TWO

Cheese-A-Go-Go!, SoHo

'Wow. I thought I'd seen the biggest mountain of cheese in New York at Zabar's, but this is something else.'

Bea giggled as she watched Jake take in the high stacks of every conceivable type of cheese rising around their table in the SoHo 'cheese-and-coffee' shop she had brought him to. 'I don't think I've ever seen anybody so impressed by cheese before.'

'Are you kidding? This is heaven for me! How come I've never heard of this place before?'

Bea took a bite of warm cheese scone. 'It's only been open a few years. They started off with a grilled cheese sandwich truck in Brooklyn, which Russ and Imelda made a pilgrimage to every week, and then when they found these premises we followed them here. Pretty impressive, isn't it? Although I imagine not so much if you hate cheese.'

'Or are lactose-intolerant,' Jake added.

'Oh, they have lactose-free cheese here, too,' Bea corrected him.

'I should've guessed. This is New York, after all. Hey, do you have The Pact list?'

'I do.' Smiling, Bea retrieved it from her bag. The list of reasons to be single had been steadily growing since their first trip out in New York and now stood at nearly thirty items.

'I just thought of another reason: "The ability to choose and eat cheese at any time of the day or night". My ex hated me eating cheese after eight p.m. Seriously, I had to wait until the Steinmann family Christmas celebrations until I could indulge in late night cheese feasts.'

Bea wrote it down at number thirty. 'Otis was lactose-intolerant.'

'At least he'd be at home here,' Jake observed. 'This is *such* a great place, Bea. Your best yet, I reckon.'

Bea was surprised that every time it was her turn to nominate a venue, Jake seemed to be genuinely impressed by her choice. For instance, today she'd had a sudden crisis of conscience in the cab on the way to SoHo when she realised she had never asked Jake if he liked cheese. Cheesecake, yes, but the subject of his dairy likes and dislikes hadn't yet arisen in conversation. What would happen if he hated it? Cheese-A-Go-Go! was definitely an acquired taste, not least because of the strong cheese aroma that bombarded you as you drank your coffee.

Thankfully, Jake had been unmasked as a true cheese devotee, and Bea was finally able to relax knowing her choice had been a good one.

'Do you realise we've become regular explorers of this great city?' Jake asked suddenly.

'I suppose we have,' Bea replied, surprised by how

quickly she'd become accustomed to their New York trips. 'And you're still having fun?'

'Of course I am.' His brow furrowed a little. 'Are you?'

'Definitely.'

'That's good.'

Bea had been considering talking to Jake about something for the last week and now she sensed her opportunity to broach it.

At the beginning of the week, one of Hudson River Books' regular customers had arrived with an unusual request on her young daughter's behalf. She had been so apologetic for her visit that Bea had made her a coffee and sat her down on the kids' section beanbag sofas to make her feel more comfortable.

'I'm really so sorry to have to ask, but Bronagh insisted,' she said, clutching her coffee mug so tightly Bea was concerned it might shatter in her hands.

'Rita, it's fine. You know Russ and I are Bronagh's biggest fans. We've never met a ten-year-old with such a passion for books before.'

'She's always loved your bookstore, ever since you opened on 8th,' Lulu Chambers smiled. 'She thinks it's magical.'

'Then she's a girl after my own heart,' Bea replied. 'So what did she want you to ask me?'

Lulu took a breath and turned to face her. 'Bronagh will be eleven next Tuesday and I asked her what she wanted to do for it. Since Clive works away so much these days I offered her the chance to have a party. We haven't held one for a few years and I thought it would be something she would like to do. The thing is, we've

255

talked about lots of venues but there's only one place she wants to celebrate her birthday.'

'Where?'

'Here.'

'Oh.'

Nobody had ever asked to hold a birthday party at the bookstore before, but Bea loved that her young customer thought so much of Hudson River Books. Her mind began to spin with ideas and practical considerations: could they clear the centre of the store to accommodate tables and chairs? Who would cater for the party and what kind of food would an eleven-year-old girl and her friends want to eat, anyway? Could she pull everything together in a week?

Lulu interpreted her silence as a bad sign and instantly began to backtrack. 'Of course, it's too short notice and I really didn't think it would be possible. Please don't feel obliged, Bea.'

'No, I think we could do this. Would you want the party on Bronagh's actual birthday or the weekend after?'

'On the day, preferably. Clive returns from Denver next weekend but he's only in town for a couple of days before he leaves for Dubai for a month. I'd like him to be able to share it with her.'

Bea smiled at her nervous customer. 'That's settled then. Next Tuesday it is. Give me an idea of your budget and Russ and I will get our thinking caps on . . .'

Jake was watching her intently as Bea retold the story. 'So the upshot is that we're going to host our first kids' party next Tuesday evening, from six thirty till eight thirty. And I know it's not a weekend and you'll probably be busy, but I wondered if you fancied coming along.'

'Me? At a kids' party?'

Bea's heart sank. *Of course* it was a ridiculous idea! Why had she even asked? 'It was just a thought. Sorry, ignore me.' *Great way to scupper a successful day out, Bea . . .*

Jake's smile widened as he considered her crazy request. 'What the heck? It might be fun.'

Bea was shocked. 'Really? I mean it will be a case of all hands on deck – I might need you to help serve drinks and food.'

Jake grinned. 'Hey, I think I more than proved my bartending skills at the party, didn't I?'

'Yes, you did. Although you might not be serving much whisky and champagne at Bronagh's eleventh birthday party.'

A wicked glint flashed in Jake's blue eyes. 'Depends how bad the party gets.'

'Suit Man.'

'His name is Jake.'

Russ didn't move, blocking the entrance to the bookstore as they stood in the office. 'You asked *Suit Man* to help us at the party?'

Bea stood her ground, secretly wishing she hadn't chosen this morning to break the news to Russ. There was so much to organise and little time to do it in: plus they had a visit from a local kindergarten that afternoon when she wouldn't be able to do anything other than control crowds of overexcited youngsters. 'Yes, I did. Now can you let me pass, please?'

'Not until you tell me what's going on.'

'Well, I don't know about you, but I have a ton of arrangements to make this morning before Sunnyvale Kindergarten invades.'

'You know what I'm asking, Bea! What is it with this guy?'

Bea smiled her best apologetic smile. 'I've been hanging out with him.'

'Excuse me?'

'Well, you know I told you I've been out exploring New York with a friend? Jake is that friend.'

Aghast, Russ stared at her. 'I thought you said you weren't going to contact him. When he brought his card over.'

'Yes, well, things change.'

'And you didn't think to tell me?'

The truth was Bea had been too busy enjoying her new friendship with Jake to fill Russ in on the pertinent details. Seeing his expression now, she wished that she had. 'I'm sorry, Russ. I *meant* to tell you . . .'

Russ rolled his eyes. 'See, I knew something was happening. You've been different for weeks: lost in your own thoughts, distant. And now I know why.'

'I made a mistake, OK? I should have told you. But now you know. He's a friend – nothing more – and so I asked him to come and help us because there is no way you and I can handle fifteen eleven-year-olds by ourselves. Believe it or not, I was *trying* to be helpful.'

Chastened by her outburst, Russ attempted a smile. 'So Suit Man's just a friend?'

'That's what I said. And for the last time, his name is *Jake*. Can we get on now?'

That evening, exhausted from Bronagh's party planning and the relentless joy of twenty little kindergarten kids descending for games and story-time in the bookstore, Bea sat at the small, flea-market-find desk in her apartment. She needed to quantify her wandering thoughts on paper – and there was only one person who she knew would help her make sense of it all . . .

Hi Grandma Dot,

I'm sorry it's been a while since I last wrote. Thank you for my lovely parcels and letters - it's so lovely to have the Book Mice back in my life!

Everything is good here. I've been organising HRB's first children's party today! One of our young customers asked if she could celebrate her eleventh birthday at the bookshop: remind you of anyone? I remember my eighth birthday party that you threw for me at Severnside Books. It was perfect for a little bookworm like me! I'm determined to make it a success, even though we now have less than a week to organise everything. If it goes well, who knows? Maybe it will be something we can offer as an extra service.

I've been spending my weekends with Jake, exploring New York. Oh, Grandma, it's been so much fun! We take it in turns to choose where we go and there is always a personal reason behind it. For example, *this week I took Jake to the daft cheese shop café in SoHo I told you about; last week Jake took me to Coney Island, which was great fun. I feel like our friendship has appeared serendipitously, just when we both needed it. Not having the usual pressures and concerns of the dating thing hanging over us has been wonderful. He doesn't want a relationship and neither do I - so our outings can just be about fun and friendship.*

I know you think I shouldn't rule out future relationships, but this is the happiest I've felt in a long time. You've always told me to follow my heart: right now it's telling me that I'm doing the right thing.

Write soon!

Lots of love,

Bea xxxx

Bea threw herself into preparations for the children's party, roping in Imelda to help dress the bookstore, inspired by her success with Celia's book launch decorations. They decided to transform Hudson River Books into an enchanted story forest, complete with hanging tree branches, hidden fairies and, of course, more twinkly lights than the bookstore usually held at Christmas. Russ worked on wooden animals to scatter through the centre of the shop: a wise owl with bright yellow eyes, baby deer, rabbits and hedgehogs.

For catering, Bea visited Sugar Rush Cupcakery, a new

cupcake bakery that had opened a block from her apartment in Boerum Hill, and ordered a delectable feast of sugar treats to ensure Bronagh and her friends could celebrate in style. Luc from Stromoli's also agreed to provide a couple of trays of canapés for the parents of the partygoers. According to Bronagh's mother, word had quickly spread about the unusual party venture and parents were eager to attend to experience the event for themselves.

On top of the day-to-day running of the store, planning the party claimed much of Bea's time, but she didn't care. She loved being busy and was excited to see where this new development would lead. Even when she was at home her mind was abuzz with finishing touches she could add to give Bronagh a birthday party to remember.

Three days after she had posted her letter to Grandma Dot, a parcel arrived. The Book Mice were dressed like Musketeers – or, as Grandma Dot had written beneath them on the brown paper package, *Mouseketeers* . . . Inside was a vintage copy of Edmond Rostand's *Cyrano de Bergerac* in a printed blue and red slipcase. The yellow Severnside Books bookmark wasn't marking a place this time: instead, Grandma Dot had written on it: 'All is explained in the letter, darling!'

Dearest Bea,
  Thank you for your letter. I'm delighted that things are going so well for you and that you're happy, which is all I care about. And yes, I remember that birthday party! You were very excited because I

dressed up as a storyteller and read chapters from George's Marvellous Medicine to you all. You were in love with Roald Dahl then, as I recall.

You will see that the Book Mice have chosen a wonderful play to send you. This is a 1941 translation of Cyrano de Bergerac, by Edmond Rostand. I rather fell for this edition when I found it. It's the story of the ultimate sacrifice the hero makes for the woman he loves. Sometimes we choose to lay aside our own wishes for the ones we love. Your letter reminded me of this story - and also a real one of my own.

I feel that now is the time to tell you about something that happened to me, many years ago. It is a secret I have held for over seventy years. I am trusting you to keep it, too.

Before your grandpa, there was another love in my life. An all-encompassing, passionate love, the like of which I never again experienced. And even though so many years have passed, I still think of him every day. Please be assured that I loved Grandpa George with all of my heart and I don't regret a single moment of my life that I shared with him. But this love happened first.

When I was seventeen years old, I met

Abel Flanagan at a village dance. He was the son of a local farmer and I had never seen him before that night. In our village, we had a Harvest Dance every year to celebrate the harvest being brought in successfully and for us young girls it was often the place we met our future husbands.

The irony is that I didn't want to be there. I was headstrong and independent, even at that young age, and I didn't think I needed a man in my life. I had watched my four sisters before me marry and lose any identity they had: I didn't want that to happen to me. I dreamed of owning a bookshop and making my own way in the world – which is why I feel we are very much cut from the same cloth, Bea. But my best friend Lillian begged me to go: her father had said she could only attend if she had a companion. So, under duress, I went to the dance.

Abel was late arriving to the dance. He and his brothers had been held up in their father's field bringing in the last of the barley crop. But when he did, my world changed.

He was six feet tall with thick, black hair and eyes the colour of sea-glass. I had never seen anyone so beautiful in my life and I couldn't take my eyes off him. He asked me to dance and my heart was beating so quickly I thought I would die in his arms. Does that shock you, darling? Forgive an old woman for being candid, but it's important you understand how strong my emotions for him were, or else you will never fully appreciate what I tell you next.

I believe I fell in love that night, even though I hardly knew him. He could have asked anything of me and I would have given it to him. It was as if everything I thought I knew was wiped away in an instant and all I could see in my future was Abel Flanagan's smile as we danced together.

He asked me to meet him the following Saturday and I agreed, knowing only too well that I couldn't tell my parents about him. Your great-grandfather was a proud man with strict ideas about the kind of men his daughters should marry. My sisters married men of business: a grocer, a butcher, a bank manager and a grain merchant - all of whom fit the bill nicely. He would never have approved of a farmer's son, even though several farmers in our community had become wealthy. My father had been born on a farm and vowed from an early age that no child of his would be forced to live the life he had endured there.

So, we met in secret: after I had suppos-
edly gone to bed, I would climb out of my
bedroom window and meet Abel just down
the lane from my home. That is how it
began - and how it continued for over a
year.

I will tell you more next time. For now,
know this: if I had known what fate had
in store for us then, I would have had
the courage of my convictions to tell my
father I had chosen to spend my life with
Abel. I would have wasted no time in
marrying him. Because time was not on
our side.

Live life for every minute, darling Bea.
You never know when your world may
change.

Fondest love,
Grandma Dot xxx

Bea turned the last page of the letter over, expecting
to find more, but it was blank. Why had Grandma Dot
withheld this part of her life from everyone? Bea – along
with all of her family – had assumed that Grandpa George
was Dot's first love. To discover that her ninety-two-year-
old grandmother had a secret past was a shock. But as
she read the letter again, Bea felt honoured that Grandma
Dot had chosen her to share it with.

What did she mean about sacrifice, though? She
couldn't be referring to Jake, surely? If anything, Bea
could accept that she was being selfish: enjoying her time

with Jake without any expectation of reciprocal feelings or giving anything back. How was *that* a sacrifice?

Grandma Dot said she would continue the story in her next letter. Until then, Bea would have to wonder what it meant – and deal with the discomfort it gave her . . .

CHAPTER THIRTY-THREE

Hudson River Books, 8th Avenue, Brooklyn

When Jake arrived at Hudson River Books nerves were beginning to get the better of him. Why had he agreed to this? Kids' parties were hardly his speciality: even at Steinmann family gatherings he was the 'Uncle Least Likely to be Picked' by the tiny Steinmanns for their party games. It wasn't that he didn't get on with children; rather that he wasn't altogether sure how they worked past a certain age. There was a window of opportunity between the ages of twelve months and three years when he officially *rocked* in their eyes, but as soon as they could really talk and think for themselves, Uncle Ed and Uncle Dan became flavour of the month. Jake wasn't entirely sure why.

On that evidence, how was he going to be received by fifteen discerning eleven-year-olds?

He was considering how easy it would be to leave when a large slap on his back made him turn. *Great.* Bea's hipster business partner friend was grinning at him from the sidewalk. What *was* his name? Ross? Reece?

'Hey,' he said shakily, frantically wracking his brain for the guy's name.

'Left the suit at home today, I see?' There was a distinct note of mockery in his tone.

Jake forced himself to ignore it. *This is playing into your insecurities about the party*, he told himself firmly. *Don't attribute your own thoughts to this guy*. 'Yes. Yes, I did.'

'Come in,' Russ said. 'But I'll warn you, Bea's like a whirling dervish in there.' There was *that* smile again. Did they teach it to people in Brooklyn? Was it something the cool people used to gain dominance over everyone else?

He couldn't leave. He'd made a promise to Bea. This party meant a lot to her and, as her friend, he wanted to support her. If that meant putting up with her self-righteous business partner, so be it. 'Lead the way,' he replied, flashing his most confident smile.

The transformation inside the bookstore was incredible. Swags of chiffon in shades of green hung from the high ceiling, giving the impression of sunlight dappling through a dense forest canopy. Tiny green and white lights were threaded through the fabric and looped along every shelf, shimmering as the chiffon moved with the passing of people through the store. Silk tree branch boughs hung down from the top of the bookshelves and woodland animals peeked out between gaps in the leaves. A smoke machine behind the counter pumped out puffs of white smoke in an impression of woodland mist, giving the whole space an ethereal quality. It was a child's dream: breathtaking in its execution.

'Do you like it?'

Jake smiled as Bea approached, dressed in a rich green velvet medieval-style dress, her red hair braided and fixed into a loose bun at the nape of her neck, from which a delicate, moss-green veil draped down her back. She looked every part the magical princess.

'This place is stunning! The change is unbelievable.'

Bea flushed. 'Thank you. There was a lot of teamwork to achieve this. Russ, Imelda and I were up till the early hours this morning putting it all together. Listen, thanks so much for volunteering to help. I know the prospect of so many kids is scary, but between us I think we'll be fine.'

Jake gave a nonchalant shrug, hoping Bea couldn't see the trepidation in his eyes. 'Totally. So, I'm at your command, m'lady. You point me where you want me and I'll be there.'

'Such a *gent*,' Russ smiled as he walked past.

Jake resisted the urge to respond. *You're here for Bea, not him.*

'I do actually have a bit of a costume for you, if you don't mind,' Bea ventured, a sheepish smile on her face. 'But there's absolutely no pressure to wear it. I thought it might be fun.'

A costume? Jake swallowed hard. Would smug hipster guy be dressing up, too? He considered how much Bea's friendship meant to him: was it worth his humiliation in front of a whole bookstore of people he didn't know? The last time he'd dressed up for anything was back in high school when he was roped into playing Romeo in the end of year production, mainly by virtue of the fact that he was the tallest and could remember the script. The memory of standing before his peers in bright red tights still haunted him . . .

But Bea was looking at him with such faith that he couldn't disappoint her. *This is the first major test of your friendship, Jake Steinmann. Survive this and you'll survive anything . . .*

'Sure. Why not?'

To Jake's immense relief, the costume Bea had selected for him was relatively manly and didn't involve coloured tights – his biggest fear when she opened the box in the office at the back of the bookstore. Her choice was revealed to be a midnight blue cloak and gold-edged green tunic with a pair of black trousers: most respectable by costume standards.

'I think I work this well,' he grinned, as Bea reached up to tie the gold braids on his cloak. Suddenly, their closeness hit him: the gentle touches of her fingers on the bare skin of his neck caused shivers to wriggle across his shoulders and he was acutely aware of the undulating pulse in his throat.

'There. Perfect.' Her voice was distinctly softer and Jake noticed that her gaze drifted to his chest as she spoke. 'Would you – um – would you set up a tray of juice on the coffee counter, please? I've left everything you need there.'

Was it his imagination, or was Bea blushing more than before?

'Sure, no problem,' he smiled down at her, a sudden urge to touch her hair assaulting him. She was close to him and it would be so easy to take advantage . . .

'You have *got* to be kidding me.' Russ' loud exclamation broke the moment and Jake stepped back to reveal Bea's business partner fuming in the office doorway, wearing a bright red and yellow jester's outfit.

Shaken by what he'd just experienced, Jake stared as Russ stormed past.

'*This* is the costume you ordered for me? What happened to the wizard outfit you promised?'

'The costume hire place was all out of wizards, I'm afraid.' Bea reached out to touch his arm. 'Sorry, hun.'

Russ jabbed his hands onto his hips, the bells on his three-pointed hat and harlequin collar jingling merrily as he did so. 'They were *out* of wizards? Is there a major wizard convention happening in Brooklyn that I wasn't aware of?'

'I tried,' Bea protested, 'honestly, I did. But I thought the jester's outfit was apt for you, being a comedian and everything.'

'*Fantastic*. There could be single women here today, Bea! You are seriously damaging my chances of making a good impression. Next time when we share out responsibilities, remind me to take control of the costumes.'

'Well, I think you look adorable,' Bea smiled innocently.

Russ was far from impressed. 'Just remember, I'm doing this for you, Bea James. I wouldn't do it for anyone else.' With that, he grabbed a handful of party bags from the office desk and flounced out.

Jake was glad to be given a job to do and busied himself with pouring drinks. The moment he had experienced in the office had unnerved him, not least because it had taken him by surprise. *You're projecting again*, he analysed. *You're feeling exposed in an unfamiliar situation: Bea is a friend and you trust her. You're confusing a moment of reassurance in vulnerability with something else. It isn't real.* Once the children arrived he would get into the swing of things and it would be fine.

Spending time with Bea *was* reassuring. Her friendship was just what he needed as the dust continued to settle on his feelings for Jess in the wake of their divorce. He needed to have fun, to smile and forget that the woman he thought was the love of his life was doing her best to surgically remove him from her life. It was obvious that Bea didn't want to be reminded of her ex any more than he did. It was the perfect arrangement. During the few weeks he and Bea had been sharing their favourite places, she had always surprised him. Even the more obvious locations – such as Central Park and a cupcake bakery in the Upper West Side – revealed unexpected reasons for Bea choosing them. The bakery was a people-watching paradise for Bea and had become a firm favourite due to the crazy owner who put a photo of his beloved dachshund dogs in different fancy dress on the counter each week. On the day Bea and Jake had visited, the dogs had been dressed as 'Sonny and Cher *Bonio*'. Had anyone else shared this with him, Jake would have laughed them off the streets of Manhattan. But Bea's unbridled joy at such cheesy kitsch was – *endearing*. He had assumed she would be reserved, considering her English heritage, but she seemed to find wonder in the smallest detail. He envied her that: in his line of work so much attention was given to cataloguing every nuance of life that it could steal any spontaneous joy from the act. Bea revelled in the absurd,

272

and her amusement was infectious. Jake felt like he was learning to do the same – and, given the alternative of moping around while his divorce steamrollered on, it was a far better use of his time.

At six p.m., Lulu and Bronagh arrived, the birthday girl's rapt expression when she entered worth every hour of work invested in the party.

'This is *awesome*,' she exclaimed, her eyes brimming with tears.

'Do you like it, lovely?' Bea asked, laughing with surprise as Bronagh threw her arms around her, sobbing loudly.

'That's a "yes",' her mother smiled. 'It's beautiful, Bea. I can't thank you enough.'

The transformed bookstore elicited similar responses from Bronagh's friends when they arrived, the sum total of conversation for the first ten minutes of the party consisting of '*Wow*'s and '*Awesome*'s and '*Unbelievable*'s. Bronagh beamed in the middle of it all, her position as the giver of the coolest birthday parties firmly established in the eyes of her friends.

Jake served paper cups of 'Forest Nectar' – a mixture of pomegranate and apple juice concocted by Russ, while Bea read stories to the party guests. She seemed to shine from within when she read: it was no wonder that you could hear a pin drop as Bronagh and her friends listened. He was fascinated to watch his new friend at work, doing what she loved in the place she and Russ had built together.

The bookshop *was* magical: but Jake sensed that this came more from the passion injected into every aspect by its owners than any of the impressive decorations adorning its fittings and fixtures today. Even with fifteen overexcited eleven-year-olds filling the space with joy and laughter, Hudson River Books had an overarching sense of calm, a peace that Jake had never experienced in a bookstore before. No wonder their young customer had wanted her birthday party here: it was a place unlike any other.

Russ led a treasure hunt after the story was finished, much to the delighted screams of the young party guests, followed by the Forest Feast of cupcakes, pinwheel sandwiches decorated with poppy seeds to resemble cut logs, and pizza slices covered with lizards cut from green and red bell peppers. Jake served canapés to the parents while Russ and Bea brought out an enormous three-tiered cake covered in sugar craft flowers and foliage, topped with a flurry of delicate sugar butterflies and eleven gold candles.

It was almost nine o'clock when the happy-but-weary guests, parents and birthday girl departed. Bea, Russ and Jake flopped down on the beanbag sofas, Russ producing a hidden bag of beers to toast their success.

'Now I know how movie directors feel at a wrap party,' he said, handing bottles to Bea and Jake. 'That was *exhausting*.'

'But successful,' Jake interjected. 'You guys did an amazing job.'

'Thanks, Jake. And thanks so much for coming to help us. I don't think we could have managed without you.'

For once, Russ appeared genuine when he leaned across to shake Jake's hand. 'You did good, man.'

'My pleasure.' Weariness began to tug at his body and Jake looked up at the clock above the counter. 'I should be going. I have a client arriving early tomorrow and I need to prepare my notes.'

Bea was disappointed. 'Do you have to leave right away? Russ and I are ordering pizza.'

Tempted as he was, Jake was ready to go home. 'You guys deserve to celebrate.' He stood slowly and went to the office to change out of his costume. Five minutes later, he returned and Bea walked him out of the bookstore.

'Thank you again. And thanks for wearing the costume.'

'It was a good costume. Just relieved I didn't get the jester's suit,' Jake grinned. He wondered if he should tell her that she looked beautiful in her outfit, but didn't think it wise. But another thought struck him and, not wanting to overanalyse his motives, he decided to act upon it. 'Hey, Bea?'

'Yes?'

'I was talking to Rosie and Ed and they'd really like it if you'd come to their wedding. It's the day before Christmas Eve at my parents' house on Long Island. I'd be honoured if you'd accept as my guest.'

Did it sound too much like a date? Would being Jake's 'plus-one' be too threatening for her? Jake almost took it back, until he saw Bea's smile.

'I would love to,' she replied.

'You would?'

'Of course I would! I think the world of Rosie and Ed and it means a lot that they would want me to be there when they get married.'

'Great. I'll tell them yes, then?'

'Yes. Please do.'

Knowing he would have a friend and ally at the wedding was a source of great relief for Jake. Bea would be the perfect person to share the day with: not only fun to be with but also a perfect foil to dissuade the attempts of well-meaning Steinmann relatives to set him up with their unmarried friends. They could be a safety net for each other. It was a perfect arrangement.

Back in the blandness of his apartment, Jake poured a double whisky and drank it quickly. He was tired and tomorrow's early start would be a test, but it had been worth it for the experience. The party had been fun and he had surprised himself with how much he had enjoyed it. One of the many new experiences of his New York life. In the dimly lit interior of his home he caught himself wondering what Jess would have thought of him volunteering to work at a children's party. How different from the person he had been in San Francisco!

Maybe I'm changing for the better, Jess, he told the frozen image of his ex-wife that sat in a frame on his still-empty bookshelf. *And maybe I like the change.*

CHAPTER THIRTY-FOUR

The Comedy Cavern, 7th Avenue, Brooklyn

'. . . So I said to her, "You mean this *isn't* the line for Ellis Island?" . . .'

The small audience in the dimly lit comedy bar erupted with laughter and applause as Russ ended his stand-up set.

'You've been a great audience and I've been Russ O'Docherty. Goodnight!'

He hopped down from the low stage nodding his appreciation at the audience's congratulations and bounded over to Bea and Imelda's table. 'How was that?'

'Great,' Bea replied, hugging him. 'You were so good.'

'The crowd were on fire tonight,' he grinned, kissing Imelda's cheek and sitting down. 'It helps the flow, you know?'

'Let me buy you a drink, Mr Comedy Central,' Imelda offered.

'That's kind. A Bud would be great.' As Imelda headed to the bar, Russ turned to Bea. 'Thanks for coming tonight.'

'Wouldn't have missed it for anything. You really are good, hun.'

'And the new material? Because you haven't heard it before.'

'It's great. So much slicker than the last time I saw you perform.'

Russ beamed. 'Isn't it? The guys who run the club reckon it's my best yet.'

'I'd have to agree.' Bea was proud of her best friend. She didn't know how he did it: even reading to groups of children at Hudson River Books, while she loved it, brought her out in a stress rash. When she knew how nervous and paranoid Russ was before a gig, the change in his confidence when he was in front of an audience was phenomenal.

'Hey.' A smiling blonde appeared by their table, smiling at Russ.

Playing it cool, he turned to look at her. 'Hi.'

'I loved your set,' she purred, her body language completely focused on him.

'Thanks,' Russ replied, clearly flattered by the compliment.

Bea smiled to herself as the woman handed Russ a business card.

'So – call me. OK?'

As Russ watched his latest admirer's waggling behind sauntering away, Bea shook her head. 'What it is to be a man in demand, eh?'

Russ shrugged. 'You know what they say about women and comedians.'

'What's that?'

'I have no idea,' he grinned, inspecting the number on the card, 'but I'm gonna have fun finding out.'

Imelda returned with a round of drinks and, after joining Bea in mocking Russ about his comedy groupies, the three friends quickly settled into their usual banter. Bea loved nights like these, having fun with her closest friends. It had now been over a week since she'd last seen Jake – his new practice calling him away from New York sightseeing for the next few weeks – and Bea was keen to redress the balance of time missed with her best friends by spending time with them now.

From the Comedy Cavern, they went to GiGi's, a friendly local diner that specialised in serving enormous hamburgers around the clock. Russ set about demolishing two bacon double burgers with spicy pepper jack cheese, his ability to shovel food after a gig still impressive to Bea after years of witnessing it.

'I hear the party was a success,' Imelda said, trying her best to ignore the loud munching from across the table. 'One of the kids' moms came into my store today raving about it.'

'We've had three enquiries about parties already.' Bea knew Bronagh's party had turned out well, but even she had been surprised by the response following the event. 'I think we could offer it as a new service. If we did, would you be up for helping dress the bookstore for each one?'

Imelda grinned as she sipped her iced tea. 'Always. It was a lot of work, but fun, too. Just say the word and I'm there.'

'We ought to start planning our Christmas campaign,'

Russ said. 'It's October next week. I have some ideas already.'

Where had the year gone? Bea couldn't believe so much time had passed and how differently her life had turned out from the path she'd expected. When the year began, she had still been with Otis, ignoring his broken promises and listening to his veiled hints that this might be the year he moved their relationship to the next level. But March had arrived and with it the series of events that would lead Bea to call time on their relationship. And then, she had discovered a new friend in Jake . . . She couldn't have predicted any of that and yet, as she looked at it now, she felt more contented and confident than ever before. It had been a strange year so far, but a good one: and it wasn't over yet. What did the next three months hold in store?

'Why don't we arrange an evening to discuss it?' she suggested.

Russ nodded. 'OK. Come to mine tomorrow evening and I'll make dinner for us. We can go over all our plans and work it out.'

The following evening, Bea and Russ closed the shop and walked the five blocks to his apartment. Unlike Bea's apartment block, which had all the charm and crankiness you would expect in a century-old building, Russ' home had only been built fifteen years ago: a sleek glass, wood and stone building with open-plan, loft-style apartments that looked out over the fringes of Prospect Park. It was too stark for Bea's taste, but suited Russ down to the ground.

While Russ juggled pans in the kitchen, Bea sat on the wide leather corner couch looking over lists of possible ideas to tempt Brooklyn's residents into Hudson River Books for Christmas. It felt very early to be thinking of the festive period but in retail it was essential to be ahead of the times. Ordinarily they would have begun planning their Christmas campaign at the end of August, but this year Bea and Russ had opted for a more relaxed approach. The introduction of their monthly-changing zones in the bookstore had kept customers coming back and business felt decidedly more stable than in previous years. Bea was pleased with how much they had achieved: Christmas would be the crowning glory of an excellent year's trading.

Russ brought in bowls of steaming Thai food and Bea cleared a space between the plans on his teak coffee table for him to put them down.

'This looks great,' she said, inhaling the sweet spicy aroma of lemongrass, peanut and chilli from the glazed beef and pork dishes.

'Well, I *try*. I have more rice if you need it.'

'And generous catering, too. Is there no end to your talents?'

'Probably not. I am the great, untapped potential in Brooklyn.' He handed Bea a pair of chopsticks.

A thought struck Bea. 'Talking of untapped potential, have you spoken to Frank about our end-of-year accounts? We should probably check where we are with him before we commit too much money to the Christmas campaign.'

Russ dismissed this with a wave of his chopsticks. 'I'm

sure it'll be fine: The weekly books have been very healthy so far.'

Accounts had always been Russ' domain with the bookstore and he had worked closely with Frank Folds, the long-time keeper of Hudson River Books' financial affairs. Bea, who found accounts scarier than anything else, was glad to not have the responsibility – another example of how well she and Russ worked. While Russ hated ordering stock, Bea loved dealing with every catalogue, order and delivery. It worked perfectly. But Bea still worried every time end-of-year accounts were due.

'All the same, we should check. I know you think I'm paranoid but everything's going so well at the moment. I just want to make sure we're covered.'

'Relax. I'll call him tomorrow.'

'We really need it sorted, Russ.'

'I know. And I said, I'll call him tomorrow. You worry too much.'

'When it comes to the IRS, yes, I do. They aren't the kind of people you go around upsetting.'

'Leave it to me, OK? I'll do it. So, Christmas. Thoughts?'

'I think we keep it simple,' Bea replied. We don't want anything that will require too much organisation. The store will be busy for most of the month, hopefully, so I was going to suggest we dress the store mid-November and maybe have one or two new things appearing each week till Christmas.'

'I like it. *Or* . . .' his eyes lit up as an idea struck '. . . we could turn the store into a giant advent calendar.'

This was a typical Russ O'Docherty idea. It sounded

brilliant but was bound to entail a lot of work – exactly what neither of them wanted for the busy festive season. 'How do you propose we do that?' she asked, careful not to hurt his feelings.

'Chill, Captain Cautious,' he grinned. 'We dress the store early, like you say. Then we advertise that there will be something new every day from December 1st through 24th. It can be something small, like free candy or a discount off novels if you buy a coffee. The main thing is we're offering *something*. That way, every time people come into HRB there's something new.'

Bea considered this. 'We'd need to draw up a list and have everything ready to go on the first day of December.'

'Naturally. Think about it, Bea: one small change every day will keep customers guessing. We throw in a few larger deals to mix it up a little and people will love it. Trust me, this could work.'

Persuaded by his enthusiasm, Bea agreed and after they had eaten they compiled a list of advent surprises to integrate into the bookstore's Christmas schedule. An hour later, Russ made peppermint tea to celebrate a job well done.

'That's business over – and we are officially bookselling superheroes,' he proclaimed, raising his mug. 'So, how's everything else in your life?'

Bea felt her shoulders tense. Was this heading towards another Otis lecture? 'Good, thanks.'

'Oh no. You don't get off that easily. I need *details*.'

'Actually, I'm happy. The happiest I've felt all year.'

'But there's something else going on, isn't there?'

'*Russ . . .*'

'It's a valid question. I've been watching you for the last couple of weeks, Bea James. You've got something on your mind.'

How could Russ be so wrapped up in his own worries one minute and blindingly perceptive the next? Bea knew he was right: since the birthday party she hadn't heard much from Jake, only that he was busy with his new practice and having to work weekends to keep on top of it all. His absence had given her time to think, not least about the last time she had seen him. When they had stood in the office together, Bea could have sworn that a moment passed between them. He'd looked so unbelievably handsome in his costume and she had suddenly found herself wanting to be closer to him . . . But that was completely out of the question. The Pact stood between them, a safety curtain to prevent any romantic notions that might try to sneak past. Jake was adamant he didn't want another relationship: and considering how awful his impending divorce sounded from the little he had told her, who could blame him?

She didn't need to be battling with this, she had told herself over and over. The happiness and peace of mind she'd discovered since The Pact was entirely due to *not* thinking of Jake as a potential boyfriend. So why couldn't she get the image of him gazing down at her in the darkened office out of her mind?

For a few moments, Bea debated whether to mention Jake to Russ, but decided not to. Nevertheless, she felt the need to address her conflicted feelings. Perhaps, she thought, if she could broach the subject without being specific, Russ might be able to offer insight that would help her without descending into cheap 'Suit Man' jibes.

'You're right,' she began. 'I do have a – *situation* – on my mind.'

'I knew it!' Russ almost jumped off the sofa in triumph. 'Spill.'

Bea took a breath, suddenly shaky. 'It's a bit embarrassing, actually. There's someone I like. He's a really good friend and I love what we have. But recently, I've started to wonder if there could be more.'

'Go on.' Russ was watching her carefully.

'It can't happen: I know it can't. But a part of me wishes it could. Does that sound crazy?'

Russ shook his head. 'Not at all. It's natural to want something you feel you can't have. Could you – is there any way you could let the guy know?'

'No. The lines of friendship between us are very clearly drawn. And it's past the point where it could change, I think.'

'So you've known this guy for a while?'

Bea hesitated. If she said how long she had known Jake for, Russ would guess who he was and she would never hear the end of it. Since the birthday party, Russ seemed to have finally accepted that Bea and Jake's friendship was strictly casual. She hadn't mentioned him after that, so Russ was none the wiser. *Keep it vague, Bea* . . . 'Yes, I have,' she replied, aware that the truth was being stretched by the omission.

'And I'm guessing you're scared you'll lose this friendship if you admit your feelings?'

'Mm-hmm.'

Russ moved to the edge of his seat, his voice softer

285

when he spoke. 'Oh Bea. This happens, sometimes. We begin with the best intentions and life has other ideas.'

'But how are we supposed to move forward if life keeps throwing spanners into our plans?'

'We just – do. This guy, do you think he knows how you feel?'

Panic tightened Bea's stomach. 'I'm not sure. I think he might . . .'

Russ didn't speak for a while, sipping tea as he considered what Bea had said.

'Actually, I hope he doesn't know,' Bea added, before Russ could reply. 'That way I can deal with how I feel without it threatening our friendship.'

'I don't think it would be threatened, personally. I think, if you've laid the foundations of your friendship first, a relationship could be stronger.'

'You think?'

'Yes, I do. I mean, look at your previous relationships: out of all of them how many of your previous boyfriends were you friends with before?'

Bea thought about it. He had a point: the longest she had known someone before dating them was a couple of weeks with Otis, and even then most of that time had been spent flirting towards the inevitable. 'None of them.'

'Exactly! Maybe that's part of the problem. If you had a solid foundation to begin with, it could make all the difference.'

Bea rolled her eyes. 'Brilliant. So the reason my relationships have failed in the past is because I didn't make friends first? That makes me feel a whole lot better.'

'That's not what I'm saying, Miss Pity Party. I'm simply

suggesting that you could try something different next time you enter a relationship. If you already know somebody, a great deal of guesswork is removed. You know their bad habits and their annoying traits, all because as friends they aren't out to impress you. When you date somebody you hardly know, all you see is the version of themselves they want you to see. The bad stuff comes later, once you're committed. And that's when it becomes hurtful – because you feel as if you've been hoodwinked. You don't get that with a friend.'

'So what should I do?'

Russ smiled. 'Keep doing what you're doing. This guy's friendship obviously means the world to you. But look for opportunities. My guess is, he's battling exactly the same dilemma. If he is, you'll see signs. Then you'll know what to do.'

Was what had happened between Bea and Jake before Bronagh's party a sign? Bea mulled this over for the next few days as she and Russ began to pull together all they needed for the bookstore's Christmas advent campaign. There was no way she would know until she saw Jake again. And that might not be for a while. His most recent text message apologised for another weekend without a New York excursion, the practice commanding all of his time. Bea wondered if his absence might also be necessitated by the ongoing divorce proceedings. If so, she completely understood. At least with her and Otis the only thing to sort out following their split were the boxes of their belongings at each other's apartments. Dividing up almost a decade of life together, while a court looked on, must be horrendous.

She replied to Jake's text wishing him all the best with his demanding schedule, saying she looked forward to seeing him when time next allowed. With nothing more she could do, she turned her attention to her own business.

Almost a fortnight after the last letter from Grandma Dot, a new parcel arrived. This time, Bea laid the book aside – a copy of Jane Austen's *Persuasion* – to read Dot's letter first. She wanted to know more about Abel Flanagan and Grandma Dot's secret courtship and try to understand why her grandmother had kept the story to herself for so long.

> Dearest Bea,
> I hope my last letter didn't shock you. I hope you will understand why I wish to share this with you now. I am merely illustrating my belief that you should never rule out the possibility that you might find love again.
>
> You will see that the Book Mice have selected Jane Austen's *Persuasion*, one of my all-time favourite novels. We think we have time to waste, but life proves we have not . . .
>
> Abel Flanagan wanted me to marry him but not until he'd saved enough money to support us. I believed that when he had the means to provide a home for us, my father would see he was a man true to his intentions. Oh, how I wish I hadn't delayed our happiness!

Abel finally proposed to me in July 1939. I accepted, of course, but then faced the decision of whether or not to tell my father. I considered elopement – with the worrying events in Germany several of the village girls had run away with their sweethearts, fearing the worst. But I loved my father and had no intention of bringing shame on our family. So I asked Father if I could talk to him and he agreed.

As you can imagine, he was furious that Abel and I had carried out our courtship in secret. As the youngest in the family, he was always the most protective of me and had hoped I would secure the best marriage of all my sisters. Once his anger was spent, he listened to Abel's plans for us, saying nothing in return. When I pleaded with him for his answer, he said he would only give his blessing once Abel could prove he had earned enough money for the down payment on a house. I was devastated: this meant at least another year of hard saving and sacrifice before we could be together. But Abel assured me that a year would pass quickly. He said it would give us time to plan and dream. We thought that time was something we had. We were wrong.

That September, Britain declared war

on Germany. At first I was terrified Abel would be called up to the armed forces, but we soon learned his profession was to be classified as a 'reserved occupation': farmers were needed in order to safeguard food supply to the country. Even my father was pleased by this news and I began to hope that he might relent on his stipulations for our marriage.

By Christmas many of the young men from my village had either volunteered or been conscripted to join the Allied forces to fight. I thanked God every day that my Abel would not be joining them, already hearing awful tales of young men who went to fight, never to return. I planned my wedding and my mother and I began to work on my wedding dress and trousseau. Late into the night, we stitched and embroidered, talking about the wedding day and what might follow afterwards. Mother wanted at least two grandchildren from us: a girl and a boy. I remember her tears as she spoke of her own ambitions for my happiness.

I thought we had a lifetime to see those ambitions fulfilled. But within a year, I would see every one shattered.

Again, I must say, Bea, don't ever think you can put off affairs of the heart. You may have all the time in the world, but

*you never know what might be around
the next corner for the one you love.
I will write again soon.
Fondest love as always,
Grandma Dot xxx*

With tears streaming from her eyes, Bea opened the copy of *Persuasion* to the place marked by the yellow bookmark. A Book Mouse in Regency soldier's uniform pointed towards a pencil-underlined sentence in Captain Wentworth's letter to Anne Elliot:

Tell me not that I am too late, that such precious feelings are gone for ever.

If Bea was falling for Jake, would time prove to not be on her side? And how could she ever know, given his insistence on The Pact? For the first time that year, Bea feared that she might lose him. Grandma Dot had lost the love of her life in a way she never expected: could Jake disappear from hers as easily? The intensity of the fear shook her to the core, yet until she could see Jake again, how could she know whether it was real or not?

CHAPTER THIRTY-FIVE

Jake's practice, McKevitt Buildings, Broadway

'I can't see the divorce as anything other than rejection. My husband doesn't want me in his life any more, and he's willing to pay to be rid of me. My friends say I should be grateful. Most of them didn't sign pre-nups and lost everything when their husbands traded up. And sure, I'll be more than comfortable financially. But I truly don't care about the money. They don't believe me: I even lost one friend over it because she accused me of bragging about the settlement. Fact is, I still love my husband. Even after the affairs, the lies, the rejection. I swear, Dr Steinmann, if Bill walked into this room right now and asked me back I'd do it. I'd give up the millions and the house in St Lucia and I'd run back into his arms. Am I crazy?'

Jake rubbed his forehead. 'No, Joanie. You're not.' The session had begun with his client wanting to talk about her issues with her mother but had quickly become a heart-wrenching confessional over her recent marriage breakdown. Jake could tell her initial problem wasn't the main issue, but he hadn't been expecting this. With new clients it was impossible to know what Pandora's box lay in store for him to unpack until they volunteered key information. Consequently, he had spent the past thirty minutes feeling increasingly uncomfortable. Of course he knew how she felt: part of him wholeheartedly identified with Joanie Viners' wish to be reconciled with her ex. Jess had dug her roots deep into his heart: he couldn't remove them as easily as she appeared to be able to.

'Then what do I do?'

Jake took a moment to regain his professional composure. Joanie wasn't paying one hundred and fifty dollars an hour for him to indulge his own neuroses. 'You have to start looking forward. The mind is a powerful tool, but it can't influence the way anyone thinks apart from you. I would love to tell you that you can make somebody want you back in their life, but it just isn't the case.'

'What if I want it to be? What if I can't think of anything else?'

Jake sighed. 'Have you always defined yourself by the success or failure of your relationships?'

Joanie stared at him, debating whether to be offended by this or not. 'I – I don't know . . .'

'Then where do you source your self-esteem?'

'I guess from what I do . . .'

'For yourself or for others?'

Joanie blinked. 'I'm not a selfish person, Doctor.'

'I'm not suggesting you are. But how often do you feel

good about yourself because of something you've done purely for you?'

'Hardly ever. But I don't understand how this applies to my divorce.'

Jake put down his notepad. 'If you only ever feel good about yourself because of something you *do*, you never learn to accept yourself for who you *are*. You feel the need to justify your existence by what you can give to other people, because who you are doesn't carry as much weight in your mind. Therefore, Bill cutting you out of his life implies that what you *did* for him – for example, ignoring his lies and turning a blind eye to his infidelity – wasn't good enough for him to want your marriage to succeed.'

Joanie began to cry, her sobs reverberating around the office. Jake handed her the box of tissues he always kept nearby. 'I . . . *don't* feel good enough. If I was, he wouldn't have looked to other women, would he?'

Jake's heart went out to his client. Her words resonated with him; he had gone through the same conversation in his head since Jessica walked. It was a natural instinct, the human mind invariably prone to accept blame, rather than appreciate its lack of power over anyone else's decisions.

'Your husband made his own decisions and there was nothing you could have done to change his behaviour. Much as we'd like to, none of us can control whether someone else loves us or not. What we *can* control, however, is how we view ourselves. How we talk to ourselves. Where we draw our sense of wellbeing from. I propose we start to work on making Joanie Viners love herself for who she is, not what she can or can't do. What do you think?'

Joanie nodded, dabbing her eyes. 'I like that.'

'Good. You did good today. The hardest part is identifying what needs to be addressed. From here on in, you'll start to feel more positive. Same time next week?'

Desiree was waiting by the consulting room door with a hot cup of coffee as Joanie left. Jake accepted it gratefully: his brain hurt and caffeine was the only thing that could help.

'Thank you.'

'You look like you need it.'

Jake winced. 'That session was a little too close for comfort.'

'Oh, her divorce? I should have warned you, sorry.'

So much for client confidentiality . . . 'How did you know about that?'

Desiree observed him as if he'd just asked her what colour the sidewalk was. 'Don't you read the society pages? Bill Viners' divorce is all over them. He's paying thirty million dollars to Joanie to end their marriage. He hired one of the best lawyers and they were trying to get him to annul the pre-nup. But he refused and offered her over half his fortune.'

'Um, *wow* . . .'

'You ask me, that rat's after getting his reputation back. If he looks benevolent now, maybe the media will forget his cheating lies.' She sucked her teeth disapprovingly. 'Ain't gonna work, of course. But at least that poor woman gets what's owed to her.'

Jake took a gulp of coffee, wincing as the heat prickled

his throat. 'Sure. Because money solves everything.'

Horrified at her insensitivity, Desiree held up her hands. 'Forgive me, I'm so sorry! I didn't think—'

'Don't worry about it.' Jake's head had begun to throb. He sat down in the reception area and wished he'd brought a packet of Advil to work today.

'But I *have* to. There I was, spouting off about divorce when you're . . .' She sat down beside him and patted his knee. 'How is that going?'

'I have a meeting with my wife's lawyer next Tuesday. It won't be the highlight of my week.' He had told Bea the practice was keeping him away, but in reality he was trying to process both his unexpected emotions caused by the birthday party and the most recent letter from Jessica's lawyer, calling him to the first 'commodities discussion'. He couldn't think of both and still function with his packed client schedule; it was easier to put a temporary distance between him and Bea while he dealt with everything else. She was his friend: she would understand.

'Until I know how I feel about her, I can't move on.'

'Oh, Jake . . .'

A heavy ball of nausea dropped in Jake's stomach as he realised he had given voice to his thoughts. 'I mean, I—'

'Shh. No need to explain.' Desiree was speaking to him like a mother to a child, an approach that did nothing to comfort Jake.

'But you don't understand—'

'I'm beginning to. You have unfinished business with her.'

'Yes, I do.'

'And you don't know whether you can accept the way things have been between you.'

Jake looked at his PA with a new appreciation. She had worked all of that out, just from what he'd said? He knew she was perceptive, but this was a new level. 'She said that's what she wants, but I'm not so sure. The last time we met I felt something there between us. It isn't what we agreed, but how can I carry on until I know for sure?'

'You care about her,' Desiree said gently. 'You've invested so much in your relationship.'

'I wouldn't call it a relationship . . .'

'Maybe not now, but the potential is still there. I know you psychiatrists say you can't make somebody care for you, but what if she's feeling the same way? What if she's scared to go there, believing that you're OK with the way things are?'

Forgetting the professional distance he had tried so hard to keep between him and Desiree, Jake responded to her questions. It was good to be able to talk about his feelings for Bea with someone who wouldn't judge him. Avoiding specific details, he talked with her about the frustration he felt; that the possibility for more was just out of reach.

'Hey, Doc, we all want what we can't have.'

'I know. And this could just be a case of wanting the impossible. So why am I hoping she'll reconsider her decision?'

'Well, you're the expert. But here's what I know: hoping

is what makes us human. Even if every other voice around us is screaming that we're wrong. When my boy's father walked out I hoped for him to come back. *For years.* Now you could say that man deserved no second chances, no such hope. And I would agree with you. But we'd been in love once: I couldn't shake the hope he might turn up at our door again one day.'

Jake was surprised by Desiree's candidness. She had shared few details about her own life until now, save that she had a nine-year-old son and had raised him by herself. 'And now?'

Desiree rolled her eyes. 'Well, of course my hope didn't come true. I just learned he was the no-good bum everyone else said he was. But that doesn't mean I was wrong to hope for better.'

'So where does that leave me?'

'Still believing. Being true to yourself beyond all else. And if your wife has any sense, she'll see her husband still loves her and call off the divorce.'

Every muscle in Jake's body tensed. *His wife?* Too late, he realised that Desiree thought his conflicted feelings were towards Jessica, not Bea. And now he saw that, he kicked himself. Of course she would have thought that! Their conversation had begun with the mention of Joanie Viners' divorce: Desiree must have assumed Jake was struggling with losing Jess. How could he have made such a fundamental error?

I can't explain it all to her now. She won't understand . . .

'Thanks,' he said, reasoning that the best way to extract

298

himself from the conversation was to allow his PA to think her advice had been helpful. In a way, it had; even if, when he returned to his consulting room and closed the door, his thoughts were as confused as ever.

CHAPTER THIRTY-SIX

Hudson River Books, 8th Avenue, Brooklyn

Bea stared at the official-looking letter and sat down heavily in the bookstore office chair. She couldn't make sense of the words on the page: they appeared to dance as her brain struggled to control them.

> *We are writing to inform you that your company accounts have not been filed for the previous tax year. The matter has been referred to our investigations unit and you should expect a visit from an IRS representative in the next four weeks. Please be aware that defaulting on your company accounts is a federal offence and liable to significant fines or even imprisonment.*
>
> *Should you feel this has occurred in error, or wish to re-submit your account data for the year stated above, please call us . . .*

There had to have been some kind of mistake: Russ had always kept a tight ship when it came to accounts.

Every year he handed the stack of books to Frank, their trusted accountant, and he filed the company accounts with the IRS. They paid what was due and everything was settled. But now she thought of it, the IRS statement had been late arriving this year, although Frank's bill had already been paid.

Although it was only seven a.m., Bea immediately found Frank's number and dialled it. If there had been a mix-up, he could still sort it out before the IRS man came to call. She waited for the ring tone, only to hear a message informing her that the number had been disconnected. Starting to panic, she called Frank's home number. The same message played back.

Frantic with worry now, she called Russ.

A sleepy voice answered. 'It's too early, Bea.'

'We have a problem,' Bea said, her voice shaking. 'I need you to get here as soon as you can.'

'Are you serious? I haven't had breakfast yet . . .'

Bea's nerves switched to anger. 'I don't care!' she yelled. 'Just get here, *now*!'

Twenty minutes later, the bookstore door flew open and a thunder-faced Russ marched in. 'This'd better be important,' he stormed. 'I don't appreciate being summoned into work. I'm an equal partner in this store, you know, not your intern!'

Bea held up the letter. 'The IRS says they never received our end-of-year accounts. I tried calling Frank, but his home and office numbers are both disconnected. I can't reach him. What are we going to do?'

Russ paled, his fury gone. 'Hell, Bea, I . . .' He dropped his head. 'I should have told you.'

Feeling sick, Bea stared at him. 'Told me what? Did you know about this?'

Russ dropped his messenger bag by the coffee counter. He couldn't look at her as he spoke. 'Frank disappeared three months ago. I only found out because one of his other clients contacted me trying to find him. Turns out he's taken all of our money and skipped the state, maybe even the country.'

'You knew all this and you didn't think to tell me?' Bea didn't know whether to burst into tears or tear Russ limb from limb. 'We're equal partners, Russ – as you were so ready to point out when you arrived. You said everything was fine with the accounts – you told me not to worry. Why did you keep this from me?'

'Because I thought I could handle it,' he replied, still avoiding her stare. 'But the truth is, I can't. The accounts are a mess. I have invoices unaccounted for and hundreds of dollars of spending with no receipts.'

'I don't believe this.' The room began to spin and Bea leaned against the counter to steady herself. After all their hard work and everything they had invested in the business, a huge fine could finish them. What would become of Bea's dreams of success? She struggled to contain her emotions as the awful prospect hit home. 'I thought this year was our best yet. What happens if we can't sort this out? We can't afford an IRS fine – or worse. This could destroy everything we've worked for.'

'I know. But it won't come to that, I promise.'

'How? Have you found another accountant to help us?'

'Well, no, but—'

'Then *how* are we going to get out of this? Because I don't see you dealing with it!'

'I don't know what to say.'

Fuming, Bea tried to rein in her thoughts. 'Don't say anything. We don't have any time left to waste on this. Go home and fetch the account books. Then after we close tonight we'll start work on them. In the meantime, I'm going to find a professional who can help us. Hopefully without stealing our money and catching the first flight to Rio.'

For the next few hours, Bea worked her way through the Yellow Pages, calling accountant after accountant. But the short notice, coupled with an unwillingness to become involved with a business under IRS investigation, led to a pile of dead-ends. Real panic was beginning to set in: and in a last-ditch effort to solve the problem, Bea called someone she prayed would take pity on the bookstore.

'Hello, Dr Jake Steinmann?'

'Jake, it's Bea. I'm so sorry to call you, but I didn't know what else to do.'

'Bea – are you OK? What's happened?'

Bea bit back tears. 'We're in real trouble . . .'

'Who is?'

'The bookstore. Me and Russ. We've been the victims of fraud and now we're being investigated by the IRS.' She paused as the lump of emotion almost choked her voice. 'I've spent all morning trying to find an accountant to help us. But nobody will. The moment I mention the investigation they hang up. I'm no good at accounts and I've never handled them for the bookstore. Now I'm beside myself with worry and – and I'm so sorry to ask you when I know how busy you are . . .'

'Bea, take a breath! I'm glad you called. Give me all the details you have and I'll make a call, OK? We have an accountant my father has used for over thirty years. I'm sure he'll be able to help.'

Bea felt awful for dragging Jake into her business problems, not least because this was their first conversation in nearly three weeks. But the soothing calm of his voice set a tiny spark of hope burning within her; barely perceptible, but still there.

Ten minutes later, she emerged from the office. Russ was serving a line of customers and Bea joined him, refusing to make eye contact until every one had been served. When the store was empty, Russ turned to her.

'Come on, you're killing me. What's happening?'

'I spent all morning doing what you should have done when you found out what Frank had done. And nobody wanted to help us. I called fifteen firms and all of them declined to get involved.'

'So what do we do now?'

'I asked a friend and they've persuaded their company accountant to help us.'

'Which friend?'

Bea was too angry to tell Russ about Jake's help. 'It doesn't matter. I spoke to the accountant and he's coming here on Friday to go through everything with us. But because time isn't on our side, we need to get as much as we can in order before he arrives. He charges double what Frank did, so I don't want to pay for any time we don't have to. As it is it will probably wipe out most of the profits we've made this quarter, if not half the year.'

'I'm so sorry, Bea. We'll sort this tonight, I promise.'

'We'd better. Or else everything we've worked for will be on the line.'

Weary from everything that had happened that morning, Bea left Russ in charge and headed to Imelda's store. Russ didn't attempt to argue. As she walked through the October chill, gold and red leaves blowing down 8th Avenue, Bea wished she hadn't got out of bed this morning. She had been thinking for days of calling Jake, missing his presence in her week acutely, and while it was wonderful to hear his voice this morning, she was dismayed that the first he had heard from her was an overly emotional plea for help. So much for presenting the best version of herself. Would he think her needy, or – worse – using her predicament as an excuse to speak to him, when he had made it clear how busy he was?

Imelda flew into action as soon as she saw Bea's pale expression, ushering her to a table by the window and insisting she drink two large cups of coffee. 'You look like death. What happened?'

As her friend tried to persuade her to eat a huge slice of homemade key lime pie, Bea recounted the morning's events, ending with her embarrassment for contacting Jake. 'I don't know why I phoned him. I'd dialled his number before I thought better of it.'

'You were scared and you needed a friend. Jake is a business owner, the same as you. He was well placed to advise you. Makes perfect sense to me.'

'But I haven't heard from him in weeks. Why did I think it was a good idea to get him involved in our problems?'

Imelda smiled. 'Because you trust him. And, deep down, I think you knew he could help. Quit beating yourself up over this, Bea: it won't achieve anything. You asked for his help: he gave it. I don't see the problem.'

'Russ is such a moron. I can't believe he hid this from me when we could have been dealing with it.'

'He wanted to be "the man". You know Russ: his pride is legendary. My guess is he thought he could handle it.'

'Well, he couldn't.' Bea looked at her friend, tears in her eyes again. 'We can't lose our business, Immi! It's all we know; all we've worked for. Without it, what would we do?'

'It won't come to that, honey. I know you're scared, but you've found out in time to put the problems right. Any idea what you can do about Frank?'

Bea hadn't even considered this in the craziness of the morning. 'We should sue him, but it's hard to serve papers on someone who doesn't want to be found. I'll report it to the police once we've dealt with the IRS. That has to be our priority.' She dropped her head into her hands, wishing that she could make it all go away. 'I thought this year was going so well, but now—'

'But now you've had a setback. And you'll overcome it, just like you did when you and Otis split. Don't be too hard on Russ, either. He was just scared, like you are now. The best way to handle this is together: be united. Even if you think he doesn't deserve it. You guys don't need any more stress than you already have.'

Bea thought about this as she walked slowly back to Hudson River Books. She was still angry with Russ, but Imelda was right: if he felt even a fraction of the fear she had been accosted by, his actions were understandable if not wise. When she arrived back, he hurried over to her.

'How are you? Please don't let this change how you see me. I know I screwed up, Bea, believe me I do. But I did it to protect you, crazy as it sounds. I thought I could handle it.'

'It's OK,' Bea replied. 'Give me a hug and shut up.'

Surprised, Russ wrapped his arms around her and Bea could hear the rapid beating of his heart against her ear as they embraced. She didn't want to fight with him any longer. Their fight was with a much bigger foe and for that they had to work together, as Imelda had said. The important thing now was for them to do what they could to salvage the accounts before Jake's accountant arrived.

'I have something that will make you happy,' Russ said, taking Bea's hand and leading her to the counter at the back of the store. Reaching behind it, he produced a brown paper package, populated with Book Mice dressed as World War Two army officers. 'It came when you were out.'

Bea took it, grateful for the lift in her spirits it caused. 'Mind if I open it now? If it gets busy give me a shout.'

'Go. Enjoy.'

In the office, Bea tore open the paper, revealing a book of Wilfred Owen's poetry and several sheets of notepaper covered in Grandma Dot's familiar handwriting. The yellow bookmark marked a page where a solitary Book

Mouse dressed as a British soldier saluted three lines of *Anthem for Doomed Youth*:

> *The pallor of girls' brows shall be their pall,*
> *Their flowers the tenderness of patient minds,*
> *And each, slow dusk a drawing down of blinds.*

Bea opened the letter and began to read.

Dearest Bea,

By now I think you may have guessed what happened to end my dreams with Abel. Even now it feels so unfair. But it is what it is, and I can't be disappointed by my life since.

In the spring of 1940 Abel broke the news I never thought I'd have to hear. He took me to the flower meadow at the southernmost edge of his family's farm, where bluebells and primroses clung to the banks of a stream. It was our favourite place: whenever I think of Abel now I always picture him there. He took both my hands and I could feel he was shaking. He said he had something to tell me, but that I wasn't to worry or get upset. It was something he had thought long and hard about. He was convinced it was the right decision.

Then he told me he had volunteered for the British Army.

I couldn't believe it. He, out of so many of his friends who didn't have the luxury, had been given permission by the Government not to go to war. Churchill himself had proclaimed the importance of the reserved occupations for maintaining Britain's greatness in this dark hour for our nation. I pleaded with him to reconsider, to serve his country by feeding those of us left behind to defend our land.

It fell on deaf ears. Abel Flanagan was a single-minded, stubborn man with a strong sense of honour and pride. He wanted to go to war, he told me. He wanted to fight for Britain's honour, for the cause of good. Nothing I could say was going to change his mind.

I asked him to think about the plans we had made: the home we would make in one of the cottages on his father's land; the children we would have; the life we would share together. And then, I said something I have regretted for seventy-three years: I asked him to choose.

I had no right to do that. I had no right to force a decision upon him when he had already signed up to fight. But I was hurt and furious that he could have made such a decision without me. I felt what we had was worth more than giving his life for his country. I was scared, of course. But it was still the worst thing I could have said.

We parted on bad terms, Abel refusing to see me for a whole week until, at my wits' end, I confessed all to my father and he marched me to Abel's farm to demand an audience. I begged for Abel's forgiveness and, eventually, he gave in. But two days later, as I waved him off at the station, I could tell from the way he looked at me that something had fundamentally changed in how he saw me. I will never forget the expression on his face as the train pulled him away from my life. I am still haunted by it today.

Six months later, his mother came to our house in tears. And I knew, before she even spoke. Half of Abel's battalion had been slaughtered trying to defend an outpost in France. He was one of the dead. She gave me a letter, found on his body and returned by his commanding officer. It said:

Dorothy, my love
Nothing you could have said would have stopped me doing what I did. But I love you dearly and I know why you asked me to choose. When the war is over, I pray we will be able to make all of our dreams come true. But if I

don't return, know this: that you were loved beyond death.

Yours forever

Abel x

I lost my chance, Bea, not because of my actions but because life intervened to change the rules.

But here is the important thing: I thought my life was over then, but I was wrong. For eight years I refused to consider the advances of anyone else. I thought I didn't deserve to be happy. But life had other ideas.

I found my salvation in a handsome chap called George. You may remember him! He tried for a year to persuade me to go out with him and one night I confessed to him about Abel and the awful decision I had made. I expected this to make him run for the hills, but instead he listened to me and never once judged. Your wonderful grandpa was gentle and patient, coaxing my heart back into life. The love I found with him was more profound, more precious, than anything I had known before. And still, he kept my secret about Abel until he died. What mattered, he used to say, was that he loved me and I loved him. What had passed before was in the past. And he was right.

*Don't you see, Bea dear? You owe your
very existence to life's endless possibilities!
Don't give up hope with anything. And
never say 'never' to the possibility of love.
Fondest love, my darling,
Grandma Dot xxx*

It broke Bea's heart to think of her grandparents
carrying this secret for years; but she was touched again
by Grandma Dot's decision to tell her Abel's story. She
wasn't ready to consider a relationship yet, but perhaps
ruling it out for the rest of her life was wrong . . .

When the last customer had left the bookstore, Bea
locked the door and took a deep breath. She would have
loved to go home and collapse after the emotional day
she had experienced, but there was work to do. And *lots*
of it.

Russ laid out the purchase and sales ledgers, boxes of
invoices and piles of receipts on the floor in the middle
of the children's section and pulled up two beanbags.
Bea joined him and together they stared at the task ahead
of them.

'Where do we start?' Russ asked.

'I've no idea.'

'It looks bad when it's all together like that.'

'It looks bad any way you look at it.'

Russ groaned. 'I'm sorry.'

'It's OK. The main thing is that you're here right now
and we're going to work through this together.' Steeling
herself for the task, she rubbed her hands together. 'Right.
Why don't you go through the outstanding invoices and

I'll try to make sense of the account books and receipts?'

They worked solidly for an hour, slowly piecing together the disparate pieces of financial information left by the untrustworthy accountant. When the pizza Russ had ordered arrived, they took a break, Russ producing two bottles of beer from his rucksack. Bea could see some progress being made and her friend's determination to get the work done made her look more kindly on his actions. To give Russ his due, his only crime had been to put his head in the sand with the situation rather than telling her about it. The real culprit was the guy who by now was probably soaking up the sun in a tax haven, paid for with their hard-earned cash.

'Thanks for helping,' she said.

Russ smiled. 'I had to. I blame myself for not having the nerve to talk to you about it.'

'You should have. We've always talked about every-thing, Russ. I don't understand why you didn't think you could tell me what had happened.'

Dropping his head, Russ stared at the floor. 'I care what you think of me. And I didn't want to let you down.'

'Well, from now on just tell me if there's something I should know, OK?'

Russ lifted his head, a strange expression on his face. 'I will. Talking of which, have you moved on any further with that situation you mentioned?'

It took Bea a little time to work out what Russ was referring to. Then, remembering her tearful phone conver-sation with Jake that morning, she shook her head. 'No. Not really.' *That* was an understatement. After her emotional contact with him today he was probably thanking his lucky stars that he'd made The Pact. Neediness was not attractive in anyone, least of all in a potential partner.

'But you like the guy?'

'Of course I do.'

'So why not tell him?'

'Because it's not that simple,' Bea replied. *Especially after today.*

Russ snorted. 'Sounds to me like you're scared.'

'I am not.'

'I think you are. It's obvious you like this guy. Why not let him know?'

There was no way Russ could understand from the vague information Bea had given him about Jake. 'It's complicated.'

'I get it. You don't want to lose him as a friend.'

'No, but . . .'

Russ reached for the last slice of pizza, moving closer to Bea. 'You won't.'

Bea stared at him. 'How do you know that? Relationships can change everything.'

'They don't have to. Face it, Bea, you've known what you really want for a long time now. Don't you think it's time to ditch the excuses?'

It was late and the last thing Bea wanted was to have this conversation now. 'Russ, I know what you're trying to do . . .'

'Then don't fight it,' he smiled, reaching out to gently touch Bea's cheek. His face was close to hers, his breath brushing her skin.

'What are you—?'

Before Bea could finish, Russ was kissing her, toppling them both to the floor. Horrified, Bea struggled to break free, kicking his leg hard and pushing him away from her as he yelped in pain. She jumped to her feet and glared at him. 'What the *hell* was that?'

Sprawled on the floor, face flushed and eyes wide, Russ stared at her. '*That* was what you've been asking me to do for *months* . . .'

'No it wasn't!'

'Don't say that! All our heart-to-hearts, all your thinly veiled references to the guy who was a good friend: you were talking about me. It's been there between us for years.'

'We kissed once for real, that's all! And we agreed then it was a mistake. Whatever made you think I wanted you in that way now?'

'The chemistry! It's always been there, Bea, you can't deny it.'

Bea couldn't believe what she was hearing. When she'd thought Russ was being a listening ear for her dilemma with Jake, he was thinking she was subliminally inviting him to declare his feelings for her. How had she not seen what was happening?

'I'm sorry if I gave you that impression. But you're not the guy I've been talking about.'

Scrambling to his feet, Russ dusted himself down. '*Thanks* for the gentle let-down, Bea.'

'Oh come on! You can't be angry with me for your mistake,' she shot back.

'Yes, actually, I can. You must have known how I felt about you, Bea! Why do you think my relationships never work out? Because every day I come to work you're there! And you're everything I've ever wanted. Always have been. Since that first kiss at Columbia.' He rubbed the back of his neck. 'I thought you knew . . . And when you started telling me about the guy whose friendship you didn't want to lose – and wouldn't tell me his name – what was I supposed to think other than you had changed your mind and were falling for me?'

Shocked by his confession, Bea couldn't answer. Instead, she gathered up the account files and walked quickly to the office. She couldn't stay here tonight: the accounts would have to wait until the morning. Perhaps in the cold light of day she and Russ could discuss this rationally. For now it was just too – *weird* . . .

'Bea, I'm sorry.' Russ was leaning in the doorway. 'I scared you and I didn't mean to do that.'

'Can we just – not talk about this, now?'

'Don't leave.'

Bea couldn't look at him. 'I think it's best if I do.'

'Then at least tell me one thing: who's the guy?'

Bea frantically boxed the piles of invoices, her need to get away taking over. 'I have to get home.'

'Please, Bea. You owe me that much . . .'

'I don't owe you anything.'

'At least tell me who managed to get to you instead of me. I'd like to shake his hand. He must be pretty awesome for you to prefer him over the guy who has loved you for fifteen years.'

Bea felt sick. How *dare* Russ lay blame for his stupid crush at her door? She didn't know he still liked her after all this time: especially considering the steady stream of

316

girlfriends he'd seen over the years. How could he possibly accuse her of leading him on? 'That's not fair and you know it.'

'Maybe not. But, hell, what in life is? I'm not moving until you tell me.'

Was he trying to end their friendship for good? Fighting tears, Bea pleaded with him. 'Stop it, Russ! Stop pushing me!'

'It's a simple question. Why hold out on me now?'

'Because it's none of your business . . .'

'Oh really? I *thought* we were friends.'

'So did I.' She marched up to him, determined to leave even if it meant knocking him out of her way. 'But after tonight, I'm not sure we still are.'

Stunned, Russ stepped aside as Bea stormed past him. She was hurt and confused by her best friend's clumsy attempt at a pass and more than anything else she wanted to be as far away from here as she could get.

Dear Grandma Dot,

Thank you for your letter. I am so sorry you have had to carry all that pain alone for so many years and I appreciate beyond anything I can express that you chose me to share it with. I don't think you have anything to reproach yourself for: Abel loved you and that's all you need to remember.

I'm sorry to turn this back to me, but an awful thing happened this evening and it's blindsided me.

My best friend Russ, who I trust more than almost anyone in the world, made a pass at me. I didn't see it coming. And now I feel terrible . . .

I started talking to him while I've been trying to figure out the whole Jake situation. No specific information, of course, but he seemed to understand so I just told him how I was feeling. It never occurred to me that he was interpreting what I said in the wrong way. But now I can see that all the time I was talking about Jake and how I feel about him, Russ thought I was trying to tell him that he was the one I was secretly in love with.

I can't believe I didn't work this out before tonight. I feel like an idiot because now he thinks I've been leading him on. And although I'm mad at him, how can I blame him? If the roles were reversed I would have thought the same thing.

This is a disaster. I have to work with him tomorrow and I don't know if he's ever going to trust me again.

At the same time, I'm no further forward with the Jake thing. In fact, I've probably made it worse.

I'm so confused. And I wish things were different. Why does life have to be so hard?

I love you. Thanks for reading my woeful rants in these letters! I wish I could

*report better things, or work out this stuff
on my own.
Write soon.
Lots of love,
Bea xxxx*

Bea had just sealed the letter when a loud knock at her door made her jump. It was late: the only person likely to call on her at this hour was the owner of a certain smoky grey cat with a death wish. Smiling, Bea walked over and opened the door.

'What's Gracie done this time—?'

'Did the cat get out again?' There on her doorstep, as if nothing had happened, was Otis Greene. His black hair was longer and swept back from his face and his dark eyes were fixed on her.

'How did you get in?' Bea asked, the shock of seeing him again after seven months slowly permeating her consciousness.

'The caretaker guy. We go way back.'

'What do you want?'

Otis feigned offence. 'You mean you aren't glad to see me?'

Her heart contracted but she lied: 'Not particularly, no.'

'Bea. I'm hurt.'

This was not what Bea wanted. Today had been too confusing and upsetting without her ex casually strolling back into her life. All she wanted to do was sleep. 'What do you *want*, Otis?'

He stepped towards her. 'I want you, Bea. I'm being serious now. I've tried to live without you this year but

319

I keep coming back to one thing: I love you. I never stopped loving you.'

In her most private moments, Bea had imagined this happening despite everything in her wanting it not to be so. She wanted to think that she had moved on, shelved her feelings as easily as she had filed away Otis' belongings in her apartment. But looking at him tonight revealed how much of an effect he still had on her. 'Please don't say that.'

'I have to. I'm no good without you, Bea. We spent five years together: does that mean nothing to you any more?'

Bea rubbed her eyes. 'No, of course it doesn't. But I can't have this conversation tonight, Otis: I don't have it in me to fight with you.'

'Then don't fight me.'

'It isn't that simple . . .'

'I know I let you down. Hell, it's all I've thought of since we broke up. Didn't Russ give you my messages?'

'No, he didn't.'

'Why?'

Probably because he was too busy thinking I was in love with him . . . 'Ask him, not me. Please go home.'

'Not unless you agree to have dinner with me.'

Bea stared at Otis, not sure whether to laugh him out of the building or be angered by how easily he thought they could be reconciled. 'Sorry?'

'Have dinner with me. There's a lot I've worked out and I want to share it with you. Most of all, I want to apologise. You endured far more than I had any right to ask of you. I was a jerk. Please, Bea, things are different.'

Bea had heard all of this before: why should she believe him now? 'I don't think they are. You and I just don't work. I've accepted it; you should too.'

Otis gave an exasperated sigh. 'You think I haven't spent this time trying to figure out my behaviour? Trying to put it right?'

'I don't know what you've been doing. And it's too late. We said all we had to say when we broke up. I don't know what else you want from me.'

'The chance to explain: and I don't mean make more excuses. I've done more soul-searching in the last seven months than at any other time in my life. I've made some major decisions and I want to share them with you. No expectations; no pressure.'

'Things have changed for me, too. I've decided that I don't want another relationship.'

His eyes narrowed. 'I don't believe you. You're never happier than when you're in a relationship: you told me that.'

'That's where you're wrong. I've been happier without one this year than I ever felt when I was in one.'

'Well, that hurt.' Otis took a step back.

'It wasn't meant to . . . I'm sorry, it's how I feel.'

'Have dinner with me,' he insisted. 'Let's talk about this.'

'No.'

He folded his arms. 'I swear it, Bea, I won't leave unless you accept.'

Bea considered threatening to call the police, shouting loud enough for Alfonso the caretaker to hear and come to her rescue, or slamming the door in Otis' face. But none of them would get the message across to him. The fight was gone from her this evening; and she had to admit she was intrigued by her ex's sudden reappearance. If she accepted, he would leave and she could finally go to bed. She could always cancel the dinner date later. Resigned to the inevitable, she sighed.

'OK, fine.'

The way Otis lit up caused a small tug at her heart. When he smiled it was as if a million tiny lights snapped on behind his eyes. It had been one of the very first things she'd noticed about him.

'You mean it?'

'I said so, didn't I?'

He clapped his hands. 'You won't regret this! I'm going to show you how serious I am.' He backed away into the hallway, his promises still floating back towards Bea. 'I'll explain everything . . . You'll see!'

Bea watched until he had disappeared down the stairs, then slowly closed the door.

CHAPTER THIRTY-SEVEN

Javacious coffee shop, East 43rd Street

He *wasn't* hiding.

Honestly, he wasn't.

There was a perfectly reasonable explanation for Jake's decision to duck into the welcoming coffee shop on East 43rd Street that Tuesday morning. He wanted a coffee. And maybe a pastry. *Definitely* a pastry. How could he help it if the pastry in question was a contender for the World's Largest Cinnamon Bun? If it meant he had to spend more time eating it, surely that was a situation beyond his control?

He noticed an oversized clock on the wall behind the coffee counter and made sure he chose a seat with his back to it. What he didn't know, he couldn't be responsible for. A lady at the next table flashed a brief smile in his direction over her copy of the *New York Post*. Jake reciprocated.

See? This is a nice place. It would be rude of me not to give it my full attention . . .

The fact that Javacious was located directly beneath the offices of a certain Sheehan, Sheehan and Owen, attorneys of choice for the well heeled of New York City, was merely a coincidence. And that Jake was due to attend a meeting there with the lawyer he fully expected to be as detestable a sleazebag in person as his letters suggested was an unavoidable fact – even if, at this moment, he was doing his level best to avoid it. He shuddered at the thought of what lay ahead this morning. Bad enough to have to go through the legally protracted death of his marriage without having to witness the joy his wife's lawyer was taking in dragging him through it.

He stared at his mobile phone on the blond wood table and wondered if he should call Bea. She'd called him when she needed help last week. Could he do the same?

He thought back to a conversation they'd had one weekend, as they enjoyed coffee in Prospect Park. The first signs of autumn were evident in the trees that surrounded the small coffee kiosk in the northern end of the park, the tips of their leaves beginning to transform from vivid green to gold.

'I have another item for The Pact list,' Bea had said, blowing the steam from her coffee cup. 'One advantage of being single is never having to sit for hours in your apartment unpicking every conversation with your ex.' She gave a grim smile. 'Although I confess I've yet to fully master that one.'

At the time, Bea's sudden mention of Otis had seemed unexpected, a sign of their growing trust in one another. But now, as Jake remembered it, the occurrence seemed to take on a prophetic significance.

He'd added the new item to the list anyway, but then had paused, wrestling the question he really wanted to ask. The divorce had been playing on his mind, accompanied by unwelcome memories reminding him of how happy he and Jess had once been. Bea's confession made him wonder if she would understand what he was feeling.

Bea must have picked up the subtle change in the air between them because she raised her head and looked at him. 'You've gone very serious. What's on your mind?'

'Can I ask you something? About Otis?'

She gave a half-laugh – a subconsciously defensive move – but her eyes still smiled. 'Go ahead.'

'Are you still in love with him?'

The question's impact on Bea was clear: she raised her eyebrows and blew out a long, slow breath. 'Wow. That *is* a question.'

What was he thinking, springing such a personal enquiry on a brand new friend? 'I'm sorry,' he began, hastily trying to reverse the conversation. 'Forget I mentioned it . . .'

Bea had held up her hand. 'No it's – it's fine. Actually, I'm glad you asked. It's something I haven't spoken about with anyone else. And it's hard, you know, because most of me wants to be totally over him. He doesn't deserve me to still be in love with him: *I* deserve more than that.'

Jake leaned closer across the table. 'But . . . ?'

Bea shrugged, her smile sad. 'But I still do. Of course I do. I thought Otis was The One, crazy as it sounds.' She gazed out across the park. 'I spent five years of my life hopelessly in love with him, overlooking the short-comings and the disappointments, believing that the love we shared was enough. Even when it turned out it wasn't enough, I still loved him. I've just resigned myself to the fact that it will be there for a while yet.' Her sea green eyes flicked back to Jake. 'Is that how you feel about Jess? Are you still in love with her?'

Her directness hit him like a boulder. 'Yes – yes, I think so. Sucks, doesn't it?'

'Oh yes. Sucks big-style.'

They shared a smile. Jake drained the dregs of his coffee. 'Fancy another?'

'Go on, then. Actually, I'll get these.' Bea rose and grabbed Jake's mug. He watched her walk across to the coffee kiosk and noticed how differently she walked to Jess. Where his former wife strode like a lithe gazelle, Bea almost skipped, her auburn ponytail bobbing as she moved. There was something fun about the way she carried herself: it made him smile. Jake marvelled again at how much her friendship had come to mean to him. It was a relief to find someone else in the world who understood exactly how he felt – and didn't judge him for it. They were bound together by the misfortune of their own lives; their dark gallows humour a telltale currency of love lost. But it was good to be able to laugh about it instead of avoiding the subject, as his brother, Rosie, family and friends all felt the need to.

When Bea returned, she placed a fresh coffee mug in front of him and retrieved two chocolate muffins from her coat pocket. 'Extra fortification for broken hearts,' she announced, making Jake smile. 'Also, a bribe to get you to tell me more about Jessica.'

He gave a theatrical groan, but secretly loved Bea for

asking. He *needed* to talk about this – and Bea was the perfect person to hear it. 'What do you want to know?'

'When did you realise you were still in love with her?'

'Oh man, *months* ago. I just didn't want to admit it to myself. I'm still angry with her and I don't think we could be together in the way we were before, but how I feel about her hasn't changed. I wish it had.'

'I know what you mean. That's why I'm so determined to get through this and live life for myself. I don't want my heart to rule my life any more. It's had far too much time to do that already.' She broke the edge off her muffin and ate it, her eyes focused somewhere far beyond Prospect Park. 'So, would you go back to her if she asked?'

She was sounding dangerously like Desiree now. 'Wow. You really are the hopeless romantic, aren't you?'

Bea blushed, brushing the comment away with her cake crumbs. 'It could happen.'

'It could. But it's not going to.'

'Why?'

'You have to ask?'

'OK, fair point.'

'Has Otis tried to get you back?'

'He did, to begin with. Now I think he's got the message, so . . .' Her voice trailed off. 'Anyway, it's immaterial. Despite how I feel, he's not good for me. And when I take my heart out of the equation, I can see that he was never the man I needed him to be. Our relationship was mostly me doing all the hard work and him coasting through it. He said he loved me but – I don't know if his understanding of love is the same as mine. I keep thinking . . . I wonder sometimes if he loved me because I made it too easy to be in a relationship.' The sadness returned to her eyes again and Jake had to fight the urge to offer her a hug. 'I mean, I overlooked everything he did wrong and I never held him to account for it. I just rolled over, time after time, and made excuses for him. That's not love: that's being a doormat. I can't go back there if I want to have any chance of being the person I want to be. Do you know what I mean?'

Jake was nodding before she finished speaking, surprised to hear words he could have spoken of himself coming from her lips. 'That's why I like you, Bea James.'

'Mutual, Dr. Steinmann.'

Smiling at the memory now as he hid out in Javacious, Jake found Bea's number and his finger hovered over the call symbol beside it. He hesitated. What would she say that could help? She couldn't attend the meeting for him – or even with him; she had no experience of dealing with divorce. She might feel awkward, or worse, she might start to see him as a damaged separated man and not the confident, happy friend she seemed to enjoy spending time with. No, it wasn't worth the risk. *Although* just to hear her voice could help . . .

Jake jumped as the phone rang, Bea's name and number replaced by the caller ID of his attorney.

'I'm at Sheehan, Sheehan and Owen,' Chuck Willets said, the implied question mark at the end pricking Jake's guilt. 'You nearby?'

'Ten minutes away,' Jake lied, hoping that the sounds of the coffee shop weren't audible to his lawyer.

'Make it five, Jake. Don Sheehan's going nuts here.'

Jake stared at the considerable remains of his half-eaten

cinnamon bun and resigned himself to his fate. 'No problem. I'm on my way.'

Five minutes later, travelling in the elevator to the seventh floor, Jake felt his mobile vibrate and found, to his surprise, a text from Bea:

> Just wanted to say thank you for saving my skin last week. I think I might be a bit in love with your accountant. Doug has sorted everything out and settled our account with the IRS. Thank you. Russ and I owe you. Bea x

Taking advantage of his last few moments of freedom, Jake quickly typed a reply:

> Happy to help. Sorry I've been busy with work. We need another NY trip soon! Doing battle with lawyers today – pray for my sanity! Jake

If he believed in signs, Jake would have wondered if Bea had somehow sensed he needed a friendly word today. But rationally, he was simply glad that she had thought of him. As he waited for the elevator doors to open, Jake turned off his phone. For the next hour, he had to focus.

The friendly smile of his lawyer was the first thing he saw, followed swiftly by the extremely unfriendly visage of Don Sheehan. Jake congratulated himself for accurately guessing the appearance of the man intent on fleecing him in Jessica's name: he was squat, short and balding; a thin layer of sweat permanently beaded across his fleshy top lip; his expensive suit unable to contain the large gut overhanging his trousers.

Chuck stepped between them. 'Mr Sheehan, may I introduce my client, Dr Jake Steinmann.'

Don Sheehan offered a too brief, slightly damp handshake and turned his back on them both. 'This meeting is already late. I suggest we get started?'

His question didn't require an answer, sparking with repressed rage Jake would love to have unpicked. The man was a classic passive-aggressive: Jake could have used him as an excellent case study.

'Charming man,' Jake observed, as he and Chuck dutifully followed Don into the company's boardroom.

'Well-dressed sewer rat more like,' Chuck whispered back, winking at Jake as they sat down.

Don spread out a raft of papers across the desk. *Overcompensation*, Jake mused. *Width of desk covered versus the obvious lack of height in his chair compared to us*. It helped him to view the lawyer's personal behaviour as a way of gaining insight into his insecurities, because it reduced the power Don was trying his best to exert over him.

'I'll keep this brief,' Don said, avoiding eye contact as he studied the paperwork.

Withdrawal. Classic tactic to make us feel unworthy of his attention . . .

'I met with my client in San Francisco last week and she has instructed me to protect her assets in this process. The San Francisco property, beach house, car, investments in both her own name and jointly accounted for . . .'

'I'm sorry. Our paperwork indicates that Mrs Steinmann

agreed a fifty–fifty split with my client,' Chuck interjected. 'I see nothing here about sole attribution.'

Don raised his head and gave Chuck a look of pure disdain. 'If your paperwork is not the latest draft, Mr Willets, that is not my problem.'

'On the contrary, Mr Sheehan. If *your office* is incapable of furnishing me with the *correct* paperwork, that is very much your problem.' Chuck's smile was broad and unhindered, having the desired effect on his legal opponent.

'In that case, *Mister Willets*, might I suggest we postpone this meeting until such a time as the correct paperwork can be forwarded to you?'

Chuck was about to speak when Jake interrupted him. 'What does she want now?' He was tired of the legal tennis already and after psyching himself up for this meeting – not to mention booking the morning off work, which was costing him considerably – he was not going to let Jessica's lawyer draw out the process any more than was absolutely necessary.

Don stared at Jake, his puce little face puffing as he scrabbled for the advantage. Clearly he wasn't used to opposing lawyer's clients asking direct questions. 'She wants it all. She said you had agreed . . .'

'I've agreed to nothing,' Jake said calmly. His conversation with Jess in the San Francisco coffee shop many months ago seemed a world away: and if she thought she could twist his words when he had been at his lowest ebb, she could think again. 'Everything we discussed was off the record. If she wishes to proceed through attorneys she can do it officially, in writing.'

The lawyer licked his lips and held up a single sheet of paper. '*These* are her desired assets.' He slid the page across the polished oak table and folded his arms.

Chuck took the page and scrutinised it, handing it across to Jake and shaking his head. 'No. This is simply unreasonable.'

'And does your client share your *learned assessment* of this document?'

Jake knew exactly what Chuck thought about it. As he scanned the list of his former possessions Jessica was laying claim to, he weighed up the pros and cons of the question. If he wanted the divorce signed and sealed as soon as possible, he could accept all of his wife's demands and let her leave him in peace. On the other hand, he had taken a dislike to her lawyer and the bloody-minded streak in him didn't want to let Sheehan win. It would mean the process could be held up by more discussion, but perhaps that was worth it given the pleasure he would get from seeing the puffed-up attorney denied his kill.

'Yes, I do,' he said. *Take that, you self-righteous over-compensator . . .*

Don Sheehan looked as if he was on the verge of a coronary. 'In that case, I have no option but to go back to my client and review the situation.'

Chuck smiled again. 'As you wish, Mr Sheehan.'

Don scrambled to his feet. 'I'll have my office call your office and schedule a meeting next week,' he barked.

Chuck and Jake left the boardroom unaccompanied, Sheehan making a last-ditch effort to undermine their confidence. It didn't work: as was evident in Jake's lawyer broad smile as they walked through the plush offices towards the elevator.

'Well played,' he congratulated Jake. 'I'd say Don Sheehan knows we mean business now.'

'I'm not sure where that came from,' Jake admitted when they were in the elevator and safely out of earshot of Don Sheehan's associates. 'I just didn't want to let him win.'

His lawyer chuckled. 'That's as good a motivation as any to start divorce discussions. We're not looking to make Jess suffer: just to ensure you both receive a fair settlement. I know it's clinical and non-emotional, but that's the way the law works. Keep that in mind and it won't be as bad as you think.'

'Thanks. Glad to have you in my corner.'

'It's my pleasure. Oh, and one more thing, Jake?'

'Yes?'

'Next time you're hiding out in Javacious, fetch me a *venti* latte and one of those mighty cinnamon buns, would you? Might as well make yourself useful.'

Jake laughed to hide his embarrassment at being busted by his lawyer. Chuck Willets was *too good* . . .

A bell signalled the end of the elevator journey and the doors opened onto the grand, marble entrance lobby. Chuck shook Jake's hand.

'I'll call you as soon as I hear anything. Take care of yourself.'

Jake watched his lawyer walk quickly out of the building. He didn't relish the prospect of returning for round two, but he had survived his first experience of divorce discussions. With Chuck Willets representing him, he knew he could rest easy that Don Sheehan wouldn't be calling the shots.

He paused by the reception desk to turn his mobile phone back on, with the sound of ringing reception telephones and the click-clack of approaching heels on the marble floor providing a familiar New York soundscape in the background.

'Jake.'

At first, he didn't hear it, the insistent flash of his email notifications commanding his attention. But it came again, nearer this time.

'Jake.'

He looked up – and his heart stopped.

Jessica was standing in front of him, her Californian tan and long, sun-bleached hair setting her apart in the grey of the building's lobby with its pale-faced native New Yorkers. In her white dress, cream coat and heels she could have walked straight off the set of a Hollywood movie, her appearance catching the attention of male passers-by heading to and from their offices. She looked incredible.

'What are you doing here?'

Jessica smiled – and Jake noticed how much more sincere it was than the superficial gesture he had witnessed at their last meeting. 'I came to see my lawyer. And you?'

'We just met,' Jake replied, struck by a sudden urge to put distance between them.

'I had no idea.' Her eyes glazed over a little: Jake knew she was lying.

He didn't need her games today. He wasn't prepared to deal with them – or the old familiar pain her presence

334

wrought in his heart. Besides, he was already late for his afternoon clients. 'I have to go. It's good to see you.' He made as if to leave, but was halted by Jessica's long fingers catching his arm.

'OK, I lied. I came to see you. My lawyer doesn't even know I'm in New York. Don just mentioned he was meeting you at his office today and I knew this was the only place I would find you. I don't know where you live, or where your new practice is, so I had to come here.'

Jake couldn't take this in. Why, after months of silence, would Jess want to see him now? Wasn't her objectionable attorney in charge of all their communication? 'I don't understand.'

Jessica's eyes were wide as she gazed up at him. 'I *needed* to see you, Jakey. After you left, I had time to think.'

'I know that. I saw your revised list of demands.'

'That doesn't mean anything.'

'Funny. That's not what your lawyer thinks.'

'*Talk* to me, Jake. Like we used to.'

This was too much. He needed to leave, and soon. 'We used to do a lot of things that don't apply now. I have to go . . .'

'Please, just have a drink with me? Hear me out? There's so much I want to tell you.'

He should have said no. He should have used his advantage gained in the lawyer's office and swept out of the building. How could he want to talk to her when he'd been trying so hard to shelve the emotions from his marriage as he rebuilt his life in New York?

And then, there was Bea. She was a friend, but the question still remained over his feelings towards her. The message she'd sent him when he arrived for the meeting had meant more than he expected it to: what did that mean? Until he had worked that out, how could he make a rational decision about anything else?

And yet, ten minutes later he was back in Javacious, listening to the former love of his life tearfully confess the feelings she still held for him; hating himself for even being there . . .

CHAPTER THIRTY-EIGHT

Celia and Stewart's apartment, 91st Street, Upper West Side

Celia Reighton's eyes threatened to pop right out of her head.

'And you *accepted*?'

'I didn't really have a choice. If I'd refused he would have camped out in my hallway.'

Stewart handed a basket of warm bagels to his sister, but Bea declined. Her appetite had vanished in the week since Otis' late-night reappearance.

'I don't get it, Bea. Why turn up and promise to explain things at a later date? Why not just tell you there and then?'

'I don't know. Maybe because I wasn't in the mood to hear it.'

Stewart snorted. 'The guy's a *douche*. You should have sent him packing.'

Irritated as much by her brother being right than she was by the crudeness of his assertion, Bea snapped back,

'Yes, maybe I should, but you don't understand. I'd had the worst day of the year and Otis was the crowning glory. I had nothing left to fight with.'

'Oh honey, what happened?' Celia's perfectly manicured hand came to rest on Bea's shoulder.

The memory still smarted, but Bea shared it anyway. 'Our accountant absconded with our fee, leaving us in serious trouble with the IRS. Then, when Russ and I were going through the mess he had left, Russ made a move on me.'

Stewart gaped at her. 'No way! I thought you'd settled all that after you graduated from Columbia?'

'So did I. But it turns out that Russ has been waiting all this time for me to come around to the idea.'

'How embarrassing! How did he handle your rejection?' Celia's question had all the subtlety of a boot to the stomach.

'Badly. He said he understood, but we've not been the same since. I can't help feeling that this might have changed how we are with each other for good. I'm worried I might have just lost my best friend and business partner.'

'No, honey. My guess? He's licking his wounds and laying low. You've been friends for too long to throw it away over this.'

'I hope so.' Bea appreciated Celia's sentiment but still couldn't quite believe she and Russ could bounce back so easily.

Stewart wrapped his arms around Bea. 'Look at it this way, sis: it's all part of that brave new world you keep saying you're pursuing. The irony is, since you told the world you were done with relationships you've become irresistible to men.'

This did little to console Bea. 'Cheers.'

Celia ignored her boyfriend and took Bea's hand. 'Oh Bea, you shouldn't have to deal with all this. What did Otis say at dinner?'

'We haven't done it yet.' Bea had so far managed to avoid actually setting a date to meet with Otis and was hoping she could continue to put it off.

'Well, honey, don't you think you should? Better to get it over so you can move on.'

Celia was right: but Bea was still reeling from the week before and she couldn't face Otis while she felt this vulnerable. She knew from experience that he would spot it immediately and move in, like a lioness picking off the smallest, weakest wildebeest in the herd.

'I will. When I'm ready.'

Celia poured herself another coffee. 'Only you can know when that is. But if I were in your position, I'd be honest with him and cancel the date. If you don't want to hear what he has to say, you shouldn't have to. On the other hand, if even the smallest impulse in you wants to hear it, you owe it to yourself to meet him.'

When Grandma Dot's next parcel arrived the following Monday, Bea and Russ had managed to establish a dialogue based upon professional politeness. It was awful but workable: and for now it was the best Bea could hope for. There were book parties to prepare for and the mid-autumn sale to run, both of which kept them busy. Bea tried hard not to notice the gaping hole in their friendship, but during quiet times in the bookstore it was impossible to ignore.

'Parcel for ya,' Murray the neighbourhood postman sang out as he walked in, bringing welcome relief from the stilted atmosphere of the bookshop. 'Another one with the cute rodents.'

'It's a present from my grandma,' Bea smiled, passing Russ to collect it.

'Whoa, you're one lucky lady,' Murray nodded. 'All my grandma ever gives me is a headache: "When you gonna get married, Murray?", "When you gonna get a better job?" I swear that woman will bug me to my grave . . .'

'Another book?' Russ asked when Murray left. It was the closest thing to friendly conversation he had managed all day.

'Yep.'

'She certainly loves sending you them.'

'They're helpful.'

Russ shrugged. 'I didn't say they weren't.' He blew out a sigh and raised his eyes to the ceiling. 'Look, I have a stand-up gig tonight, so I was thinking I'd finish early. You know, to prepare.'

Bea kept her eyes on Grandma Dot's parcel. 'That's fine. I'll close up here.'

'OK, well . . . I'll finish pricing these sale books and then I'll head off.'

'Good. Thanks.' Every exchange was lead-heavy and cumbersome: gone was the effortless badinage they had always enjoyed. Bea wondered if it would ever return.

Wiping sudden tears from her eyes, she hurried into the office to open the parcel.

An illustrated copy of William Shakespeare's *A Midsummer Night's Dream* was wrapped within Grandma Dot's letter. Immediately, Bea sought out the yellow Severnside Book Emporium bookmark, finding it tucked into Act 1, Scene 1. A pencil-sketch Book Mouse dressed in an Elizabethan ruff and feathered cap was leaning against three lines of Lysander's speech:

> For aught that I could ever read,
> Could ever hear by tale or history,
> The course of true love never did run smooth.

Why would she have chosen those verses? Bea turned to the letter.

My dearest Bea,

It occurred to me that the only downside to our exchange of real letters is the time it takes for them to reach us. I was so sorry to hear about what happened with Russ. I hope this letter finds you both in a much improved state.

You may be wondering why I selected this gem of wisdom from William Shakespeare. To begin with, there is very little we can experience in life that the Bard has not written about. But secondly, I think this particular verse applies to all relationships in life, not just true love. We seek out those we want to love, but the obstacles and bumps in the road that life brings can throw us off-course. We just have to learn how to navigate them.

You will find a way to repair things with Russ, of that I am convinced. It might take time, and you should prepare yourself for that. But your friendship has remained strong all these years and, I'll bet, has faced more than its fair share of bumpy roads. It will survive this too. You just need to believe it will.

I know you wish it hadn't happened. I can only imagine how embarrassed you must feel. But here is where I'm going to say something I know won't be popular: Russ did the right thing. If you don't tell someone how you feel, you will never know what's possible.

That's what Russ did with his feelings for you. He found out how you felt - and even though it wasn't what he hoped it would be, at least he knows now. It was important for him to ask the question and equally as important for you to answer it. Don't be angry with him for being brave with you. There was a lot at stake.

As ever, the Bard is correct: the course of true love never did run smooth. But it is in using our courage to navigate the

bumpy roads that we discover what is real
and lasting. You may be disappointed,
but there's no substitute for knowing, one
way or the other, where you stand.
  Fondest love as always,
  Grandma Dot xxxx

Bea read the end of the letter again. Her grandma was right: she didn't like the suggestion. But it was true for Russ – and she had to believe that she could win back her friend's trust eventually. So, what should she do about Otis? Unless she asked the question of herself – and allowed him to ask it of her – she couldn't know what was possible. Putting off talking about her feelings with him was useless.

Until Bea talked with Otis there was no way she could even think about where her future could lie. And she had to admit that his unexpected arrival at her door had fanned old flames she'd done her best to bury. She didn't want another relationship, but was that just because her previous relationships weren't successful? If Otis was serious about starting again, could that be a different consideration?

Inevitably, Jake entered her thoughts. He was serious about The Pact, but if his wife changed her mind and asked for him back would he go there again? Maybe both he and Bea were in denial, hiding their true feelings behind a noble stance. Given the chance to start again, would they?

She dismissed this. Jake was proceeding with his divorce – that was all the proof she needed. As for her, unless she met with Otis she couldn't know how she felt – about anything. As she stared at her phone, she knew what she had to do.

Hi Otis. How about dinner next Friday at 8pm? You choose the restaurant. Bea x

CHAPTER THIRTY-NINE

W New York Hotel lobby, Lexington Avenue

Jake walked through impressive entrance doors into a sumptuous hotel lobby, feeling anything but comfortable. He still wasn't sure why he'd agreed to come, debating his decision during the entire cab journey from his office to Lexington Avenue.

One meeting should have been enough. Why come back for more?

That one meeting had led to his agreeing to another was a source of frustration and bewilderment to him. How had he let Jessica talk him into this? He thought back to their conversation in the coffee shop below her lawyer's office. Jessica had broken down as soon as they found a table, her sudden emotion taking Jake completely by surprise.

'I miss you. And I didn't think I would, you know? I thought I needed my own life: no marriage, no responsibilities. I managed for a while and I thought I was happy. But then Don asked me to write that list of assets

I wanted and suddenly it hit me, staring at our whole life itemised on one sheet of paper. I knew then it wasn't what I wanted. Because I wanted *you* . . .'

A waiter passed Jake and laid a porcelain tray on a low table for a businessman sitting on one of the elegant brown velvet couches. Jake noted the designer coffee cup and cafetiere, carefully placed as if by a feng shui expert, tiny indents in the tray holding everything in place. It was the kind of attention to detail Jessica loved and the reason why the ultra-stylish W Hotel was the obvious choice for her to stay in New York. It was too contrived for Jake. The lobby seating, which was designed to look luxuriously comfortable in hotel photographs, seemed to be cluttered by the people trying to be comfortable on them. Jake felt as if he was spoiling the aesthetics just by being there. His house in San Francisco had been decorated in the same way by Jess, causing more than one argument if Jake dared to put his coat in the wrong place or drink coffee without ensuring he had a coaster nearby to put it down on.

These were the tiny annoyances that had joined and spread, like hairline cracks across the surface of their marriage. If they were so easy for him to remember, why did he think seeing her again would achieve anything?

Jessica was waiting for him on a pale grey couch in the centre of the lobby and Jake ground to a halt when he saw her. She had her back to him, but it was unmistakably Jess: the straightness of her spine; the flawlessly smooth blonde mane; the proud tilt of her head. No matter where she sat, she appeared to have been placed by a photographer in order to achieve the greatest effect. And even though he should have been able to walk straight up to his wife

346

and address her as an equal, Jake found himself battling the same adolescent hesitance, hating the way his pulse still raced and his palms still sweated at the sight of her.

I'm still in love with Jess.

The realisation sat heavily on his shoulders as he dragged his unwilling frame towards her. It had been so easy to cover his feelings with anger and determination when she was in a different state, but now he was sharing the same space he knew his heart was far from fixed. He kicked himself for making such a fundamental mistake in thinking he was over her. He was *far* from over Jess. And she would know it the moment she saw him . . .

He arrived at her side. 'Hi.'

She stood and they shared a brief embrace. He was acutely aware of her pink pepper and magnolia scent: a personalised present from her father last Christmas. Nothing was too much for Mr Martin's little princess and Jake had quickly learned that if Jess couldn't get what she wanted from him, Daddy was always waiting in the wings to make it happen.

That's it: keep remembering the bad stuff, Steinmann. It's the only way to get through this . . .

Jessica sat a respectable distance away from him, managing to look completely relaxed on the not-designed-for-comfort lobby couches. She looked over her shoulder and raised a slender hand to summon the waiter. 'Could I get coffee here, please? And perhaps a basket of pastries – Jake, are you hungry?'

'I'm good, thanks.'

'Oh. Well, bring them anyway. He might change his mind.'

Jake stared at her as the waiter left. Was that how easy Jess thought this would be? That his mind could be swayed over the divorce as simply as it could over a mid-morning snack?

Jessica beamed at him. 'You might be hungry later.'

'I said, I'm fine.'

Her gaze flickered. 'OK, then.' She looked around the large hotel lobby. 'I love this place. When I knew I was coming to New York I had to stay here. I'll go home with so much inspiration for next season.' She smiled at him. 'And I'm happy you're here. I wasn't sure after – well, you know. I made a fool of myself in that coffee shop.'

'No you didn't.'

'Oh, I did! But I wanted to show you how serious I am about this, Jakey. I know I hurt you. And I'm sorry. I was just – confused.'

Jake nursed his coffee cup, aware that he was subconsciously using it as a barrier. 'You filed for divorce, Jess. You made me leave San Francisco. That can't be undone with a few tears over coffee.'

'I know it can't. But I hoped it was a start . . .'

What was she playing at? Was this some scheme cooked up with her lawyer to persuade Jake to accede to her demands? 'A start for what?'

Jessica's smile faded. 'I thought I made that obvious last time.'

'No, Jess, you didn't. Which, probably, is why I agreed to see you again.'

'Probably?' She appeared to be offended by the word.

'Just tell me what you want and we can move on.'

'I want us to halt the divorce. Get back together.'

Her words hit Jake like a wrecking ball. It was as if everything around him froze, Jessica's words hanging in the air like shards of suspended glass. Jake was aware of his breathing which drowned out the music and buzz of the hotel lobby; the steady beat of the pulse in his wrists.

Jessica was watching him for a reaction. 'Jake – please say something.'

Slowly, Jake stood, every movement requiring an unbelievable amount of mental effort. 'I should go.'

'No!' Casting a glance around her, Jessica lowered her voice. 'Stay. Let's talk about this.'

'There's nothing to say.'

'There's too much we haven't said. And I'm not leaving this city until you listen to me.'

Jake grabbed his coat. 'Have a nice stay.'

He didn't listen to her protests as he walked out of the hotel: he didn't hear anything but the furious words raging in his own head. She could have said many things to him today that he would have been prepared to listen to, but this? She had told him at their first meeting that she missed him, that she regretted hurting his feelings, but he'd assumed she was laying the groundwork for some kind of civility as the divorce proceedings began in earnest. He never thought she would ask for reconciliation.

And, actually, how dare she think she could call the shots on their future? Announcing the end of their marriage, filing for divorce and never once fighting Jake when he moved out of their home and across the USA to start again had all been on her terms. What right did she have to ask for it all to be reversed?

Jake marched on, fuelled by fury, the buildings of New York becoming a blur around him. There was no way he was giving up everything he had worked so hard to build in this city, just because Jess didn't want to let him go. So what if she wanted Jake back? More fool her for realising what she'd had after she had tossed it in the trash!

He was livid with her for even suggesting they reconcile, but behind it all one question remained unanswered: why now?

Was this a case of Princess Jessica altering her demands on a whim? If that were true, it had been an expensive whim already. She had filed for divorce and Don Sheehan's services were far from cheap. Add to that the cost of renovations she had already begun at Jake's former home and the considerable cost of a suite at the expensive Lexington Avenue hotel. Jess had never been one to appreciate the value of money – having a multi-millionaire for a father and a considerable personal fortune of her own had seen to that – but even by her standards, this was extravagant.

What had changed her mind? And how serious was she about repairing their marriage? Was this her father's suggestion to protect the precious lifestyle of his only daughter? But what about her tears? Jake had seen Jess use her emotions to win arguments before, but her tears in the coffee shop last week had been different. They didn't appear to be calculated then – they had certainly been uncontrolled; and that was remarkable as Jess could be a master of control. It had been that observation alone which had prompted Jake's agreement to meet her again today.

Far beneath his fury, a tiny voice suggested a different reason: *maybe she still loves me.*

Jake stopped walking. He had no idea where he was; his anger had powered his steps away from the hotel, causing him to lose all sense of direction. Breathing hard, he looked around for street names or familiar landmarks. A lump of raw emotion lodged in his chest and he had to fight the urge to cry. The last time he'd cried was while he was packing up his life on the West Coast, the emptiness of his home crushing him. How *dare* Jess pull this on him now?

Seeing a sign at an intersection for East 59th Street, he headed towards it, an idea forming in his mind. He followed it over Park Avenue and onwards, until the red, gold and brown flash of Central Park trees appeared ahead. Crossing the street, he walked down a path he had followed before, a few months ago. His heart was a muddle of emotion as he wound his way around curved paths beneath black iron lampposts until the Pond came into view. It was quieter today than it had been when he and Bea visited in the summer, the few people scattered around the benches wrapped up against the late October temperatures. The bridge was framed by flaming red and gold leaf clouds and chilly-looking ducks moved slowly across the water. Jake found a spare bench and sat down, wrapping his coat around his body to keep out the worst of the autumn breezes.

He wasn't sure why he had come here, but he felt calmer looking out across the water. It was strange that in all the time he had lived in New York City, he'd hardly ever come to this corner of Central Park: it had taken a woman born thousands of miles away in England to show it to him. Bea had made him appreciate a great deal about his home city. He wondered if her influence had played a large part in helping him resettle here. Certainly Williamsburg didn't feel as alien now that he knew her neighbourhood was close to his.

The red leaves made him think of her auburn hair and he found himself wanting to see her again. Finding his phone, he called her number.

'Hey, Bea.'

'Jake! Um, hi . . .'

'Are you busy?'

'No busier than usual. How have you been?'

He smiled against the phone. 'Busy – of course.'

'Those pesky lawyers aren't giving you grief, are they?'

'Well, you know lawyers. Always pulling surprises . . .' Jake flinched a little, the mention of lawyers bringing back the events of this morning. 'But I'm fine. Actually, I'm in Central Park right now. At the Pond.'

There was a pause as Bea took this in. 'The Pond? How come?'

'I was in the neighbourhood and, you know, I just thought I'd see what it looks like in the fall.'

'It's gorgeous, isn't it?'

'Pretty impressive, yeah. I was thinking, it's been too long since we last explored this great city of ours. And I believe it's your turn to choose somewhere for our next visit. So how about we pick up where we left off – say, Saturday?'

'This Saturday?'

'Mm-hmm. If you're free.'

'Um, yes, I'm free. But . . .'

'Yes?'

'No, don't worry. Saturday's great.'

Her voice sounded a little tense: had she felt ambushed by his call? 'Are you sure?'

'Yes. Absolutely. I'm just a little distracted by work.'

'Of course, forgive me. So, Saturday at eleven a.m. outside my apartment building?'

'I'll look forward to it. Bye!'

The call ended abruptly. Jake pocketed his phone and turned his attention back to the autumnal view. He would sit for a while longer, he decided. He'd rescheduled his morning clients and so, for the next hour at least, he could try to make sense of his thoughts. Pushing Jessica's bombshell to one side, he began to think about the woman who made him smile today: the one with whom any kind of future was utterly impossible.

Welcome to your life, Jake Steinmann. Now what?

CHAPTER FORTY

Imelda's apartment, 7th Avenue, Brooklyn

'You look incredible.'

'I look a *mess*.'

Imelda playfully slapped Bea's hand. 'You're panicking.'

'I'm not. It's just dinner with my ex. What's to panic about?'

'I don't think I'm the one you should be asking.'

Bea looked at her reflection in the mirrored door of Imelda's closet. 'Why am I getting so nervous about this, Immi? Otis means nothing to me now. I'm over all of the heartache he put me through and I'm finally happy with my life – apart from the Russ thing . . .'

'And the *Jake* thing,' Imelda added, a wicked glint in her eyes. 'Will you be this wound up when you see him tomorrow?'

'Oh, I hope not. I'll be a nervous wreck by Sunday. I should have told him this weekend wasn't possible.'

Imelda pinned up the last of Bea's hair and took a

step back to admire her work. 'Why? You've missed seeing him, that much I know.'

'Yes, I have. But his timing *sucks*.'

'That's men for you. Never expect them to do anything but at inopportune moments. Anyway, why not see tomorrow as your reward for surviving tonight? Let's face it, with Otis Greene you *need* something to look forward to.' She took a can of hairspray from her dressing table and sprayed a fine mist over Bea's hair. 'Are you worried he'll stand you up again?'

The thought hadn't even occurred to Bea: she had been preoccupied with what on earth she would say to him. Now, as she considered the possibility of an Otis Greene no-show, her nerves threatened to take over completely. 'What will I do if that happens? I don't think I could bear it . . .'

'OK, that's *enough*.' Imelda grabbed Bea's hand and marched her through to her living room, depositing her friend on the sofa and pouring a large glass of wine. She forced it into Bea's hands. 'Drink that. It will help.'

Bea obeyed, the warm glow of alcohol hitting her nerves head-on. She closed her eyes and took a deep breath as the wine went down. 'Thank you.'

'You're welcome. And hey, look at it this way: if Otis doesn't show up, you could always catch a cab to Jake Steinmann's apartment and tell him you love him.' She grinned as she saw Bea's shock at her suggestion. 'Tell him this pact thing is absurd and that you would drop your side of the bargain like a hot bolt if he wanted to be with you.'

Bea couldn't believe Imelda had chosen this moment to bring up her wildly unfounded Jake theory. 'You've got this completely wrong. Jake and I are friends.'

'So you've told me a million times.'

'Because that's the truth! Why does everybody assume I secretly want a relationship when I say I'm done with them? You, Stew, Celia – even Russ, back when he was speaking to me . . .'

Imelda relented. 'OK, I'm sorry. I'm just telling you what I see. I'm not saying I'm right.'

The alcohol was working its way into Bea's bloodstream and she felt a little woozy. Leaning back against the cushions she scrutinised her newly painted nails. 'I never wanted to be in this situation. I wanted to be able to walk away from Otis and rubbish relationships and just enjoy life. Why has this come back to haunt me?'

Her friend draped a peacock blue pashmina around her shoulders. 'Because you guys have unfinished business. Neither of you dealt with the issues in your relationship when you broke up: you need to do that to get the closure you want. Get through tonight, be honest with Otis about the issues you had and don't let him off the hook. Deal with it, once and for all. Then you'll be free to get on with however you want to live your life.' She hugged her. 'And now you're ready to go.'

In the taxi heading to the restaurant, Bea bumped her head against the window. Her nerves were getting the better of her, not helped by once again having to justify her friendship with Jake. This was not how she wanted to be. She had to pull herself together and return to the emotional high she had been so happy in when she wrote to Grandma Dot proclaiming her new life decision to be a roaring success.

'You been to this restaurant before?' the cab driver asked, parking outside a small restaurant lit by a canopy of white fairy lights.

'No. A friend suggested it.'

'You'll like it. It's my wife's favourite place.'

Bea smiled. 'Great.'

'And my wife has excellent taste.'

'I'm sure she has.'

'Plus, it's cheap. That's why *I* like it.'

Sounds about right for Otis. Bea paid the driver and walked inside.

The interior of O'Jay's was a little old-fashioned but welcoming with a family restaurant feel. Several large groups of families were enjoying home-style food such as chicken fried steaks, racks of sticky ribs, Philly cheese steak sandwiches with mountains of fries in red plastic baskets and huge pitchers of beer and iced tea. It was less threatening than a more expensive, more intimate restaurant would be and Bea was relieved that Otis had chosen such a venue for their dinner discussion.

She was waiting to be seated when her phone buzzed in her bag.

'Hello?'

'Bea, darling, it's Celia.'

'Hi. I'm out at the moment, hun. Can I call you tomorrow?'

'I know it's your date with Otis tonight—'

Bea bristled. 'It isn't a date . . .'

'Whatever. There's something I wanted to tell you before you go to the restaurant.'

'I'm here now . . .'

The waiter approached and stood in front of her with a menu, not wanting to interrupt the call but clearly keen to get her seated as a queue was forming behind her.

'Darling, I just need two minutes of your time . . .'

'I'm being seated. Sorry, honey, I'll call you tomorrow. Bye!' She smiled sheepishly at the impatient waiter. 'Sorry about that. I believe the reservation is in the name of Greene?'

The waiter checked the list. 'Greene party. Follow me.'

Bea walked through the restaurant to an adjoining room with one long table at its centre. At one end, Otis was seated. Seeing Bea, he stood to greet her.

'You see? I'm here early. A good change, right?'

The waiter departed and Bea sat opposite her smiling ex. She peered along the table. 'Didn't they have a smaller table? It seems odd for two of us to take a table for this many people.'

Otis smiled. 'It's part of the dining experience. Like Wagamama, only in a family restaurant. Relax, it'll be fine.'

None the wiser, Bea poured a glass of water. 'It seems a nice place. Apparently my cab driver's wife loves it here.'

'It's a little old-school, but I kinda like the charm. And the food is good.' He took a long, lingering look at Bea, making her a little uncomfortable. 'You look great, Bea. Thank you for coming.'

They ordered and Otis asked for a bottle of red wine,

which he proceeded to serve. Bea's nerves were no calmer than they had been at Imelda's apartment and she took full advantage of her glass as soon as it was poured. Throughout their meal Otis made polite conversation, asking about the bookstore, Bea's family, Russ and more, adding to the surreal nature of the evening. It was almost as if he was avoiding the very reason he had asked her to have dinner with him; and Bea couldn't decide if this was a delaying tactic while he mustered up courage to talk about it or plain head-in-the-sand avoidance of the elephant in the room.

She declined dessert, her stomach churning by this point, ordering black coffee instead. Eventually, she could bear it no longer. She had to know what Otis wanted to say to her.

'Why did you want to meet me?'

Otis looked blank. 'Haven't we had a good time together?'

'Don't avoid the question. You didn't turn up at my door at almost midnight to invite me for an evening of small talk in a cheap and cheerful restaurant.'

'You don't like the restaurant? I thought you did . . .'

Bea folded her arms. 'You know what I mean. What's going on?'

'OK.' Otis admitted defeat, putting his napkin on the too-long table and pushing his chair back to stand up.

Thoroughly confused, Bea watched him walk to the connecting door to the main restaurant area and say something to someone beyond it that she couldn't make out. Then, he walked back to his seat and said nothing. Bea was about to demand an explanation when the sound of approaching feet and voices came from the other side of the door. To her utter surprise, Bea saw the faces of her family members as they slowly walked into the room: Aunt Ruby, Gramps, Uncle Gino, Stewart, a very apologetic Celia and – last but not least – Bea's own mother and father.

Stunned, Bea stood and hugged them, tears falling freely when her parents both wrapped their arms around her at once. 'What are you doing here? I thought you were in New Orleans this week?'

'We rescheduled –' her mother said, casting a wry glance in Otis' direction '– *again*.'

'I don't understand . . .' This was by far the strangest evening of her life. None of it made any sense: and Otis was in the middle of it all, pleased with himself and chatting to her family as if the last seven months hadn't happened. *What* was going on?

Otis saw her confusion and tapped a water glass with a spoon to quieten the conversation around the table.

'I guess this is a shock to you, Bea. But don't worry: you'll see why you're here this evening.'

All eyes around the table were now on Otis as he stood.

'Seven months ago, I made the biggest mistake of my life. I let down the woman I loved – and not for the first time. But that night was *meant* to be special, which made what I did even worse. I've gathered you all here now to apologise for my mistake. I didn't just let Bea down: I let all of you down, when some of you had made considerable sacrifices to be there. I'm truly sorry. And I intend to make amends.'

'About time we got an apology,' Aunt Ruby barked, quickly hushed by Uncle Gino and Bea's mother. 'What? I was only *saying* . . .'

'You're right, Ruby. It's been too long coming. I hope you'll accept it now?'

Ruby waved her assent without smiling.

Otis turned to face Bea, who was feeling increasingly claustrophobic under the scrutiny of her family. 'Most of all, I owe you an apology, Bea. Not only for letting you down many times when we were together, but for not being the man you deserved in your life . . .'

This was getting too much. 'Otis, please don't—'

He held up his hand to silence her. 'Just let me say this. I took us for granted and you didn't deserve that. I was selfish and scared and when I had the opportunity to step up to the plate, I freaked out. I'm sorry.'

'Thank you for saying that. Now *sit down* . . .'

'I'm not done. I've done a great deal of thinking since we broke up and I've been dealing with my issues. I was selfish and wrapped up in my own life: and that meant I lost you. Not a day has gone by when I didn't regret that. And I've missed you, Bea, so much. We had five years together and I didn't realise what I had until you were gone. But I want to make amends – and show you that I've changed. I'm not scared any longer. I know what I want.'

It's too little, too late. The time for this apology was months ago . . .

'This is a nice gesture, Otis, but it doesn't mean anything. I've moved on, and so have you. I'm not the same person I was then . . .'

361

'And neither am I. That's why I called your family together this evening. I don't want to make the same mistake I made this year. I'm ready, Bea, to be everything you need and deserve me to be.'

Bea gasped as Otis dropped to one knee beside her chair, producing a small red velvet box from his trouser pocket and opening it to reveal a sizeable oval-cut diamond ring. Somewhere way in the distance, she heard her mother sob and Aunt Ruby make a noise as close to pleased surprise as she could manage. Bea felt sick with shock, her head swimming and the room suddenly impossibly hot as the light from the precious stone glinted and danced through the tears now drowning her vision.

Bea's world went into slow motion. When Otis spoke it sounded like he was talking underwater.

'I'm here and I'm yours. And I'm asking you to marry me.'

Bea stared at Otis, her heart flipping when she saw genuine love shining in his dark eyes. It was as if she had been transported back to the first six months they were together, long before the disappointments began and frustrations set in. Had she been avoiding how she felt about him all this time? Did she still love Otis?

Her gathered family were watching her with expectant hope, her brother and Celia a little more cautious than her parents, who were beaming at each other. They were waiting for her answer. Otis was waiting, too . . .

This was what she *said* she wanted at the start of the year. Otis was here, now, offering everything she had hoped for.

'I don't know.' Her voice came from somewhere else.

362

Otis, still down on his knees, said nothing.

'Can we get dessert while we're waiting?' Aunt Ruby's whisper was audible to all. 'What? Can I help it if I'm hungry?'

'I said, I don't know. You've dropped this on me out of nowhere. How am I supposed to give you an answer when I haven't seen you for months?'

Her family began to shift in their seats.

'You gotta know whether you love the guy or not, Beatrix.' Uncle Gino, usually the quietest of the American branch of the family, leaned across the table.

'I thought I did. But that was seven months ago.'

'So, he was a jerk. So what? All men are jerks at some point. He's seen his mistakes and he's trying to make it up to you . . .'

'Gino, *enough*.' Bea's mother was on her feet. 'Darling, don't listen to anything but your own heart. Only you can know how you feel. You shouldn't be pressured to perform for us.'

'Appreciate that, Mrs J,' Otis said through gritted teeth.

'You're *welcome*, Otis.'

'I just want an answer, Bea. Even if it's a maybe. I have to know if I still have a chance to love you.'

Bea honestly didn't know how she felt. But she knew she wasn't ready to commit to Otis when he had only just reappeared in her life. It was wrong of him to put her on the spot: and while she could see his logic for inviting her family to witness his proposal, it didn't help her to think clearly. This evening was meant to be about dealing with the issues they'd had, not sweeping them under a magnificent new carpet.

'Otis, get up.'

Crestfallen, he shook his head. 'No, Bea. *Please* . . .'

'I can't give you an answer now.'

'Then you'll think about it?' The ring still hovered inches from her face.

'Yes.' Had that word really come from her mouth?

Appeased by this, Otis stood. 'Then I'll wait for your answer.'

'Good. Can we *go* now?' Aunt Ruby was struggling out of her chair.

Otis nodded. 'Sure. Class dismissed.'

Casting concerned glances at Bea, Uncle Gino and Gramps waved as they followed Aunt Ruby out.

'Next time that young man invites us out anywhere, remind me to eat before I arrive,' Ruby's voice floated through the door.

Celia looked over at Bea. 'Do you need a ride home, darling? We're taking your folks back to their hotel.'

Bea realised she was shaking. It was time to leave. 'Yes, please.'

Otis kissed her cheek. 'Take all the time you need. I'll be waiting.'

Flanked by her parents, brother and Celia, Bea hurried out of the restaurant. The street outside was cold and still, the beginnings of a frost forming on the windscreens of cars parked on either side. Her breath billowed out in icy clouds as her father's arm slid around her shoulders.

'Are you OK, Bea-Bea?'

'I'm fine, Dad. It's just a shock.'

'You did the right thing, darling,' her mother assured her. 'Otis put you in an impossible situation and we all unwittingly added to it. When he called us on the road I assumed the two of you had been working through your problems.'

'No. He turned up at my door last week, late at night, and asked me to have dinner with him. I thought he was going to apologise so we could part on good terms. I never expected *this*.'

Celia took Bea's hand. 'I tried to warn you, honey. Stewart told me that Otis had called this evening and I didn't want you to be ambushed.'

Of course! Celia's attempt was badly timed but now Bea understood why Celia had insisted on talking to her when she arrived at the restaurant. 'I appreciate the thought.'

The lights of an approaching yellow cab appeared at the intersection up the street and drove towards them. Bea had never been so glad to see a taxi.

They didn't speak as the cab headed to Boerum Hill, her family understanding Bea's need to be quiet. When they reached her apartment block, her mother stroked her hair.

'Will you be all right, darling? I'm sure there's room at our hotel if you'd rather not be by yourself tonight.'

'Thanks, Mum. I think I just want to be in my own space. How long are you and Dad here for?'

'We have an early flight back to New Orleans in the morning,' her father said, his eyes sad. 'We left the Winnebago with friends there and they're going to pick us up from the airport. We could always postpone . . . ?'

'No, please don't.' Her poor parents had been inconvenienced enough by Otis' whims on their holiday of a lifetime. 'I love you both. Call me when you get there, OK?'

'I'll check in on you next week, sis,' Stewart promised.

'Wait, darling.' Bea's mother climbed out of the taxi and took her hands in hers. 'You were very brave tonight. And I'm sorry we unwittingly played a part in that embarrassing situation. When Otis called us, we thought you two had already spoken.'

'Mum, it's fine. You couldn't have known.'

'No, it's not fine. But I want you to know how incredibly proud we are of you, sweetheart. Just as you are. I know you think we're keen to see you settled down but all we really want is for you to be happy. And you seem to have been happier this year being on your own than Dad and I have seen in a long time. Only you can know what's best for you. And we love you. So you take all the time you need to work this out. And don't ever think you're a failure because you're not.'

Her mum's words meant the world to Bea and she hugged her tightly. 'Thanks, Mum. You and Dad enjoy the last leg of your holiday.' She held her smile steady and waved from the sidewalk as the cab drove away.

Up in her apartment at last, Bea climbed into bed without getting undressed. Cocooned within the private sanctuary of her bed sheets, away from the world, she turned her face into her pillow and sobbed.

CHAPTER FORTY-ONE

Empire State Building, 5th Avenue

'Are you OK?'

Jake asked the question he had wanted to ask all morning. Bea seemed to be lacking her usual sparkle today and he was reminded of her countenance when she'd first approached the bar at Rosie and Ed's party. It was strange to see her this way after months of witnessing her sunny, carefree personality. Yesterday she had sounded fine, if a little tired, when he spoke to her. So what had changed?

'Of course I am.'

'Forgive me if I don't believe you.'

'Honestly, I'm fine. I had a bit of a late night, that's all.'

'Out on the tiles?' Jake asked, hoping his joke would bring Bea's smile back.

'Um, no.' *There* was that hesitation again: what was going on with her? 'Family thing,' she added, her brief smile little consolation.

Whatever was on her mind, Jake was unlikely to be party to it. He couldn't blame her for not sharing it with him – after all, he had secrets of his own. The meeting with Jessica yesterday had thrown him and once he'd calmed down, other questions came to mind. Questions he didn't want to even give a second of his time to. But questions he knew wouldn't go away . . .

They had come to one of New York's most famous landmarks: the Empire State Building. Bea confessed in the cab on the way to Number 350, 5th Avenue that she hadn't been to the top of the famous structure since she was at Columbia. It was a definite tourist choice and differed greatly from the more personal venues she had chosen previously, but Jake didn't care. Given Bea's mood and his own battered state of mind, it was a safe choice – and might even be fun.

'We should have booked a time,' Bea said, as the long queue moved slowly towards the entrance.

'I didn't think of that.'

'You didn't know we were coming here,' Bea smiled, causing Jake's heart to lift. 'I did. I should have remembered the queues are worse from eleven.'

Jake looked at the line of international tourists and American holidaymakers with their identical shorts, white trainers, polo shirts and sun visors in front of them and chuckled.

Bea looked up at him. 'What?'

'I was just thinking: d'you think you and I will be taking pan-American coach tours and steaming pleats into our shorts when we're their age?'

Bea followed his nod and laughed a little. 'Gosh, I

hope so. I wonder how old you have to be before you learn the secret of the blinding white trainers?'

'My guess is somewhere around the age of sixty-five,' Jake replied, encouraged by his friend's willingness to play the game. 'You get a visit from the FBI and are made to swear an oath of secrecy before it's revealed.'

Her smile was a welcome sight. 'I'll look forward to that, then. This queue is taking forever. I'm sorry, Jake.'

'As New Yorkers we have failed.'

'We have.'

'You know, those guys in the visors don't look too healthy. I think we could take them down . . .'

Jake grinned as his comment had the desired effect, sending Bea into a fit of giggles. It was such a relief to hear her laugh and it meant he could stop worrying that she was growing tired of his company. It was important to him that they both had fun today and he was determined to make it happen.

With Bea's mood lightening, the next hour in the queue passed quickly. She and Jake began to discuss different cunning schemes to bypass the queue, from rocket packs to stink-bombs, ninja tactics to David-Copperfield-style stunts.

When they at last reached the 86th floor Observatory outside deck, the view of New York halted their jokes as Jake and Bea gazed out across their city.

'Hello, NYC,' Bea breathed. 'Looking good.'

'The best,' Jake confirmed. He was standing behind Bea and could see the rise and fall of her shoulders as she gazed out across the Big Apple. 'This was a great idea, Bea.'

She twisted to look up at him. 'Even though we've spent the last hour in a huge queue?'

'Absolutely. And if I had to stand in a queue in New York, I'm glad I got to do it with you.' His mind played back his comment and he realised how much like a pick-up line it sounded. 'Uh – I mean . . .'

Bea was staring at him and Jake's heart sank. Everything had been going so well . . .

'Jake Steinmann, that was the *worst* line I've ever heard!'

She was smiling! He hadn't blown it! 'I tried to scoop it back inside my head where it sounded *so much better*, but it snuck out.'

'Good job we have The Pact to protect us from any misunderstandings, eh?' Bea said.

'Yeah. *Phew*.'

As Jake turned back to look over Bea's head towards the sentry-like skyscrapers stretching away into the distance, he suddenly felt flat. The Pact was still a firm focus for her and her mention of it reminded him of how impossible his deepening feelings for her were.

Nevertheless, as they spent time pointing out buildings and neighbourhoods from one thousand and fifty feet above street level, Jake couldn't help but compare Bea to Jessica. When he was with Jess, he scrutinised every word she said. It was as if he had lost his trust in her ability to tell the truth. Consequently, every conversation was a verbal minefield of conspiracy theories and over-analysis. But with Bea, the only words he occasionally mistrusted were his own, the relative newness of their friendly relationship heightening his resolve to avoid saying the wrong thing. He laughed when he was with her: she made him smile and wasn't afraid to mock him at will. With Bea he felt he could be himself.

The fact that Jess had laid her cards on the table and wanted to rekindle their relationship confused matters, but so did Bea's insistence that they adhere to The Pact. There were no answers to be found today, Jake decided. Instead, there was only the mandate to spend time with somebody who made him smile. After the week he'd endured, this was just what he needed.

'Did I tell you I'm planning a bachelor party for my brother?' Jake asked later, when he and Bea were munching salmon teriyaki with multi-grain rice and cucumber kimchi in a Korean restaurant near the Empire State Building.

'No. How did you get roped into that one? Didn't you learn your lesson with the engagement party?'

'You'd think I would have. Thing is, I figured Ed would never get around to planning it and his friends have been bugging him already over what he wanted to do. Being close to Christmas I knew it would be hard to find a date to suit all the guys if he'd left it any later. So, I stepped in.'

Bea took a sip of lemon ginseng green tea. 'What are you planning?'

'Can't divulge specifics, I'm afraid. You are, after all, too close to the *opposition*.'

'I won't be going to Rosie's hen do.'

'You will. I'm pretty sure she's put you on the list.'

'Oh – *wow*. That's lovely . . .' The news seemed to impress Bea. Jake congratulated himself on another smile earned. 'Just promise me you won't take Ed to a strip club.'

Jake almost choked on his Korean beer. 'I did *not* expect that to be the next thing out of your mouth.'

'It's a valid request,' Bea replied, feigning innocence. 'If and when Stew ties the knot I know his mates from the UK will try to drag him somewhere seedy for his stag night. It's just not very nice.'

This fascinated Jake. Beyond the usual male-female acceptance of such things, why did Bea care where he took his brother? 'When you say "not very nice", what do you mean?'

'Nothing, *Dr Steinmann*.' She wagged her chopstick at him. 'It's a personal thing. I just think there are better ways for bridegrooms-to-be to celebrate.' She looked at her watch. 'Will that confession cost me on your bill?'

Jake laughed. 'I'll give you that as a free sample. And don't worry: Ed would be bored to death at a strip joint. His bachelor party will revolve around sport and liquor. Strictly old-school partying. That OK with you, *Mom*?'

Bea made a swipe for him with her napkin. 'Cheek. When do you think the parties will take place?'

'Just after Thanksgiving, I guess. After the family commitments are over and before the holiday season arrives. It's a tight window, but we'll make it.'

'And you don't mind organising everything? I mean, not that I think you can't do it: the engagement party was wonderful. I just wonder if you'd rather be celebrating with Ed than herding the rest of the partygoers around.'

Bea's concern that Jake might miss out on the fun of

Ed's party was touching – and another check in her favour. 'I'll be better having a job to do. Besides, I owe it to Rosie to look after my brother and get him home without being arrested.'

'Then I reckon Ed will be in safe hands.'

That evening, as he relaxed with a beer at Ed and Rosie's apartment after dinner, Jake was still smiling. He noticed the amused glances exchanged between his brother and Rosie and, after spotting it several times, challenged them.

'What's with the looks?'

'I don't know what you mean, Jake.' Rosie Duncan was about as good at feigning innocence as her fiancé was at resisting cracking jokes.

'Don't think I haven't noticed. Psychiatrists see *everything*.'

'Can we help it if we like seeing you happy?' Ed asked, handing his brother a fresh bottle.

'Touching, bro, but I don't believe you.'

Rosie sighed and sat on the arm of the couch. 'We were just speculating about who might be responsible for that smile of yours.'

'I'm high on life.'

'You're fooling nobody, Jakey-boy. You've seen Bea again, haven't you?'

Jake lifted his eyes to heaven. 'Man, not this again.'

'We're just happy for you,' Rosie protested. 'You have to admit you've been smiling all evening. And it's lovely to see. I'd just like it to become a permanent feature for you again, that's all.'

'I appreciate your goodwill. And for the record, I did

see Bea today. We waited in a queue that most intelligent people would have given up on and went to the top of the Empire State. Then we shared Korean food and walked up to Times Square. A New York tourist double-whammy. It was fun.'

Rosie and Ed were sharing *that look* again. Jake laughed and took a swig of beer. He disliked feeling like a biological organism being studied in a Petri dish, but beyond that it was good to feel those closest to him wanted him to be happy. For all their unashamed meddling in his new single life to this point, Ed and Rosie cared for Jake and he had come to appreciate again the importance of having family close by. When he had lived in San Francisco he'd always felt a certain sadness that such a considerable distance existed between him and his loved ones. He'd made friends easily on the West Coast, but nothing could rival the times when he saw his family. Thanksgivings and Christmases had become sacred times when he could reconnect with those who knew him best. This year he was looking forward to being in New York for these celebrations, rather than rushing with half of America to get home in time for the holidays.

'Bea is a lovely person,' Rosie said, draining the last drop of red wine from her glass. 'I like her a lot.'

Me too, Jake thought. *And that's the problem* . . .

CHAPTER FORTY-TWO

Hudson River Books, 8th Avenue, Brooklyn

November arrived and with it the busiest retail time of the year was ushered in. It never ceased to amaze Bea how trade at the bookstore was boosted at this time. It was as if a switch had been flicked which unleashed a torrent of customers into Brooklyn. Every store, bar, restaurant and café on and around 8th Avenue heaved with festive shoppers, while a red and white army of Santas invaded every corner, the ringing of hand bells becoming as familiar a neighbourhood sound as the honking taxi horns and passing aeroplanes heading to John F. Kennedy International Airport.

As if to add to the holiday feel, this year the first snow fell during the second week of November: just enough to add a delicious dusting to the Brooklyn streets, making the coloured lights in every shop window twinkle a little more.

Bea loved looking at the snowy scene through the

windows of Hudson River Books as she worked with Imelda and Russ to transform the interior into a sparkling winter wonderland. Imelda had brought length upon length of semi-opaque chiffon with a subtle sheen like that of a soap bubble. Draped from the ceiling over a net of tiny white lights, it gave the impression that the whole bookstore was nestled beneath a covering of ice and snow. Russ sourced a box of white feather boas and laid them along the bottom of the shelves and bookcases to resemble a fresh snow fall, while Bea sprinkled silver sequins along the edge of each shelf. This caused a magical shower of sparkles to fall whenever customers pulled books from the shelves – much to their delight. Imelda and Bea hung strings of white tissue paper pompoms in the window and down from the ceiling throughout the bookstore, while Russ made a forest of book-print paper trees, amongst the branches of which nestled delicate brown and red papercraft robins. White and blue fairy lights were everywhere, reflecting in frosted baubles made of palest pink, green and blue glass. As a final touch, a beautiful silver fretwork star hung over the counter.

Bea was delighted with the finished effect, a reaction shared by every customer that entered the store. The atmosphere was vibrant and happy, and even though queues at the counter were longer than at any other time of year, the shoppers seemed less inclined to complain. This might have had something to do with the plates of free cookies that were available on the coffee bar and the large jars of brightly wrapped sweets placed at strategic intervals where queuing customers might pass.

Seeing their plans realised so breathtakingly had a positive effect on Russ and Bea's friendship, too. After a month of near deadlock following his declaration of love, Russ had begun to mellow towards her, but the weekend where they dressed the store finally broke through the barriers he had built around himself. In the middle of their preparations, he had walked over to Bea and hugged her, wordlessly, for a long time. When he finally let go, his rueful smile was like those he'd given her before the misunderstanding happened.

'I've missed you,' he said. 'I'm sorry.'

'Me too. I never meant to hurt you, Russ.'

'So, let's just forget it ever happened and move on, yeah?'

Bea was relieved to hear this. After that things still weren't quite as easy between them as before they had fallen out, but they were a lot closer than in recent weeks. For that, Bea was thankful.

The demands of the store meant that Bea didn't see Jake again that month. They shared the occasional phone conversation to catch up with each other, but both were necessarily preoccupied with their respective businesses. It amused Bea no end that Jake should experience a Christmas rush in his line of work, but he explained that the approaching holiday season brought with it many problems for people. His clients were in a hurry to try and deal with their issues before doing battle with the demands of the season in the same way that Bea's customers rushed to settle their gift lists before Hanukkah and Christmas arrived.

'This time of year often magnifies the cracks in relationships because we try so hard to adhere to an idealised view of what the holidays should be,' Jake told her.

Bea could appreciate how talking to Jake could help his clients make sense of their worries and concerns. Even though they were too busy to meet, Bea looked forward to Jake's calls, the sound of his voice brightening her day no matter how stressed she felt. She hoped that she did the same for him, enjoying the sound of his laughter as they spoke.

Otis had taken to calling her, too: usually late at night when Bea was unwinding with a book at home after a long day working at the bookstore. This new development was taking some time to get used to, but Bea was impressed that he never once pushed her for an answer to his proposal, although he did, of course, talk often of seeing her soon. Instead he asked about her day and shared news of the art sales his gallery was handling. As November drew on, Bea could feel her defences softening towards him. In the last week she had even caught herself looking forward to his call. Their late night discussions began to remind her of those they had shared in the early days of their relationship, back when everything Otis Greene said to her seemed to have been written in the stars. She made sure she held a healthy dose of cynicism in reserve this time, not wanting to make the same mistake as she had then; but as the days passed, Otis was proving himself in ways she would never have thought possible.

A week before Thanksgiving weekend, Bea received an elegant invitation to Rosie's hen party. The celebration would last all day, beginning with relaxing massages, facials and a champagne breakfast at an exclusive Upper

West Side day spa, followed by a sumptuous afternoon tea at a quirky British teashop and dinner at a gorgeous penthouse restaurant overlooking Central Park. The day was pure Rosie and Bea didn't hesitate in accepting.

'It's going to be great,' Rosie said, when Bea called her on the day the invitation arrived. 'My cousin Harri is coming over from England to be with us and Zac's looking after the twins so that Marnie can come.'

'How are the babies doing?'

'Really well. They're gorgeous little girls. Mae is the most vocal at the moment and Maia is the cutest thing. Zac can't stop talking about them when he brings our flower deliveries, although he's like a zombie from the sleepless nights, poor bloke. Be warned: Marnie will bring a bagful of photos so make sure you're comfortable before you ask to see them.'

'I'll remember that.'

The excitement in Rosie's voice was palpable. 'I'm so glad you can come, Bea. A good natter is long overdue: I want to hear *all* your news . . .'

On the morning of Rosie's hen party, Bea arrived at the Upper West Side day spa and was ushered into a beautiful waiting lounge, where three women were chatting. Everything in the room was white: from the walls and wide sofas to the thick natural fibre matting beneath her feet. Huge spherical paper lanterns hung from the high ceiling and folds of white voile at the long windows shielded the room from view of the street. Bea raised her hand in greeting, a little nervous of meeting a group of people she didn't know but was about to spend the day with.

'Hi, I'm Bea. Nice to meet you.'

One of the women stood to kiss Bea's cheek. Her blonde hair was tied back in a simple ponytail and she was dressed in a loose white shirt and skin-tight black jeans. 'Hi Bea, I'm Evie. This is Catriona and Kirsty.'

'How do you know Rosie?' Catriona asked, her bright smile instantly putting Bea's nerves at rest.

'My brother's partner Celia introduced us,' Bea replied. 'We've become good friends recently.'

Evie grinned. 'Oh *we* know Celia. Everybody does.'

'Rosie designed our wedding flowers,' Kirsty said. She was pretty and her smile lit up her features when she spoke. 'For all three of us. We all got on so well that we've kept in touch.'

It said a lot about Rosie's passion for her job that half of her hen party guests were former customers she had struck up friendships with. As they settled down to wait for the bride-to-be, Rosie arrived, accompanied by Marnie and another woman whose red curly hair was almost the same shade as Bea's.

'I'm so sorry I'm late,' Rosie grinned. 'We had to wait for a certain new mum to say goodbye to her babies.'

'They're still so tiny,' Marnie protested, her deep pink bunches bobbling with indignation. 'It feels like I've abandoned them.'

Evie hugged Marnie. 'I was exactly the same with my boy, don't worry. Just think of the champagne waiting for you.'

Marnie brightened a little. 'That is a *little* consolation.'

'Ladies, may I present my cousin, Harri.' Rosie put her hands on the redheaded woman's shoulders. 'She's a Brit like Bea and I, so we have a real transatlantic gathering.'

'Hi,' Harri smiled, and Bea was struck by the family resemblance between her and Rosie.

'Is Celia joining us?' Bea asked Rosie.

'She's coming for dinner. Unfortunately her editor scheduled an important meeting today and she can't get out of it. She sends her profuse apologies and has sent us great champagne, so I think we'll forgive her.'

A startlingly handsome male consultant arrived, clad completely in white, and led them through to a beech-panelled changing room that smelled of patchouli and rose. Enormous white towelling robes, white fluffy towels and comfortable slippers waited for each of them in the lockers, together with unbleached cotton tote bags to carry their belongings and baskets of expensive toiletries for use after treatments. Soon, they were padding through to an elegant room with a small infinity pool and fresh water fountain at its centre. Pale woven wicker recliners with soft white cotton cushions were arranged around the room and gentle Oriental music drifted serenely in the air.

'This is *heaven*,' Harri breathed, taking it all in. 'You're going to have to drag me away from here.'

A personal schedule had been prepared for each of them, with treatment times, rest periods and details of the spa's facilities. Bea loved that the day spa had gone to the trouble of printing each guest's name at the top of the schedules: the kind of attention to detail that was highly frivolous but designed to make each person feel special.

'Would you like your breakfast served here?' the therapist asked.

'That would be lovely,' said Rosie, amused by the rapt expression on Marnie's face. 'Marnie, you're dreadful.'

'I'm sleep-deprived and sex-starved,' Marnie replied, admiring the beautifully pert backside of the therapist as he walked away. 'This is the best therapy I've had in *months*.'

Breakfast consisted of fresh fruit, wafer-thin folds of deli meats, exquisite flaky pastries, green tea and a huge bottle of champagne on ice. Rosie's friends pulled several of the wicker recliners together around the low table and quickly descended upon the feast set before them. After breakfast, Evie, Kirsty and Catriona went to their first treatments of the day, while Rosie, Bea, Harri and Marnie lay on the recliners to chat.

'I'm looking forward to the sea salt and rosemary massage,' Bea confessed. 'It sounds so indulgent.'

'And just what the two of us need after working for festive shoppers,' Rosie added. 'My shoulders are so knotted the therapist will think they're made of macramé.'

Marnie stretched out her arms. 'It's the facial and manicure I can't wait for. Since the twins arrived my skin and nails have taken a total backseat. I'd like to look less like a wild-woman at the end of it.'

'You have twins?' Harri asked. 'How lovely. Boys or girls?'

'Both girls. Actually, I have pictures . . .'

Rosie winked at Bea as Marnie gleefully produced three photograph albums from her cotton tote, thrusting them into a startled Harri's hands. With her cousin thus occupied for at least the next forty minutes, Rosie grinned at Bea.

'So, how's everything with you?'

'Good. Just so busy, you know.'

'Tell me about it. I'm starting to question my sanity planning a wedding at our busiest time of the year. That's why today is such a godsend.'

'How are the wedding plans?'

'Better, now that Jake managed to wrangle Dr Steinmann Senior into line.' Rosie grimaced. 'The wedding's at his house and he decided to have a hissy fit about it all. At one point I thought we'd have to call it off. But Jake saved the day.'

'He's good at doing that,' Bea replied, quickly qualifying her remark when she saw Rosie's eyebrows lift in surprise. 'He helped Russ and I when our accountant did a moonlight flit without filing our end-of-year accounts.'

'No! That's awful. You must have been so worried.'

'We were. I thought we would lose the business: it was only through Jake's family's accountant Doug that we avoided serious trouble. Jake was brilliant.'

'Sounds like Jake. Speaking of whom . . .' Rosie sipped champagne and Bea knew exactly where she was heading next, 'I hear you two have been having fun in the city.'

Rosie's question was so good-natured that Bea didn't mind it. 'We have. Or, rather we were.'

'Oh?'

'Nothing bad, don't worry. It's just difficult to find free time with the holidays approaching. I'm sure we'll manage to do it again when the Christmas rush is over. It's been nice getting to know him.'

'Just *nice*?' Rosie gave a wry grin.

'OK, *very* nice. I like him. And it's good to spend time with someone who loves this city as much as I do.'

Rosie sipped her glass of champagne. 'Jake's a lovely bloke. I've always thought so. I'm glad he's back in New York: Ed loves having him near again. It's a shame about what happened between him and Jess, though: we got on with her really well.'

'What is she like?' If it had been anyone else Bea was talking to, she wouldn't have dreamed of asking this, but in all the time she had spent with Jake he had spoken little about his former wife. Bea was interested in the kind of woman who had captured Jake's heart for a significant part of his life.

'Jess? She's beautiful, but then anyone who's ever met her will tell you that. She has an interior design practice and a list of celebrity clients, so their home always looked like something straight out of a magazine. She comes from a wealthy family and I think that was sometimes a cause of tension between her and Jake: he grew up with parents who believed you should earn money and spend it wisely; but she is her daddy's little princess used to snapping her fingers to get what she wants. That said, I never felt she was spoilt; she just knows what she wants.'

Knowing what she did about Jake, she couldn't picture him beside the image of his wife Rosie was portraying. Jake was laid-back and witty, as happy in a diner with four-dollar hotdogs as he was in an expensive restaurant.

He was well dressed but not obsessed with designer labels. Perhaps it was a case of opposites attracting. 'You and Ed liked her, though?'

'Oh yes, Jess was a sweetie whenever we met. And you could tell how in love with her Jake was. I always thought they were the perfect married couple. It's a shame they broke up, but I suppose you never know what goes on with people behind closed doors.'

Bea kept returning to the image of beautiful Jessica Steinmann as she enjoyed a facial, manicure and the most relaxing massage she'd ever had. She didn't know why learning about Jake's ex-wife interested her so much, but it did. The woman who had caused Jake to swear an oath to avoid future relationships must have been considerable to warrant such action.

At three o'clock – pampered, polished and happy – Bea, Rosie and the hen party guests were chauffeured in a beautiful silver Bentley to a chic little English-style teashop two blocks north of Kowalski's. The interior was more 'Hollywood-does-Miss-Marple' than a true reflection of a British café, but it was fun, with jaunty 1940s music and a great atmosphere. Shelves of vintage china teapots lined the walls, pastel-coloured cotton bunting looped across the room and the waitresses wore starched white broderie anglaise aprons and frilled mob-caps. There was much excitement when the owner, Portia, realised she had 'three genuine English' in her teashop and her staff then proceeded to bombard Bea, Rosie and Harri with questions for a full thirty minutes.

'. . . Did you grow up in a house like Downton Abbey?'
'. . . How many servants do you have?'

'. . . Is it true that people in England take afternoon tea every day?'

'. . . My cousin lives in Berwick-upon-Tweed: do you *know* her?'

When they were eventually allowed to enjoy their afternoon tea, Harri nudged Bea. 'I think I've disappointed them as a Brit.'

'You told them you lived in a village,' Bea said. 'You earned far more points than Rosie or I did.'

Harri chuckled. 'You know Stone Yardley: no one could accuse it of being "quaint".'

'It's *quirky*, though,' Rosie corrected her cousin. 'And that's the next best thing.'

'Do you miss England, Bea?' Catriona asked. She had an infectious smile and Bea liked her immensely.

'Sometimes. But I've been living in New York for a long time now, so it feels like home.'

'If I lived in London, I'd never want to leave,' Evie said. 'We visited last spring and I felt like a princess.'

'Because, of course, *all* English people live in London,' Harri whispered, making Bea hide her smile behind a slice of Victoria sponge.

It wasn't a surprise that Rosie's friends were so easy to spend time with and Bea was enjoying being part of their easy chatter.

Marnie clinked her china teacup with a teaspoon. 'Ladies, I'd like to make a toast: to Rosie Duncan, one half of the Upper West Side's cutest couple!'

'And her fantastic taste in men!' Harri laughed.

Rosie giggled as teacups clinked across the table. 'Oi, hands off! That gorgeous man is *mine*.'

'How did he propose?' Kirsty asked, her eyes sparkling. 'I don't recall you telling me.'

The hen party guests agreed loudly, applauding Rosie until she gave in.

'OK, OK! Well, we were working late on a huge order for a wedding and Ed said he had to go back to the apartment for something he'd forgotten. He'd been weird all day: distracted, vague whenever I asked him anything; and to be honest he was getting on my nerves. I was tired and just wanted done with work so I could go home. I was furious at him for leaving me with the job half-finished and he didn't come back to Kowalski's for nearly two hours, which made matters worse. When he walked in I tore a strip off him and I was so angry that we walked home in complete silence.'

'Didn't you have any inkling of what he was planning?' Harri asked. 'When Alex proposed to me he'd been acting so strangely all weekend that I strongly suspected he was leading up to something.'

Bea noticed the sparkling diamond on Harri's left hand.

'I suppose the fact that he'd whisked you both off to Venice at very short notice might have given you a clue as well,' Rosie smiled.

Harri reddened a little, her red curls falling across her face. 'Well, yes, that *helped* . . .'

'I didn't have a clue. It was the furthest thing from my mind. Of course, now I look back it was obvious. But not at the time. Anyway, we arrived back at the apartment building – still not talking – and I went inside first. From the lobby to the stairs and all the way up to our apartment pale pink rose petals had been scattered.

Ed said nothing, just silently followed me. Then, when I opened the door, I found that he'd filled our entire apartment with white fairy lights, candles and more roses. I have no idea where he'd got it all from but it explained why he'd been away from Kowalski's for such a long time.'

Marnie, Harri, Evie, Catriona and Kirsty sighed as one at Rosie's description. Bea felt their emotion and was moved by Rosie's expression as she told the story.

'What did you do?' she asked.

'Nothing – for ages. Literally, I just stood there, frozen to the spot, still in my coat and holding my bags, staring at this incredible scene in my apartment. I didn't know what to say, whether to burst into tears or laugh . . . It was such a shock. Then Ed moved in front of me and took my hands in his. He told me he loved me more than anyone else he had ever loved and couldn't imagine his life without being with me. He said a lot of other things as well, but by then I was in tears and so was he. We were wrecks, the pair of us!'

Kirsty dabbed her eyes. 'Did he do the one-knee thing?'

'Oh yes. As he knelt down I knew what he was going to ask me and I almost didn't give him time to produce the ring before I said yes. It was perfect: just the two of us, in our home, promising to share the rest of our lives together.'

'You're killing us!' Catriona exclaimed. 'You should bring Kleenex whenever you tell that story.'

'I told you they were cute,' Marnie grinned. 'So sweet I couldn't spend too much time with them during my first trimester for fear of extending the morning sickness.'

As she listened to the women discussing the happy couple, Bea found her heart was heavy. Rosie was so happy she shone, her expression serene and excited when she talked about her fiancé.

That's how you should look when you're talking about the man you're going to marry.

Bea remembered the way Otis had gazed up at her in the restaurant when he was promising her his love. That wide-eyed wonder was the same as she saw in her friend's expression now. It wasn't contrived or forced: it was *real*.

Otis really loved her. He asked her to marry him because, like Ed had said to Rosie in their magically lit apartment, he didn't want to go through life without her by his side. It was what Bea had longed to hear from him for years; and yet, now he had confessed it in front of her family, she wasn't sure what to do. They had been happy once. Could they be again?

The party moved to Rosie's apartment so that everyone could change into evening wear for dinner. Bea hadn't been here before, but Rosie's description from her proposal story made it feel familiar. It was strange to be standing in the place where Ed had asked Rosie to marry him, but it also gave Bea further insight into her new friends. Harri made pots of tea as everyone took turns to change in Rosie's bedroom. Bea changed first and wandered back into the living area to apply fresh make-up.

'Hey Bea, are you OK?' Rosie sat beside her on the couch.

'Yes, I'm having a great time,' Bea replied. 'More to the point, are *you* having fun?'

'Absolutely. But you've been a bit quiet this afternoon. What's up?'

Bea hesitated. This was Rosie's day, not hers. She didn't need the complications of a guest's love life clouding her enjoyment today. 'Honestly, it's nothing.'

Rosie's brow furrowed. 'I don't believe you. So this is what's going to happen: I'm going to give you *this*,' she handed Bea a mug of tea, 'which, as we all know, is the only truth serum that works for English people, and you are going to talk to me. Deal?'

There was no avoiding the topic now, even if Bea didn't know how to express her muddle of thoughts. 'I loved hearing how Ed proposed,' she said. 'And most of all, seeing how much in love with him you are. It's a beautiful, rare thing and you should always cherish it.'

'I will. Thank you. Keep talking, Bea.'

'You don't give up, do you?'

Rosie laughed. 'No, I don't. And as today is meant to be all about me and you're sitting on my couch in my apartment, I don't think you have any grounds to refuse. So – you were saying?'

Bea took a deep breath, trying to summon her thoughts into some semblance of order. 'I've dated for most years since I was seventeen years old and I don't think I've ever experienced that kind of love. That's why not looking for a relationship makes sense to me now. But the thing is, I think I still wonder what it would be like to be loved like that. You know, *really* loved by someone who can't imagine not being with me?' Her words made her cringe and she chastised herself for saying them out loud. 'I'm sorry. I sound like a daytime soap script.'

'No, you don't,' Rosie said. 'Thing is, I know where you're coming from. I spent years telling myself that relationships weren't for me. Ask Ed – it infuriated him. When I arrived at the florists' he and Mr Kowalski were forever challenging me about it. But I'd had a bad experience and I thought my chance was over. I told myself I was perfectly fine with it, but in truth I was lonely: too burned by what had happened before and too proud to move on from it.' Looking straight at Bea, she continued, lowering her tone so that the others couldn't overhear her. 'I see that in you, hun. And I know that it's not a fulfilling way to go through life.

'Mr K used to tell me that, no matter what I did or where life took me, the most important thing was that I follow my heart. He told me not to give up on the possibility of finding love. For a very long time, I didn't want to hear it. But now I know he was right all along. I believe it will happen for you, Bea. You just have to take the chance when it arrives.'

Rosie's words played on Bea's mind that evening as the hen party – with the added energy of Celia – enjoyed a sumptuous evening meal at a beautiful restaurant on the top floor of a hotel overlooking Central Park. During five courses served by attentive waiters, the group traded laughter and tears over Rosie and Ed's relationship and forthcoming nuptials. Bea was struck by how moved all the women were by the details of Rosie and Ed's love story. It was more than friendly affection: every guest at the elegant frosted glass table appreciated why their relationship meant so much. The old man who had established Kowalski's had certainly been right about Rosie accepting a new chance of love. Bea wondered if it might one day be true for her, too.

'That couple are made for each other,' Celia proclaimed loudly, as Rosie blushed and begged her to stop. 'Although it took long enough for them to realise. But when I think of the guy she *could* have ended up with . . .'

'What guy?' Kirsty and Catriona chorused.

'There were *several*,' Marnie grinned, ducking as Rosie's linen napkin flew across the table in her direction.

Rosie laughed, her cheeks pink. 'You're meant to be my friends!'

'Ah, but true friends always speak the truth,' Celia replied. 'Don't worry: I'll spare your blushes, darling. The fact is you found the one who deserved to love you.'

The laughter around the table became sympathetic exclamations at Celia's sentiment. Bea turned her head to gaze out across the darkened silhouette of Central Park, dotted with patches of light from the roads traversing it and the skating rink at its centre. New York could steal your breath at any time of the year, but the lead-up to Christmas was Bea's favourite time of all. It came from the many Manhattan-set Christmas films she had watched as a child and the wonder of the Macy's Thanksgiving Day Parade, which she had always longed to see. New York came alive in December with light and life; and when snow fell as it had begun to this evening, no city on earth could compare with it.

She thought about Otis and the surprise of his behaviour in recent weeks. Could a parallel be drawn between him and Ed? Certainly both men had been patient in their pursuit of the women they loved. Was Otis her chance of happiness as Ed had been for Rosie?

Bea had hoped that being at the hen party might bring some clarity to her thoughts, but as she returned home that night she felt more confused than ever.

'It will happen for you,' Rosie had said.

But how could *anything* happen when Bea didn't even know what she wanted?

CHAPTER FORTY-THREE

Harry's Bar, Midtown Manhattan

'A toast! To freedom!'

Raucous cheers met this suggestion as seven considerably inebriated men raised their umpteenth shot glasses and raced to drain them first.

'But I don't want freedom,' Ed protested, wobbling on the top of a bar table like an unsteady tightrope walker. 'I want *Rosie May Duncan* from *In-ger-land . . .*' Grinning, he attempted to down his brimming shot of tequila, managing to throw most of it down his dark blue shirt instead. 'Ooops . . .'

'He's beyond rescue!' one of the bachelor party guests yelled.

'So declare him lost already!' Laughter boomed across the group.

Behind the bar a wry-faced barman pointedly consulted his watch. Jake, nowhere near as drunk as his friends, took the hint and raised his hand.

'Guys? Guys! I think it's time we call it a night . . .'

This was met by a cat's chorus of impassioned booing.

'OK, I know, I'm a killjoy. But you fellas have homes to go to and wives and girlfriends waiting for you . . .'

'Apart from Lou,' one guest said, laughing as a short guy next to Ed flicked a hand gesture back at him.

'Yeah, but I heard Lou's *mom* is waiting up!'

'*Plenty* of people still live with their parents. I have stats to prove it . . .'

'Guys! Lou has *stats* now . . .'

'I can't go home!' Ed wailed, as he half-climbed, half-fell off the table and was caught by three of his friends. 'It's too full . . . of *women* . . .'

Wolf-whistles sounded across the bar.

'No – wait – 's not I meant . . .'

Jake grabbed his brother's shoulders to steady him. 'I know, dude. You're at mine tonight.'

Head wobbling, Ed turned to Jake in surprise. 'Really, Jakey-boy?'

'Really. Now let's call a cab.'

'You're a good boy, J-J-Jake,' Ed slurred, patting Jake's face like a puppy. 'Hey! Guys! My brother's a good boy! A s-sh-*well* guy . . .'

It took Jake almost twenty minutes to get every bachelor party guest out of the sports bar and into cabs, a feat not aided by his own alcohol-induced lack of co-ordination that became magnified when the cold New York night air hit him. When he had offered to arrange Ed's night out it had been an attempt to keep himself busy and his brother safe: Ed's other friends were most certainly incapable of ensuring Ed got home in a state fit to marry anyone. The plan had worked to begin with. Jake had consciously paced himself, ignoring the impassioned pleas from the other guests to enter into drinking challenges. But as they had moved from the steak restaurant to the gig bar and finally to Harry's, he had found the lure of plentiful alcohol too tempting to resist. With Ed's friends generously funding every round, it was easy to drink far more than he'd intended. But it felt good to have a real blowout: the last time he'd been this drunk was on the night Jess announced their marriage was over. That time he'd been alone – and that was dangerous.

Jessica.

She had been calling him since he'd walked out of their hotel meeting and it was messing with his mind. He hadn't replied yet, but he knew through the family grapevine that she was still in the city. Her voicemail messages confirmed that she intended to remain in New York until he agreed to talk to her about their future.

Because of this, alcohol was his friend this evening. Alcohol helped to erase her face from his memory. It reminded him he was in sole charge of his destiny and – for tonight at least – that made him feel good. Nevertheless, he was pleased to finally get back to his apartment and complete his last grown-up responsibility of the night by steering a wheeling brother to the safety of his couch.

'Women. *Everywhere*,' Ed wailed, waving his arms above his head as he sprawled across the couch. 'Can't 'scape them. 'S like my home's become a Ladies' Room.'

'It's only one more woman,' Jake corrected. 'And good for Rosie that she has her cousin with her.'

'Ah, Cousin Harri . . . short for Har-ri-et. From good old Blighty. She's nice,' Ed conceded. 'But *smells* . . .'

Jake spluttered a laugh. 'Harri smells?'

'Mm-hmm. Harri smells *good*. Sprays and perfumes and – and –' he frowned as the word he needed evaded him '– that stuff that sticks up your hair . . . Everywhere. All over our apartment.'

'Her hair is all over your apartment?' Jake was reaching the point in his semi-drunken state where everything bordered on the hilarious. A few more drinks and he would be sniggering at lampposts . . .

'Ha! No! Good hair, though. *Red*. Like *Bea's*.'

'Bees aren't red.'

'No-no-no, not *bees*. *Your* Bea.'

Jake stared at Ed, his vision hazing around the edges. 'My Bea?'

'Yep. Pretty *Bea* the Book Lady of Brooklyn. Though you won't admit you like her.'

'I do like her. She's become a good friend.'

'Not like *that*, Jakey-boy. Like, you *like* her.'

In the encroaching fog of his mind, Ed's comment dazzled Jake like a searchlight. Suddenly, he needed another drink. He stumbled into the kitchen and rummaged in a cupboard until he found a bottle of bourbon. Grasping it like an old friend, he collected a pair of glass tumblers and returned to Ed, who had managed to wobble himself upright on the couch.

'Ah! That's my bro!' Ed exclaimed, receiving his glass with relish. 'Cheers . . .'

Jake downed half his glass, hoping it would wash Ed's comment away. Instead, it burned brighter. 'What did you mean?' he asked.

Ed was trying to see his reflection in the amber liquid filling his tumbler. 'Eh?'

'What you said about Bea: what did you mean?'

'Oh, *that*.' He looked up at his brother. 'We're the same, Jakey, me and you. We wait too long to admit how we feel. We hope it'll go away if we ignore it. But it doesn't. You know that, I know that.'

Jake felt his shoulders drop. 'It doesn't matter how I feel.'

'Liar.'

'It doesn't!' He raised his glass. 'Impossible relationships. That's what I get for *feeling*, bro. Impossible with Jess. Impossible with Bea . . .'

'*Bull*. That's what I told myself with my Rosie. That it was impossible. That she was falling for someone else and there was nothing I could do to stop it. I didn't want to let her hurt me. So I waited. I waited a *long* time, bro. And I wish I hadn't – because that woman is everything to me. I'm going to marry her like she's never been married before!' With a snort of laughter he took another sip of bourbon. 'Nothing's impossible, man. You have to tell her how you feel. 'S the only way.'

'She doesn't want a relationship.'

'So you say.'

'So *she* says. We made a pact.'

'Pact! Who dragged you from Camelot? Lemme ask you something, Jakey: in all the time you've been hanging out with Bea have you ever asked her straight out if she wants to be with you?'

The question sent cold icicles of fear spreading across Jake's shoulders. 'No!'

'Why not?'

'Because I know she's not looking for that . . .'

'How do you know?'

Jake groaned. 'If she wants a relationship with me, how come she always mentions The Pact every time we meet?'

'Probably 'cause she doesn't know how you feel. But how you feel could change it, like – like –' he made several attempts to snap his fingers, finally resorting to waving his hand instead '– *that*. You just gotta take the chance, bro.'

It had been a long night and now alcohol was slowly taking over his ability to think of anything at all. As Jake closed his eyes, the sound of Ed's snoring filling the room, one thought rose and fell on a blurred, spinning carousel:

Until I tell her, I'll never know what's possible . . .

CHAPTER FORTY-FOUR

Hudson River Books, 8th Avenue, Brooklyn

The first significant snow of the winter fell the week before Christmas, blanketing the city and either ruining New Yorkers' travel plans for the week or enhancing the festive feel of last-minute Christmas shoppers, depending on which taxi driver you listened to. For Bea, it was beautiful – even if it did mean some customers coming into Hudson River Books were more interested in keeping warm and enjoying the complimentary Christmas treats that changed with each day of the bookstore's advent calendar theme rather than buying anything.

'Watch that guy,' Russ said, sidling up to Bea behind the counter.

'Which guy?' asked Bea, gift-wrapping a stack of books for Mrs Ovitz, a long-time customer of the store and owner of a startling selection of New York one-liners.

'*Beard Guy*. Over by the biographies.'

Bea looked across the bookstore to see a bearded older man wearing a blue baker-boy-style cap and long grey belted cardigan over baggy jeans and army boots. 'Why am I watching Beard Guy?'

'He's taken five candy canes in the last fifteen minutes.'

'They're free gifts, Russ.'

'Sure. One per customer, like the sign says.'

'Which sign?'

'The sign I just put up.'

Bea squinted. 'I don't see it. Where?'

'There. By the biographies.'

'*Russ* . . .'

'What? Look at him: I don't think he's even reading those books. It's a ruse to steal our candy.'

Bea groaned as she handed over the bag of books to Mrs Ovitz. 'Thanks, Mrs O. Have a lovely Christmas.'

'I'll try, Bea. Although if my kids don't stop yelling at each other I might forget these books are gifts and use them as weapons instead.'

Grinning at the mental picture of Mrs Ovitz barricaded in her living room throwing books at her children on Christmas Day, Bea turned to Russ. 'It's Christmas. We're meant to encourage our customers to stay and buy, not scare them away with rules and signs.'

Russ was unrepentant. '*If* he buys anything. Right now he's too busy enjoying our heating and free candy. He was in here last week when we had sugar cookies, too. Trust me, Beard Guy is a browser, not a buyer.'

Mrs Ovitz tapped Bea's arm. 'I'm with Russ. Bill the guy for the candy before he leaves.'

Bea laughed as her straight-talking customer left. When she looked back at Russ, she saw he was smiling at her. 'What?'

'Us.'

'What about us?'

'We're doing *that thing* again.'

'What *thing*?'

'The Russ and Bea *shtick*. We haven't done that for weeks.'

It was true, but until Russ said it Bea hadn't realised how easily they had both fallen back into their old rhythm of conversation. She wasn't certain what had changed, but to see signs of a restored friendship meant the world. 'You're right,' Bea smiled. 'It's good to have us back.'

Russ wrapped a stack of books for a timid-looking lady who looked ready to scurry away at the slightest sound. 'Today's a day for celebration, Miss Jackson.'

The nervous lady blinked back at him. 'It is?'

'Oh yes. The two people you see behind this counter are, quite possibly, the best double-act on 8th Avenue. Bogart and Bacall, Hepburn and Grant, Kermit and Miss Piggy: they've got nothing on us.'

'Oh . . .'

'Good, huh?' Russ handed Miss Jackson her purchases in a Hudson River Books cotton bag. 'That'll be forty ninety-five, please.'

When a lull in business settled around four p.m., Bea made coffee for Russ and brought it over to where he was restocking the gift books section.

'You're an angel,' he said. 'We got so busy earlier I didn't think we'd survive.'

'Ah, but you forget we're the A-team of 8th,' Bea smiled back.

'Yes, we are. Talking of which,' he sat on the floor and

motioned for Bea to join him, 'I just wanted you to know how sorry I am. For the misunderstanding. For my dumb ego.'

'We've said this already. It was just one of those things.'

'I meant it, though, at the time.' He frowned. 'At least, I think I did. My dating life's been slow for ages now. Scratch that: it's been awful. For the record, I *hate* first dates. I get so sick of having to introduce myself over and over again, only to find I either don't want to see the woman again or she doesn't want to see me. I hate the endless carousel of questions. And I think I just looked at us – where everything's so easy and you know me and I don't have to feel like I'm going through a résumé – and I thought we'd be perfect for each other.'

Bea squeezed his hand. 'You don't need to explain.'

'I think I do. I love what we have, Bea. When I thought I'd lost you, I hated myself.'

'You never lost me. But we would never have worked out as a couple. We'd have killed each other in a week.'

He laughed. 'I guess.'

'Anyway, it's done. I'm glad we're back to where we were before.'

'Me too. You're going to marry Otis, aren't you?'

His question came out of the blue and Bea didn't know how to answer. For one thing, she wasn't aware that Russ knew about the proposal; discovering he did was unnerving. 'I haven't decided yet.'

'Hey, it's OK. You have a chance to be happy. And Otis has changed beyond recognition.'

'Russ?'

'Mm-hmm?'

'Why would you want me to marry someone else if . . . ?'

'If I thought I had feelings for you?'

Embarrassed, Bea looked down at the silver sequin-strewn floor beneath the shelves. 'Yes.'

'I want you to have the best deal possible in life. I know you don't believe your "no-relationship" rule, even if you still think you do. The right guy will change your mind. If that guy is Otis, you should say yes.'

'I don't know. My life is more than whether I'm in a relationship or not, and I've learned a lot about myself while I haven't had to think about that aspect of my life.'

'Bea.' Russ took her hand and, surprised by the comfort it brought, she didn't pull away. 'You're successful and smart and you've achieved so much in life already. You've proved to everyone what an awesome person you are. Don't you think you also have the right to be loved by somebody who sees all that? Otis sees it. He's willing to change everything to have you in his life. That's not dating, that's *love*. We don't get too many chances to find that kind of devotion: but now you have this incredible opportunity, waiting for your reply. Now, if it's not what you want, you should absolutely refuse. But if you want to be loved by a man who will change anything to have you in his life, you know what you should do.'

At the end of the day, Bea wrapped up against the elements and walked out onto the snowy street. Snowflakes patted against her face and the air was still. All along 8th Avenue traders were closing for the day, waving to Bea as she passed. Usually the season would fill Bea with excitement, but this year nerves tugged at her insides.

When she was halfway home, her mobile phone rang.

'Hey Bea.'

Bea's heart flipped a little. 'Dr Steinmann, this is a nice surprise.'

'I'm practising my unpredictability.'

'Oh, I see.'

'And on that note, are you busy?'

'We have been. Last week of Christmas shopping is always manic, even with this snow.'

She heard Jake cough. 'No, I don't mean at your store. I mean *now*.'

'You mean right this second?'

He paused. 'Yes.'

'Um . . .' This was certainly unexpected. 'No. I was just on my way home.'

'Meet me for coffee?'

Bea stopped walking, thick snowflakes illuminated by the coloured lights strung across the street settling on her hair, hat and coat. It had been a long day and the promise of a long, hot bath and early night was tempting – but so was Jake's offer. 'OK. Where?'

'There's a great place I found on 6th Avenue. Meet me there.'

Bennett Roastery was warm as toast, the heated interior steaming up the windows and filling the air with the holiday scent of chocolate, coffee and peppermint. It was a cosy sanctuary after Bea's walk in the Brooklyn snow and she peeled off layers as Jake ordered at the wood-panelled counter. Her face stung from the sudden reintroduction of heat and surprise meeting with Jake and as she waited for him to return she put her cold hands against her cheeks to cool them.

'I bought us candy cane mochas,' Jake proclaimed as he returned to their table, his face as flushed as Bea's. 'I figured this close to Christmas it was permissible.'

Bea accepted the cream-topped mug sprinkled with crushed peppermint candy. 'Perfect. Good job I needed a sugar rush.'

'This will be kill or cure, I reckon. Crazy day, huh?'

It's certainly turning out that way, Bea thought. 'The last week before Christmas always is. How's business for you?'

Jake scooped a spoonful of whipped cream from his mug. 'Busy too.'

Bea decided to broach the question burning as brightly as her skin from its snow-battering. 'So how come you thought to ring me?'

'Honestly? I have no idea. I just got back to my apartment and the idea hit me that it would be great to see you before the wedding. We've both been busy so I figured a catch-up was in order.' He took a sip of peppermint mocha and grimaced at the intense sugar hit. 'Along with us getting our week's quota of sugar in one beverage. *Wow*.'

Bea was amused by his reaction. 'It is a little OTT. You didn't want to sleep before Christmas, did you?'

'This is going to keep me buzzing into New Year. Hey, let's do something.'

'For New Year?'

'No, sooner. Tomorrow evening.'

Was this the sugar rush talking? Jake Steinmann was proving to be full of surprises today. Bea observed him carefully. 'What did you have in mind?'

'Nothing specific. But it should be something fun, don't you think?' He frowned as he considered the possibilities.

'OK, what about this: is there something you've always wanted to do in New York at Christmas that you've never gotten round to?'

Bea thought about it. During her years in New York City she and Russ had covered most of the classic holiday traditions: wandering around shopper-packed Bloomingdale's and Tiffany's with no intention of buying anything; drinking frozen hot chocolate at Serendipity 3; watching the lighting of the gigantic Rockefeller Center tree; buying a real Christmas tree from a Brooklyn tree yard and dragging it home through the snow Then, a possibility popped into her mind. 'Actually, there is one thing. But it's a bit of a cliché.'

'Hey, Christmas in New York was made for clichés. Shoot.'

'I've always wanted to skate on the Wollman Rink in Central Park. You remember, I mentioned it before? I'm ashamed to say it comes from religiously watching *Serendipity* every Christmas.'

Jake pulled a face. 'Man, when you said it was a cliché you weren't kidding. Skating, huh?'

'Skating. Russ and I have visited the rink in Brooklyn and the Rockefeller Rink but I only ever skated with him once – which lasted a grand total of fifteen minutes before he fell and gave up.'

'Then that's what we'll do. But I should warn you: I am no Olympic champion.'

Bea grinned. 'That makes two of us.'

The Wollman Rink in Central Park – renamed the Trump Rink, which caused Bea such hilarity that she couldn't quite bring herself to use the name – was framed by illuminated trees and the looming figures of Manhattan skyscrapers beyond. It glowed bright white in the early evening dusk against an eerily orange-black sky, heavy with burgeoning snow clouds. Like everywhere else in the city this evening, the rink was packed with people. A few spun and twirled like professional skaters but most were content to wobble and wiggle around the perimeters of the ice in giggling, arm-linked groups. Couples tumbled together or argued mid-ice, while kids dragged unwilling parents around like reluctant sleds in a husky race.

Bea laughed at Jake's expression as he fastened his skates on the wooden bleachers at the edge of the rink. 'You can smile, you know. This is supposed to be fun.'

'Tell that to the guys out there,' Jake replied. 'The ones trying to impress their friends and girlfriends. I don't see many of them smiling.'

'That's hardly surprising: it is New York, after all. And you don't have to impress anyone.'

'Hey, I have a certain reputation to maintain,' Jake grinned, holding out his hand to Bea as she helped him to stand unsteadily on his blades. 'What would happen if one of my clients saw me falling over?'

'I wasn't aware psychiatrists were judged by their skating ability,' Bea giggled, as Jake wobbled and grabbed hold of her arm. 'Although if you're this unsteady when you're not even *on* the ice, perhaps we should find you a disguise before you try to skate?'

'Way to boost my ego, Bea,' Jake replied.

Bea couldn't help but smile at Jake as they headed out onto the ice. His suggestion that they do something she'd always wanted had taken her by surprise last night, and she had been like a coiled spring all day waiting to finally add another New York holiday tradition to her list. The frozen December air pinched at her face as they began a slow circumnavigation of the ice rink and she was very aware of how tightly Jake was gripping her arm. He hadn't exaggerated his lack of skating ability, but his vulnerability on the ice and constant laughter at his own ineptitude was undeniably endearing.

It felt good to be laughing with him, adrenaline pumping as they narrowly avoided being knocked over by more proficient skaters, who appeared to be using those trying it out for the first time as slow-moving chicanes for their speedy circuits.

'These guys are *nuts*,' Jake said, almost losing his balance again and only rescued by Bea's fast reflexes. 'You know if I'm going down I'm taking you with me.'

'I'm well aware of that. Just keep putting one skate forward at a time and I'll do my best to keep us both upright.'

A girl of no more than fourteen wheeled in front of them, performing a perfect pirouette before racing away. Jake stared at her, then at Bea, and they both descended into giggles again.

'Reckon I'll be doing that by the end of the night?' Jake asked.

'Baby steps, Steinmann: baby steps.'

She was having the best time and even though the reality of skating in Central Park wasn't quite as glamorous or easy as it was always portrayed in the movies, Bea felt as if an ambition had been achieved. That she was skating with a handsome man who was relying upon her ability to stand on ice only added to the experience . . .

'So is this everything you'd hoped it would be?' Jake asked, confidence injecting a little more speed into his steps.

'It's lovely. Thank you for bringing us here.'

'Hey, I'm happy to help. And also happy to fake terrible skating prowess in order to make you feel protective of me,' he smirked.

'Oh, is *that* what you're doing?' Bea said. 'Now I get it.'

'My master plan. What can I tell you?'

'Genius. Well, it's working. You can show me what you've really got now, if you like.' Before Jake could protest, Bea unclamped his hand from her arm and skated a small distance away.

Alone on the ice, Jake's shock turned to horror when a group of skaters moving against the flow headed straight towards him. Flailing out his arms he lunged forward to avoid them, catching Bea's shoulder and bringing them both crashing down to the ice in one decidedly inelegant heap. Bea's head cracked against the hard surface as Jake landed awkwardly across her body and for a moment both were stunned by stinging, frozen pain. Bea struggled to catch her breath – an attempt not helped by the heavy hulk of Jake's shoulders across her chest; when she did so it quickly changed from short, sharp bursts to uncontrollable laughter.

Jake raised his head to look at her, concerned, then quickly followed suit, until they became a freezingly damp, aching heap on the fringes of the Wollman Rink, sprayed by frosty blades as other skaters wove around them.

'I am *so* sorry, Bea, are you OK?' he gasped, raising his gloved hand to stroke frost away from Bea's hair.

And that's when it happened.

Bea's laughter faded as she gazed up at Jake. The lights from the rink threw his face into silhouette, but she could see the chilled puffs of breath coming from his mouth, his eyes catching the light as he stared at her. The cheerful Christmas music, loud voices of the passers-by and sound of metal traversing the ice around them retreated to a muffled hum and Bea could hear the steady thud of her heart.

'I – I think . . .' Jake began to speak and Bea almost didn't want to hear it. This moment was profound enough without words. Despite the pain in her head and back and the encroaching cold seeping up through her coat, jumper and jeans, she could have happily remained where she was, feeling the slow, gentle motion of Jake's fingers as they brushed her cheek . . .

Suddenly, hands grabbed Jake's shoulders and lifted him bodily upright, Bea squinting as the full beam of the rink spotlights filled her vision before another pair of hands helped her to her feet.

'You folks all right?' A large, middle-aged man, made wider by the many layers of clothing he was swathed in, was looking at Jake and Bea as a diminutive woman wearing a fur hat brushed the ice from their coats. 'Y'all came down like a sack o' flour back there.'

'We're good, thanks buddy,' Jake replied, reaching out to shake the man's hand.

'That ice can be unforgiving. I know. Back home we see many sprained ankles and dislocated arms when the creek freezes over,' the man replied. 'I'm a doctor, by the way. Are you sure you two don't need checking over?'

'He's very thorough,' the woman nodded. 'And trustworthy, too.'

Dazed from her fall and strange moment on the ice, Bea managed a smile. 'We're fine. Nothing broken. Thanks for helping us, though.'

'My pleasure, li'l lady.' The man shook Bea's hand, which disappeared inside his huge gloved shake. 'I'm Bobby Ray and this is Lily, my wife. We're from Silver Springs, Maryland, here for the holidays. I must confess, I thought everyone from New York could skate.'

Jake gave a wry smile. 'Not everyone. Myself in particular.'

'Then it's good to learn, sir. O-K. Well, you folks take good care of yourselves, y'hear?'

Bea smiled, her heart rate still erratic as she tried to make sense of what had just happened. 'We will. Thanks for helping us.'

'Oh you are more than welcome, dearie,' Lily replied, patting Bea's arm. 'And if you're ever in Silver Springs, you be sure and look us up.'

As the couple skated away, Bea turned to Jake. 'Do you think we should . . . er . . . ?'

'Yes,' Jake replied quickly, offering Bea his arm. 'And find a hot drink maybe?' He hesitated, as if there was more he wanted to say, but started to skate unsteadily towards the exit of the rink instead. As Bea held his arm there were a thousand things she felt she should be saying, but no words came. They reached the safety of the bleachers in stultified silence and wobbled towards a hot chocolate hut at the side of the rink. Jake paid and Bea couldn't summon the words to stop him. As he handed her a lidded takeaway cup, she followed him wordlessly to the bleacher seats and they sat, both lost in their own thoughts for some time.

What was he going to say just then? The question haunted Bea. Her own reaction surprised her, too – not least because, had the moment prevailed, she could very easily have kissed him.

When they regained their ability to speak, neither was willing to refer to what had, hadn't or – more to the point – *could have* happened.

'At least we'll have something to show for tonight's experience,' Jake said, staring resolutely at his takeaway cup.

'What's that?'

'Bruises. Loss of dignity. Absolute confirmation that I will never represent my country in the Winter Olympics.'

'Probably for the best,' Bea nodded, wondering why eye contact was suddenly so challenging for both of them, a fact at odds with the joviality of their words. 'Good job Rosie and Ed didn't plan a skating party wedding.'

'I heard it was a close call,' Jake replied. 'My parents tell me there's a real freeze on Long Island. We'd better hope for warmer temperatures between now and then.' He finally managed to look at her. 'Are you looking forward to the wedding?'

Bea was. From what she had seen of Rosie and Ed's floral design work the event promised to be stunning in every sense. Rosie had told her about the many arrangements, garlands and displays she and Ed were working on and this, coupled with the unmistakable happiness the couple shared, made Bea excited to witness their special day. 'It's going to be fantastic. I'm so touched that Rosie invited me.'

'Rosie loves you. I'm glad you're going to be there.'

Bea smiled, pushing the memory of their closeness on the ice away. 'The only two singles at a couple event again, eh?'

Jake shrugged. 'I think we've gotten that down to an art now.' He paused, watching the twirling, wobbling and speeding crowd moving in circles around the illuminated Wollman Rink. 'And as our Pact still stands . . . we'll be safe from – you know . . .'

Bea's heart plummeted to her numb toes. 'Yes, we will. Lucky us.'

That night as she lay in bed fighting the urge to cry, Bea's memories of the evening were bitter-sweet. For a moment there – the smallest moment – she had almost believed that Jake had forgotten their agreement; that he wanted to be with her and forget they ever swore an oath. There was no point pretending any longer: if Jake Steinmann had asked her to be his tonight she wouldn't have hesitated.

'. . . our Pact still stands . . .'

That was his way of telling her no, wasn't it? At the time she had been so consumed by confusion she'd missed it: but now, with the lights from the street pooling into her darkened bedroom, Bea realised Jake had told her exactly where he stood.

Unable to sleep, she put on her dressing gown and slippers and went into the living room. Opening her laptop, she began to type an email.

From: Bea.James@hudsonriverbooks.com
To: Dot.James@severnsidebookemporium.co.uk
Subject: I think I know now

Hi Grandma,

Please forgive this message arriving by email. I know we agreed matters of the heart should only be discussed on paper, but it's late, it's too close to Christmas to post a letter and I really need to tell you what just happened.

Tonight, I found out how I felt about Jake. I think you might have known all along and I'm sorry I didn't see it. I was taken aback when it happened and if I'd had more guts I would have confessed to him what I was feeling. I didn't, of course, but almost immediately he gave me his answer. I just wasn't prepared for how painful that discovery would be. Now I understand how Russ must have felt when I told him I couldn't love him like he wanted me to. It's awful and I must apologise to him again tomorrow.

If this were the plot of a movie then tonight would have been the picture perfect almost-Christmas finale to the tale of the two leads. We went skating in Central Park,

415

he fell and took me with him and then –
there was a moment where I swear we
might have kissed. He seemed to want to
say something to me but the moment
passed. Later, he said, 'our Pact still stands'.
And now, I'm in no doubt at all. Jake likes
me as a friend, nothing else; which should
be fine to discover, not least because until
this evening I didn't fully understand what
he meant to me.

But it's *not* fine. Part of me is devastated.
And I have no idea why.

It turns out I wasn't ready to throw in the
towel on relationships. I *want* to be loved
by somebody.

I'm not expecting an answer, by the way. I
just wanted to tell you. Thank you for
sharing your story with me and making me
understand why I should never rule out the
possibility of love in my life.

I'll call you on Christmas Eve, like always.
Lots of love,
Bea xxxx

Sending the email, Bea placed the laptop on the coffee
table and listened to the muffled sound of early morning
traffic outside. She felt emptiness within but for the first
time didn't question why it was there. It was necessary
for her to move on: through Christmas and into a brand
new year that promised much in all other aspects of her
life.

She could go to Rosie and Ed's wedding now with every loose end tied and every question settled. She could enjoy Jake's company for what it was: a deep, shared friendship. And then, she could move forward into whatever life had in store.

Couldn't she?

CHAPTER FORTY-FIVE

The Steinmann family home, Hampton Bays, Long Island

Jake yawned and prayed that his fourth cup of coffee of the morning would help him focus on the day ahead. Being Ed's best man was an honour he took very seriously, but the large amounts of warm spiced bourbon the men of the Steinmann family had enjoyed last night gathered around the back garden fire pit in the Long Island snow were now pummelling his brain to a pulp. It had been a good night: Joe Steinmann as ready to joke with Ed as he was with Jake and Daniel. Ed, in turn, had responded well to his father's efforts. As they relaxed together, stories of winters gone by fizzed and sparked around the fire.

'You should be getting ready, Jacob.' Martha Steinmann, already dressed and looking as if she'd stepped from the society pages of the *New York Times*, nudged Jake to one side as she helped herself to a cup of coffee from the percolator in the kitchen. 'The guests will begin arriving soon.'

'Yes, Mom.' Jake kissed the top of his mother's head, smiling as he did so. 'I was just attempting to unscramble my brain.'

Martha gazed up at her son with unbridled pride. 'There's never been anything wrong with your brain, darling. Nothing that avoiding your father's lethal spiced bourbon toddies couldn't solve.'

'They were strong last night.'

'Mm-hmm. He was celebrating.' She reached up to straighten Jake's tie in a way that only women long trained in the art can. 'You made him see sense when you visited last. Thank you, baby boy.'

Jake shrugged. 'He needed to hear it. Besides, he loves Ed. They're just too alike.'

'That I know.' Martha looked at the slim gold watch on her small wrist. 'Heavens, is that the time? Go and drag your brother down to the garden room, Jacob!' Clapping her hands, Martha shooed her son out of the kitchen.

Ed was standing in one of the Long Island house's eight bedrooms, frowning at his reflection in a free standing dressing mirror when Jake arrived.

'Bro, it's time. Do you have everything you need?'

A wistful look passed across his brother's face. 'I think I always have. Can you believe that today she'll be mine for life?'

Grinning, Jake rested his shoulder against the doorframe. 'She loves you. She's always been yours.'

Ed groaned and shook his head. 'No, you don't understand. I never thought this day would come. I wanted her for so long when she didn't know it and I figured she would always be one of those "almost" people in my life. A what-if; an if-only . . . Last night it hit me: if I'd never told her I might still be waiting. I was *this close* to losing my chance to be with her. And today . . .'

'Today you make it happen. I get it. But you won't get to marry Rosie if you don't haul your butt downstairs before Mom kills you.' Jake was smiling when he said it, but secretly Ed's words were making him uncomfortable and he was keen to move away from the subject.

Ed turned to embrace Jake. 'You're the best, bro.'

'I know I am. Now grab your jacket and let's *move*.'

The garden room of the Long Island house was the largest of its three sitting rooms, with full-length windowed doors that opened out onto the garden. Today it had been transformed into a vision of white, leading guests into the heated marquee beyond. Rows of silver chairs with deep green cushions had been arranged in the marquee, with a snow white, thick pile carpet runner forming an aisle towards a rose-and-ivy-strewn altar where Ed and Rosie would promise their lives to one another in less than two hours' time. Delicately etched glass baubles were suspended from the draped marquee ceiling, spinning and catching the light of a thousand tiny white lights that lit the whole space. Looped along the sides of the marquee and into the garden room itself, sumptuous garlands of ivy, holly, pine, eucalyptus, rosemary, white and cream roses, gardenia flowers and white freesias hung, filling the room with their beautiful bouquet. A forest of Christmas trees stood sentry-like along the length of the marquee on either side, covered in fairy lights and frosted with powdered sugar to resemble snow. At intervals between the silver chairs, large chrome and glass lanterns containing tall cream altar candles were waiting to be lit, each one decorated with ivy trails and a single white rose. It was as if a spell had been cast over the garden room and marquee, creating a magical, sparkling, frost-covered forest lit by hundreds of tiny white fireflies.

'*Wow.*'

Jake turned to see his eldest brother Daniel strolling into the garden room. His pale green cravat and dark grey morning suit emphasised his closely cropped dark hair and denim blue eyes. 'You and Rosie outdid yourselves this time. It's incredible.'

Ed flushed from the compliment. 'That, my friend, is the result of countless hours of planning and pre-wedding battles in floral form.' Catching his brother's wry smile, he relented. 'Rosie designed it all. Gorgeous, huh?'

'Nothing but the best from Kowalski's,' Daniel smiled, slapping his brother's back. 'This is a good day, bro.'

'It sure is.' Ed's eyes glistened and he turned his head back towards the marquee. 'A perfect day.'

'Are you boys ready?' Joe Steinmann boomed, striding into the room. 'Our guests have already begun to arrive.'

Ed shared a look with Jake and Daniel, his nervous smile telling them all they needed to know about how much this day meant to him. 'I'm ready. Let's do this!'

Within minutes, the Steinmann family home became a jostling, laughing mass of bodies as guests were ushered into the garden room by polite waiters carrying silver trays of sparkling champagne flutes, a single raspberry resting in the bottom of each glass. The marquee and surrounding decorations were met with gasps of surprise and exclamations of admiration, every guest already in no doubt of the special nature of this wedding.

Jake circulated, sharing anecdotes and small talk with family and friends. He was enjoying the happy atmosphere and it was good to be with people he hadn't seen for years. The inevitable questions and commiserations over Jessica prevailed but today they didn't seem to hit him as deeply as they had in the past. He had made a decision in the spiced bourbon haze of the early hours of the morning that today was about focusing on the future. Memories of his own wedding and the questions that still remained over Jessica could wait for twenty-four hours. This was a day to be happy. He received the well wishes politely, his eyes drifting over the guests' shoulders to the garden room door. There was only one person he wanted to see today, but as yet there was no sign of her.

'And you're looking so *well*, considering,' the over-dressed wife of one of Joe Steinmann's practice partners said, her cheeks reddened by a little too much enjoyment of the free champagne.

'Thank you, Nora, I appreciate that.'

'My niece is newly divorced – I could hook the two of you up . . .' Nora's voice floated above the guests as Jake beat a hasty retreat.

Reaching the relative safety of the kitchen, he leaned against the central island and looked at his watch. Where was she? Their last meeting had been a little awkward after their tumble on the ice, but surely not embarrassing enough to cause her to think better of coming to the wedding? Bea had been quiet in the taxi as they returned home, but Jake assumed it was the result of a long day and bruises incurred in the fall. She'd hit her head when he pulled her over: could that have been the reason she didn't speak much?

But then, there had been *that* moment: when he was lying across her and their faces were so close only one movement in the right direction would have resulted in a kiss. She had looked so beautiful, despite the tears of laughter and shock streaming from her eyes. Her red hair had settled across the ice and Jake had been struck by a sudden longing to know what it felt like. If the well-meaning couple from Maryland hadn't intervened, would they have kissed? And would Bea have pulled away?

There was something else, too: something that concerned Jake more than he wanted to admit. His descent to the ice had given him more than an awkward moment of indecision and bruised pride: it had brought back a memory long hidden. One that called everything into question . . .

There had been another wintry night, ten years before, on the Wollman Rink. A different face had gazed up at him when they'd tumbled down: pale blue eyes and a riot of blonde curls beneath a dark grey beret. That time he hadn't hesitated in kissing her, setting into action a course of events destined to shatter his heart and turn his life upside down. His fall had been accidental both times: so why had history repeated itself a decade later? Ten years ago, aching from the sudden fall to the ice, Jake had told Jessica he loved her for the very first time. A few days ago, he had been moments away from repeating himself in more ways than one.

In his apartment the half-unpacked possessions from his former life were beginning to find homes in his new rooms. Back there after his trip to the Wollman Rink with Bea, Jake had opened another box, looking for distraction, and had found the one memento from his time with Jess that he'd never been able to let go of. The small snow globe was a cheap tourist souvenir he and Jess had bought the day after he told her he loved her. Over the years its clear plastic surface had been scratched and dented, but the night-time scene of New York in the snow was still visible through the fog of its war wounds. As soon as he saw it, Jake was transported back to the time when Jess was all he could think of. And now she was in his city again, this time the one thinking of him. Had her presence and the coincidence of his return to the Wollman Rink clouded his judgement? Could he even trust the sudden emotion he'd experienced with Bea that night?

Only one thing would settle the warring factions of his brain: the sight of Bea, today, at his brother's wedding. Here he couldn't compare the experience with any of his memories of Jess: only then could he be sure of how he felt about Bea.

But if she didn't arrive, how could he be certain of anything?

CHAPTER FORTY-SIX

The Steinmann family home, Hampton Bays, Long Island

Bea ran up the drive to the elegant coastal property, cursing her luck again for finding the only taxi driver in New York with no sense of direction. He had made four wrong turns during her journey to Long Island and, with his cab sat-nav broken, Bea had resorted to bringing up directions on her mobile phone and directing him to the Steinmann house herself. By all accounts, he should have paid *her* for the privilege, but when they eventually pulled up outside the correct address she had been so relieved to arrive that she'd thrust a handful of notes into his hand and scrambled out onto the frosted driveway.

This was not how she wanted to arrive at Rosie and Ed's wedding – red-faced, out of breath and her hair turning frizzy in the freezing winter temperature. But she was *here* – and that was all she cared about.

Handing over her coat at the door and receiving a glass of champagne, Bea hurried through to the garden room just as the master of ceremonies called for the guests to take their seats in the gorgeously decorated marquee. She found a seat and only then allowed herself to take in the full view of the wedding venue.

It was beautiful, in sight, sound and scent: every detail a delight. It was evident in the reaction of the assembled guests, eagerly awaiting the beginning of the ceremony as they talked in hushed voices. Outside the light had begun to fade into the early evening, bringing the tiny lights and candles along the length of the pure-white aisle into full effect. A string quartet began to play as the remaining conversations fell silent and a sense of expectation filled the space.

Bea felt her heartbeat quicken when she saw Jake walk briskly down the aisle, accompanying the celebrant and registrar. He looked so handsome in his dark grey morning suit, pale green cravat and silver waistcoat, so different from the casual wear she had always seen him in. From her seat towards the back of the wedding marquee, Bea watched as Jake laughed with the celebrant, occasionally bringing his hand up to his cheekbone, which she had learned he did when he was nervous. He kept looking back across the guests as if he was scanning their faces.

Could he be looking for me?

She dismissed the thought the moment it arrived. Jake was best man at his brother's wedding. He had far more important things on his mind today . . .

The portly celebrant looked towards the garden room and nodded, stepping in front of the altar.

'Ladies and gentlemen, we're ready to begin. Can I ask you all to rise?'

Bea followed the guests as the string quartet began to play 'Someone to Watch Over Me', the lilting tune bringing tears to her eyes. She turned towards the back of the marquee to see two little flowergirls dressed in white with silver and pale green sashes, scattering handfuls of white rose petals and silver sequins along the aisle runner. Marnie, Celia and Harri followed, their simple pale green sleeveless dresses elegant as they walked past holding bouquets of white roses, freesias and trails of deep green ivy. Bea looked to the altar: where was Ed? Alarmed, she turned back as a gasp went up from the wedding guests. Holding hands with the woman he had loved for many years, Ed Steinmann was leading his own bride up the aisle towards Jake, two groomsmen and the celebrant as the strings swelled to herald their arrival.

Bea had never seen this happen before, but it was a beautiful gesture that seemed to resonate with the guests who broke into spontaneous applause as Rosie and Ed reached the altar. Laughing, they turned to acknowledge the guests' reaction. Rosie was every inch the radiant bride: dressed in a long, slim-fitting silk gown decorated with fine strands of silver embroidery across the bodice and a line of delicate silver ivy leaf shapes which tumbled down the centre back seam to the bottom of her flowing train. Her dark hair had been scooped into a loose bun with a single white rose at the back, a simple sparkling silver chain around her elegant neck. In her hands she held a stunning bouquet of white gardenia flowers, pale green and shell pink roses with frosted eucalyptus sprigs surrounded by deep green leaves. She appeared to glide along the aisle beside Ed and now, as she stood facing him by the altar, it was as if her face shone brighter than any of the candles or lights illuminating the space.

The celebrant smiled at the guests. 'Welcome, everyone, to this very special day.' She turned to Rosie and Ed. 'So – shall we begin?'

Bea held her breath as Rosie and Ed made their promises to each other. Ed stopped halfway through his vows as emotion overwhelmed him and Rosie raised her hand to wipe a tear from his cheek.

'I do love you,' she giggled, as the wedding guests dabbed their eyes and smiled at one another.

'I love you too,' Ed replied, shrugging apologetically at the celebrant. 'I'm sorry – she just looks so incredible.'

The celebrant laughed. 'I don't think anyone here will argue with you.'

A ripple of laughter passed through the marquee.

'Are you ready now?' Rosie asked, her face full of love for her bridegroom.

Ed nodded. 'Sure.' He looked out at the guests. 'It's Rosie's fault for being so beautiful.'

Bea could see Rosie's eyes filling with tears. 'Get on with it!'

In the presence of their assembled friends and family, Ed and Rosie promised to love and cherish one another for life and nobody present doubted their ability to fulfil these vows. Bea was swept away by the intensely personal ceremony she was privileged to witness as she watched her new friends begin the next chapter of their lives together.

When the vows had been made, Ed barely waited for the celebrant to pronounce them husband and wife before gathering Rosie into his arms for a long, passionate kiss which elicited whoops of delight and wild applause from their wedding guests who spontaneously stood to welcome the brand new Mr and Mrs Steinmann into married life.

After the ceremony, Ed and Rosie headed out to the snow-covered jetty at the front of the house where a photographer worked quickly to capture special images of the couple before they froze. Bea watched them from the warmth of the Ocean Room as the guests milled around, the waiting staff furnishing them with delicate canapés and mulled wine.

'They're braver than I am.' Celia appeared beside Bea. 'I'd last two seconds in the snow.'

Bea smiled. 'How did you ever come to be born a New Yorker if you hate the snow?'

'Honey, we have warm apartments and heated cabs,' Celia replied. 'There's no need to be out in these temperatures any longer than is absolutely necessary. Besides, I like the winter parties.' She sipped her mulled wine. 'They look so happy, don't they?'

Rosie and Ed were trying their best to control their giggles as the winter wind whipped snow flurries around them. It was an intensely private kind of happiness that Bea wondered if she would ever find.

'Yes, they do.' She turned to Celia, a question from the ceremony springing to mind. 'I meant to ask you, was there a reason Ed walked Rosie down the aisle?'

Celia's expression grew serious. 'A very personal one.

It was Ed's idea. He said he wanted to do it so Rosie knew, without a doubt, that he was going to be there.'

It was a lovely thought, but Bea was still confused. 'The wedding's at his family's house, though: was there ever any chance he would miss his own wedding?'

'Trust me, honey, that one thoughtful gesture will have meant more to Rosie than she could ever explain.' She glanced over the heads of the gathered guests. 'I wonder how long they'll be setting up the marquee for the food? I'm so hungry.'

'Didn't you eat earlier?'

Celia stared at Bea. 'Are you kidding me? In *this* dress? I needed to look good standing up: once we sit to eat it's every woman for herself.'

The master of ceremonies put Celia out of her misery twenty minutes later when he announced the marquee was ready for guests to be seated for the wedding breakfast. Bea was checking the seating plan when she felt a tap on her shoulder.

'I found you.' Jake's blue eyes seemed to call her closer. Instinctively, Bea looked back at the plan.

'I can't seem to find my place,' she said, nerves evident in her voice.

'You're here,' Jake replied softly, leaning across Bea to indicate a table near the top table. 'Next to me.'

Of course. Why didn't I work that out?

Bea was here as Jake's guest: where else would she have been seated? 'Ah. Only two singles at the wedding, right?'

Jake grinned. 'Enduring the shame together.' He offered her his arm. 'Shall we, fellow singleton?'

Bea felt as if all eyes were upon her as she and Jake walked through the middle of the seated guests. She could smell the fresh green scent of his cologne mingling with the newness of his suit jacket and had to resist the urge to lean into it. When they reached their table, she busied herself with arranging her napkin in her lap, not wanting to look directly at Jake in case he saw the battle within her. How could he be so attentively flirtatious now when he'd made it clear at the Wollman Rink that The Pact was alive and well?

The master of ceremonies announced the arrival of Mr and Mrs Steinmann, and Rosie and Ed entered to hearty cheers from the guests.

Over dinner, Bea and Jake stuck to safe ground, sharing anecdotes from their respective businesses. Bea was glad of this: she loved spending time with Jake and didn't want questions from the other night hanging over their heads. Their conversation was aided considerably by course upon course of delicious food: scallops in dill and apple coulis; delicate apricot sorbet; spicy beef paprikash with buttered winter vegetables; a trio of white chocolate desserts with silver leaf-covered sugar *tuile* biscuits; and frost-like peppermint wafers that melted in the mouth served with smoky espresso.

'Can you believe this menu?' Jake asked, clutching his stomach. 'I won't need to eat for a week.'

'It's wonderful. Like everything else at this wedding.'

'Even the strictly single company?'

There was the mention of The Pact again. And yet, Jake's closeness to Bea and occasional touch of his fingers on her arm as they talked were at odds with this. More confused than ever, Bea returned Jake's smile. 'Even that.'

When it was time for the speeches, Bea welcomed the opportunity to look away from Jake, although she still felt the warmth of his gaze on her as Rosie's mother stood nervously at the master of ceremonies' invitation.

'I'm not one for public speaking,' she began, jumping when Ed gently moved the microphone she was waving in her hand back towards her face. 'Oh, thank you, Edward, I *hate* these things . . . As Rosie's father isn't part of our lives now, I just wanted to say how proud I am of my little girl. It's been many years since Rosie left England to start her new life here and when I see what she's achieved I'm blown away. And Edward, I wanted to thank you because you've always been there for Rosie. I thank heaven that in you my little girl has found a man truly worthy of her. Love like yours doesn't happen very often in life: I know this better than most.' She raised her glass. 'To Rosie and Ed!'

Rosemary Duncan's speech brought tissues out of guests' handbags and jacket pockets once more, the atmosphere charged again with shared raw emotion. Then, Jake joined his brother Daniel for a double-act roasting of the groom, causing laughter to break out at every table.

'We love Ed,' Daniel said as the bridegroom shot him a wary look. 'We do, bro. But it has to be said that the day he found the nerve to declare his love to Rosie, the collected single women of New York could finally breathe a sigh of relief . . .'

'Because, as we're all aware, our brother was the terror of the Manhattan dating scene for many years,' Jake added.

'As psychiatrists we observed this phenomenon carefully,' Dan smiled as he and Jake donned stethoscopes and produced notepads. 'What would you call it, Dr Steinmann?'

'Classic denial, Doctor,' Jake nodded.

'Indeed, Doctor. I made some observational notes of each of his dates to support our findings . . .' To raucous laughter, he unfurled an enormously long roll of paper, which spilled over the top table and down onto the carpet. 'As you can see, Ed Steinmann the Serial Dater was *rather* busy . . .'

Bea was struck by how much love she could see between the Steinmann brothers as they entertained the crowd and embarrassed Ed. She found it impossible to stop looking at Jake as he and Daniel chuckled their way through the speech, her own eyes misting when Jake brought it to an emotional close.

'Edward, Rosie, you're wonderful. You deserve the very best that life can offer you and we both wish you every happiness in the world. We love you!'

Ed's speech almost didn't happen when emotion overwhelmed him again, but when he was able to speak he charmed the guests with his unconstrained love for his new wife. 'She's my every waking moment, my deepest dreams and all the best things I hope for the future. Rosie Steinmann, you're perfect and I love you.'

As music drifted through the marquee, Jake returned to his seat next to Bea. 'Man, am I glad we don't have too many weddings like that in the year. I don't think my delicate emotional state could take it.'

Bea wasn't fooled. 'It was beautiful and you loved every minute.'

'Yes, I did. It's been a great day. And it looks like my brother and his new wife are about to impress us with their dancing skills.'

Bea followed his gaze to the front of the marquee. A five-piece band had set up where the string quartet had been earlier, a dance floor replacing the top table from the wedding breakfast. Walking slowly into the middle of the floor, Ed swung Rosie into his arms and they began a slow waltz to 'Let's Fall in Love' as the guests stood to watch, the happy couple sparkling in the light of camera flashes. Bea couldn't take her eyes off Rosie and Ed, their shared joy a powerful symbol of the love they were celebrating today.

She was watching them move across the floor when a sudden memory of Otis on one knee holding a ring towards her flashed into her mind. Where had *that* come from? Trying to unpick the link, Bea remembered how Otis had looked at her as he asked her to marry him. Despite his unwise choice of venue – and spectators – his actual proposal had been heartfelt. Could the love that he professed to feel for her be real? Bea paid close attention to Ed as he whirled his wife around to the delight of their wedding guests. The way he looked at Rosie left no doubt in her mind how much he loved her. What if Otis meant what he said this time? Could he be to her what Ed was to Rosie?

Wait: why am I thinking about Otis at a time like this?

Until this moment, Bea hadn't allowed herself to think about him today, wanting instead to enjoy the wedding without questions she still didn't have answers to. Now, as she reeled from his sudden reappearance in her mind, she wondered if she would ever know for certain how she felt. Determined to ignore it, she was about to say something to Jake when she realised he was standing.

'Do you want to dance?' He held out his hand, the candlelight from their table catching the contours of his face.

It was such an unexpected question that Bea found herself accepting. Others had joined Rosie and Ed on the dance floor: why not join them? She nodded, accepting his hand, and let him lead her towards the dancing wedding guests. The band began a slow rendition of 'Ain't Misbehavin'' as Jake slipped an arm around Bea's waist, drawing her gently to him. Laughing away her nerves, Bea placed her cheek against his shoulder, her hand reaching around to rest across his back. Together they began to move to the soft jazz song and it was as if everything and everyone else melted away. Bea was completely at peace in his arms, smiling at the naturalness of their embrace. When she lifted her head from his shoulder, she saw that Jake was smiling, too. She wanted to say something, to express what the moment meant, but he was already opening his mouth to speak.

'Bea,' he said, his breath warm across her face. 'I want to be honest with you . . .'

She saw tenderness and fear in his eyes, their faces so close that the smallest movement could change everything.

'There's something I need you to know . . .'

'Jake, I want to tell you something, too . . .' Bea's mind was racing at a hundred miles an hour, every thought and emotion she had experienced today converging *en masse* until one sentence made its bid for freedom. She had to honest with Jake, to tell him how she felt. But the words that emerged took her by surprise:

'Otis came back. He's asked me to marry him . . .'

CHAPTER FORTY-SEVEN

The Steinmann family home, Hampton Bays, Long Island

Jake's world ground to a halt. In that moment, everything he had planned to say to Bea evaporated as her words sank into his consciousness.

Otis came back. He's asked me to marry him.

His arms still held her against him but she might as well have been on the other side of the universe. He had stopped dancing and was staring at her, not knowing what else to do.

She gazed up at him. '. . . And I don't know what to do.' Her eyes glistened in the candlelight. 'What do you think?'

Why is she asking me? What the hell am I supposed to say?

'I'm not the best person to ask—'

'But you are, because . . .' She looked down at their motionless feet on the dance floor. 'Maybe we should sit down?'

Reeling, Jake agreed. His arms dropped to his sides as

he released Bea and followed her back to their table. He felt sick, knowing how close he had come to telling her what she meant to him. All the signals he thought she'd given today had been wrong: how could he have assumed she wanted anything other than friendship from him?

'I wanted to tell you the other night, but I thought you might be disappointed,' she said, her eyes still scrutinising him.

'Why would I be disappointed?' His head hurt.

'Well – our Pact.'

'What does that have to do with anything?' Was she trying to rub his nose in it?

She frowned. 'It has *everything* to do with it. Doesn't it?'

Now she was talking in riddles. And no matter how much Jake hated what she had told him, he was her friend. She had trusted him with so much and listened to him when no one else had: now she needed his advice, how could he refuse? He had to rise above his feelings. This wasn't the time to wallow in what might have been.

'Do you love him?'

She didn't look at him. 'I did – once.'

'Could you again?'

'I–I don't know . . .'

He cared about Bea. She deserved to be happy. 'Then I think you should go for it.'

She was close to tears when their eyes met again. 'You do?'

'If Otis can make you happy, you shouldn't hesitate.'

'But I don't understand: we made a Pact. No more relationships for us, ever. We even shook on it.'

438

Suddenly, Jake understood. All her mentions of The Pact today had been seeking his permission to break it in light of her former boyfriend's proposal. She cared what he thought of her – even if she didn't care for him in the way he'd dared to hope she might. Therefore it was his responsibility to put her mind at rest.

'Bea,' he said, reaching across the table to take her hand in his, ignoring the pain the touch of her skin caused his heart. 'We made The Pact to protect ourselves when both of us were hurting. But now, it's served its purpose for you. If you love this guy, nothing should stop you from being happy.'

Bea shook her head. 'We promised each other we'd stick to The Pact.'

'I know we did. But, hand on heart, can you say you'd be advising me differently if the tables were turned?'

'I want you to be happy, of course. But you said life was better without the pressure of considering someone else. You said . . .'

He *had* said that. But if Bea really loved Otis, no clever arguments could stand in the way of her being with him. 'Listen to me. If you love someone enough, nothing else matters.'

'Nothing?' Bea didn't look convinced; neither did she seem happy with what Jake had said.

She thinks I'm just saying this to appease her . . .

He had to put her mind at rest: there was only one way he could demonstrate how much she could trust him.

'Actually, I have a confession of my own. Jess is back in New York.' He looked at her, noticing how still her gaze had become. 'She – uh – she wants to stop the divorce.' *No response: nothing at all.* 'She said she still loves me. I met her, the day I called you from Central Park. I was angry, of course: how could she march back into my life and call the shots again? I don't know if it's possible to trust her again, Bea, but . . .'

'. . . But you want to know if she's serious?'

Jake nodded. 'Is that how you feel about Otis?'

'Yes.' She twisted the stem of an empty wine glass beside her on the table. 'How did we get in this complicated state when our Pact was going so well, eh?'

The bitter-sweetness of their respective situations made Jake laugh. 'It seems life has other ideas for us, Bea James.'

At last, he saw Bea's smile return. 'Yes, it does.'

Jake needed to lessen the tension between them and return to how they had been before setting foot on the dance floor. 'So, this proposal: was it a good one?' Seeing her expression he pressed on. 'Come on, we're friends. You can tell me.'

A slow smile appeared as she leaned closer. 'It was in an awful, cheap family restaurant. In front of my own family, whom he'd invited to witness the event. Even my parents, who were meant to be in New Orleans in a Winnebago.'

'Ouch.'

'I *know*. I thought I was meeting him to go over what happened between us, to gain some closure to allow us to move on. Then all of a sudden he was on one knee with an engagement ring and . . .'

'And you don't think he's serious?'

'The thing is, I don't know. He's made promises in the

440

past that haven't happened. How do I know I can trust him this time? I mean, you must feel that way with Jessica?'

'A little, yes. I just don't know if forgiving her will be that easy. When she left me, there was no hint that she'd ever change her mind. I never saw it coming.' It was strange to be discussing his former wife with Bea, but in the light of what he now knew, it seemed appropriate. 'Now I can't figure out what her true intentions are.'

'Perhaps she made a mistake and she wants you back.'

'Hmm.'

'I mean you said it yourself when we talked about what you'd do if she ever came back: a part of you still loves her.'

How could she be so perceptive at a time like this? Jake shook his head. 'That's true. But my loving her shouldn't be the deciding factor. And it shouldn't be for you. Both Jess and Otis have a lot to prove.'

'I suppose the only way you can know for sure is to talk to her.'

She was right, but he didn't want to hear it from Bea – not tonight.

By midnight, a fleet of local taxis had arrived to take weary wedding guests back to the hotels scattered along the ocean road. They parted on good terms, Bea kissing Jake's cheek as they stood in the freezing night saying their goodbyes. He watched her walking away from him; his heart heavier than it had been in months. Bea had found the relationship worth breaking The Pact for: but it wasn't with him. Taking a long breath of night air, he turned and walked slowly back into the house.

CHAPTER FORTY-EIGHT

Apartment 18D, 142 Allen Street, Lower East Side

Bea gazed up at the apartment block and felt sick. Since Rosie and Ed's wedding she had thought of nothing else but standing here; now it was a reality, she wanted to turn and run away.

It had taken hours of heart-searching to reach her decision, begun in the early hours of the morning in the family room of the Long Island guesthouse as Celia and Stewart slept soundly in the adjoining room. She had been crushed when Jake didn't even attempt to talk her out of marrying Otis, instead giving her his blessing . . .

'If you love Otis enough, nothing else matters . . .'

That was the point, wasn't it? Jake was willing to stick to The Pact because he didn't want Bea enough to break it for her. He clearly still loved his wife and her sudden arrival in New York had brought with it possibilities he hadn't thought he would be offered. Was that enough to make him reconsider his side of The Pact? Was his long-suffering love for Jessica about to receive a second chance?

In the cold light of day, The Pact was revealed as little more than protective rhetoric, keeping Bea and Jake from making mistakes while their hearts healed from their respective break-ups. Jake said it had served its purpose and it had: bringing them together as friends with a common goal and allowing Bea to view her life from a perspective that wasn't dominated by the state of her relationships. She had obviously mistaken their closeness for something else – that was the only possible explanation.

A lone Santa Claus was ringing his bell on the opposite side of the largely deserted street, bidding to attract last-minute Christmas Eve donations before the Lower East Side residents retreated to the comfort of their homes to enjoy the Christmas holiday. Bea took pity on him, wandering across the snow-covered road to drop a handful of one-dollar bills into his bucket.

'Thanks, lady.'

'You're welcome. Merry Christmas, Santa.'

The man in the red and white suit chuckled. 'I'd ask ya to sit on my knee but I think we might freeze. I hope you get what you want for Christmas.'

So do I, Bea thought, saying goodbye and crossing back to stand outside the apartment block. There was only one way she was going to find out what she wanted . . .

The buzzer sounded as a resident of the building stepped out onto the street. Bea hurried over, catching the entry door before it slammed shut, and ducked inside. The lobby was deserted, so she headed across the hallway to call the lift. Once inside, she selected the sixth floor button and waited for the lift to reach its destination.

Nothing else matters, she repeated to herself as, heart thundering in her head, she walked along the narrow corridor to reach Apartment 18. Smoothing down her hair, she knocked.

A few moments later, the door opened. 'Bea! I didn't hear you buzz up.'

'That's because I didn't.'

'It's so good to see you! Come in.' Otis rubbed a towel across his shower-damp black hair as Bea followed him into his apartment. His crumpled white T-shirt and jeans looked as if he had pulled them on in a hurry, his feet bare and the clean scent of shower gel still on his skin. Bea kept her breathing steady as she sat down with him. 'I got up late,' he apologised. 'Shouldn't you be at the bookstore about now?'

'Russ is holding the fort for me. I have a couple of hours before I need to be back.'

Questions were raging in Otis' expression. 'There's a fresh pot of coffee in the kitchen. Want some?'

'No,' Bea said quickly. She didn't have time for distractions this morning. It was time to deliver what she'd travelled to the Lower East Side to say. 'I wanted to see you because I've been thinking about what you said.'

The hope in his eyes couldn't be hidden.

She continued, her pulse thudding in her ears. 'I didn't want to say anything until I was sure. But – now I am . . .'

'Go on.'

Otis was still as gorgeous as he had always been, his effect on Bea taking her back years to their first meeting. And now he was looking at her with such longing Bea knew her decision was the right one.

Nothing else matters . . .

She took a breath. '*Yes.*'

'Pardon me?'

'I said, yes. Yes, I'll marry you.'

The apartment fell silent as Otis and Bea faced each other. She could see the rise and fall of his chest, the piercing stare of his dark eyes. Her heart powered like a freight train as she willed him to respond.

Please say something, Otis . . .

And then, he was pulling her into his arms, his insistent kisses falling on her lips and neck, his fingers caressing her cheeks and moving up to tangle in her hair. On Christmas Eve in the Lower East Side, Bea forgot everything that had gone before and lost herself in Otis Greene's kisses as the sound of a single hand bell tolled from the street below.

CHAPTER FORTY-NINE

Jake's practice, McKevitt Buildings, Broadway,

'Well, Desiree, I think we're done.' Jake smiled at his PA as he handed her a completed stack of client files.

'Hallelujah!' she exclaimed. 'I'll file these and then, if you don't mind, I'm going home for the holidays.'

'Don't bother. We can manage that in the New Year. Go home. See your kid.'

Desiree frowned. 'Are you sure? I don't like unfinished work . . .'

'Totally sure. You've worked harder than anyone else in this practice since we opened. I think you've earned the right to finish early for one day.'

'What happened with you?'

'Eh?'

Desiree folded her arms. 'You've been acting strange since the wedding. One minute you're miles away, the next you're so happy I'm wondering what drugs you're taking.'

'Can't a man just be happy?'

'A man *can*, but you ain't no ordinary man, Dr Steinmann. You're a professional who should know that he can't spend all day analysing others and not expect to be analysed right back.'

Jake knew when he was beaten. 'OK, fine. I finally found clarity on a situation this week. It's something I've been working through and the other day had a breakthrough. I know where I stand and that's brought everything into focus. Satisfied?'

'This is about your wife.'

Her comment floored him. How could she possibly have worked that out? 'I – uh – I didn't say that.'

'You didn't have to. It's written on your face as clear as day.' She smiled broadly. 'Well, I'm glad you got it clear in your head at last. Now perhaps you can do something about it.'

Jake thought about Jessica and the fact that she was due to arrive here in less than an hour. Knowing his PA's infamous perception, he needed to ensure Desiree was well on her way home when that happened. 'Maybe so.' He reached down behind his desk and lifted up an elaborately wrapped hamper from Dean & DeLuca. 'This is just a little something to show my appreciation for everything you've done this year.'

'Oh!' Desiree welled up instantly, springing from her seat to hug Jake. 'Thank you! You didn't have to.'

Jake laughed as she grasped him to her. 'Whoa! I'm not sure grabbing your boss is in your job description.'

'I don't care: you need to be hugged, Jake! Not just for your kindness but because I believe in you. I wish you every happiness for Christmas. Sincerely.' She released him and took hold of his hand. 'You make sure you take that chance to be happy, you hear me? It's never too late to change a situation. Just you remember that.'

'I will. And I hope that for you, too.'

Desiree paused to observe him. 'I'm getting there. There's a guy in my building I've been on a date with. He might just be a new start for me. We'll see.'

Jake grinned. 'Well, I'll expect to analyse that in the New Year. Deal?'

She patted his arm. 'Deal. And I'll bring New Year cookies for you as my belated Christmas gift – no arguments.'

'You'll get none from me. Merry Christmas, Desiree.'

'Merry Christmas, Doc.'

When Desiree left, Jake set about tidying the desk in his office. He wanted Jess to see his new practice in its best light and, while his PA always ensured the reception and other consulting areas were kept in military-precise order, his desk had become a dumping ground for the detritus of his day.

As he worked, he considered the twists and turns of the last few days. He had been devastated when Bea blurted out her news about her boyfriend's proposal and had spent the best part of the next day attempting to sweep up the pieces of his shattered illusions. But now he could see it had all been for the best. He had come dangerously close to declaring his feelings for her, when in reality only one man was enough for her to break her side of The Pact. It was what it was, and Jake didn't need to spend any more time considering what might have been.

And then there was Jessica: still in New York and

resolutely committed to addressing the issues that had splintered their marriage. Jake reasoned that his unwillingness to hear her out weeks before came from a place of defence: the confusion over his feelings for Bea merely a tool to allow him to discount anything Jess might want to say. If he didn't have to listen to her, she hadn't the power to hurt him. It was a classic case of evasion. He would have recognised it instantly in anyone else.

'Hello?'

He looked up from his cleaning to see the familiar figure of his estranged wife standing hesitantly in the doorway to his practice.

'Jess, hi.' He walked into reception and greeted her with a polite kiss on her cheek. 'Thanks for coming.'

'I wanted to see you. So, this is your new practice?'

Jake looked around the calming interior of his offices. 'Not bad for a few months' work, huh?'

'It's great. And right on Broadway, too. I imagine it's a good location.'

'It's worked so far. Won't you sit down?'

'Thank you.' Jessica took off her camel-coloured wool coat to reveal a delicate lace shirt, figure-hugging blue jeans and tan boots. 'It's cold out there. Snowing again.'

Jake hung her coat on the stand by the door and poured two mugs of coffee from the percolator. 'It's a shock after so many West Coast winters. But I kinda like it. Christmas works better with snow.'

'You always were a big kid.' She took a sip of coffee, her eyes never leaving his. 'I was surprised to receive your call yesterday. Have you thought any more about what I said?'

Ordinarily, her directness would have kicked Jake's defences into action, but not today. There was much to discuss and very little time to waste avoiding the inevitable. Better to jump in . . .

'I have. And I'm sorry for leaving like I did before. I wasn't ready to hear it then. But I think I am now.'

Slowly, they began to pick apart the events of the year, beginning with Jessica's decision to leave and working through to her recent change of heart. There were many questions Jake needed answering and for once he didn't hold back, willing to hear the bad things as much as the good. He needed to understand why their once so seemingly perfect marriage had crumbled.

'It was never you,' Jessica confessed. 'I know you've thought it was. I was unhappy, but you didn't cause it. I saw what all my friends were doing and wanted what they had. I saw them either divorced or still single, managing their own lives and having fun. Setting up the design practice took its toll and I had begun to feel like an automaton caught in an endless circuit of activity. None of it felt like *me* any more. And then I came home to you every night and I could see how relaxed and fulfilled you were in your job . . . And I guess I was jealous.'

'But my job was just one aspect of me,' Jake protested. 'Our marriage mattered more.'

'I know. But at the time all I could see was you living your life and me feeling trapped with nowhere exciting to go.'

It was hard to hear. Jessica had always given the impression that her career was paramount, that it challenged her and gave her reason to keep forging forward.

450

Jake never considered she could feel hemmed in by it. 'Did I make you feel that way?'

'Not directly, no. But I wanted more than the routine we'd settled into. I wanted excitement, something new to work towards.'

'Then why didn't you tell me?'

'Because –' she looked away, emotion catching the edge of her voice '– I didn't want you to see me as weak.'

Jake stared at her. How could anyone in his right mind think Jessica Steinmann was weak? 'I would never have thought that. I was in awe of your career and drive, Jess. Always was. I thought that was what you wanted.'

'It is – it *was*. To be frank, I didn't know what I wanted.' Her baby blue eyes met his again. 'But I do now.'

Jake ignored the knots his stomach was contorting into. 'What do you want?'

'I want to start again.'

The pull of her words on Jake's heart stole his breath. 'Oh Jess . . .'

'I mean it. We were in love for almost ten years of our lives, Jake, and I can't believe I was ready to throw that all away. But we still have time. The final divorce consultation is on December 29th. We can call it off then. Both our lawyers will be present and they'll see that we're agreed this is the best course of action for us. If I told Don now that I was reconsidering he'd pressure me to continue. This way, we make sure they know what we want.'

Jake considered her suggestion. A week ago he would have argued that the 29th couldn't come soon enough:

that he wanted the divorce over and Jess out of his life for good. But that was when he was confused about Bea. Now, they needed more time: if for no other reason than to fully discuss what went wrong so they could learn from the experience. 'I think you might be right. I don't want to rush this any more than you do.'

Jessica's smile was like the sun rising over the San Francisco Bay. 'Then shall we do it? Call off the divorce at the meeting?'

Thrilled and terrified in equal measure, Jake agreed.

Harry's Bar was packed with New Yorkers seeking refuge before the festive season finally arrived. It was five o'clock in the evening and already several of the drinkers were three sheets to the wind. Ed grinned as he slid a beer bottle to his brother.

'I think we earned this, bro.'

'I think we did. So how come Rosie let you out so soon after the wedding?'

'Hey, I'm the man of the house, I'll have you know,' Ed protested. 'OK, truth was she thought it would be good for me to see you. She's worried about you, what with Jess back in town and Bea doing – well, that's what I'm here to find out.'

Jake might have known that his new sister-in-law would be behind the surprise invitation from his brother. 'Bea's ex proposed. She asked me what she should do, so I told her to go for it.'

'Really? Wow.'

'Why are you so surprised?'

'Nothing. It's just – OK, I kinda have a confession to

make. Rosie and I were hoping you guys would get together at our wedding. I know, you never needed us meddling in your life, but you and Bea had a *connection*, man! I mean it: both Rosie and I saw it and we were sure that, given the right conditions, it would grow into something special. I saw how you danced with her and the look on both your faces. You can't manufacture that. It was more than friends.'

Jake turned his beer bottle on the polished wooden bar. 'Turns out, it wasn't. She didn't want me that way: if she did she would have broken The Pact. As it is, she was willing to do that for Otis. And that was the answer I needed to hear. So, I told her to accept his proposal, if it was going to make her happy.'

Ed raised his eyebrows. 'Well, your advice triumphed again, Dr Steinmann.'

'I don't follow . . .'

'She accepted his proposal. Their engagement party is happening on the 28th. Rosie spoke to Bea this morning and she invited us to the party. I'm sorry, man.'

Jake found it hard to swallow as he knocked back his beer, but forced himself to smile. 'It's all good. Besides, Jess wants to call off the divorce.'

Ed nearly choked. 'Say what? When did that happen?'

'This afternoon. She came to my office and we talked it over. I think she's right: things are happening too fast for us to take stock of it all. A little more time might help us repair what broke before.'

'And this is what you want?' Ed clearly didn't buy it.

'I think it is. I love Jess, bro. I always have. And yes, she hurt me, but nothing is ever irrevocable, is it?'

His brother said nothing, but Jake guessed his reaction to the news.

'And look at it this way: both Bea and I will have what we truly want by the end of this week. She'll be engaged, I *won't* be divorced. Next year could be pretty significant for both of us. And we're still friends, which means the most to me.'

Ed patted Jake's shoulder. 'Sure. If you say so. Just be certain this is what you want, OK?'

So much had changed this week and Jake felt he was still coming to terms with it all. But today had galvanised his decision: he was calling off the divorce.

CHAPTER FIFTY

Christmas in New York

From: Dot.James@severnsidebookemporium.co.uk
To: Bea.James@hudsonriverbooks.com
Subject: Please be happy, darling!

Dearest Bea,

Forgive the use of blasted email for this purpose, but I am writing a quick note to let you know that I won't be at home over Christmas for our annual telephone chat. I am so, so sorry, darling, but I'm afraid it is unavoidable. Suffice to say that I will call you myself, very soon.

Well, even in the era of electronic mail, it seems life moves at a speedier pace! Since your last message I hear you are engaged? Congratulations of course and you already have my blessing if this is what you really want. I suppose the clarity afforded you by your recent experience with Jake helped your decision?

All I will say for now is this: please be happy, darling! You owe it to nobody but yourself to make the very best decisions for your life. Trust an old lady when she tells you that. My wish for you is that you never waste a second of precious time regretting decisions you made or should have made. To dust off an old cliché, life really is too short.

I trust you, my beautiful Bea, and I know that whatever your heart tells you to do will make you happy.

Have a glorious Christmas and I will speak to you soon.

Fondest love as always,

Grandma Dot xxxx

Bea had to hand it to Otis: once he'd received her answer to his proposal he had sprung into action. Before she knew it, the engagement party was planned, booked and paid for, Otis insisting on taking care of everything himself. Even Russ had been surprised by the speed with which his friend had organised everything. He had taken Bea's hands in his after they closed the bookstore on Christmas Eve and smiled.

'This is what you both needed to happen. I truly believe that.'

'Do you think so?'

He nodded. 'I do. And I'm happy for you. I know you

think this is happening so fast, but maybe you've both been working towards this all along.'

Now, enjoying the cosy, romantic Christmas Day Otis had arranged for them at his apartment, Bea smiled to herself as her new fiancé worked in the kitchen putting the finishing touches to a lavish meal. Snuggled up beneath a faux fur throw with *Merry Christmas, Charlie Brown* playing on television, she looked at the sizeable diamond on her left hand. It was a beautiful ring and one she would have chosen for herself: maybe Otis knew her better than she had given him credit for. He certainly seemed happy. Last night she had woken in the early hours to hear him whispering promises to her. Lying still in bed, not wanting to break the illusion, she had listened as he had spoken of his determination to put her first, to give her the love he had failed to deliver in the past. When he finally rolled over to sleep, she had sobbed soundlessly into her pillow.

This is what you wanted all along, Bea James. This is the stability you need.

After a romantic Christmas Day with Otis and a riotous Boxing Day with Russ and Imelda, featuring too much alcohol and too many awful jokes, the day of Bea's engagement party soon arrived. It was to be held at a gorgeous loft-style restaurant, which Otis had booked exclusively for the celebration. Bea dreaded to think how much it had cost him, but this – along with everything else Otis had arranged this week – indicated that money was no object to the delighted art gallery owner.

'You look beautiful,' he told her as she nervously awaited the arrival of their guests that evening.

'Thank you.'

'Smile, baby. This is what we both want, remember?'

Bea smoothed down the gunmetal grey satin of her Fifties-style evening dress, straightening the diamanté-studded black velvet sash at her waist. 'Of course it is. Just pre-party jitters, that's all.'

The restaurant waiters were hard at work making last-minute preparations for the party and Bea retreated to the bar to gather her thoughts. On one hand she was relieved to see everything happening so quickly – the concerns of the past week lost in the whirlwind of activity. But on the other, she felt a little like a leaf caught in a tornado, tossed and turned by forces beyond her control. Everyone had seemed to support her decision to marry Otis, which led her to believe that any reluctance she felt was down to nerves alone. Jake had given his blessing, Rosie had called to congratulate her and Russ and Imelda seemed convinced that her decision had been the right one.

So why did she feel so shaky this evening?

I'm just getting engaged, she reassured herself, *it isn't like this is my wedding day . . .*

She and Otis had discussed possible ideas for their wedding, but she had made him agree that they would take their time before setting the date. After their roller-coaster relationship history, she needed to feel they had time to establish the new path they had embarked on. To be fair to Otis, while he would quite happily have married her on the spot, he accepted her suggestion to wait. So, once the engagement frenzy died down, they would be free to focus on the important task of building their lives on firm foundations.

Downing a small glass of brandy to calm her nerves, Bea prepared herself to meet her guests.

Celia and Stewart were first to arrive, Celia marching straight over to Bea to hug her so violently she was almost asphyxiated.

'Darling, I'm so happy Otis came through for you. This is going to be a success, I can feel it!'

Otis strolled over to Bea's side and shook Celia's hand. 'Thanks for being here, Celia. I know it means the world to my fiancée.'

Rosie and Ed arrived soon after and Bea was glad of their encouraging smiles. As the guests slowly filed in, Otis and Bea were wished happiness for their future and Bea could feel her confidence growing with every blessing bestowed.

When a lull in the arriving guests appeared, Otis moved a stray copper-red hair from her cheekbone and kissed her. 'Baby, I have a surprise for you. Come with me.' Taking her hand, he led Bea out of the main restaurant area to the entrance hall, where a noisy group of guests were peeling off coats and jumpers to hand to the startled cloakroom attendant.

Bea gasped and burst into tears.

There, laughing with Bea's mother and father, was Grandma Dot. When she saw Bea she beamed and walked stiffly towards her, holding out her hands.

'Bea, darling! Surprise!'

Overcome, Bea hugged her grandma. 'I thought you couldn't travel?'

'I made an exception for my darling granddaughter,' Grandma Dot replied, her watery blue eyes welling with tears as she cupped Bea's face with her cold hands. 'Your mother and father insisted I should join them. Me, a jet-setter, at my age!'

'Did we get you, Bea-Bea?' Bea's dad scooped her into a large bear hug.

'You did! It's so wonderful to see you all. Especially when you'd only just got back home after your American adventure.'

'Wouldn't have missed it for the world,' her mum grinned, joining in the family embrace. 'This is a very special day: our little girl, settled and happy at last!'

Aunt Ruby, Uncle Gino and Gramps were next to arrive, Ruby already disgruntled about being 'dragged out in the snow in the middle of the holidays', but pacified with a glass of warm winter punch hastily thrust into her hand by Otis. As the family moved through to the restaurant, Grandma Dot held back, catching Bea's hand.

'I want to talk to you, darling, most urgently. That's why I agreed to come to New York with your mother and father.'

Bea was delighted to have a few precious moments with her grandmother. 'Of course, Grandma. Let's hide out here for a while.' She led the way to a candy-striped silk sofa in the reception hall and they sat down. 'I can't believe you're actually here! It's amazing . . .'

'I don't think this is what you really want.' The abruptness of Dot's statement stole the wind from Bea's sails.

'What?'

'I don't think you want to be with Otis.' Her pale hand was cool as it rested on Bea's.

'I do, Grandma, I'm wearing his ring – look . . .'

Dot ignored Bea's hand as she held it out. 'A ring means nothing if there is no love behind the gesture. It might as well have come out of a Christmas cracker for all it's worth.'

'I think Otis spent a small fortune on it,' Bea replied, suddenly on the defence. 'He really *has* changed. I've never seen him like this before. We've talked so much about everything that's happened and he's determined to be the man I want him to be. I trust him. I know he'll make me happy.'

'But will he, really? I didn't see that from your letters, darling. Or in the emails you sent. In fact, at no time have I ever had cause to believe that Otis Greene was the man you were destined to marry.'

Why would she come all this way to see Bea celebrate her engagement only to drop such a bombshell? This was unfair: Bea had made her decision. Why couldn't Grandma Dot be happy for her? 'I think he is. That's why I accepted his proposal.'

'Nonsense. You accepted his proposal because the man you truly loved didn't want you. I know this is hard for you to hear, Beatrix, but when should it be said if not now? In every correspondence we've shared since the spring, one name has come up, time and time again: Jake Steinmann. Oh, you said he was a friend, a *great* friend, someone you felt unthreatened by, and someone who understood you. But you were crushed when he appeared to say he didn't want anything more. You emailed me at four in the morning, for heaven's sake! If he meant nothing to you, surely you would have waited to tell me what happened?'

Bea could feel tension claiming her neck and shoulders. 'Grandma, this isn't helpful. We're at my *engagement* party . . .'

Grandma Dot gripped her hand. 'I know, my love. *That's* why you need to hear it now.'

Bea fought her anger back. She didn't want to argue with her grandmother but what else could she say to change her mind? 'Grandma, I appreciate what you're saying, but the thing is—'

'Everything good here, ladies?' Otis was smiling as he walked up to them, offering Bea and Grandma Dot his arms.

Dot maintained her insistent stare on Bea, who turned to her fiancé.

'Everything's fine,' she stated firmly. 'Isn't it, Grandma?'

Dot didn't smile. 'Apparently.'

Otis missed the tension, grinning broadly at them both. 'We're ready to get started. Shall we?'

The guests were seated in the middle of the loft restaurant, each one smiling at Bea as she entered the room with Otis and Grandma Dot. Giesla and Gudrun from 12B waved at her, wearing their best frocks for the occasion; Celia, Stewart, Ed and Rosie raised their glasses; Bea's parents beamed with pride, her mother rising to escort Grandma Dot to the family table, leaving Bea with Otis in the middle of the room. Imelda and Russ wolf-whistled from the nearest table, Russ winking at Bea to indicate his blessing. All around the beautiful space the people Bea loved most were waiting for her new fiancé to make his speech. And Bea's heart was racing as her grandmother's grave expression dominated her vision.

'Ladies and gentlemen, family, friends, I want to thank you for coming out in the snow to be here this evening. This beautiful lady on my arm is the love of my life. And I am over the moon that she's agreed to become my wife next year . . .'

Next year? Despite their decision to wait, had Otis already settled on a date without telling her? Bea pushed her doubt away, her fingers cradling the diamond on her ring finger.

'. . . Now, I'll admit, at the start of this year if you'd told me I would be planning a wedding by Christmas I'd have said you were nuts. But here we are. And I couldn't be happier. This woman –' he turned to face her '– this *incredible* woman endured more than most would have done because she believed I could be a better man than I was. She saw in me what no one else did: potential for more. In life, my friends, there are few greater things we can aspire to. Bea loved me – and, thankfully, still loves me – enough to see past the disappointments to this one, immovable truth: that we are meant to be together . . .'

Bea's eye fell on the diamond ring. All of a sudden, it looked out of place on her hand. Throughout Otis' overblown speech, she had been growing increasingly uncomfortable and had tried her best to dismiss the feeling as nerves. But it refused to leave her and now, as Otis invited her to speak, one sentence screamed loud in her mind:

This isn't what I want!

' I'll hand you over to my beautiful fiancée Bea, who I know wants to say a few words to you all.' Otis ushered Bea forward.

With every eye on her like a hundred follow-spots, Bea froze. 'I . . .' she began, battling to assemble words in her mind.

'She's so in love she's lost the power of rational speech!' Uncle Gino quipped, causing a ripple of laughter to cross the room.

'Go Bea!' Russ shouted, as Imelda applauded.

Beads of cold sweat were forming on her palms and at the nape of her neck; her heart beat so rapidly she felt faint; but this was her only chance to express what every atom of her being was feeling. 'It's so good of you all to come tonight and I'm really touched you wanted to be here . . .'

'We wouldn't be anywhere else, darling,' her father said, eliciting appreciative murmurs from the party guests.

Bea didn't want to see their encouraging smiles. 'That's why this is *so hard* . . .'

Imelda and Russ were the first to sense something was wrong, closely followed by Ed and Rosie, who exchanged worried looks.

'The thing is, I honestly thought this was what I wanted. It was all I thought about at the beginning of the year and then, when Otis asked me to marry him a few weeks ago, I thought he had finally come to his senses. What I didn't know was that I was about to come to mine . . .'

Grandma Dot was nodding slowly, willing Bea onwards, her gaze full of compassion for her granddaughter. Otis remained at Bea's side, the corners of his wide smile just beginning to tighten as the guests looked on.

'This isn't what I want. I'm so sorry, Otis. I made a

mistake. You're wonderful and I've appreciated everything you've done for me. But I can't marry you.'

Stunned silence filled the room.

'What do you mean? Everyone is watching us . . .' Otis hissed, his eyes darkening further beneath a frown.

'This – us – it isn't right. If I married you we would end up unhappy.'

'But I *love* you! You said you loved me too . . .'

She hated doing this to him now, after everything he'd done to prove his love to her, but she had to be true to herself. Grandma Dot was right about that.

'I don't love you like you need to be loved,' she whispered back, slowly sliding the ring from her finger, placing it in his palm and folding her fingers over his. The words stung her, but they were the right ones to say. 'I'm truly sorry. Goodbye, Otis.'

Without another word, Bea turned and fled from the room as behind her utter chaos broke out.

CHAPTER FIFTY-ONE

Sheehan, Sheehan and Owen offices, East 43rd Street

Jake waited alone in the stylish reception area of the legal practice, trying his best not to obsessively watch the second hand of the oversized clock on the wall as it marked the passing seconds to the biggest decision of his life this year. He hadn't slept well the night before, his thoughts inevitably turning to Bea celebrating her engagement to a Lower East Side art dealer last night. He should have been at the party as her friend to support her, but he understood why she hadn't invited him. It would have been painful beyond belief to see her so happy with another man. Staying away was the sensible choice.

His phone buzzed and he peered at the display. Ed, *again*. His brother had been trying to call since six a.m. and it was getting to be beyond a joke. His support was always welcome, but this level of compassion was bordering on stalker-like.

'Stop calling me,' he growled at his phone, rejecting

the call. Almost immediately the display lit up again, this time with two text messages. The first, unsurprisingly from Ed, read:

Dude, call me as soon as you can.

Ignoring it, Jake flicked to the second message, instantly relaxing when he saw the sender's name:

Jake, when something is worth having, you just know.
Thinking of you today. Desiree x

That's more like it, Jake smiled. Real support, at the perfect time he needed it. He congratulated his decision to tell Desiree about his intentions this morning.

'Jacob!' Chuck Willets smiled as he walked from the elevator towards him.

Jake stood and shook his lawyer's hand. 'Hey Chuck.'

'Are you ready to do battle one last time?'

'Actually, no. Maybe you should sit down.'

Puzzled, Chuck did as he was told. 'Now you're not going to tell me you want nothing from the settlement again, are you? Because we talked about this . . .'

'No, nothing like that. But Jess and I . . .'

Chuck's bushy eyebrows made a bid for the high ceiling. '*Jess* and you?'

'We've been talking. And we've decided to call off the divorce. For the time being, at least. We haven't had the chance to really address our problems and I'd like to do that before I sign away our marriage.'

Chuck frowned at his client. 'Kinda late to be making that kind of decision, isn't it?'

'I'm sorry, Chuck, I know you've put so much work into this for me.'

'It's your money, Doc.' Jake could almost see his lawyer's mind working. 'Well, O-K, if you're certain that's what you both want?'

'It is.'

'Alrighty then. But this is how I advise you both to play it: we don't mention this to Don Sheehan before the moment presents itself. Trust me, that guy's out for his pound of flesh. If we spring the news on him too soon, he'll retaliate, try to talk Jess out of it and into a stronger position for demands. All I ask is that you wait for my signal. Agreed?'

'Agreed.'

'Good. You've no more curveballs waiting for me, have you?'

'No, we're good,' Jake assured him, relieved to have told Chuck about the plan. He respected the man and didn't like withholding things from him. Now, with his lawyer on side, he could go into the meeting confident of no nasty surprises. This was what he wanted: to be able to concentrate on what was real and attainable, not impossible and doomed to failure.

An associate approached them. 'Mr Sheehan will see you now.'

Chuck turned to Jake. 'Ready?'

'Absolutely,' Jake replied, surprised by the resolution in his answer. 'Let's make this happen . . .'

CHAPTER FIFTY-TWO

Bea's apartment, Boerum Hill, Brooklyn

Everything in Bea's body hurt. After a night with no sleep and enough tears to flood her apartment, she felt completely wrung out. Her phone was off the hook, the unobtainable tone droning in the corner, her coffee table strewn with discarded tissues and empty wine glasses. Her family would want to see her, but this morning she wasn't ready for their inevitable questions. She would call them later, she decided, when she felt stronger.

Sick of the darkness in her apartment, she picked her way across the living room floor to pull up the blind, blinking as the too-white light flooded in from the snowy street outside. Fresh snow had fallen overnight, leaving local motorists to plough at a snail's pace in a long, impatient line along St Marks Place and 4th Avenue. It was still early but already several neighbours were out with shovels moving the worst of the snow from the roads and sidewalks. It was a feature of life here that had first attracted Bea to this neighbourhood: while her neighbours might not be as close as those she'd known back in Shropshire, when situations arose that affected the whole area in Brooklyn, everyone banded together.

Staring out at her snow-covered neighbourhood, Bea felt alone. She hated that, once again, her family had been dragged into the mess of her romantic life, especially as her nonagenarian grandmother had travelled against doctor's orders to be there. But then, she reasoned, out of every member of her family, Grandma Dot was probably the only one smiling this morning.

She had to put it all behind her – to see the New Year as a new start in every sense of the word. There was much in her life she was proud of and she resolved to invest her time and energy in building on her success. As she had told herself countless times during the months of The Pact, there was so much more to Bea James than her relationship status. It was time the world saw it.

Staring at the wreck of her apartment, Bea set to work. She pulled empty boxes and rubbish bags from the cleaning closet and started to pack away all traces of Otis. It surprised Bea how much of Otis' belongings remained in her apartment from their acrimonious split earlier in the year. Her resolve to rid her life of him had clearly not been as strong then as she'd assumed it to be. For an hour she worked steadily, her confidence growing with each new item discarded, until a familiar wailing sound from the fire escape beyond her window caused her to stop.

An icy blast of freezing air hit her as she slid up the sash window and reached out to rescue the snow-laden, smoky grey furball, hugging it to her as she shut out the winter wind once more.

'Enjoying the snow, eh Gracie?'

The cat shuddered and buried her head further into the crook of Bea's arm.

'Let's get you warmed up, shall we?'

After towelling the terrified feline dry, Bea made a makeshift nest of blankets and cushions on one end of her couch and Gracie climbed into it with the tiniest hint of a purr.

'I'll take you home to Giesla and Gudrun when I've finished this, OK?' Bea asked, but Gracie was already fast asleep in her cosy hideaway. If Bea was honest with herself, the last thing she wanted to do today was visit her neighbours who had been at the party last night and witnessed everything. Their concern would be genuine, but Bea wasn't ready to study the scattered remnants of her engagement party just yet.

As she filled the fourth box, a pile of her former fiancé's art books balanced on the arm of her chair toppled over, knocking her vintage phone to the floor. Irritated, Bea picked it up, replacing the receiver without thinking. Instantly, it began to ring.

Please don't be Otis. Or Mum and Dad. Or Aunt Ruby . . . 'Hello?'

'Bea, it's Rosie. I'm so glad I caught you. I tried your mobile but there was no answer. I only realised you'd given me your home phone number when Ed reminded me. How are you?'

Bea sank into her favourite armchair, curling her legs up underneath her and pulling a tartan rug over her knees. 'I'm OK. Tired, but OK.'

'I wanted to come after you last night but Ed said to

let you go. I just didn't want you being on your own after something like that. I know how awful it can be . . . Is there anything you need? Anything at all?'

'Thanks Rosie, but I'm fine. I appreciate you calling, though.'

'Come to Kowalski's? A change of scene might help.'

'I don't think so . . .'

'OK, hear me out: right now you need friends who aren't going to grill you for the juicy details of what happened yesterday. You don't need to be alone in your apartment going over and over it all. I can promise, hand on heart, that neither Ed nor I have any wish to go over that ground. We just want to be there for you. Come for an hour, even. Have coffee with us, perhaps a bit of a laugh? You'll feel better for it, I promise.'

The half-packed boxes and bin bags sat in Bea's apartment like tombstones, the atmosphere in her living room heavy with the smell of last night's alcohol and regret. Suddenly, Bea wanted nothing more than to be out of there. She would return Gracie to her hapless owners and head for the Upper West Side.

'I'll be there in an hour.'

Kowalski's looked even more picturesque in the snow than it had in the midsummer sun. Its windows were filled with festive flowers, cut-paper snowflakes and twinkle lights, and the welcoming smell of coffee as Bea pushed open the door made her smile.

Rosie hurried over to hug Bea immediately, Ed raising his hand in greeting from behind the counter.

'I'm not going to mention last night, I promise,' Rosie

472

reassured Bea as they sat down. 'Old F has been busy preparing his finest coffee for you and Ed's been pretty handy with the snacks.'

Grinning, Ed produced an M&H Bakers' bag. 'Frankie had a special on doughnuts. It would have been un-neighbourly not to support him.'

Bea's appetite, which had been missing-in-action since yesterday morning, was soon coaxed back by the deliciously spiced, glazed ring doughnuts and strong coffee from the flower shop's resident percolator. 'Thank you. This is wonderful.'

Rosie sat beside her. 'I'm so glad you came over.'

'It's been an odd year,' Bea admitted, wanting to talk about what had happened after all. 'But I know I made the right decision. I had to test my feelings for Otis to discover what I really wanted. Jake was right about that.'

Rosie flinched a little but covered it quickly. 'Be honest with me: what was the deal with you and Jake?'

There was no point denying anything in Rosie and Ed's presence. Bea was aware they already knew more than anyone else. 'I really liked him,' she admitted with a sigh. 'I hoped he would reconsider his "no-relationship" rule for me. But I was wrong.'

'What "no-relationship" rule?'

'The one we made at your engagement party. We made a pact. I meant it and for a long time it seemed to be working. But then we had a moment in Central Park and I realised how I felt about him. I was going to tell him at your wedding but it came out wrong . . .'

'And this pact of yours?'

'I would have dropped it in an instant if he'd asked me to.'

Surprised, Rosie exchanged glances with her new husband, who disappeared into the workroom at the back of the store. Taking hold of Bea's hand, Rosie shook her head. 'Bea, I hate to tell you this now: Jake liked you, too.'

Bea stared back. 'What?'

'But he thought you'd sworn off relationships. That's why when you told him about Otis he assumed you loved him enough to break your rule.'

'We both made The Pact! He suggested it in the first place and we shook on it. I told him about Otis because I think I wanted him to talk me out of marrying him. When he didn't, I assumed it was because he didn't feel anything for me. I thought that was my answer.'

Bea's head swam. Had she been working under a wrong assumption? Her heart sank as she realised her mistake; and worse, that it was now too late to do anything about it. She'd more or less given Jake her blessing to rescue his marriage.

Ed returned, his face ashen. 'I called Jake's office. His PA says he's with his lawyer and Jess, calling off the divorce. I'm sorry, Bea . . .'

Devastated, Bea buried her head in her hands and sobbed.

'Oh, mate. I'm so sorry. I wish I could have told you this earlier . . .' Rosie squeezed Bea's shoulders to try to comfort her.

Bea couldn't believe it: Jake could have been hers. That moment they'd shared on the ice rink in Central Park was *real*; and the way she'd felt when they danced at the wedding was her heart telling her exactly what she should do. How had she missed so many obvious signs?

'It doesn't matter,' she replied, wiping her eyes and attempting to smile at her concerned friends. 'It's too late now.' She had lost maybe her first real chance of happiness with a man who was completely her equal. And why? Because of her stupid pride! If she'd told Jake how she felt, maybe he would have confirmed that he felt the same. There had been so many opportunities, but she had talked herself out of every one.

She had to learn from this, to prevent her from making similar mistakes in the future. It was too late for her and Jake, but maybe the next time fate provided blindingly obvious clues she would be ready to spot them.

Finishing her coffee, she looked at Rosie and Ed. 'Thanks so much for this. I think I'll make a move now.'

Rosie scrambled to her feet. 'No – stay a bit longer? I feel like we've just compounded things for you.'

'You haven't. In fact, you've helped a great deal. I mean it. Ed, thanks for the doughnuts. And the sneaky phone call to your brother's office.'

Blushing, Ed gave her a hug. 'You're welcome. Take care of yourself, OK?'

'I will.' Bea turned to Rosie. 'And you can stop worrying about me, too. When you're back from your honeymoon, let's meet for dinner. Hawaii sounds divine: I want to see all the photos.' She bent to pick up her bag, which had fallen off the leather sofa when she stood. 'I love you both. Happy New Year and have a great honeymoon.'

The little silver bell over the door rang out as Bea

hurried out of Kowalski's onto West 68th Street. She wasn't ready to go home just yet: it was early and the sky was still light. Wrapping her scarf around her chin to keep out the bitter wind chill, she set off through the snow. Ahead of her, the snow-heavy trees of Central Park beckoned and she smiled against the wool of her scarf. This place had always been her sanctuary and today she needed its peace more than ever.

She walked a little way into the park until she found a bench, swept the snow from its seat and sat down.

A young couple walked past Bea, hand in hand. They paused beneath the snow-laden branches of a fir tree to kiss, laughing when a lump of snow fell onto their heads. Instantly, Bea was transported back to the night of Rosie and Ed's wedding. Jake had begun to tell her something before she'd blurted out about Otis: was that his chance to express how he felt?

It didn't matter now: it couldn't matter any more. Because, at this moment, Jake was in a Manhattan law firm office fighting for his marriage. Bea had told him to do it, and he had done as she suggested. Just as she had taken his advice and agreed to marry Otis.

In the bright daylight, the full extent of Bea and Jake's misunderstanding became clear. They had come so close to being together, but had never known it. Sitting in the frozen park, Bea made a vow to never make the same mistake again . . .

CHAPTER FIFTY-THREE

Sheehan, Sheehan and Owen offices, East 43rd Street

Don Sheehan was verbally pacing the floor as he ramped up to his *tour de force* takedown of Jake and his lawyer. Jake could see the glint in the pig-faced attorney's eyes as he pontificated and strutted his legal speak in an attempt to claim the higher ground. By contrast, Chuck Willets remained calm and softly spoken in this war of legalese. *It must be driving Sheehan mad*, Jake thought, hiding his smile as best he could. He glanced across the broad boardroom table towards his wife, who was sitting perfectly composed next to her red-faced lawyer. She was playing the game well, giving nothing away. Don Sheehan was in for the shock of his year . . .

The meeting had lasted for an hour already, Jessica's lawyer more than happy to spell out his client's demands before Chuck offered his counter-arguments. As Jake had listened to their verbal combat, his mind had drifted to wonder what Bea was doing today. He hoped she was happy.

Sheehan reached the end of his speech, pausing dramatically to down a glass of water like a prize-fighter in between rounds. He must have imagined himself as a bloodied Rocky Balboa of the legal ring, receiving a shoulder rub and pep talk from his team as he prepared to annihilate his opponent . . .

Chuck turned to Jake and winked. 'We appreciate your *thorough* statement of demands, counsellor,' he offered, the very picture of professional politeness. 'As for my client, his stance remains as laid out in the documents before you. He wishes for a fair settlement to be reached by both parties, in order that they may emerge from this process in as amicable a fashion as possible.'

Sheehan snorted. Jessica didn't move.

'And, to that end, I wish to afford my client the opportunity to add anything he thinks pertinent to the proceedings at this stage.' He turned pointedly to Jake. 'So, Dr Steinmann, is there something you would like to say?'

Jake was about to speak when the boardroom door opened and one of Don Sheehan's associates hurried in.

'What?' Sheehan barked, his face turning crimson.

'Pardon the intrusion, sir, but I have an urgent message for Mr Willets' client.' The associate turned to Chuck. 'May I?'

'Sure. Go ahead.' Chuck cast a wry glance at his legal opponent, suspecting foul play at work.

Nodding her thanks, the associate handed a folded note to Jake and scurried out of the room.

Jake shrugged at his lawyer and opened the note.

From: Ed Steinmann
To: Dr Jacob Steinmann
  Message:
  Engagement off. She's free and she's at Kowalski's.
  Get here.

Jake felt his heart stop. Was it true? How did Ed even know? What had happened to break her engagement? His head swam as he struggled to make sense of Ed's message.

'Dr Steinmann? *Jake?*'

Jake raised his eyes from the note to see Chuck staring at him expectantly. Sheehan was leaning forward, watching him with interest; Jessica was beginning to look concerned.

'I need a moment, please,' he said, weighing up his options. He'd been so sure calling off the divorce was the right decision, but was it? If it was, Ed's message wouldn't change his mind. So why was his heart pounding now? Turning to his lawyer, Jake lowered his voice. 'I need to speak to Jessica.'

'Kinda the wrong time to be doing this,' Chuck hissed back. 'We have Sheehan's nuts on the block.'

'I *really* need a moment with my wife.'

Still not understanding, but loath to deny his client's request, Chuck agreed. 'Mr Sheehan, my client requests a private consultation with your client. Shall we step out for five minutes?'

'This is out of order . . .' Sheehan began, but Jess touched his arm.

'It's what I want, too, Don.'

Unable to argue with the woman paying his considerable fee, Sheehan bustled out of the room, followed by Chuck.

'What's going on?' Jess asked, moving round to Jake's side of the table.

Jake looked at her and for the first time asked himself what he really wanted. Was he here to prevent the loss of the love of his life, or to buy him more time before their ineluctable separation? The answer should have come immediately, but it didn't: and *that* was the answer he was looking for.

'Jess, I don't think this is going to work.'

'The divorce? I know, Jake. That's what we agreed.'

'No, you don't understand.' With a deep sigh, Jake reached for her hand. '*This* isn't right for us. You said you weren't happy but you didn't know why. That's not going to change if we stay together.'

Panicked, Jess shook her head. 'No, Jake! This is what I want. It's what I *need* . . .'

'What you need is to find what makes you happy. You didn't find that with me. You want to call off the divorce because you're scared. I get that. I'm scared, too. But if we stop this now, I know that in a year, a few years maybe, we'll be back in another lawyer's office with a far more acrimonious divorce in progress. Look at me: you know I'm right.'

Her eyes made a sweeping search of his. 'But we've been together for so long. We've *loved* each other for so long . . .'

'And I'll always be grateful for the ten wonderful years

480

we had, Jess. But you know it wasn't enough for you, not in the end. I've loved being a part of your life, but I want you to be happy.'

Blinking back tears, Jess dropped her head and nodded. 'Me too. Thank you, for everything. I'm sorry we didn't make it, Jake.'

He reached out to lift her chin, their eyes meeting for the last time. 'Nothing to be sorry for. Just be happy, Jess.'

'You too.'

Seeing his lawyer's surprise when he walked out of the room, Jake shook his hand. 'You have my permission to proceed. Don't let Sheehan call the shots but don't fight what you think isn't important.'

'I kinda need you in there,' Chuck argued.

'No, you don't.' Smiling, Jake began to walk towards the elevator.

'Where are you going?'

'I have to be somewhere,' he called back.

There's somewhere else I need to be . . .

CHAPTER FIFTY-FOUR

Central Park, Manhattan

Central Park was still, the fresh fall of snow covering everything in sight and glistening in the early afternoon sun. The longer she remained in its soothing presence, the more Bea could feel the park working its magic on her bruised spirit.

In the distance through the trees she could just make out the shores of the Jacqueline Kennedy Onassis Reservoir. As a student she had come here often to read and study, enjoying picnics with Russ and their friends in the summer, leaf-fights in the autumn and hard fought snowball tournaments in winter. The quality of the snow today would make excellent ammunition, she thought, smiling to herself.

So many things had changed for her this year, but sitting in the timeless beauty of Central Park gave her hope. No matter what happened, it was comforting to know that New York remained constant. She might have lost her chance with Jake, but she would be forever grateful to him for making her get out and appreciate her adopted city again.

The time for thinking of what could have been was over: now what mattered was what Bea did next. She had begun a list of plans she wanted to put into action at Hudson River Books, some of which she had discussed with Russ as they had served Christmas shoppers over the last few weeks. Here in the park was where their first dreams of owning a bookstore were born: it seemed fitting to continue the list today.

She reached into her bag to retrieve the embroidery-covered notebook Imelda had given her for Christmas where she was keeping the list . . .

That's odd: I'm sure I brought it with me . . .

She had definitely packed it when she left her apartment. So where was it now? It could have fallen out in the taxi on the way to Kowalski's. Or—

Her mobile rang and she smiled at Rosie's picture on the screen. 'Hi, Rosie. I don't suppose I left my notebook at Kowalski's, did I?'

'That's why I'm calling! How spooky! We must have some ex-pat British telepathy going on, Bea.'

'Maybe so.'

'Can you pop back and pick it up?'

Bea looked at her watch. She wanted her notebook back to be able to focus on positive plans in the future, but by the time she'd returned to Rosie and Ed's store it would be reaching rush hour and the taxi journey home would be arduous. 'I'm not sure . . .'

'The thing is, Ed and I leave for Hawaii tomorrow morning. If you don't collect it today, it's going to be three weeks before we're home.'

That was enough to persuade Bea. Brushing the snow from her coat she began to walk out of Central Park towards Kowalski's. 'OK, I'm on my way.'

CHAPTER FIFTY-FIVE

A yellow New York taxi, travelling west, Manhattan

In the cab swerving through mid-afternoon Manhattan traffic, Jake called Ed.

'I got your note. What happened?'

'Bea called off her engagement last night.'

'She did?'

'Uh-huh. In front of her whole family. Said she thought it was what she wanted but she'd made a mistake. It was *carnage*, bro.'

Jake tried to picture the scene. Poor Bea. 'How is she today?'

'Upset, naturally, but convinced she's made the right decision. Then, she confessed she'd hoped you guys would get together. Turns out she only accepted the other guy's proposal after you told her to go for it.'

It was exactly as Jake had feared.

'She said that?'

'Yep. And then she left.'

Jake slapped a hand to his forehead. '*What?* But I'm heading for Kowalski's now.'

'Bro, *chill*. She left her notebook by mistake. Rosie's just called her and Bea's coming back to collect it.'

Jake's heart jumped. 'OK. Keep her there, Ed. I don't care what it takes, just don't let her leave until I arrive.'

'Consider it done, bro.'

Jake felt as if his heart had scaled a military assault course today. Hope followed realisation followed disappointment followed possibility: how was one man meant to cope with so many emotions veering in and out of his life like that?

He was supposed to be an expert on the human mind: how then had it been so easy for him to miss the obvious signals Bea was sending? She didn't want The Pact any more than he did, but it had become a convenient currency of conversation whenever they were together and now was nothing but a barrier to the real issue he and Bea needed to address. It would be laughable if it didn't scare him so much. He had almost lost her: but life was waving one last opportunity in his face – one he couldn't miss.

The question was: would he make it to Kowalski's in time?

'Can you drive any faster?' he begged the driver.

'In case you hadn't noticed, *sir*, we happen to be crossin' Manhattan during rush hour,' the taxi driver replied drily. 'And, unfortunately, my *flyin'* taxi is at the auto repair today.'

Jake tried another approach. 'I'm sorry. You're doing a swell job. But it's kind of an emergency. There's a girl . . .'

The driver's eyes widened in the rear view mirror. 'A girl, you say? Now *that's* a different matter. Hold onto your hat, sir, this could be a bumpy ride . . .'

Jake clung to his seat as the taxi overtook a school bus and made a sharp swerve right down a side alley, narrowly missing dumpsters and bags of rubbish.

'OK, maybe slow down just a little?'

'No can do, sir. You say there's a girl and I'm guessin' she ain't waitin' for ya. So here's what's gonna happen: I'm gonna take care of the driving and you, sir, are gonna to hold on. OK? Here we go . . .'

CHAPTER FIFTY-SIX

Kowalski's, corner of West 68th and Columbus, Upper West Side

The little silver bell rang out as Bea walked back into Rosie and Ed's florist store. Rosie waved the notebook at her from behind the counter as she served a customer with poinsettia plants.

'Make sure you water them once a week, but keep an eye on them if the room you have them in is very warm.'

'Thanks Rosie. My husband always loved these. We put them near the chair where he used to sit. At this time of year it's when you miss them most, isn't it?'

Bea waited until the shop was empty before approaching the counter.

'Thank you,' she smiled, taking the notebook from Rosie. 'I thought I was losing my mind when I couldn't find it.'

'It was lying by the sofa. I suppose it must have fallen out of your bag earlier. What do you keep in it?'

Bea was impressed that Rosie hadn't looked inside. 'Plans. Mostly for the bookstore. Russ and I have always had a wish list of ambitions for our business – since the first year of university when the dream began. It's become a tradition. This is the latest in a long line of notebooks we've filled. I'm so glad you found it: I need to be dreaming of the future right now.'

Rosie smiled as Ed arrived at her side. 'It's funny you should have lost and found your notebook here. Ed and I know from experience that Kowalski's seems to have a habit of reuniting people with their dreams.'

The silver bell rang out as the door opened. Rosie and Ed were suddenly grinning at Bea.

'Speaking of which . . .' Ed said.

'Hi Bea.'

Startled, Bea swung round to see Jake Steinmann standing in Kowalski's doorway. He was breathing like he'd sprinted to the store, his blue eyes fixed on her.

'Jake . . .' Flushed and not knowing what to say, she looked over her shoulder to Rosie and Ed for help, but they had disappeared – just as they'd done the very first time she and Jake had been reunited in the neighbourhood florists'. Slowly, she turned back. But Jake's stare was too intense for her. Instead, she gazed out of the window to the lines of red lights as traffic queued in the snow. 'I thought you were stopping your divorce.'

Jake stepped into the store, the front door closing behind him. 'I thought you were engaged.'

'Well – I'm not.' She could feel the weight of his stare even though she wasn't looking at him.

'And neither am I.'

What else was she supposed to say to him? How much did he know about last night?

Heart pounding wildly, Bea closed her eyes . . .

CHAPTER FIFTY-SEVEN

Kowalski's, corner of West 68th and Columbus, Upper West Side

She was beautiful. Jake couldn't take his eyes off her as they stood in Kowalski's, the sound of the building traffic jam drifting through the window that looked out on Columbus Avenue.

Why won't she look at me?

She had when he arrived but now she kept her gaze resolutely away from him. Did she know that he knew the truth about her allegiance to their Pact?

'Ed said I'd find you here. I wasn't sure if you'd want to see me . . .' *Please look at me . . .* 'I heard about what happened last night. I'm so sorry, Bea.'

'I made a mistake. It happens.' She shrugged, snatching a glance in his direction then averting her eyes once more. 'Of course, I wish my parents and grandma hadn't flown over from England to witness it all fall to pieces. But I know I made the right decision.'

'I think you did, too.'

Now she was staring at him at last, her sea green eyes

blazing with indignant fire. 'You *told* me to marry him!'

He could see the pain in her face and wanted so much to gather her into his arms, to kiss away every hurt. Instead, he inched closer, praying she wouldn't back away. 'I said to do it if he made you happy. For what it's worth, I think you did the right thing. I think we both did, in our own way. Jess and I – we're over.'

Bea frowned as she took in the news. 'But I thought you were calling off the divorce? Starting again?'

Jake shrugged. 'It wasn't what I wanted. When the time came to say it, I couldn't do it. There's a reason I did that. An important reason . . .'

'You have to be happy, too,' Bea said. 'I'm sorry things didn't work out with Jess.'

'I'm not,' Jake confessed. 'I'm glad you're here, Bea, because . . .'

Bea's eyes widened and she held up a notebook. 'I came back for this . . .'

Unsure of everything except what his heart was telling him, Jake took another step towards her. 'I came back for *you* . . .'

CHAPTER FIFTY-EIGHT

Kowalski's, corner of West 68th and Columbus, Upper West Side

Was it true?

'I don't understand.'

Jake took a breath. 'I was about to halt the divorce when Ed's note arrived. And when I read it, I had to know if there was a chance . . . If *we* had a chance.'

What note? And was Jake really saying what Bea thought he was? 'If we had a chance of what?'

'Ed sent a message to the lawyer's office saying that you weren't engaged any more. That you were free. And I needed to tell you how I felt about you. Truth is, I haven't believed in our Pact for some time.'

Her heart skipped a beat. 'Me neither. When did you change your mind?'

'At the birthday party in your bookstore,' he confessed. 'At least, that's where it started. You?'

'When we were skating at the Wollman Rink.'

He smiled. 'That *was* an opportunity.'

Suddenly weary from the flood of revelations, Bea sat

on the arm of the leather sofa. 'So where do we go from here?'

Jake shook his head. 'I don't know.'

Bea thought about all their conversations this year and the countless valid reasons they had found for *not* getting involved. 'The thing is, a lot of what we said made sense. There are aspects of relationships I don't want to experience again.'

Jake raised his hand. 'I hear ya. All the needless point-scoring and jostling for supremacy . . .'

'The false expectations and unspoken laws . . .'

'Not to mention the minefield of male-female differences to navigate.'

'I don't want another argument over who has control of the TV remote, or whose turn it is to put out the rubbish.'

'Me either.'

Bea stared back at Jake. 'Then it's hopeless?'

He shook his head. 'On the strength of that, perhaps it is.' His eyes met hers and Bea felt her heart pulse. How was it possible to want someone so much and *still* not be able to express it? Even now, when both Jake and Bea knew the truth, they were still using The Pact as common ground. Something had to change . . .

You wanted a second chance, Bea James. This is it . . .

Slowly, she stood. 'Unless . . .'

'Yes?'

Her confidence was growing as he held her gaze. 'Unless we choose to ignore how awful, embarrassing and downright frustrating relationships can be and just take our chances with each other? Because I *really* want to take my chances with you, Jake. And I'm sorry I wasn't brave enough to tell you until now.'

He was moving closer, his eyes telling her everything she needed to know. 'I think we have a chance to be happy. Sure, it might all go wrong and we may end up hating the sight of one another. But I'm willing to take the risk if you are.'

Bea had never been more certainly uncertain about anything in her life, but her decision was the easiest she'd ever made. Bravely, she held out her hand.

'Then let's shake on it.' Smiling, she lifted her little finger. '*Pinky shake.*'

Laughing, Jake locked his little finger with hers – then pulled her into his arms. The last few inches of distance closed between them as their lips met at last, their arms encircling one another as they drew closer still.

And there, in the middle of Kowalski's flower store, another two souls were reunited with their dream . . .

Dearest Bea,

This will be the last package from the Book Mice for a while. They tell me their mission has been accomplished. And I am inclined to agree with them.

There was really only one choice the mice and I could make – another nod to the great Bard himself. If ever there was a couple that endured the ups and downs of life, Romeo and Juliet fit the bill. (Needless to say, please don't follow their example for the end of the story: your

family heartily approves of this union.
Deadly poison and daggers will not be
necessary!)
Love each other like the verse the Book
Mice have chosen suggests, and you won't
go far wrong.
Fondest love to you both,
Grandma Dot xxxx

The yellow Severnside Book Emporium bookmark lay against a verse from Act 2, Scene 2 of William Shakespeare's *Romeo and Juliet*. Two Book Mice had been sketched in the margin, their tails entwined into a heart, gazing up at the lines:

> My bounty is as boundless as the sea,
> My love as deep; the more I give to thee,
> The more I have, for both are infinite.

THE END

Miranda's five must-see films set in New York

New York has been the setting of so many amazing films it's difficult to only choose five. But, for me, these are the five films that have inspired me most and kindled my love of the Big Apple . . .

1. *You've Got Mail* (1998) – Tom Hanks. Meg Ryan. Nora Ephron. Practically the holy trinity of romantic comedy, set in the City That Never Sleeps. It was this film that inspired me to start writing my first novel, *Fairytale of New York*. And here's a fact that links this amazingly witty, feel-good movie with my first book: Kowalski's is set one block up from the film location used for The Shop Around the Corner. This film made me fall in love with the Upper West Side of New York and led me to set my story there. So really, it's all Nora Ephron's fault that I'm an author . . .

2. *When Harry Met Sally* (1989) – from Meg Ryan's famous faked orgasm scene in Katz's Diner to Billy Crystal's Harry running to find Sally before the ball drops in Time Square, this film is as much a love letter to New York as it is a tale about two people trying not to fall in love with each other. A perfect movie and perfect story in a perfect location.

3. *Serendipity* (2001) – John Cusack and Kate Beckinsale trust fate to bring them back together after meeting in New York at Christmas. In *I'll Take New York* there is an unapologetic nod to this brilliant romantic comedy, as Bea has always wanted to skate on Central

Park's Wollman Rink after 'too many hours spent watching *Serendipity*'.

4. *Miracle on 34ᵗʰ Street* (**1947 and 1994**) – I really can't choose between the original classic and the feel-good Nineties' remake, so I'm naming both. Christmas in New York is famous the world over and features in so many films, television programmes, books and music that whether you've experienced the season in the city or not, it feels familiar. The Santa ringing his bell on the corner oppo-site Otis Greene's apartment is my nod to this film.

5. *Definitely, Maybe* (**2008**) – When I pictured Jake Steinmann in his new apartment, surrounded by unpacked boxes and facing an ominous brown enve-lope from his estranged wife's lawyer, I was inevitably reminded of Ryan Reynolds as Will Hayes, trying to make sense of his disastrous history of relationships for his eleven year-old daughter (Abigail Breslin). New York through the decades provides the backdrop to this bittersweet story, and April's (Isla Fisher) apart-ment in Brooklyn inspired Bea's apartment in *I'll Take New York*.

Miranda's playlist while writing *I'll Take New York*

For every book I write, I put together a playlist to inspire me. For *I'll Take New York*, these are the songs I listened to:

1. World Spins Madly On – The Weepies
2. Tourist – Athlete
3. Fall for You (Single Mix) – The Whitlams
4. Sing – Travis
5. Amsterdam – Imagine Dragons
6. Every Little Thing – Delirious?
7. My Waltz – Bailey Tzuke
8. U + Me = – Dan Black
9. Stars – Dubstar
10. Pulling Teeth – Newton Faulkner
11. Audience of Souls – Emily Smith
12. Caught Up In Circles – Chesney Hawkes
13. Loud and Clear – Olly Murs
14. Umbrella – Scott Simons
15. Where to Go from Here – Teddy Thompson
16. You Can Close Your Eyes – Carole King & James Taylor
17. Someone You Need – Howard Jones
18. Panic Cord – Gabrielle Aplin
19. Ashes On Your Eyes – Deb Talan
20. The Last Song (Acoustic) – Ben Carrigan

Interview with Miranda

Is *I'll Take New York* a sequel to your debut novel, *Fairytale of New York*?

It's the closest to a sequel I could get without breaking up the characters who spent so long trying to find each other in *Fairytale*, or killing someone off! I'm calling it an *almost-sequel* because it answers many of the questions I've been asked over the last six years by readers who loved *Fairytale*, but in a brand new story that can be read as a standalone novel. I wanted Ed and Rosie to be continuing their love story while also supporting Ed's brother Jake and Celia's partner Stewart's sister Bea in their own story.

In the past, you said you didn't think you would write sequels. Why now?

Fairytale of New York was my very first novel and for many years nobody knew I was writing it. By the time it was published in 2009, the Kowalski's gang had been in my life for the best part of ten years – so they have always been special characters to me. I wrote the story (which I originally called *Coffee At Kowalski's*) to indulge my long distance love affair with New York – I couldn't afford to go there, so I bought a guide book and researched the city, setting the story around places I wanted to visit. It meant hundreds of hours of research (thank goodness for Google Earth!) to make the settings as authentic as possible, but I was very relieved when people asked me how long I'd lived in New York!

For the past couple of years, I've had a hankering to write about New York again and the idea came about making Kowalski's the setting for a brand new story, weaving in the stories of my much-loved characters. After six years of writing professionally, it felt like the right time.

How have you found the experience?

I've *loved* it. Every minute. It has been so much fun to find out what Rosie, Ed, Celia, Marnie and others have been up to and wonderful to write about Kowalski's flower store again. After spending so many years dreaming up the characters and settings for *Fairytale*, I had a really strong mental picture of what Kowalski's and Rosie's neighbourhood looked like – going back there for *I'll*

Take New York has felt a little like coming home. These characters and locations started my entire published writing journey and it's been wonderful to go back.

This is the first book you have written from a male and female perspective. Why did you choose to tell the story in this way?

Every book I've written has been different from the last in terms of perspective, generally alternating between first and third person, with my second novel, *Welcome to My World* using both present and past tenses. I use whatever feels right for the story. For *I'll Take New York*, I felt very strongly that Jake needed to have as much a voice as Bea; I liked the idea of seeing a friendship from two simultaneous perspectives. Jake has been an incredibly fun character to get into the head of and his voice was very strong from the beginning.

You wrote *I'll Take New York* while expecting your first child. Did being pregnant alter the way you wrote?

Yes! I had to write very quickly because I was determined to get the book written and edited before I had my daughter Flo. But being pregnant seemed to focus my mind and I certainly had a greater drive to complete the novel than I've experienced before. It did mean that writing was far more tiring than before I was pregnant, but I discovered the joy of afternoon naps, which helped a lot!

Why has New York inspired so many authors, artists and musicians?

I think it's the personality of the city. It has a definite character that sets it apart from other American cities. New Yorkers are a unique breed; their unapologetic drive, opinions and sense of humour give the city its colour and vibrancy. The idea of the American Dream is a bit of a cliché, but in New York I think it's most evident. New York is a magnet to people from all over the world, which gives it a sense of romanticism because of the hope invested in the city – whether people find their dreams or not.

Books play an important part in *I'll Take New York*. Why did you choose to make Bea a bookshop owner?

I always try to give my characters 'real' jobs – I've written about florists, travel agents, radio station jingle writers, wedding singers, café workers and even council planners before! I want readers to identify with my characters and for them to have real-life concerns, work and working environments. I adore bookshops and believe very strongly in the need for great independent booksellers. There is something magical about walking into a shop filled from floor to ceiling with books – the possibilities contained within the pages of those books are endless. One thing I noticed when I visited America was how many wonderful bookshops there were and what a community they harbour. Brooklyn – where Hudson River Books is located – seemed the perfect place to have a really funky, independent bookstore. I discovered a fantastic bookshop in Brooklyn, called Powerhouse on 8th (http://powerhouseon8th.com) I loved the look and feel of it, so set Bea's bookstore there.

Why did you decide to make Jake a Doctor of Psychiatry in *I'll Take New York*?

Jake had to be a psychiatrist because of the story I'd established for Ed in *Fairytale of New York*. The Steinmann family have been psychiatrists for several generations, but Ed broke the mould (and his father's heart) when he decided to pursue a career in floristry. Jake and eldest brother Daniel followed their father into what Ed calls 'the family business'. In *I'll Take New York*, Jake is rebuilding his practice in the city following his wife Jessica's shock decision to file for divorce. I liked the idea of seeing some of the neuroses of New York residents as Jake works his way through his unwanted new situation. Also, by making Jake an expert in the human mind, it allowed me a much deeper insight into his thoughts and emotions, because he is more likely to analyse how he is feeling.

Do you have plans for sequels of any of your other books?

Not at the moment. I think it would have to be another standalone story that incorporates some of the original characters for it to work – unless you set out to write a series, I think trying to do a sequel when you've resolved so much in the original novel can be tricky. Having said that, in *I'll Take New York* I do mention what happened next for Harri and Auntie Rosemary from *Welcome to My World*, as an extra gift for the lovely readers who have read all my books. As for my future plans, I'll never say never . . .